# 183 TIMES A YEAR

### EVA JORDAN

Copyright © 2021 Eva Jordan
The right of Eva Jordan to be identified as the Author of the Work has been asserted by her in accordance to the Copyright, Designs and Patents Act 1988.
First published in 2016.
Re-published in 2021 by Bloodhound Books.
Apart from any use permitted under UK copyright law, this publication may only be reproduced, stored, or transmitted, in any form, or by any means, with prior permission in writing of the publisher or, in the case of reprographic production, in accordance with the terms of licences issued by the Copyright Licensing Agency.
All characters in this publication are fictitious and any resemblance to real persons, living or dead, is purely coincidental.
www.bloodhoundbooks.com

Print ISBN 978-1-913942-82-3

ALSO BY EVA JORDAN

All The Colours In Between

Time Will Tell

*This book is dedicated to my children, family and friends. Thank you for your continued support and enthusiasm.
Special thanks to Steve for giving me the time to (finally!) finish the book; to my Mum for her never-ending optimism; and to Jade and Callum for your endless supply of inspiration.*

PERFECT: PERFECTION:
*Someone or something that is FAULTLESS.*

*"But no perfection is so absolute That some impurity doth not pollute."*
— **William Shakespeare**

# PROLOGUE

*I* don't like my daughters very much. Don't get me wrong – I love them, and would lay down my life for them should the need ever arise – but right now my teenage daughters are a pain in the proverbial backside.

I look forward to the day when my attempts at communication with my daughters are not met with sulky, surly indifference. When my requests for help are not preceded with phrases like "for god bloody sake" and the loud slamming of doors.

When that day comes my life will be perfect…

For god bloody sake – why are adults so stupid? Okay – they're not all stupid. Nan and Grandad are pretty sick – and Mum's friend Ruby is okay too. But the rest of them can go to hell – especially Dad.

And Mum – I swear she's done nothing but nag me since the day I was born. Was she ever young? She sucks the fun out of everything so I doubt it. Why can't she just leave me the hell alone? Dad seems to manage it without any problem at all – so why can't she?

I wish I was like Chelsea Divine – her life is perfect. One day maybe? One day I will have the perfect life and everything will be ... well ... perfect.

## CHAPTER 1

FEAR AND LOATHING

I open my bedroom door and thrust my head into the hallway. Fearful, I look from left to right, my heart thumping hard against my chest. All is darkness except for a slit of light radiating below the door of HER room. I take a deep breath and with tentative steps I begin my journey. Although we live in a modest house with four-bedrooms, it is not particularly big or grand. However, at moments like this, when my mission is to get from bedroom to kitchen without detection, the distance between the two rooms feels huge. This requires covert military precision.

Stealth like and bare-footed, so as not to make any flapping or clacking noises with said slippers or shoes, I wander along the unlit hallway. I am determined to reach my destination without alerting the monster residing in the bedroom next door. I truly can't face another telling off tonight. It really is about time she stopped talking to me as if I were a child and treated me like an adult.

My eyes adjust to the darkness and I continue my potentially explosive journey. I grimace, tiptoeing past her room. Her TV is switched off. This can mean only one thing. She is reading THAT book. The one that is as shady as its title – or at least something of that ilk. I roll my eyes to the darkness and feel my cheeks burn with embarrassment. Oh god, what am I supposed to tell my friends when they ask me if she's reading it?

I chastise myself. What does it matter? I've been told it's very educational – maybe I should read it too? Purely for research purposes of course.

I descend the stairs but my thoughts have momentarily distracted me from my mission. I trip and miss a step. My stomach leaps into my mouth and before I can stop myself I yell out as I grab the banister to prevent my fall. I quickly steady myself, clasping both hands across my mouth.

*Oh shit. That's surely done it.*

I freeze, rooted to the spot. Not daring to move, not daring to breathe. I look up into the darkness. All remains quiet. I breathe a sigh of relief.

*I've got away with it.*

Then I hear her; the familiar thud of heavy footsteps across her bedroom floor.

My heart sinks. Her door swings open and the hallway is filled with a blinding light. The monster has awoken.

Defeated, I squat on the step nearest me, clutching and rubbing my now twisted ankle. The sound of her footsteps grows ever nearer. I screw my eyes shut and duck my head into my hands, mentally preparing myself for what is about to come. 'MUM?' she yells, her voice as unceremoniously loud and uncouth as ever. 'Mum,' she repeats. I lift my head from my hands.

*Oh well – here we go again.*

'MUUMMM!' my petulant, obnoxious and hormonal first-born shouts for a third time, the intonation of her voice clearly marked with her ever-growing impatience. 'Is that you?'

Foghorn Lil from over the hill, my Dad calls her.

"Cor blimey," he once said. "No-one's ever likely to kidnap her; she'd drive em round the bleedin bend – begging ya to take her back."

I thought his observation a little harsh and told him so but right now I find myself agreeing with him. My beautiful but hormonal 16-year-old daughter is on transmit.

'What the hell are you doing up? I thought you had a migraine? Why are you making so much noise for god bloody sake? Don't you understand I have exams to revise for? It's all right for you; all you have to do is go to work. I'm only doing this for you anyway. You're the one that puts all the bloody pressure on to "get a good education, go to university". Most normal Mums just want their kids to be happy but *no*, that's not good enough for you is it?'

This barrage of information is being downloaded at alarming speed, and she hasn't even reached the bottom of the stairs yet. I am both mildly amused and slightly terrified at the same time. Subjugated, I stand up and hobble to the kitchen. The whirlwind that is my daughter follows me – to enlighten me no doubt – with yet more of her wisdom and knowledge.

'See the dishwasher,' she points, her arm outstretched and stabbing the air, 'I did that. Me. I loaded and unloaded it,' she yells. 'I did that for you. *For you*. Not the Emo freak, not the "perfect child" but me. Me!'

I could be wrong but as far as I can remember, everyone in the household eats and drinks – some more than others – and everyone likes to do so from clean cups and plates. Why then does the loading and unloading of the dishwasher benefit only me? I'm far too tired to think of a witty reply.

'Thank you Cassie,' I say in a voice much softer and calmer than my internal one.

I have a sneaky suspicion this latest outburst is down to yet another text war with her supposed best friends.

My red-faced daughter wears an expression of indignant astonishment. 'Thank you? Is that it?' she asks.

The front door bursts open and a gust of cold air rushes through Cassie's animated soliloquy. It's Maisy (or as Cassie so fondly refers to her, the Emo freak) my 17-year-old stepdaughter. Equal parts petulant, obnoxious and hormonal.

Both girls nod at one another before Cassie continues her rant. Maisy observes the commotion through heavy, eye-lined eyes. Somewhere beneath that thick, black liner lurk the beautiful green eyes I was first introduced to almost six years ago.

I turn away from Cassie to look at the clock on the kitchen wall.

'You're very late Maisy,' I say, relieved to have an excuse to interrupt Cassie's histrionics. I try to sound assertive but the remnants of an earlier migraine and Cassie's ranting have left me deflated and it shows in my voice. Maisy's black eyes stare at me, her bright red, lip-sticked mouth opening and closing as an irritating, brisk, smacking sound emanates from her violently juddering jaw. She is chewing gum. Masticated and annihilated at a deadly pace. She remains quiet for a moment then shrugs her shoulders.

'Whatevs,' she eventually replies. 'And I told you before, don't call me Maisy.' She lowers her voice and mumbles. 'What idiot would call their daughter Maisy? It's Mania!' she shouts as she climbs the stairs. 'I told you before, my name is Mania.'

I half-heartedly attempt a stern response. 'Well don't be so late again *Mania* otherwise I'll speak to your Dad, and you'll be grounded.' Her unintelligible reply is followed by the loud slam of a door, once to a bedroom but now to something more akin with a refuge collection. A floordrobe of clean and dirty clothes, empty boxes and assorted make-up as well as sullied plates, cups and glasses, some with their own furry growths.

It had taken me some time to work out why Maisy had resorted to calling herself Mania. Surely she'd just missed the 'c' off the end of her new name? Cassie eventually informed me that Mania was the name of the Etruscan Goddess of Hell. A name discovered by Maisy while surfing the net for an alternative name for herself. Her search led her to female satanic names because, apparently, Maisy is as bad and black as Beelzebub himself. In a world where – according to Maisy – tyrants, mostly in the form of politicians, bankers and reality TV stars, are blindly worshipped by the uneducated masses, Maisy has taken it upon herself, along with a few others, to beat these narcissistic rulers at their own game. Maisy et al plan to override and rule with their own brand of evil. Although, quite what their manifesto is hasn't exactly been made clear yet. Maisy now prefers to be known as Mania – Princess of Darkness, Goddess of Hell.

This title of insidious, sinister royalty conjures up an image of a medusa type seducer of men. Of one that eats babies for breakfast and drinks the blood of mere mortals as an afterthought. An image completely at odds when juxtapose to the surly, self-assured but anxious woman-child I know so well. For, despite her fiery rhetoric, this is the same young woman insistent the reason she needed me to accompany her to the dentist the other week had nothing whatsoever to do with her fear of needles. She is also equally adamant that I did *not* catch her crying at the slightly sentimental yet endearing movie about a dog-called Marley. Any idiot could see she just had make-up in her eyes – apparently.

Cassie, who has temporarily suspended her ranting, looks

from the stairs to me, from me to the stairs and I know what's coming.

'Oh. My. God. Oh my actual god,' she declares. 'You so *would* have grounded me if I'd done that. You always treat her differently to me – and *him*.' I turn to look in the direction of her dramatically waving outstretched arm. *Him* is Connor – my second born – or "your perfect child unlike me" as Cassie often refers to him.

Connor stumbles into the kitchen. His large eyes appear startled and his unruly shock of blonde hair is sticking up in all directions.

'I heard a noise,' he says in a voice not yet tainted by puberty.

'I heard a noise,' Cassie repeats in a raised voice to mimic her brother's.

'Enough Cassie,' I snap.

'Can I get a drink Mum?'

I look at my 11-year-old son with affection. 'Course you can love.' His daily declarations of love for me are – for the moment at least – genuinely altruistic. I glance up the stairs in the direction of Maisy's bedroom before I look at Cassie again, finally resting my eyes on the retreating back of my son. I sigh inwardly. One out of three isn't bad I suppose.

Cassie coughs loudly. She has folded her arms and wears an expression of disgust.

'Right,' she shouts across the kitchen. 'I'm going to bed because unlike *some* people who only have to go to work in the morning, I actually have important exams to do.'

Cassie sticks her nose in the air and haughtily pushes past me. Connor clumsily carries a glass of water, sloshing half of it on the floor before he stops to hug me.

He squeezes me hard, then looks up at me. 'Love you Mum,' he declares through a brilliant grin.

I wrap my arms around him and squeeze him back. 'Love you too my Little Big Man.'

Why do I feel as though I want to cry? Connor disappears. All is quiet again.

## CASSIE

It's Wednesday 17th April 2013. The day Nan starts radiotherapy for her Cancer, Margaret Thatcher's funeral, Chelsea's Birthday and another stupid exam. God she is such a cow! Chelsea I mean, not my Nan or Margaret Thatcher; although a lot of people seem to be pretty mad at Margaret Thatcher and are calling her a cow even though she is dead.

Some people have posted things on the internet like "Ding Dong the Witch is Dead". Ha ha very funny – NOT! Why do old people even try to be funny? Wasn't Margaret Thatcher the first woman President or Prime Minister or whatever the title of the top manager in this country is? Exactly. So why is everyone being so harsh? What about girl power and all that crap? I don't really care anyway, she's just some old woman who died and is having a bloody expensive funeral as far as I can see.

I hope Nan doesn't die. They say the cancer hasn't spread but adults lie – a lot.

Dad lies all the bloody time.

'We can't take you and Connor abroad on holiday,' he said, 'because we can't afford it. And we don't have to pay for your little sister because she goes free.'

Then don't go abroad you idiot. Go somewhere we can all go, as a family. Oh yeah that's right we're not really part of your new little family are we? Stupid bloody dickweed. Arrggghh – just thinking about it makes me angry.

I couldn't bear it if Nan died and left me here all alone with them. Mum, Dad, "Simple Simon" and the Emo freak.

I wish I could talk to Nan about Chelsea. I usually talk to Nan about everything but Mum said I can't coz we have to let her rest. Cow! My Mum I mean, not my Nan.

I love my Nan.

## CHAPTER 2

EXAM HELL

**LIZZIE**

*I* feel worn out. Like I've done a day's work already. Cassie couldn't find the all-important piece of paper containing her Student ID and Centre Number for her English Exam this morning. I could hear a strange wailing noise coming from one of the bedrooms and for one ridiculous moment I imagined Maisy performing some sort of ritualistic sacrifice on the cat. As I made a panicked dash for the stairs I realised the dirge of noise was in fact coming from Cassie's room. Normally spotless, her bedroom looked a bit like the Emo Freak's as anything within reach was frenziedly thrown in a desperate bid to find the small piece of paper. A pair of frilly, pink knickers – clean thankfully – landed on my head as I opened the door. Mild amusement danced across Cassie's eyes but it was a mere split second before anguish contorted her features yet again.

'This is all *your* fault,' she shouted.

*Of course it's your fault. Why are you always so surprised when she says this? Her entire existence is your fault and she'll blame you forever more.*

I watched my very angry daughter as her poor bedroom flinched from her brutal interrogation. A jumble of words I could barely make out fell from her mouth. She sounded like a tortured animal. Taxidermy sprang to mind. I imagined her here but stuffed and quiet. She would stand with her arms out – welcoming. And she would smile – permanently.

'Are you even listening to me,' Cassie demanded. 'If you hadn't come into my room last night to talk to me I wouldn't have put the stupid piece of paper down in the first place. I was putting it in my bag when you rudely interrupted me.'

'Have you checked your bag?' I asked. Cassie stopped her ranting and stared at me, as if I'd just graduated from Stupid School with Honours.

'Of course I looked in my bag,' she yelled back. Despite her angered protest I reached into her bag to check anyway. After a short rummage around I pulled out a crumpled piece of paper with the words "candidate ID and centre number" clearly printed in bold black type. Cassie looked at me in utter disbelief, as if I had planted it there. She snatched the piece of paper from my hand and headed for the door. She hesitated before turning back to look at me.

'Thanks,' she said.

This small crisis has made me a couple of minutes late for work. I stuff my bag into my locker and head towards the back office. Amira, my manager, a twenty-something older version of my daughter looks up from her desk towards the clock on the wall before looking at me and frowning. I offer some hurried explanation about the security door for staff entry at the back of the building not working properly again (thank god it plays up sometimes) and she appears happy to accept my excuse, rolling her eyes and nodding her head in agreement. I key in the four-digit code to release and open the office door and before I know it I'm back on the frontline, ensconced amongst the arena that is the city library.

I'd always, as far as I can remember, wanted to work with books and had done now, on and off, for the last 25 years. As a child growing up in the 1970's most of my schoolgirl dreams were filled with boys, make-up and pop stars. Posters of Donny Osmond and David Cassidy adorned my bedroom walls and that all-important thirty minutes on Thursday night TV was always eagerly anticipated. If you missed Top of the Pops on Thursday evening, then Friday morning would be hell at school. Discussions and arguments would ensue about who the best performer was, what song Pan's People (later Legs & Co) danced to and if the number one slot was indeed deserved. To miss out was to be a social outcast.

Playground songs also developed around some of the more famous boy bands. Chanted by zealous pre-teenage schoolgirls like some sinister pubescent war cry to taunt the boys. The Bay City Rollers one still stays with me to this day.

*B-A-Y, B-A-Y, B-A-Y—C-I-T-Y—with an R-O—double L—E-R-S—Bay City Rollers are the best. If the boys don't agree, flush them down the lavatory, with an R-O—double L—E-R-S—Bay City Rollers are the best!*

However, although my youthful imagination was filled with being the next Mrs Donny Osmond or Mrs David Cassidy and as I entered my formative years Mrs Martin Kemp or Mrs Simon

Le Bon, my love of books also flourished. Music and boys could be shared but reading was a solitary indulgence and had been my escape to strange and wonderful places like *The Magic Faraway Tree* or magical kingdoms at the back of old wardrobes such as the one described in *The Lion, The Witch and the Wardrobe*. When that sinking Sunday evening feeling descended and I was ushered to bed – always before the good TV programs started like *The Sweeney* or *Van Der Valk* – I sought solace with *James and the Giant Peach* or I imagined a whole tribe of little people living under our floorboards, just like *The Borrowers*. Later as puberty beckoned and strange things began to happen to my body, Judy Blume's *Are you there God? It's me, Margaret* helped me address issues like buying a first bra, starting my periods and jealousy towards another girl – Fiona Ramsden in my case. I watched in awe as her body changed from its straight up and down shape like mine to one that was noticeably curved and developed, my envy as inflated as her growing breasts. Thankfully, *Margaret* knew how I felt.

As the years rushed by I continued to read with great voracity; Charles Dickens, Shakespeare, John Steinbeck, Louisa May Alcott, George Orwell, The Bronte sisters and Jane Austen to name but a few. I even attempted to read writers like Angela Carter with her allegory, symbolism and surprise – although I must confess I didn't fully understand her writing at the time – I loved them all. I loved to escape.

My passion for books was passed on and cultivated by my Baby boomer parents.

Married young with a common desire to reject the stuffy values and traditions of their parents, they forged their own path in life. They had their own ideas about bringing up children. Money was tight though and with only a portable black and white TV and three channels to choose from, music and books played a key role in my childhood. Both my parents were avid readers, providing them with the means to create weird and wonderful worlds for both my brother and I. Worlds that at any other time were only experienced on our rare trips to the cinema.

Over the years though, Dad excelled in the eccentricity of his preferred reading.

In between his shift work at the shoe factory he created his very own bolthole at home; a garage converted into a mini library of the classics as well as obscure books about philosophy and alchemy. Dad also acquired (for reasons as yet still unknown to me) the odd Bunsen burner and collection of test tubes. This sanctuary has come to be known as Grandad's laboratory and Connor for one thinks it's pretty cool to have a mad professor type Grandad.

My love of reading never waned over the years. I knew I wanted to work with books in some capacity and no one was particularly surprised when I began working at the campus library after I finished my English degree. My secret ambition was to be a writer but as a teenager growing up in a small town I was contemptuously directed by the resident school careers advisor (who preferred to play Olivia Newton John getting *Physical* on repeat on the school's newly acquired VCR during our careers guidance lessons (allegedly for the one girl in our class considering a career in Dance) than actually give any careers guidance) to aim for something a little more realistic. "Being a writer is not for the likes of people such as you Lizzie Lemalf" he'd said. Arrogant prick. Despite his advice though, I did hold onto that dream, at least for a while. Wrote the odd short story, a poem or two, then I met Scott and life just got in the way. Married, then children, then divorced.

It was way back though, at junior school and Miss Fenn – our school librarian – who had planted that seed and inspired me to work within the library service. As far as librarians go she most definitely broke the mould, a far cry from the older librarians at the local town library. They had stern faces with wiry grey hair and defunct reading glasses that dangled around their neck from a chain. They were always smartly dressed but their clothes were dour and old fashioned; frumpy pullovers and scratchy tweed jackets. Miss Fenn however, was like a breath of fresh air.

Young and beautiful with very long, straight, red hair, she didn't need to wear glasses but she did wear make-up and her clothes were really trendy. Miss Fenn liked me and would sometimes let me help her. I quickly developed the idea that shelving books at a sedentary pace and checking them out for the occasional patron wasn't particularly hard work. Oh the naivety of youth.

'Oi, scuse me,' someone shouts in my ear. 'That stupid machine has stopped working again.' A rather irate looking gentleman is pointing at our all new, all dancing, state of the art self-service checkout. I conjure up a smile and take his books from him.

'Let's have a look shall we,' I say. I try to sound helpful but I'm not at all confident I will be. The black metal boxes stand to attention at the main entrance. On first sight they look a little foreboding and soulless. Older customers are cautious. They follow the on screen instructions with trepidation, unsurprised if they fail to navigate this new piece of jiggery-pokery, a suggestive smile of victory if they do. The kids of course are completely unfazed. This machine is positively simple compared to their X-Boxes, Wii's, Smart phones, iPad's, iMac's, laptops and various other 21st century technology at their disposal.

Much to my relief, I successfully manage to check the irate customer's books out for him. I pass them back to him with his return-dated receipt.

'There you go and not to worry, the machines are still new, you'll soon get the hang of them.'

'Stupid bloody things,' he replies. 'What's wrong with real people checking your books out with a proper date stamp instead of these bits of bloody paper that I ALWAYS lose? Besides, it can't leave too much for you lot to do can it?'

'Oh don't you worry sir, I'm sure I can find something to do,' I call after him as he walks out shaking his head.

The day has barely started and my legs are already aching. I have a computer course to run, shelving in the archives to do, the holds list to complete and I've offered to cover Story Time with twenty-five under-3-year-olds because Angie is off sick and as usual we are short staffed. I need a coffee.

**CASSIE**

Oh god that English paper was so bloody hard. God help me if I fail. I can just see Mum's face if I do, full of disappointment, which in actual fact is at least something. Dad won't give a shit whether I fail or pass. He's too busy looking after my little sister. Why doesn't he love us, me and Connor, like he loves her?

Chelsea's bloody bragging again about how easy it was. Why do some people have everything? She's so pretty and everyone likes her. All the girls like her and all the boys fancy her. None of the boys fancy me. They think I'm weird because I play the piano and ugly because I have a bump in my nose. I have the same nose as Mum – Roman she says. Well I'm not bloody Roman, I'm English, and would prefer an English nose thank you very much. It suits Mum though. It wouldn't really matter if it didn't though coz she's like *old* now, well not as old as Nan – I think she's 68 or something so she's ancient – but 45 is pretty old.

Mum's life is done really so she doesn't need to look attractive or anything, although all the boys in my year say she's a MILF, the sickos. And she's divorced and we've got "Simple Simon" as a step-dad, although he's not really our step-dad coz he can't even be bothered to marry Mum. I don't blame him though; she is pretty annoying.

Chelsea's Mum and Dad *are* still married and still together and just to top it off Chelsea's brother Ollie is gorgeous and good at everything. Good at science, good at English, good at Football, good at playing the guitar (the guitar is sick unlike the piano apparently). Perfect like his perfect sister and his perfect Mum and Dad who are *still* perfectly together.

Everyone keeps talking about what they are going to wear to the end of exams party at Chelsea's house. The perfect family live in a mansion of course and the perfect parents have offered to throw a party for the perfect daughter. Apparently she messaged everyone that was invited. I wasn't invited. Phoebe showed me the message on her phone coz she is invited.

*Message for all my boys and bitches. End of exams party at my house, Saturday 23rd 8pm. Message me back all those coming. Get ready for a sick night. Bring it on!!!!!*

Feel a bit gutted Chelsea didn't include me coz I thought we'd been getting on well good. Pheebs told me not to worry about it and said that maybe Chelsea just forgot to add me in and she's sure I'll get an invite. Secretly, I think Pheebs loves that I've been left out. She thinks she's well better than me now. And Joe has started talking to her. He was talking to me before she got drunk and flashed her boobs at Marcus Longthorpe's party. Now he's started ignoring me and talking to Pheebs all the bloody time. Come to think of it all the boys have started talking to Pheebs – a lot.

Oh my actual god, I don't believe it. Chelsea has just tweeted:

*£50 for every A I get. A trip to New York if I get all As! #SORTED!*

Bitch.

※

## LIZZIE

Where did it all go so wrong? I'm standing midway on the stairs, stunned at the sudden eruption that has just taken place. I merely asked Cassie how her English exam went. Forgetting to ask about her Maths exam had resulted in accusations of failing to take an interest in her life so I was pretty confident remembering this one would surely score me a few brownie points. How wrong could I be? I'm still not entirely sure what I said, or did, that was so wrong. Maybe I shouldn't have corrected her when she said Shakespeare wrote in Islamic pentameter instead of iambic pentameter. Or perhaps it was when the conversation turned to Chelsea and her "undivorced" parents. It doesn't seem to matter that Scott *left me* for another woman and had another child, side-lining ours; it's my fault anyway. Everything's always my fault.

I stare at the photo of Cassie hanging on the hallway wall. She's about 6 years old, her hair is in pigtails and her nose is wrinkled from smiling. No, actually she's laughing. I feel sad. She loved me then. Maybe Scott leaving us was my fault and my teenage daughter's malaise is entrenched in me?

How had I failed to notice Scott's avarice and ambition? I don't remember him being like that when we first met. The house, the cars, the golf club, the other women all took priority over us. I – we – were never going to be good enough for him.

God only knows why he married me? I feel wretched. Right now the only emotion I can remember from our marriage is worthlessness. What the hell was it all about Scott?

I look at a photo of Simon (I know Cassie calls him "Simple Simon") on the same wall and smile. The irony is, he IS far simpler than Scott. He doesn't buy into all that status shit. He loves me for me and he loves the kids – all three of them – and that's certainly not easy at times. I was burned and frightened when I met Simon but he promised me he was in for the long haul. He didn't lie.

I run my fingers along the collection of framed snapshots of times past, ephemeral moments gone but not forgotten. I look at a smiley, fat cheeked Connor held, almost in a vice like grip, by an equally smiley but toothless Cassie. My thorax tightens and my vision blurs. It was shortly after that photo was taken, Scott left us. I still don't get it though. Can't get my head around his complete lack of interest in Cassie and Connor. I understand his apathy towards me but not the kids? Why Scott? Why?

I use my hand to reach up behind me and rub the back of my neck, twisting my head from side to side in a bid to banish the stresses of the day. It's not really working so I perch on the stairs for a moment staring into space. An unwelcome feeling washes over me. The black dog has made an appearance and looms at my feet. I shake my head, suddenly angry. I use my hands now resting on my knees to push myself to a standing position again. I will not give in to this ridiculous melancholy threatening to descend upon me. Yes, Scott is a fully-fledged, first class arsehole but as far as I'm concerned it's his loss if he chooses to miss out with Cassie and Connor. And besides, the bottom line is simple – teenagers, whether you are married or divorced, single or co-habiting, straight or gay, rich or poor, simply don't like their parents. And that's official. Every parenting book I've ever read clearly states that any parent hoping to be liked by their teenage children is on a damned path of discovery.

Looks like I'm fucked then.

## CASSIE

For god bloody sake does she do this to me on purpose? Why? Why does she even ask about my exams if all she wants to do is make me feel shit? Dad and all my *so-called* friends do a bloody good job of that. There really is no need for you to jump on the band wagon, wagon wheel, whatever the bloody saying is, too Mum. You have a degree in English (you've told me since the day I was born – boring!) so you know damn well I meant to say Virginia bloody Woolf instead of Canary Wharf (shit, did I call her Canary Wharf in the exam?) and you know I meant imbecilic, whatever the bloody word is, pentameter when you asked me about Will.i.am Shakespeare.

Wish we had been writing about Will.i.am, would have been a lot more bloody interesting than *"To be or not to be"*. What kind of stupid question is that anyway?

Arrggghh Dad's so right, you think you're such an academic but only an idiot wouldn't know what I meant. Not that he's any better. Knob head. You promised you'd ring me, but you didn't. Again!

Chelsea still hasn't invited me to her party. I hate it coz everyone keeps whispering about it behind my back. I don't even care about the stupid party, I really don't. I just feel so ashamed I haven't been asked. It makes me look like such a loser. And Joe still isn't talking to me, much. Maybe I should gate-crash the party, snog Ollie and flash my tits at all the boys. Bet they'd bloody like me then? My tits are not as big as Pheebs though, and I'm pretty sure one of them is smaller than the other. Scrap that then, they'd probably think I was an even bigger loser. Pheebs is texting me:

*Hey there besteee. Come to mine for a sleepover on Friday. We'll get takeaway pizza and I'll get my mum to buy us some boooooze! Shots maybe. Well Lambrini at least. Xxxxxx*

Shit, I wanna go but I have so much revision to do. Mum's bound to get pissy at me if I ask. God she is such a fun sucker. She so doesn't know how to have fun. She must have been born old. But I have to go to Pheebs. She may be able to get me an invite to the party.

I swear to god I'll bitch slap Mum if she says no.

# CHAPTER 3

## GOOD FRIENDS AND CHEAP WINE

**LIZZIE**

'My legs look good when I'm lying down,' Ruby says.

I look at my best friend who has dropped by for a chat and glass of wine and is now stretched out on one of our reclining garden chairs. I had asked Cassie to help me get the chairs from the shed where they'd been patiently waiting, collecting dust, amongst the other fallow garden paraphernalia, but she fled, screaming like a banshee, when a tiny spider glared at her for disturbing his web.

It's been a long winter and for the first time in a long time the sun shines with promise. It's the kind of day that catches you out though. The morning still has a sharp bite to it and lures you into dressing accordingly. The thick tights that earlier seemed like such a good idea have now left one uncomfortably moist. Such a day also (as is typical of the British) finds everyone emerging from their centrally heated cocoons to bask in its warmth. I'm convinced it's actually now a part of our DNA. An innate, built-in, obligatory need to expose our anaemic bodies at the first sign of the sun's rays, along with wild abandonment of all other garments. The reason for this evolutionary response? We only have two seasons in this country; namely July and winter. And, as we are still only stepping into June there's always the distinct possibility of snow tomorrow.

'What?' I reply, unsure where Ruby's conversation is leading.

'When I'm lying down like this,' Ruby continues, 'I don't have to worry about gravity do I?' She stretches out a milky white, slightly plump leg and looks admiringly at it. 'Everything stays where it should, so my legs look good. It's standing up that causes the problems.' Ruby stretches out her other leg and points her toes. She wrinkles her nose, her expression one of disgust as she continues to study both legs. 'God, look how white I am though. Need to book a spray tan I think.'

I laugh and enjoy another mouthful of wine. It's cold going in, warm going down. I look at my friend and bask in our comfortable, benign drivel. Ruby has known me only slightly less time than my parents. She's an honest friend – more like a sister really. Not the sort who'll tell you you look good on a bad hair day but always there when the chips are down.

'It's standing up that's the problem,' Ruby continues. 'Forces everything south you see, so my knees fall to my ankles and my tits hang around my waist. And god help me when I look up into the bathroom mirror every morning, it's like my face has slid off and just hangs there, gathered and crumpled, waiting for some miracle to force it back to its rightful place.' I laugh again. 'It's true,' she implores. 'What is it about hitting your forties and the gravitational pull of your skin? And wrinkles? Don't even get me started on those. Wrinkles, wrinkles everywhere! Where did they all come from?'

'Mark Twain said, *"wrinkles should merely indicate where smiles have been"'* I reply.

'Yeah and isn't that a load of bollocks.'

'Yep. More like *"Age, with his stealing steps, Hath clawed me in his clutch".* Hamlet, I think.'

'Botox and fillers, that's the way forward. Inject it, pump it, plump it all up and smooth it all out.'

I sit upright, horrified. 'No!' Don't you dare!' I imagine my lovely friend like so many of the ageing celebrities splashed across gossipy, coffee-table magazines. Their stretched skin pulled across faces only slightly resembling someone they used to be but more akin to a cartoon waxwork of themselves, with huge, comedic bee-stung lips.

'Yes but look,' Ruby continues, yanking her bottom lip down. 'Don't you think I'd suit pouty lips?' Wine dribbles from the corners of her mouth. I grimace. She lets her lip bounce back up to its rightful place and uses the back of her hand to wipe her mouth.

I sigh and use my hand to rake the hair off my face.

'You may as well accept it my old friend, time is passing and with time we beget that terrible curse of ageing.'

'Speak for your bloody self. I'm never going to get old and if I really have no choice in the matter I'll be doing it disgracefully, right to the very end.'

I laugh at Ruby's indignation. 'I don't doubt it for a second.' I take another swig of wine and enjoy the slight burning sensation it makes as it slides down my throat.

'Andy still loves me though.'

'Yes he does doesn't he, and after all these years.' Ruby shoots me a look of mock outrage. 'No but really,' I continue, 'he still adores you doesn't he?'

Ruby smiles. 'Yeah, I suppose he does.'

'Despite all your ups and downs, Andy's stuck with you

hasn't he?' I pause for a moment and shrug my shoulders. 'Wasn't enough for Scott though was it?'

'Don't make Andy out to be such a bloody martyr; I've had to put up with him and his shit over the years. Did I tell you about his latest purchase?'

'No, what is it this time?'

'A snake. Called Terry. He thinks it's hilarious.'

I don't say a word but clearly my face speaks a thousand words.

'Yep, that's exactly what I thought,' Ruby says. 'I told him if he ever gets it out in front of me, or if it gets into the rest of the house, I'll kill him.'

'Does he keep it in the house then?'

*Was my voice really as high as it just sounded?*

Ruby sighs. 'Yes, in the spare room. But don't worry it's got a huge lock on the door.'

I shudder. 'What kind of snake is it?' I'm both intrigued and appalled at the same time.

Ruby shrugs her shoulders, derision scored into her face. 'I don't bloody know. A snake's a snake isn't it? It could be a python, I'm not sure.'

I flinch and am reminded of Kaa from Rudyard Kipling's Jungle Book.

*"Kaa was not a poison snake – in fact he rather despised the poison snakes as cowards – but his strength lay in his hug, and when he had once lapped his huge coils round anybody there was no more to be said".*

Thank god the only thing I have to worry about with Simon is a sweaty gym kit left in the hallway.

'Why he couldn't get a sports car or have an affair like any normal man managing a mid-life crisis is beyond me?'

I jerk my head quickly to look at Ruby. I feel rattled and if I'm honest, slightly wounded.

Ruby looks back at me and frowns. 'What?' she says raising both her arms. 'Oh come on babe, don't be so sensitive, you know what I mean.' She pauses for a moment to light the cigarette now precariously balanced between her bright red, perfectly manicured fingers. Once lit, the tip of the cigarette glows bright orange as she draws heavily on the other end. 'You really missed your calling in life you know?' she continues, squinting and exhaling smoke from the corner of her mouth. 'You should have been a stage actress then you could have put all that depth and drama to good use. In fact, that's what you should encourage Cassie to do, she's so like you.'

I look at my friend in genuine disbelief.

'She is *not*.' She's, we ... Cassie's nothing like me.' A faction of emotions has quickly gathered around my thoughts. It's true Cassie looks like me. She's inherited my large nose with the same bump she detests as much as I did at her age, but at 45 years of age I've grown into mine. But our personalities couldn't be more different. 'She's loud and dramatic,' I add. 'And, despite being quite clever, says the most ridiculous things at times. I'm much more quiet and reflective.'

Ruby almost chokes, then laughs so hard she actually snorts wine from her nose. 'You then my old friend, have a selective memory. Your stupidity and intelligence used to floor me in equal measures. An enigma old Digby the chemistry teacher at school called you.'

'Did he? I don't remember?'

'Absolutely. Don't you remember when he asked you, his A star student, to explain to the class what hard water was? I swear you just said the first thing that came into your head.'

'Really? What did I say?'

'Ice. Hard water is ice.'

To my dismay I can hear sniggering from the back of the

classroom. Zinc and hydrochloric acid fizzes in my ears infused with the ardent smell of lit Bunsen burners.

'Then there was the time in Biology,' Ruby continues, 'when you said a fibula was a lie.'

I flush with embarrassment. My friend has conjured up my 16-year-old self and in doing so has released an anthology of emotions that are mostly alien to my older self; opinionated and bolshie with my parents, awkward and shy with my peers, brilliant on paper, bumbling and flustered in public. Boys shouting along disinfected school corridors; "Oi Lizzie, you want ice with that?" or serenading me with their rendition of Foreigner's *Cold As Ice*.

This excavation of my formative years brings with it waves of humiliation and insecurity that wash over me with surprising immediacy. I see my clumsy adolescent self and, much to my dismay – I see Cassie.

'Course, if they'd been my responses, I'd have been sent to detention for being insolent but with you – well – Digby just rolled his eyes and asked someone else because he knew, like everyone else it was just you.'

'Okay, okay,' I laugh, 'you've made your point. You weren't much better if I remember rightly. I barely said a word whereas you always said too much. Still bloody do sometimes.'

'Bloody cheek, but nonetheless true. Why use three words when you can use ten? I do like the sound of my own voice after all.'

By rights Ruby and I shouldn't have been friends at all really. Meeting at infant school in the small town of Great Tosson (where I'd now moved back to with the kids after Scott left us) Ruby was always loud and extrovert. She was continually curious about *everything* whereas I was more introvert and introspective. We were good for each other though – Ruby made me push the boundaries and I reined her in.

I turn to Ruby, suddenly serious. 'They hate me you know?'

'Who do?'

'Cassie and Maisy. They hate me.'

Ruby shakes her head and laughs. 'They do not.'

'They do. Maisy can barely bring herself to talk to me, unless it's to contradict *everything* I say. And Cassie? Well, she just argues with me all the time. She blames me for Scott leaving you know?'

'Lizzie, they're just teenage girls being teenage girls for god sake. It's quite normal for a girl to argue with her mother. Up to 183 times a year I read just recently.'

'Well they got that wrong then,' I snort. It's more like 183 times a day.'

Ruby laughs, emptying her glass of its contents and passing it to me for a refill. 'The girls seem just fine to me, don't worry about them. And don't worry about that fuckwit ex of yours either. Cassie knows it's not your fault he left. She's just angry and trying to figure it all out. And she's also just a teenager just being ...well ... a bloody minded teenager.' She sits back taking another, final drag of her cigarette before stubbing it out.

Ruby's right of course, always the voice of reason. But she hasn't finished yet. 'And anyway – bet you didn't know this – troublesome traits like haste and idiocy are just part of the developing teenage brain apparently.

I smirk and throw her a quizzical look. 'How do you know that?'

'Andy read it somewhere; one of those high-brow Academic Magazines I think it was?' Ruby pauses for a moment, her brow creasing into a thoughtful frown. 'Well, anyway,' she continues, 'the adolescent brain is a work in progress, which sort of makes sense really. Some psychologists actually call it a neural clumsiness. Sort of like the physical clumsiness most teens have, a bit like you did.'

'Thanks.'

'Others,' she says tapping her forehead with her finger, 'actually question whether the developing teenage brain is akin to mental retardation.'

I think of Cassie and Maisy and laugh harder than I have all afternoon. 'Oh. My. God.' I reply, desperately trying to catch my breath. 'That explains so much.'

It feels good to laugh. My jaw actually aches from so much merriment. I'm grateful for good friends and cheap wine.

Quiet descends and our extreme cackling subsides. We sit back for a moment and enjoy the warmth of the sun. It's a breezy, cordial heat, without any strength to it as yet, but it warms the soul nonetheless.

Two white collared doves are perched on our dishevelled, weather beaten fence, cooing softly to one another and the sanguine song of a lone blackbird carries through the air. Even the birds are happier when the sun shines.

Ruby looks at me, using her hand to shield her eyes from the sun. 'And you know your problem babe,' she adds. 'Your profundity knows no limits. You care too much Lizzie and it's just not sustainable. Don't get me wrong, that wanker Scott never deserved you – superficial, twat. Did I tell you he sent me a friend request on Facebook?'

'No,' I try not to show the surprise in my voice. 'Did you accept it?' I try to hide my pain when she tells me she did.

'You know me, nosey cow. Andy's always telling me he's finding my nose...'

'Finding your nose?'

'Yeah, you know, in someone else's business.'

I try to force a smile but fail. 'Humph,' is the only response I can muster.

'Oh, don't be angry,' Ruby pouts. 'I was intrigued.'

I can't look at my friend for a moment. My throat feels tight and I suddenly have the urge to cry. It's a stupid, childish emotion but I feel betrayed. I can't decide if I want to know what she's seen or not. The silence between us hangs heavy.

'Well?' I say eventually, scrunching my eyes behind the sunglasses I've just put on.

'He's still a pretentious knob,' she retorts. 'God, he has so many selfies, it's like looking at Cassie or Maisy's profile for god sake. Scott standing by the pool. Scott standing by his car. Scott on his bike. Scott at the Eiffel Tower. Scott on the beach. Scott drinking at the bar. If you ever wanted a case study for narcissism he's your man.'

'Were there pictures of her, or their daughter?' I ask, slightly more sober than I was five minutes ago.

Ruby shrugs her shoulders. 'A few.'

'What about Cassie and Connor?'

She pauses. 'I didn't see any, but then I didn't really look for too long. Look Lizzie the only person Scott will ever truly love is Scott and the only reason he stays with his second wife is for her money. Pure and simple. The problem wasn't – isn't – you or Cassie or Connor. It's him. Don't you get that? And bleeding for the world won't change things.'

'What do you mean? I don't.'

'You do,' she continues. 'Take your job for instance, you're only supposed to check out books, but you can't leave it at that can you? You feel obliged to help the homeless, the jobless, the bereaved, and the uneducated. Christ if I didn't know better I'd have sworn you were a social worker, not a bloody librarian. It doesn't stop there though does it? You try to be the perfect Mum, perfect step-mum, perfect daughter, perfect friend and perfect partner.'

I look at Ruby in dismay. I was laughing five minutes ago and now I feel like shit. 'Are you saying I'm wrong to care?' I try not to sound angry. Ruby smiles at me.

'You sounded just like Cassie then. No, you are so right to care. I wish there were more people like you Lizzie, but just look at you. Unlike me you're still as skinny as the day you left school, but I swear that's because you run round after everyone and spend most of your life worrying. And you never stop trying to make up for Scott's shit. It's exhausting Lizzie – give yourself a bloody break will you? And besides,' she adds, 'all it does is reinforce how flawed us mere mortals are.'

I look at my friend, confused.

'I still don't understand, what are you saying?'

Ruby sighs and runs a hand through her long dark hair. 'I dunno. What am I saying? Maybe – just maybe – try and worry a little less about everyone else and take more care of you for once? Cassie, despite her prick of a father, will be okay, you know? She has a tough time with him, I'll grant you that, but she's also just a teenager. It's normal to be filled with all that angst and anxiety. Christ don't you remember?'

I digest my friend's words – slowly. Part of me feels furious. I want to shout at her like Cassie shouts at me. How dare she knock me for caring?

'It's easy to preach Ruby but you haven't got a bloody clue what it's like to live with two damaged teenage girls.' My words have barely finished tripping off the end of the tongue I now want to bite off. My response was instant but my regret is equally so. I look at the face of my lovely friend and see the pain I've caused.

I place the heel of my hand on my forehead and sigh heavily. 'Shit. I'm – so – sorry,' is all I can manage to say. Three pathetic words, never more meant. Ruby lowers her head for a moment and the quiet is deafening.

Thankfully (for once) I'm relieved to hear that all too familiar voice. 'Mum,' Cassie shouts, 'Mu-um!'

'Outside Cassie,' I shout back. Cassie emerges at the back

door, Maisy behind her. Maisy's eyes are lined with thick black liner out of choice, Cassie's because her – I suspect – make-up has ran from crying again. Cassie spots Ruby and out of nowhere, in a sweet angelic voice totally alien to me, greets her. Cassie then turns to me again and her demonic intonation returns.

'I'm going for a sleepover at Pheebs,' she states.

'Cassie, please don't *tell* me where you are going, please ask me.'

Cassie rolls her eyes and sighs heavily. '*Please* can I go to Pheebs for a sleepover?'

'What about your revision?' I ask, slightly anxious. Fully aware of Ruby's words only moments ago. Cassie's eyes begin to fill up, threatening to erupt into tears.

'I knew you'd do this to me,' she replies. Cassie looks defeated, her voice tinged with anger but for once she seems resigned. She turns to go back to her room but I'm moved by her sadness.

'Okay, you can go,' I call after her. Cassie turns back and looks at me in disbelief.

She smiles like the little girl she once was and still struggles not to be.

Her eyes are wide. 'Really?'

'Yes really, but make sure you're back bright and early to get on with your revision.' She sighs again but she has to, it's compulsory for teenagers. She's still smiling though. I smile back. Maisy's giving her a lift. Having recently passed her driving test Maisy wants to drive everyone everywhere – except me of course – which is great, except I can't extricate the driving instructor's comments to me just before her test. "Maisy, or should I say, er, ummmm ..." He paused and coughed at this point, his face reddening a little. "Maisy or Mania" he eventually continued, "is err, well ... ahem ... a slightly over-confident driver, who talks very little except to call other drivers expletive words". I can feel myself worrying already.

'Please drive carefully Maisy,' I plead. She looks at me, the regular, rhythmic movements of her jaw viciously chomping on the gum in her mouth.

'My name is *not* Maisy, its Mania' she states, 'and yeah, whatevs.'

The girls, like a tumultuous cyclone, are gone as quickly as they came. I look across at Ruby. She is, thankfully, laughing.

'I'm sorry,' I say again. 'That was a shitty, thoughtless thing for me to say.'

'No, no, it wasn't.' She sighs. 'And you're right I don't understand, I sometimes wish I did though.'

# CHAPTER 4

## WHEN THE GOING GETS TOUGH

**CASSIE**

So bedroom, it's just you, me, my books for revision, my laptop, my phone, and Mum doesn't know it but I've nabbed her iPad too. One more stupid exam to go then I'm free from this life of pain. I *was* nicely spread out across the kitchen table. I like it there coz the light's good, and I can see if anyone comes to the door. But Mum said I had to move my crap – can't believe she called my stuff crap – coz they are having friends round for a meal. It's only Ruby and Andy for god sake and having them round for a meal basically means they'll all eat too much, drink too much and laugh too loud.

Arrrrgh it's okay for them they don't have any real stress in their lives. I mean really, how hard can it be working in a library? I mean basically it's just,

'Can you help me find this book please?'

'Of course I can, here it is.'

And Simple Simon's job can't be much harder; he works in

IT or consulting or something. Andy and some other idiot own the company, so he just gets to sit in front of a computer all day. Although he does travel a lot, so he isn't here much during the week, thank god. Try doing eleven GCSEs I say. Then you lot would know what hard work really is. Of course, Mum loves to remind me that she did do it, so she does know – but that was like a trillion years ago and it doesn't count coz it was easy for her.

I'm only doing this for her anyway. She's the one that keeps saying *"education is the key Cassie."* The key to what? She's got all the brains and no money and Dad is an idiot and has loads. Mum thinks she's a prophet and Dad's all about the profit. Ha that's quite funny – for me.

Dad's always saying he doesn't have any money though, says it's all the Step-Monster Sharon's money. Bell end. I know that's a big lie. It's just something you say Dad so you don't have to pay for me and Connor. Knob head.

I remember how excited I felt when you said you were moving to a new *bigger* house. You said there would be a bedroom each for me and Connor but as usual it was another lie. You got a huuuuggge bedroom with its very own walk-in shower, an office for Sharon, a playroom for Harriet (even though she also got her own bedroom too), a cinema room, two dining rooms, three living rooms and enough money left over to install some of those fancy bisexual, bi-folding stupid doors for your massive kitchen. But, once again, no bedroom for us. We have to make do with the stupid sofa bed in Sharon's office if we want to stay. Don't wanna stay at your stupid house anyway. It stinks of bullshit.

Arrggghh now I'm too angry to revise. Only one thing for it…

## LIZZIE

I'm so tired tonight; I really could have done without Cassie's attitude. Asking her to kindly remove all her books from the kitchen table was not without the usual drama. For one delicious moment I did consider asking Andy to bring Terry the snake round to give Cassie a hug.

I tried to explain to Cassie that her idea of a carpet picnic was not really good etiquette for our dinner guests, even though it did work quite well for Richard Gere and Julia Roberts in *Pretty Woman*. She then asked what the hell petticoats had to do with anything and proceeded to storm upstairs, which she had to do three times in total, as she couldn't carry all her books at once.

I'd almost forgotten what the table looked like, so voluminous and spread out were her remnants of revision. Heavy text books sat amongst dog eared copies of Shakespeare's *Hamlet*, George Orwell's *Animal Farm* and John Steinbeck's *Of Mice and Men,* as well as numerous past papers of various subjects which lay scattered amongst page after page of intense handwritten notepaper. Boredom and indifference were clearly evident as scribbling's such as Shakespeare stinks, Chelsea is a bitch and I love Joe were threaded throughout correct and legitimately attempted answers. Heart topped letter I's and the black and white keys of a piano were also generously dispersed throughout. One particular question caught my eye, 'describe in detail what hard water is,' and scrawled underneath the words, *ice you idiots*, made me smile.

Why Cassie chose to sit in the kitchen and revise I'm still none the wiser. Personally, I think it was to persecute everyone else in the house. If she was miserable then goddamn it, we were going to be too. I caught poor Connor blue from holding his breath the other morning. He was afraid Cassie would hear him breathing and shout at him again.

Oh god, she's playing the piano. Simon looks at me and raises his eyes. Clearly something's rattled her because she's playing *Rolling in the Deep* by Adele. The performance is faultless but the keys are being hammered senseless.

Undoubtedly a great tragedy has befallen her that would dwarf even the likes of Shakespeare's *Macbeth* and Sophocles *Oedipus Rex*. Probably another text war with said friends or someone's disliked her Facebook profile. Whatever it is, the poor piano is being played to within an inch of its life.

I'm suddenly aware of Maisy at my side. We stand, quietly listening to the dark and dramatic performance unfolding in the living room.

'She's actually very good when she's angry isn't she?' I say.

Maisy is silent for a moment, listening intently. 'Yeah, she's like a tragic enigma.'

I turn to look at Maisy. Her hair is now as black as the thick make-up around her eyes and her bottom lip is newly pierced with a small silver hoop. She has just spoken three more words to me than she has all week. I seize the opportunity to communicate with my surly step-daughter but she senses it and is heading for the door.

'Going out,' she says.

'Where?'

'Friends.'

'Stay safe.'

'Whatevs. Bye Dad.' And with an obligatory slam of the front door she is gone.

Simon, who has just witnessed my attempt to fraternise with the enemy smiles at me. It's a warm, safe smile without agenda. He shrugs his shoulders, lifting and holding his hands up in question.

'Don't worry about them love,' he says. 'Now, do us a favour and pour us both a glass of wine will you while I finish burning this lasagne?'

I smile at him and make a beeline for the fridge. As I bend to open the door I realise how much my back is aching. Despite what many may think, working in a library can be really heavy work, and I've been doing it now for more years than I care to remember. And I'm not getting any younger. Perhaps I should look for a new job, something less physical. What the hell else would I do after all these years though?

Ruby and Andy are at the door. I ask Cassie to stop playing the piano for a while, just so we can hear ourselves talk. She scowls at me.

'Do you realise I have a Grade Eight piano exam in two months? You never support me in anything I do.'

*No, I only pay for and drive you to all your lessons, and have done since you were 6 years old. Then there's all your books and exam fees, but no, I never support you do I?*

'You can practice later,' I promise. 'Maybe you can play Cannon in D or Fur Elise? You're always so happy when you play those two.'

'Oh. My. God. Oh my actual god, and what, may I ask, is wrong with Adele?'

'There's absolutely nothing wrong with Adele. She's amazing, it's just you...'

Cassie cuts me off before I can finish.

'You know your problem?' she glares. 'You're a bloody Palestine.'

*I'm a what?*

After a few seconds the penny drops and I can't help laughing. 'Don't you mean Philistine?' Cassie looks at me with disgust, gives her best dramatic pause and haughtily barges past me. 'Don't be so bloody condensing,' she says.

'Don't you mean condescending?' I shout after her. 'Oh just shut bloody up.'

## CASSIE

Oh my actual god, how many followers does Chelsea have? It's like she's some sort of celebrity. I mean really, what does she have that I don't? Well besides like being really pretty, having a washboard stomach, junk in her trunk, hair like the shampoo adverts, long toned, tanned legs, *and* big boobs (not that I've seen her boobs in real life. All the boys would love it if I had though). All the boys at school love it if girls are lesbians. Chelsea's not a lesbian though and neither am I – although Chelsea does sing that Katy Perry song a lot. The one about kissing a girl. So ... I dunno? Whatevs. She's clever too and her brother is gorgeous and her parents are still together and they live in a mansion and her Dad drives an Aston Martin.

OMG she *is* a celebrity.

She still hasn't invited me to her party. Not that I care. I'll just check my Facebook again in case she's left me a message. I scroll quickly through my phone. Nothing. I don't care. Oh no, she's just tweeted. I really can't be bothered to read it.

I look at my revision notes. History – another one of Mum's favourite subjects and sooooooooooo booooooooooooooooooooring. I mean really, what is the point of it. What's done is done. It's not like anyone seems to learn anything from it is it? I mean pick a year, any year from now back to pre-historic times when the Romans were around and you can bet somewhere there's a war going on. Some country thinks they're better than another one and uses excuses like trying to make them civilised or religious or whatever to make them do what they want. But it's like, not really about any of that crap is it? It's usually about taking stuff, like people or money or animals, or gold or oil, or sugar or tea, or coffee or diamonds, or bananas and just, well... stuff. The powerful and the powerless. What's changed?

I spread myself across my bed and try to make a start. I will not read my phone. I will not read my phone. Maybe I should do some Buddhist chanting and make that my mantra or maybe I could add some piano music to it and send it to Beyoncé. It would of course be a world-wide hit and I would become Beyoncé's best friend and rich and famous overnight.

Everyone would want to know me then. Dad definitely would, although, I'd tell him he'd have to sleep on the sofa bed in my enormous mansion if he ever visited. And Joe would definitely fancy me then, and when he asked me out I'd say, "no thanks, I'm going out with Jay-Z's brother." I don't even know if Jay-Z has a brother but that's what I'd tell Joe.

My history revision fights with my phone for my attention. Some of it is quite interesting I suppose. Women's rights and getting women the vote really like, opened my eyes. I didn't realise how depressed, or is it oppressed (probably both) women were. I mean like, throwing yourself in front of horses or going on hunger strike was like a bit extreme but women had no voice, no rights, and they were owned by their husbands. That's like, well out of order. I'm never going to be owned by anyone. I'm strong and independent like Beyoncé. That reminds me I must ask Mum for a lift tomorrow.

I suppose that's why Mum says it's important to vote. She said this bit of history is just one small part of a much bigger picture. She said that when Nan was my age I am now, she got paid half the wage of a man doing the same job. She also said abortions were illegal and you couldn't go on the pill unless you were married. I secretly like that Mum knows and tells me all this stuff but sometimes it makes me feel different to a lot of my friends.

Mum looks like she's been on hunger strike sometimes. I swear she's even thinner than normal lately. I think she does it on purpose to make me feel even fatter. Yeah, thanks Mum, you can't just put me down mentally, you have to put me down physically too, by being thinner than me. I mean really, what kind of mother does that to their child?

I try to concentrate, not really sure if the ball of sticky tac I'm snapping between my fingers is really helping. I don't actually know where I got it from but I find it strangely comforting to roll, stretch and snap across my notes.

I stare at the words on the pages before me. Okay, so there's the 1832 Reform Act, the 1835 Municipal Corporations Act, the National Union of Women's Suffrage Societies or the NUWSS and the Women's Social and Political Union or the WSPU.

'Arrggghh.' I screw the grubby piece of tac back into a ball and aim it at a blank piece of wall. I give it my best shot. I'm not very good at throwing so instead of making the part of the wall I aimed for it actually hits Ed Sheeran smack in the mouth – the poster that is. I wish Ed Sheeran was here with me, in my bedroom.

'Arrggghh, DILLIGAS! Work that one out Mr Examiner.'

Oh shit, what the hell, I'll read Chelsea's stupid tweet. Then maybe I can get on with my revision proper.

*Hey ladies, do I wear the blue or the red for my fabulous party?*
*#Dior or Chanel?*
*Decisions, decisions!*

Cow.
My phone pings. It's a text from Pheebs.

*Hey babe. Think I may have got you an invite to the party.*
*Laters xxxx*

Oh my actual god! Yay! Chelsea is actually really nice. OMG what will I wear?

※

## LIZZIE

God I feel tired tonight. Maybe I really am getting old?
*Have another glass of wine. What a good idea.*
I'm happily conversing with myself because Andy is prattling on and is actually pissing me off. I didn't realise how blinkered he is, how narrow his perspective is. He's actually preaching the virtues of sterilising young teenage mothers.

'Well while you're at it lets sterilise the young teenage fathers too then, shall we?' He actually ignores my comment and continues his one-man argument.

'I mean *not* having a baby takes planning and intelligence,' he states, in a voice that always seems too high for his build but never more so of late due to his ever increasing physical demeanour. He was never particularly slim but he's let himself go a bit recently and definitely carries his share of middle age spread.

I look across at Ruby. Her grin is impish. She rolls her eyes but seems content to sit this one out. She drinks greedily from her wine glass then excuses herself from the table in search of more.

'Do you know the teenage pregnancy rate is so high in this country we are now officially the worst in Europe. It's a disgrace,' Andy continues, safe in his knowledge of statistics.
*Who comes up with these bloody stats anyway?*

I sigh heavily.

'So you want to bring in mass sterilisation do you, Andy? State interference in women's reproductive lives? Did you – do you – even read your history books? You're an educated man. Don't you realise how far women have come in the western world and how fragile that progress is? You must have *some* idea of the struggles of women to get to a place where we finally have some control; or at least some choice about our own bodies?'

I feel my anger escalate within me. It's a small but intense heat rising rapidly from the pit of my stomach.

I stare at Andy and marvel at how my dislike of someone's bigoted point of view manifests itself as an aversion to his or her physical flaws. What I would usually see as a minor physical imperfection – and certainly of no consequence under normal circumstances – suddenly appears positively grotesque. In Andy's case it's his stomach I've focused on. His visceral fat, bloated, pot-bellied, beer-guzzling gut protrudes far more than mine ever did during both my pregnancies. His abdominal obesity is, if only for that moment, as offensive to me as his smug attitude.

'So you like the idea of eugenics?' I continue. 'Why don't you just start preaching Mein Kampf, establish a few concentration camps and be done with it?' My intonation is curt but controlled. 'Why does everyone blame the underdog, the weaker members of society for our country's problems?'

The room is uncomfortably quiet for a moment. I should leave it at that but I can't.

'Free money,' I state.

Andy looks puzzled. 'What do you mean free money?'

'That's what Amber, one of the young women that visit's the library a lot, equates having a baby will provide.'

A look of triumph flashes across Andy's eyes. 'That's exactly what I'm saying. So they're *not* controlling their bodies are they?

They're churning out kid after kid and expecting the state to foot the bill.'

'Do you know why Amber sees having a baby as access to free money?' I continue; my exterior voice far calmer than my internal one. 'Because she lives in a system that's set up to fail her.'

Andy nearly chokes on his wine. 'How does free money, which is made up of *my* taxes incidentally, fail her?' he snorts.

'Because,' I reply, inhaling deeply. 'If Amber's been through and seen half of what she says she has in her 17 years, then that's far too much for any one lifetime. Right from the word go, the people that should have loved and cared for her abused her. The system set up to protect her from those abusers failed to do so. Now, add to that an absent father unwilling to pay a penny towards her upbringing and Amber is the end product. What about mass sterilisation for absent fathers then, eh?'

Andy opens his mouth to speak but changes his mind again. 'Then of course there's her education. Have you noticed how it's always those that have nothing that fall through the safety net? If the same amount of time was given to her education as it was to her continued isolation and being suspended or expelled, the poor girl may have actually learned to read and write properly.'

'Well, what was she doing getting herself expelled? She should have had a better attitude.'

'Of course, yes, you're *so* right. She shouldn't have let minor things like her mother's boyfriends trying to rape her – again – or her uncle using her arm as an ashtray for his cigarettes, affect her attitude. No, she shouldn't let any of that affect her attendance or attitude towards school should she?'

Andy is taken aback, his face flustered and red. He coughs and smooth's his tee shirt over his fat belly.

'God, no, no, of course not,' he says. 'What ... where were Social Services?'

I roll my eyes and shake my head. 'Overstretched, understaffed and at breaking point, like every other public sector service.'

'Couldn't she at least try and get a job?'

'Doing what? What has her poor education left her qualified to do? I'll tell you shall I? Drifting from one meagre minimum paid job to another, scratching around for a fulltime contract but most probably offered one of those god awful zero hour one's. The sort so many employers now seem to be so fond of. Legal contracts that specify workers must be flexible and available at short notice but are only paid for the hours they work on the days the employer stipulates. These would be the same contracts that mean a disposable, throwaway workforce walking down a one-way street where employers bear no risk, avoiding sickness and holiday pay and overtime? Christ Andy, even Maisy has had trouble getting employment and she's got us behind her. Add to that the breakdown of many industries in this country and we're left with a whole section of society where many options are non-existent or just not available.'

Andy looks thoughtful for a moment. I look across the kitchen. Ruby appears to be guarding the second bottle of wine she's now opened and Simon is conversing with her. They both look in our direction from time to time, grinning and raising their eyes in mild amusement.

'So,' I continue. 'What does Amber and girls like her, see as their way out? Yep, you've guessed it, to get pregnant. This leaves respective mothers dependent on a system where yes, they receive a level of child support three times what it was twenty years ago, but that was done in a deliberate attempt to reduce child poverty. But for a lot of young women, having a baby is an opportunity to break away from their surrounding misery and start their own life, albeit a life dependent on the state. It's a well-known fact that a lot of the young mothers you seem to be referring to, mostly come from poorer backgrounds and communities.'

'Look Lizzie, step down from your feminist soap box. I was merely stating...' I cut Andy off mid-sentence.

'And you, Andy, step down from your thinly veiled, crude, cruel and misogynist one.'

'I'm not a misogynist.'

'Really? I have two teenage daughters that god knows I'm trying – and struggling sometimes – to help navigate, negotiate and fight when needed, their way through this crazy world we live in. A world where despite, and thank god for, the definite advance of women's rights and freedoms over the years, is still a world where advertising, the internet, celebrity culture, television and the media at times, pose a real problem to young and impressionable young women. If any of those ridiculous reality programs are anything to go by for god sake we're in real danger of cultivating a whole generation of unstable, over-sexualised, bullied young women with very little or no self-esteem. And, as if that isn't hard enough, you, one of my oldest friends, is trying to preach to me the virtue of sterilising young women.'

'Well,' Andy stutters, 'I didn't mean Cassie or Maisy, they wouldn't be that foolish.'

'How do you know?' I exclaim. 'It's true neither of them appear to have a maternal bone in their bodies but what if one of them did get pregnant? There is so much grey area, Andy, between your narrow black and white views. A lot of these young women are vulnerable and any belief or politics that excludes vulnerability is bound to have a spiteful, authoritarian edge. I don't understand you Andy, you had a daughter. Do you really believe what you're saying? And more importantly what would she have thought of you if she was here today?'

I feel like this question is hitting below the belt but it had to be said. I don't expect a response. Andy is quiet but looks stunned. It's a victory for me but not one I feel good about. I no longer see the grotesque round belly. Instead I see a wounded, moth eared, oversized teddy.

Andy swirls the red wine he's drinking diligently around the large wine glass he's holding, bringing it up to eye level. He pretends to examine the glass before finally putting it to his mouth and taking a large gulp. He then puts the glass down, looks at me and grins.

'You're right. I'm ashamed of myself. I'm a complete and utter twat.' I smile and he takes another swig of wine and bangs the empty glass on the table.

'Bloody hell, no wonder Scott bloody left you. I bet he could never win an argument.'

I grin back at Andy.

'Touché,' I say. 'Touché, Andy.'

## CASSIE

Right that's it for tonight, I've done enough revision. If I don't know it now I never will. Besides, I'm too excited to concentrate. It's official – Chelsea texted me and I'm now going to the party. I was a bit offended by the text though.

**Chelsea:** *Pheeb said u keep hassling her about my party? Must admit I didn't even think of u but Em can't make it so u can take her place I spose!*

**Me:** *Thanx Chelsea, that's well sick. What time does it start? Xxx*

**Chelsea:** *8 but drinking with my bitches at 7 – if u can handle it?*

**Me:** *I can handle it. See u at 7. Thanx again xxx*

What the hell Pheeb? I wasn't hassling you. Was I? Whatevs, it's obvious I'm an afterthought but I don't care coz now I'm going to the party like everyone else. At least I won't look like such a loser tomorrow when all and sundried – or is it laundry? No, it's sundry. Yeah, when all and sundry is talking about what to wear.

Oh my god what *will* I wear? I don't have anything decent. I'll have to ask Mum to take me shopping. Oh no, she'll take me to all the cheap shops. Not that there's anything wrong with that. It's just that, this is Chelsea Divine's party.

Oh god, I'm stressed already. Okay, okay, take a deep breath Cassie. Mum will just have to help me out for once in her life. Or maybe Dad could buy me a dress, if I explain how important it is? He won't though. I know he won't. The idiot will just say he's got no money – as usual. I'll just have to be nice to Mum for a few days. I'll start now by going downstairs and playing *Fur Elise* for her.

I open the kitchen door my mouth starts watering. I can smell the lasagna Simon's cooked. He's quite good at cooking, makes pretty good Italian food. Simon is loading the dishwasher. He looks up and asks me if I want some lasagna. I greedily accept, taking over the dishwasher loading while he dishes some up for me. Revising is hungry work.

Ruby is standing by the cupboards pouring herself another glass of wine. She smells of wine a lot lately. Mum and Andy are being a bit weird, just staring at one another across the table. Oh god, I hope they don't fancy each other?

Simon passes me a plateful of lasagna and I carry it towards the table.

'Hi Andy. How are you?' I haven't seen him in a while, he looks quite fat.

'Oh hey Cassie, I'm fine thanks love. How are you?'

Urrggghh, I am *not* your love. I smile sweetly. 'Yeah, I'm okay thanks, or at least I will be when I finish my stupid exams. Hey Mum, you look well pretty tonight. Would you like me to play *Fur Elise* for you?'

Bloody hell, she doesn't have to look so shocked. Mum smiles at me. She looks really happy. I can see why the boys in my year call her a MILF – sickos – she does have a really pretty face. Nan and Grandad say I look like Mum. Nobody thinks I'm pretty though, except Nan and Grandad and Mum, but that doesn't count.

'Yes please Cassie, I'd love that,' Mum says.

I finish shovelling lasagna into my mouth then go into the lounge and sit at our old piano or "old Joanna" as Grandad calls it. I tell the perfect child to turn the bloody TV off and bugger off while I play.

'Okay Cassie,' he says. Why does he have to be so bloody nice?

I begin to play. Mum walks in and is smiling. I have one exam to go and I am going to Chelsea's party. All is well with the world.

## CHAPTER 5

### THE GOOD NEIGHBOUR?

**LIZZIE**

The flat monotonous sound of Tabitha's voice is offensive to my ears. She is building up to something and I'm dreading it because Tabitha only ever comes round for two reasons; the first is to borrow something, the second is to be the bearer of bad news (as long as it doesn't involve her).

Something in her voice, despite its complete lack of colour, suggests it's most definitely the latter. Maybe it's the slight ripples of excitement that just lifts her words – barely noticeable to the untrained ear, ubiquitous to a skilled listener – that gives the game away.

Some unfortunate individual's calamity has excited my next-door neighbour and it's still only 7.30 in the morning. She is prattling on about something and nothing, no doubt building up to it, so I continue getting ready for work around her.

As she drones on I look up from time to time and marvel at

Tabitha's excessively chattering mouth. Bright red lips frame bleached white teeth; teeth that protrude a little but not enough to disrupt the generic Barbie doll look Tabitha so obviously covets. Her hair is long (hair extensions I believe) and red today but it changes as often as Cassie changes outfits when going on a night out so there is every possibility it could be short and any one of a number of other colours tomorrow.

Tabitha owns her own Hair and Beauty salon – Scissortly Love – and never has a hair out of place. Her perfectly manicured locks match her perfectly manicured nails. It is the perfect profession offering the perfect opportunity for her to glean and gloat about the latest gossip and misfortune of others. Unfortunately, Tabitha's need to gossip perpetuates the urban myth that all hairdressers are brainless, shallow, gossipmongers; which, of course, many are not. Tabitha pauses.

*Here we go, get ready for the bombshell.*

'Well, anyway, the reason I came round, is well...' Another pause.

*Could she make this any more dramatic?*

'Well, don't be angry, but Mark and I caught Cassie smoking yesterday evening, and, well...' She lowers her voice and continues to talk from the corner of her mouth. 'It smelled a bit, sort of funny, herbal – if you get my drift? It was quite late, we were taking Fortuna out for a walk because she had colic, and we bumped right into Cassie.' She makes a poor attempt at a half-hearted laugh. 'We really did make her jump. Bless her.'

*Yeah, and bless you too.*

'She looked very guilty so we didn't say too much. Just that it was rather disgusting.'

*Disgusting? You – a parasitic amoeba greedily feeding off the misfortune and insecurities of others – is calling my daughter disgusting?*

'We didn't want to trouble you with it last night,' Tabitha continues. 'But Mark and I discussed it at great length and we both agreed it was something you needed to know.'

*Err no, I don't think so. What you mean is, you decided and Mark, who lost his balls the day he met you, did as he was told.*

My mind races, quickly searching for a response; a forceful anti-climax is what's needed. My internal voice is on full rant.

*Yeah, I bet this kept her awake last night. Long moments of wakefulness punctuated by small snatched moments of sleep, thinking about the various ways she might deliver this terrible news. I'm sure she was positively delighted when that alarm clock went off this morning.*

I am disappointed with Cassie but not particularly surprised, she is a teenager after all. A child developing into an adult is, by definition, the process of a gradual managed parting of parent and child, and at the very core of those adolescents is the need – within reason – to try new things.

Barely a second has passed but it feels like an age and I'm still searching for my reply. For the briefest of moments I see myself poking a lighted spliff into Tabitha's perfectly made-up eye. I quickly reprimand myself and somewhere from the library of my mind I'm reminded of a non-violent technique promoted by Gandhi, whereby he suggests the liquidation of the antagonisms rather than the actual antagonist.

I have my reply. 'I know,' I smile.

'Pardon? You know?' I can hear the bitter disappointment in Tabitha's voice.

'Yes, I know.' I didn't, but I'll deal with it later.

'Oh. Well, isn't she a little young to be smoking cigarettes … or otherwise?'

'Two years older than your husband was when my Dad caught him doing the same thing, if I remember rightly?'

'Yes, well, as you know I thoroughly disapprove of smoking and...'

I cut Tabitha off mid-flow. Devilment and sarcasm has grabbed me by the throat and I can't help my response.

'Did I tell you Cassie's getting her tongue pierced in a couple of weeks? Come to think of it, I might go with her and get mine done too. Would you like to join us?'

'Err, what? No, I don't think so, not really my thing.'

'Go on,' I goad. 'Live a little.'

'No really,' Tabitha replies. 'Anyway I have to go now, Mark's watching Fortuna.' Tabitha strides towards the door.

'Good for him. How is little Tuna?'

Tabitha wrinkles her nose in disgust. 'Her name is Fortuna, *not* Tuna,' she states. 'Anyway Mark needs to get to work so, I'll, um, see you soon,' she finishes, irritation and disappointment evident in her farewell.

'Yes, goodbye Tabitha,' I reply, mischief clearly evident in mine.

My revenge is sweet but short lived. Cassie is almost – from out of nowhere – on top of me, gangly, flaying arms trying to wrap themselves around my neck, practically choking me in the process.

'Thank you, thank you, thank you,' she squeals. I'm confused to say the least.

'Thank you for what?' I reply.

'For letting me get my tongue pierced. I heard you, just now, talking to Tabs. I didn't even know you knew I wanted it done?' she continues, thoroughly delighted.

*Serves you right. Let's see how you get out of this one.*

'No, I didn't mean you Cassie.' Her smile vanishes. I take a deep breath. 'Tabitha came to tell me she caught you smoking, what she thinks was, cannabis last night?' Cassie immediately pulls away from me.

'For god bloody sake,' she shouts. 'I'm going to Nan and Grandad's and why don't you just leave me a-bloody-lone.' Cassie grabs her jacket and with one almighty crash, slams the front door behind her.

## CHAPTER 6

UNDER PRESSURE

**CASSIE**

'It's not a life, it's an adventure!'

'Oh shut up Salocin,' Nan snaps at Grandad. 'You can't apply that stupid motto to every bloody thing that happens you know. Having cancer is not an adventure.'

I open the back door of my second home, still seething about the bloody tongue piercing and smoking weed thing with Mum, and catch my grandparent's sort of arguing.

I know what Nan means, Grandad does say that a lot, but he does make me smile all the same. Somehow, nothing ever seems that bad when Grandad puts his arm around me and says, "Dan chu worry sweedheart. Remember – it's not a life, it's an adventure."

Nan is right though, cancer isn't an adventure, but she still smiles at Grandad when he says it. It's his way of trying to cheer someone up when they're sad or down. Grandad pulls Nan to him and kisses the top of her silver hair. They have been together like, forever, but they still love each other. Which is so cute. They managed to stick at it. Pity their daughter couldn't do the same. Although, to be fair, it was actually Dad who left Mum, but she probably drove him to it.

'Cassie gal, how are ya?' Grandad shouts when he sees me.

Grandad puts that old style Frankie & Benny's restaurant music on that they listen to sometimes and starts dancing and twirling Nan round the room. Nan pretends to be annoyed but she's laughing.

Everyone says Grandad is grumpy but it's grumpy in a funny way. He moans a lot but it's different to Mum's nagging coz he makes me laugh. Grandad swears quite a lot too, much to Simon's annoyance, which makes it all the more funny. His favourite words are "fuck off", which he always says when he disagrees with someone or something but because of his cockney accent it always sounds like "fack orf". Grandad says that all the kids from my generation are spoilt, but I know he loves us.

Freddy – Nan and Grandad's black and white cocker spaniel – sits next to me and looks as amused, if not a little confused, as I am, as Grandad continues to spin, whirl and twist Nan around the room. If Nan was sad before I walked through the door, she isn't now.

Freddy barks enthusiastically at them both and I can't help laughing along.

'See Cassie,' Grandad shouts, 'I wasn't always a grumpy old git. Bit of a dapper dancer in the day ya know?'

I sit back on their comfy old sofa, kicking my shoes off, curling my feet under my big backside that has too much fat dimpled junk in it, and let that lovely safe feeling wash over me. I can't explain what it is but all my stress seems to stop at my grandparent's door. No one is nagging at me to do this or that, or promising me stuff then letting me down. Everything's just warm and chilled and safe.

And they don't let me use my phone when I'm with them but for some reason I don't mind. I can't explain it but it really pisses me off when Mum tells me to stop using my phone but I respect it when Nan and Grandad ask. Besides I don't really mind coz I always feel like my head's had a rest when I've been here.

It's not that Nan and Grandad don't like technology though. Nan has one of those Kindle thingies to read with but Grandad still prefers real life books. They have a computer too, which they're quite good at using. Except Grandad does get like, a bit confused from time to time and sometimes ends up shouting at it, which is actually like, well funny. Nan has Facebook too, which is like dead embarrassing coz sometimes she posts things on my wall, then everyone takes the piss of me. I want to unfriend her but like, she's my Nan and everything, so I can't.

Nan and Grandad like music too and love listening to me play the piano. They say music is good for the soul. They're quite cool and like a lot of chart music. Mumford and Sons is their favourite band at the moment, although Grandad quite likes some dance music. They also like a lot of the music Mum grew up with in the 80's but they say the 60's were the best. It's thanks to them I have a real dyslexic (or is it electric? Whatevs) taste in music.

When they stop dancing I make us all a cup of tea (or Rosie Lee as Grandad calls it) and Nan cuts us a slice of her homemade bread pudding. Grandad gets some of Bob Dylan's songs up on the computer. He says he wants to show me Bob Dylan coz he knows I like Adele and he knows Adele sang a Bob Dylan song. It's the one that always makes Mum cry. The one she says she dedicated to me and Connor. She should bloody well listen to the words of that song then sometimes, when she's like nagging at me.

I talk with Nan and Grandad for a while, listening to some Bob Dylan and then to some of the early stuff by Grandad's favourite band, The Rolling Stones. I dedicate *Paint It Black* to Maisy and *19th Nervous Breakdown* to Mum, coz she always acts like she's having one. I make the dedication in my head though of course. Not out loud coz I have to respect that Mum is Nan and Grandad's daughter, after all. It's not their fault they made such an idiot.

Nan looks tired; it's the radiotherapy I think. Thankfully the Doctors have caught the cancer early so she doesn't have to have chemotherapy which I'm like well pleased about coz Nan has lovely hair and it would be like well bad for her to lose it. I told her I'd chop all my hair off too if she did lose hers to make her feel better. So I'm like well chuffed she hasn't. It would be like sooooooo embarrassing if I had no hair. No boys would *ever* fancy me then.

Nan lies down on the sofa and Grandad covers her up with a blanket. He kisses her head and tells her to rest for a while. He also tells me I can stay for a few more minutes, and then I have to go, so Nan can sleep.

Grandad goes outside to his laboratory in the garden – well, it's an old garage converted into a room with hundreds of books really. He's not a scientist or anything, but he is a bit mad I suppose. Eccentric Nan says.

## LIZZIE

Can someone please tell me who, when writing the rulebook for teenagers, felt that slamming doors was compulsory and should be adhered to at all times? And we're not just talking the front door or their bedroom door. Although they are often the preferred choice and never more so than when trying to make a statement of sorts. But teenagers are not picky.

It can be the bathroom door:

'I'm taking a shower.' Bang!! 'Arrggghh, get it out, get it out, get that bloody spider out.'

Or the front door:

'I'm going out.' Crash!

Alternatively, there's the back door:

'For god bloody sake, why do *I* have to get the washing in?' Whack!!

There's the washing machine door:

'For god bloody sake, why do *I* have to put the washing on?' Thud!!

Let's not forget the car door:

'What? Oh yeah, thanks for the lift, I suppose. Don't forget to pick me up.' Slam!!

And last but not least, the bedroom door:

'I bloody hate you. You never let me do anything.' Smash!!

I contemplate a life without doors? Not practical. I contemplate a life without teenage daughters? Not possible, at least not just yet, but I am working on it. I contemplate a glass of wine and chocolate. Very practical, very possible. Happy Days!

## CASSIE

Nan has fallen asleep so I pull my phone out to check the time. One hour until my final exam. If I leave now I can take a slow walk to school.

Pheebs has texted and asked me to meet her but I've made up an excuse about not being able to coz I'm here with Nan.

She's with Chelsea and her lot and they're probably all smoking and I really can't be arsed with it.

Freddy is sleeping next to Nan but opens his eyes as I stand up to go. I walk quietly towards him, stroke his head and whisper goodbye. He licks my face, rolls back slightly and lifts his paw. He's waving goodbye to me, I know he is. I love Freddy coz he loves me just for being me.

As I step, outside I take a deep breath. It's a warm day but still a bit crisp and the sky is a lovely blue instead of that horrible grey it can be sometimes. I start to walk, relieved this is going to be my last exam. I swear to god I'm going to sit around in my onesie for a whole week when this exam has finished and I'll do it eating ice cream and watching those ridiculous reality programmes, as Mum calls them.

She's already nagging me to get a job for the summer. As if. Like, *no* one has worked as hard as I have for the last year. I actually deserve a year off from everything. I still don't really know if I even want to go to Sixth Form in September. Think I'd rather go to college and study music, but Mum would flip.

Can't believe bloody Tabitha, what a cow, a boring, fun sucking cow; bet she couldn't wait to spill the spaghetti. Oh god, Mum's bound to interrogate me when I get home. I don't even bloody like smoking. It was Phebe's brother's spliff and it was her who told me to have a drag. She said I needed to know how to do it properly, ready for Chelsea's party. She said it makes you look proper grown up and everyone will take the piss if I can't do it right. It tastes rank though. I mean proper disgusting. Give me a bar of chocolate any day. It didn't even do anything for me either coz I only took one bloody drag for god bloody sake and now Mum thinks I smoke weed!

Oh god, she'd better not ground me. I like sooooooo need to go to this party, more than life itself. If I don't go I could lose all my friends and it's a well-known fact that not having any friends is as harmful as smoking. It was on UberFacts or something, so it *must* be true.

So, if Mum doesn't let me go she's making it as bad as me smoking anyway.

She'll have to take responsibility for making me ill if I have no friends. So she'll have to let me go for health reasons.

I check my phone. Mum hasn't wished me luck for my exam yet?

I look up and feel the sun on my face. It's been nice to get some fresh air. I feel like I've got a clear head and I'm ready for my exam. However, that feeling quickly fades as I turn a corner and the building that's been my prison for the last five years comes into sight. My tummy flips. The nerves are starting and I have butterflies threatening to flutter my memory away. Oh god, now my stomach is like making rumbling noises, but I feel too nervous to eat. I feel dead panicky. I'm trying to remember what Mum said:

'Take a deep breath Cassie – then exhale – nice and slow.'

I hate to admit it but she's right, it does actually help, a bit.

I can see Pheebs up ahead. She's waiting with Chelsea and some of the others and it looks like they're all passing a ciggie around. My stomach flips again coz I really don't want to join in. I just don't like it. But then, if they don't offer me a drag, that'll make me look crap anyway. Oh bloody hell. Pheebs has spotted me and she's waving. Chelsea turns to see who she's waving at and glares at me. She looks away again and says something to everyone, then they all look towards me and laugh, including Pheebs.

I don't think Chelsea really likes me anymore and I'm like, not quite sure why, coz I thought she did a couple of months ago. I miss not going round her house coz the truth is I like sooooo fancy her brother – not that I'll ever be good enough for someone like him. Her Dad was nice too; he talked to me, quite a lot actually.

Once, when Chelsea nipped to the loo, her Dad put his arm round me and said I had a stunning body. Which made me like blush a bit, and if I'm honest, a bit uncomfortable. None of the boys at school have ever said that to me though. His hand brushed near my boob as well, but I'm pretty sure it was an accident. He was always really nice to me though.

As I join them all, Chelsea is drawing heavily on the ciggie they've been sharing. She blows smoke from it in my face, which makes me cough a bit and everyone else laugh. Then she thrusts the disgusting thing in my face.

'Smoke this or you can't come to my party,' she demands.

I reluctantly take the lighted fag from her and put the stupid thing to my lips. I try to remember what Pheebs showed me to do with the spliff (which is like the same I think) and I suck hard on the stupid cancer stick. My nightmare comes true though, and I cough and splutter like the virgin smoker idiot I am. Everyone around me erupts into raucous laughter, including Joe. I feel humiliated. I try to laugh but it's not easy to do when you're gasping and choking.

'Oi Miss,' Chelsea shouts. 'Miss, over here, Cassie is smoking inside the school gate.'

Before I know it Chelsea has dragged me past the metal gate and is holding onto me. I'm mortified when Miss Jay marches up to me and takes both me and the cigarette inside. She gives me a stern talking to which makes me late, and almost miss the start of the exam.

My phone vibrates, just as I grab my pen to take into the main hall. I hope it's Dad wishing me luck. I look at the screen. Oh, it's a text from Mum.

*Hey there lovely girl, lots of luck in your final exam today. I'm very proud of you. Don't worry about Tabitha, we'll chat about it later. Love you xxx*

Arrggghh, why does she have to be so bloody nice and why do I feel like crying?

Why hasn't Dad text me – again?

# CHAPTER 7

## DIVIDED BY A COMMON LANGUAGE

**LIZZIE**

My back hurts. This job is far more physical than most realise, but really, I should be able to manage a bit of stock rotation. I load my trolley with yet more books but stop for a moment to straighten up and massage my lower aching lumbar region. My thoughts turn to Mum, tough as old boots, and brave. Clearly I'm not cut from the same cloth. Mum has cancer, I have backache.

*Man up you wus!*

I look across at my colleague Joan and am mildly amused as a customer attempts to converse with her.

'Excuse me lady, I need card please.'

'Certainly sir, you will need two forms of ID to join.' The customer continues to smile but just waits quietly.

Eventually he speaks again. 'So, you give me card please?'

'As I've said sir, you need two forms of ID.' A puzzled look replaces the customer's smile.

'What you mean?' he says.

'I mean sir we need to see some ID, something with your name and address on, like a passport and a utility bill or a driving license?' The penny has dropped. Or has it?

'Ahhhhh yes, yes, yes, my name is Bolek Adamski and my address is 71 Gilamorey Street.'

'No sir, you cannot tell me your details, we must see some ID.'

'Eh?'

Joan sighs heavily and taps her head with her fingers, slight exasperation evident in her weary voice. 'Some ID. We need to see some I – Deeeeee,' she repeats.

The customer sounds irritated. 'Yes, yes, yes,' he replies. 'My name is Bolek...' and round and round they go.

'City of the bloody poles innit?' Raj, one of my other work colleagues whispers in my ear.

'What do you mean?'

'Immigrants innit. Eastern Europeans. This city is flooded with em. Thanks to all this open border ideology shit.'

'Isn't there room enough for all of us?'

'Nah man, there aint. There aint enough jobs for us Brits – never mind that lot as well. And you know what really pisses me off? They don't speak a bloody word of English and they don't even try.'

Raj is a young, enthusiastic third generation Indian. He's a natural comedian, but, thanks in part to his age, can sometimes be both passionate and fixed in his views.

'Raj, your grandparents were immigrants,' I remind him. 'People probably said the same about them too, when they first came to this country.'

'Yeah, I know, I know,' he replies. 'It was like well hard for them. People called them Paki bastards and all that, which was like well out of order man. Indian people are nothing like those lazy Pakis.' I purse my lips and frown at Raj. 'But you know what the difference is between my grandparents and these bloody eastern Europeans?' he continues.

'No, but I'm sure you're going to enlighten me Raj?'

'They learned to speak the lingo and they integrated. This lot seem to think they can get by on "I want card please" or "I want money please" or "I want toilet please". Then spend the rest of the time keeping themselves to themselves and talking about us in their own bloody language.'

I'm annoyed and slightly disappointed with Raj. 'I think you're generalising there a bit.'

I'm about to remind him of the library's policy towards equal opportunity and discrimination – of any nature – but before I can he's left my side and is volunteering to help a struggling elderly customer. I listen to their conversation and smile. The customer has a Polish accent and Raj, as always, is going out of his way to help her.

Immigration has always been a bit of a hot political potato, especially in this city but Raj's comments make me think. It wasn't so long ago when immigration and race were inextricably linked but the recent arrival of many white, Christian, Europeans has completely changed all that.

I look back across at Joan. After a small amount of patience and some very basic sign language, an understanding is finally reached: despite the long and winding queue that has now formed behind this particular customer. The self-issue machine has stopped working – *again* – and the rather cross-faced waiting customers are, shall we say, a little less understanding.

With such a diverse, multi-cultural society, barriers will always need to be broken but even two people speaking the same language will sometimes struggle, especially when it transpires across one or two generations. God knows I struggle to understand the girls some days. When they talk to each other I'm lost.

Divided by a common language, Mum always says and this was never more evident than when I overheard Dad and Cassie talking the other day about music.

Dad, not knowing the title and performer of a particular song he'd heard, was trying in his usual brusque manner to hum the tune to Cassie. Her confusion at the slightly offensive whining of my aging father manifested itself as a number of distorted faces worthy of winning a Gurning competition at National level.

Eventually, Cassie seemed to grasp some semblance of a song amongst the noise that gradually became so offensive to the ear even Freddy the dog had to leave the room.

'Ohhhhh,' Cassie suddenly replied, 'it's Otto Knows.'

'Who knows?'

'Otto Knows.'

'Otto? Otto? Who's bleedin Otto?'

Cassie rolled her eyes and sighed heavily. 'No Grandad, I *mean* its Otto Knows.'

'So you keep telling me but I don't bleedin care what bleedin Otto knows, I'm asking you what the bleedin song is.'

'Arrggghh Grandad, that's what I'm trying to tell you! It's called A Million Voices.'

'What?' Dad responded slightly agitated. 'What do you mean a million voices? I'm asking you about one bleedin voice and one bleedin song.'

I watched, amused and slightly dizzy at the ability of two different generations to confuse one language. This verbal tennis match continued for several minutes before grandfather and granddaughter finally understood one another. I laugh out loud at the memory, the song now firmly imprinted in my own mind, *A Million Voices* by Otto Knows.

My thoughts are interrupted by a commotion over by the Science Fiction and Fantasy section. I recognise the shrill, angry shouting. Amber is clearly having a bad day. I excuse myself from the patron I'm serving and head with some urgency towards the disturbance. Bill and Dave from Building Security race ahead of me.

Amber seems to be involved in some form of tug of war with one of our more bedraggled visitors. The item in question appears to be a bottle. When I reach the scene I am relieved to see the Buildings Officers have separated the duelling pair but expletives are being spat fiercely at one another. Both customers are dragged towards the main entrance.

Mr Gray smells, if it's at all possible, more pungent than ever; a putrid mix of sweet, rotting fruit, stale urine and strong tobacco oozes from his every pore. Priding myself on enduring some of the more unpleasant smells that sometimes waft among the shelves of the public library (even during the hottest of days of summer), I'm unable to prevent the heaving sensation in my abdomen as the stench of Mr Gray hits my quivering nostrils.

I gather myself together and turn my attention to Amber. She is a year older than Cassie, the same age as Maisy, but has had to grow up so much quicker. Her face is flushed with fury and wet from tears. Her anger reminds me of Cassie but it's tenfold and actually makes Cassie appear quite tame in comparison. I attempt to talk to her but I can see my words are useless today. Her glazed eyes suggest a riotous rage and ferocious fear bubbling inside. Her prose is jumbled as she screams something about the crazy bastard stealing her vodka and something about "being in for it now, the last of his giro until the end of the week". She looks at me, eyes wide and wild.

'Can't you see?' she shrieks. 'He'll make me pay and I can't stand it anymore. It hurts, it fucking hurts.'

Amber has gone. The commotion in the library is over, but

it's not over in my head. My mind races as I imagine all kinds of scenarios to befit her last haunting comment. Her words stay with me, dragging me down. I think of Cassie and Maisy with their grumpy, surly faces and for once it brings a smile to mine. I don't know if they are, or ever will be, but I'm grateful they have Simon and me, grateful they have us.

# CHAPTER 8

## GOURMANDISE

**LIZZIE**

It's not enough that my nosy neighbour tells me Cassie is smoking, now the school has too, phoning me to say she was caught smoking inside the school gates before her exam. It's been a long day at work and Amber's words are still disturbing my thoughts. Do I tackle this smoking thing tonight or pick another day to be the bad mother again?

I pull up to the drive. Despite having seen better days I still love my little, old yellow Beetle. The same one I've been driving for the last 10 years and very unlike the new BMW Scott drives despite, apparently, not having any money.

*Bastard.*

I switch off the radio and sit in complete silence for a moment. The calm before the storm?

I eventually get out of my yellow cocoon and head for the front door. I shiver, despite it being a warm evening, and look round. My senses feel heightened and the hairs at the back of my neck stand on end. I expect to see someone watching me but other than Joyce, opposite, pruning her roses and Dan next door cleaning his car, the street is relatively empty and quiet. I shrug it off and throw a courteous nod at both my neighbours. I open the front door. It looks tatty with its peeling paint; we really should replace it. Perhaps I can slip in unnoticed and disappear upstairs until tomorrow morning.

'Mum, is that you?' Cassie demands. 'Mu-m,' she shouts again.

*Fat chance of disappearing anywhere.*

'Yes it's me,' I reply in a borrowed, much chirpier voice than my internal one. 'How was your exam?'

'Good, good, it was all good. Another one bites the crust eh?' she says, flustered and almost colliding with me in the hallway. 'Right take your coat off and come into the kitchen,' she orders.

I'm suddenly aware of a strange combination of smells wafting from the kitchen; there's a definite burning smell but also seared or roasted meat and something sweet, possibly apple? The table is set, there are candles burning and Connor is standing wide-eyed with a tea towel over his arm.

'Hi Mum,' he says, 'me and Cassie have made dinner for you.'

'No, I *made* dinner,' Cassie snaps, 'Connor just helped – a bit.'

'But, but…' Connor stutters but Cassie abruptly pushes him out of the way.

'Get out of the way you idiot. Let Mum sit down.'

'Okay Cassie,' Connor replies.

Cassie has cooked for me. Why?

'Well, well, well' I say, 'what have I done to deserve this?'

'It's just to say thanks for being such a great Mum,' says Cassie.

I raise my eyes. Suspiciously.

*Oh my god it's a trap, get out immediately, you are in serious mortal danger. Just pick up your coat, nice and slow, make some excuse to go to the front door, then ...R U N !!!!!!!!!*

I pull out the chair Cassie insists I sit on.

*You're in for it now, you should have got out while you had the chance.*

'Me and Connor, or should I say Connor and I,' Cassie continues, attempting to add some plum to her accent, 'are going to wait on you tonight. We'll be the butlers and you can be the Lady, like in Down Town Abbey.'

I smile.

'Where's Maisy tonight?' I ask, as plates, pots and pans seem to crash continually behind my back in the kitchen.

'Didn't she tell you?' Cassie says, as she continues to busy herself whilst barking orders at poor old Connor.

'Tell me what?'

'She got a job at that shop that she's been dying to work in, you know the one?

Goth Shock I think it's called.'

'Oh,' I reply, disappointed to be excluded from such good news.

'Ta Da!' Cassie shouts as she bangs a plate of something that resembles food in front of me.

*That looks interesting, smells like garlic.* 'More like arsenic,' I say out loud. 'What?' Cassie replies.

'Garlic,' I say. 'Yum yum, smells like garlic.'

Connor pulls out a chair next to me, Cassie sits opposite. I'm very aware that I seem to be the only one with food in front of me.

'Aren't you two eating?' Cassie and Connor look shiftily at one another.

'We ate when we were cooking,' Cassie replies.

I cut into and chew on a piece of chicken breast (at least I think that's what it is?), which is about as easy and tasty as chewing on a piece of old leather. The aesthetically pleasing carrots are hard as bullets but the peas are quite good. However, not even soft candlelight can disguise the burned new potatoes.

Cassie watches my every mouthful, desperate to please.

*You're just going to have to fake it. You can fake an orgasm so this should be easy, just make the same noises.*

'Mmmmmmmmm. This. Is. Soooooooooo. Goooooood,' I say with as much enthusiasm as I can muster.

I attempt to push a carrot onto my fork but fail miserably as it shoots across the table and smacks Cassie straight between the eyes. Connor cups his hand across his mouth and begins to snigger. Within a few moments this quickly escalates into a full blown belly laugh. I try to contain myself but it's impossible. Not even the wrath of Cassie can stop the laughter gushing forth. To make matters worse the carrot has stuck to Cassie's forehead like a perfect, if somewhat slightly large, bindi spot.

For the briefest of moments Cassie is mortified, her stony face threatening to explode into a terrible rage but much to my delight, she laughs. It is pure unadulterated laughter and a lovely moment; one that finds all three of us falling about in hysterics. Suddenly the front door bursts open and Maisy stares at the three hyenas falling across the table. Her confusion quickly turns to disdain before she finally shouts, 'Bloody idiots.' And then storms upstairs, slamming her bedroom door behind her.

A moment of silence descends; we all look at each other, then the guffawing begins again. We eventually pull ourselves together and agree a trip to the chip shop is a gastronomically good idea. Connor offers to go to the one on the corner while Cassie and I get stuck into clearing the bombsite that is now the kitchen.

Cassie is uncharacteristically sweet and asks me how my day

at work was. I tell her about Amber but I know she's not really listening. She has an agenda and she's building up to it. I'm happy talking though, enjoying my daughter's feigned full and undivided attention. Is this a glimpse of things to come, or will she always hate me? I continue to prattle on when she stops me mid-sentence.

'Mum?' she says, her face very serious. 'Chelsea's like having a huge end of exams party and everyone – I mean *everyone* – is going. And guess what? I've been invited too,' she squeals.

*Oh whoooopee doo, the great and mighty Chelsea Divine has dared to invite my lowly daughter to her dazzling party.*

'Isn't it great?' Cassie continues enthusiastically.

'Isn't it just,' I reply. My internal voice is on full rant.

*Hummmph, the Divine's, the kind of people Scott loved. The sort of people who measure success by money and material goods. In their world you're either a "somebody" or a "nobody." They most definitely believe themselves to be part of the "somebody" camp.*

'Oh shut up,' I say out loud. Cassie swings round to look at me, slightly confused.

'What?'

'I said hurry up, let's get this dishwasher stacked eh?'

'Oh, right, yeah,' Cassie replies. 'The thing is Mum; I really need something new to wear. For the party?'

Oh god. My heart sinks. I've only just paid off the huge repair bill for the car. And what with never getting a penny from Scott for maintenance and no sign of a pay rise at work in over four years now, we're not exactly flush. My good mood is quickly disappearing as is my temporary bonding with my daughter. I need a diversion. Maybe now would be the right time to bring up the smoking thing.

The door bursts open and Connor arrives with both arms full of delicious smelling chips. He slams the front door behind him with his foot. I sigh. Something tells me there's going to be a few doors slamming tonight.

## CASSIE

Oh my actual god that's the last bloody time I ever cook anything for *her* again. I go to all that effort and all she can do in return is have a bloody go at me about bloody smoking. Maisy bloody smokes but no-one ever moans at her, mostly coz she doesn't get caught I suppose. But it's not bloody fair. I don't even bloody like smoking anyway. We didn't even talk about getting me a new dress either and time is seriously running out.

Joe is definitely going to the party so I have to look really good. Perhaps then he'll notice me again. Not that he gets a chance to breathe with Pheebs draping herself all over him lately. She knows I like him, why would she do that in front of me when she's supposed to be my BFF?

Whatevs all I need is the perfect dress and if I do my hair like Chloe from Towie then he might, just might, notice me again. I won't look as pretty as Chelsea but then again who does? It's hard to compete with perfection so why try? Besides, she doesn't fancy Joe, even though he fancies her, all the boys fancy her. But she's only really interested in older boys, with cars and money.

I look at Chelsea's profile on my laptop. She has so many selfies and each one has so many comments, all good of course, but then why wouldn't she? She is soooo pretty, so different to me. I wonder what it's like to have such a perfect life and be soooo perfect.

She's just tweeted.

***Some people will do anything to fit in – but they never will!!! #Loser.***

Oh my god, she means me, with the smoking thing. I know she does, and – OMG – she's only just posted it and already has 27 likes. How humiliating. Everyone will know it's me.

The thing is, she's right, I don't fit in and I can't work out if that's a good thing or a bad thing. Or a normal thing? I mean, I wanna fit in, so I know I need to have the right look, the uniform. That means the hair, the nails, the clothes and the make-up. I do like all those things I suppose but we don't always have the money for them so I make do and mend (yes I was listening in my history lessons).

What I don't understand is girls like Natalie Wilson who makes herself sick to stay thin and Ella Maxwell who's saving up for a boob job. There's nothing wrong with the ones she already got as far as I can see. I know because I've seen a photo of them coz Aaron Taylor got her to send him a picture of them in a sext; which was well out of order coz then he sent it round to the whole year 11. I would have been like so humiliated, but she just laughed.

I really need to sort this dress out so that I can look just right. I'll ask Maisy – I mean Mania – if she's got anything I can borrow.

I knock and open her bedroom door. The first thing to hit me is the familiar whiff of fag smoke; the second is the state of her floor. I can't see her carpet for stuff. She has her back to me and is perched on her windowsill with the window open. She turns to look at me, blowing smoke from the corner of her mouth. Where's Mum now eh?

'S'up,' she says.

'Hey.' I reply. 'You know Mum'll kill you if she catches you smoking?'

'Let her try. I'll bitch slap her.'

'Maisy?' Mum shouts up the stairs. 'I can smell smoke? I hope you're not smoking in your room again?'

'Oh shit,' Maisy says jumping, almost burning her fingers. She quickly stubs out the roll-up she's smoking and carefully pushes it back into the fag box shoved down her bra. She flings her window wide open making a wafting motion with her hand, willing the fresh air in whilst simultaneously spraying her room with body spray.

'You sure bitch slapped her there, Mania,' I say laughing. 'Piss off,' she replies. 'Anyways, what'd ya want?'

'I'm going to a party in a couple of days and I really don't have a thing to wear. Can I look through your stuff?'

She looks amused. 'Be my guest, but you won't find anything there that fits in with that fake lot you hang round with.'

If she's trying to wind me up it's not working, mainly because I agree with her. I half-heartedly run my hands across the various items hanging in her wardrobe also aware that most of what she owns is spread out across the floor. I don't have a clue what's clean and what's not and it repulses me a little. Why is everything depressingly black? Why no colour?

'Do you really think all my friends are fake?' I ask.

'Duh! Are you really asking me that? Fake hair, fake nails, fake boobs, fake arse, fake tan, fake eyelashes, fake teeth, fake lips. Fake, fake, fake!'

'They're not all fake.'

'That bloody Chelsea Divine is. Everything about that girl is fake, including her personality. You only have to look at Malala Yousafzai to see how rank your friends are.'

'Who's Malala Yousafzai?' Maisy sighs and rolls her eyes.

For a moment she reminds me of Mum.

'Malala Yousafzai,' she repeats, 'the Pakistani schoolgirl who was shot by the Taliban for campaigning for girls' education.'

'Oh yeah, I think I remember Mum talking about her. What's she got to do with anything?'

'Are you for real? Malala nearly got herself killed trying to liberate the girls of her country. The only thing the liberated girls you hang round with want to do is out-bitch each other. They're all surface and no substance.' I throw her a quizzical look. She sighs heavily. 'Superficial,' she says. 'It's all about *"look what I've got,"* tashing off and getting drunk.'

Maisy's not a girl of many words (I think she only says about three a week to Mum) but when she does go off on one you realise she is quite a deep thinker.

'You like tashing off, and partying,' I remind her.

She grins. 'Yeah well, that's true. And there isn't anything particularly wrong with that in itself. It's just you don't need to do it with fake boobs or eyelashes or hair and you definitely don't need designer clothes and bags. Why can't they just be themselves?'

'Like you?' I ask. As far as I know Maisy isn't a natural blackhead and wasn't born with black lips and eyes.

Her face has become moody again. 'Humph!' she snorts. 'My look is art, an expression of who I am. It's a non-conformist, two fingers in yer face to the stereo typical view of what a woman should look like. The kind of look constantly perpetuated by society and the media and those bloody dumb reality shows you always watch.'

'Me? You watch em more than me.' Maisy grins at me again, loudly smacking chewing gum between her lips.

'Yeah,' she says shrugging her shoulders. 'Well whatevs, it's coz they're funny. All the women are stupid, narcissistic bitches and its compelling viewing coz they're a constant reminder of something I don't want to be.'

'Like your Mum?' I ask sheepishly, half expecting a fist in my face, but Maisy merely shrugs her shoulders again and looks away.

'She's just a bitch who should never have had kids. I'm glad she left. Me and Dad are better off without her.'

'How's the job going?'

'S'okay I s'pose. The boss is a bit of a bitch.' I suddenly have a brilliant idea.

'Do you get staff discount?' I ask. Maisy lowers her head and looks at me through her heavily black lined eyes.

'You, at Goth Shock? Really?'

She's right of course; I wouldn't be seen dead in there. Actually that's the only way I would fit in such a place, if I was like, dead. I've never actually set foot in the shop before but I've walked past it a couple of times. It's a dark, foreboding place, pulsating with what I think is loud music but sounds more like screaming to me. The staff dress positively satanic and the mannequins clearly represent their Goth style window dressers. I shiver at the thought. I look at Maisy and shake my head. We both laugh.

'Nah!' we both say at the same time.

Ooh I've got a text. It must be Pheebs responding to mine. I asked her if she wanted to go shopping with me tomorrow to sort this bloody outfit out.

**No babe, can't go with u, have already promised 2 go with Chelsea xxx**

Oh, right, thanks for asking me. Why can't I go with you? Why do I feel like I'm on the outside all the time? What's wrong with me? What's right with me for that matter?

Right, she can skate round this all she wants but Mum really is going to have to help me sort this out. I cooked for her for god sake, so she like owes me. Big time.

I fling Maisy's bedroom door open. 'Mum,' I shout. 'MUUUUUUM!'

# CHAPTER 9

Q – WHAT?

**LIZZIE**

I can't quite believe I got out of shopping with Cassie. Who knew they'd need me to cover extra hours at the library.

*Such a shame.*

Okay it's true. The theme music from the Jaws film does start to play in my head whenever Cassie suggests we go shopping together. This, I believe, is for two reasons.

The first is simply that the fantasy of mother and teenage daughter shopping trips is a world away from the reality. I did, I confess, fantasise a little about such trips on that beautiful morning Cassie was born. I projected forward in time to a place where she was grown, and mini films of our time together would run and re-run across my thoughts. I pictured us on lovely girly shopping expeditions, full of smiles and laughter. Not that I'm particularly good at or enjoy shopping but it would be more about the bonding experience between mother and daughter.

It was I've come to realise an unrealistic, unspoken expectation, borne out of rules and silent imperatives absorbed from an array of social and cultural affiliations; especially family movies and television adverts. Sadly, as with most things, fantasy and reality are two completely different experiences.

In case you're in any doubt, take heed of the following unwritten rules, when shopping with your teenage daughter:

Teenage daughters do not smile, unless they are with friends, only frowning is permitted.

Teenage daughters do not laugh, unless they are with friends, only growling is permitted.

Do not make it obvious that you are out with your teenage daughter – especially if she sees her friends.

If you do see her friends, you must run, crouch down amongst the clothes, *anything* that ensures you are *not* seen.

Yes, your teenage daughter will allow you to buy her a coffee, cappuccino, frappucinno, organic smoothie, double choc espresso or whatever the hell else there is to choose from. As long as you sit at separate tables.

Do not ever – under any circumstance – shout across the lingerie department that: "This is a lovely bra; what size are you again?"

Understand the default response from your teenage daughter to the word NO is: "But it only costs..."

And finally, the second reason Cassie, shopping and I don't

work is quite simply because I have turned into my mother. Not the calm, older but wiser version of late, but the one who blurts out comments like: "How short?" or "Is that a top or a dress?" or "How much?" or "How high?"

I swore I would never subject any daughter of mine to such questioning. After all, surely such statements were only made out of a deep-rooted need to ruin my life weren't they? How was I supposed to know at that naive but arrogant time of my life they were actually borne out of an indisputable love and genuine concern for my welfare? And anyway, such questions almost always result in your teenage daughter's face, to quote my Dad, "looking like a slapped arse". I'm hopeful for the future though. I'm sure one day will find Cassie and I on a shopping trip that doesn't find her completely repulsed by my presence and where I no longer have the urge to hurl her from the top of the multi-storey car park or under the next passing bus. Until such a time I have friends.

## CASSIE

I don't quite know how this happened but I'm now clothes shopping with Ruby. Mum has to work extra hours or something so she asked Ruby to meet me, but that's okay coz Ruby is like well sick.

I had to catch the bloody bus to the city though and all coz neither Mum nor Maisy would take time off work to pick me up. I told Mum to tell her boss it was an emergency, explain to her how important it was that I actually get a dress for *the* party of the year, and just ask for half an hour off to come and collect me and drop me off. It's a perfectly normal request. Don't know why Mum got so bloody moody about it.

It's not my fault our stupid little town is about ninety miles away from the main city. Well, actually it's only about nine miles but it feels like bloody ninety on those bloody old, juddering buses that smell of stale wee and BO and baby sick and diesel.

Ruby lives in the city. She's the same age as Mum and like an aunt to me really coz she's been in my life since I was born. And Andy has too of course. Its better being with Ruby anyway coz she's like well chilled and she spoils me. I think that's coz she lost Lilly though.

Lilly was only 4 years old when she died; of meningitis I think it was. I thought she had a cold and it like, well scared me, because she was literally here one minute and gone the next. I was only a year older than Lilly, and because Mum and Ruby were best friends, me and Lilly grew up together. Like sisters really. I couldn't believe it when she died. I became like, well paranoid for a while. Every time someone sneezed I thought I was going to lose them. It didn't take meningitis or death to lose Dad though, did it.

I keep a photo of me and Lilly in my purse. I keep it there coz I forget what she looked like sometimes. I talk about her quite a bit with Mum, but not with Ruby; she closes down if you try. Even with Mum. She just won't talk about her, which is like well weird coz Ruby likes to talk about *everything*.

Grandad says Ruby can talk the hind legs off a donkey, whatever the hell that means? But clearly she likes to talk a lot, except about Lilly. I've given up trying coz it's obvious it upsets Ruby. I don't really understand why she and Andy didn't have more children after Lilly but then again, I don't understand adults full stop.

'I don't know about you babe,' Ruby says, 'but I'm parched. Let's grab a coffee or something eh?'

We've only been looking round the shops for an hour, and I still haven't found anything, but I don't suppose it would do any harm to stop for a while. My feet are like well killing me from all this walking.

Ruby decides to take me to Catalina's, which is like *the* place to eat, but it's like mega expensive. You virtually have to be a millionaire or something to eat there, but then again Ruby and Andy do have loads of money so I guess they can afford it.

They're not flash about it though; they don't think they're better than anyone else or anything.

Okay, so like Ruby's flirting with one of the waiters, which is like slightly embarrassing coz she's at least fifty years older than him. Whatever she's saying is working though coz in only a few minutes we are being seated at a nice little table for two.

The waiter looks at me, and winks. I can feel myself go bright red coz he is pretty gawjuss. He's waaaay too old for me though. He must be at least 20, maybe even 21 years old.

He looks at Ruby and speaks.

'So ladies, can I get you a something to drinka?' His voice is low and has the soft hint of an Italian accent. 'Maybe a coffee, or a tea, yes?' he continues.

'Coffee?' Ruby asks. She sounds like well offended. 'Have we no wine here sir?' she booms.

The waiter grins at Ruby and before I know it she's ordered us both a glass of white wine each.

'Shakespeare,' Ruby says to me, as if he just walked in the room.

'Where?' I reply, looking round the restaurant slightly puzzled coz I'm fairly sure he died about a zillion years ago.

'The quote I just said,' she continues, 'can't remember which play though. Your Mum would know of course; she was brilliant at English at school. Well, she was brilliant at most things, but she loved English. And reading; always had her head in a bloody book.'

'She still does,' I reply.

I look at Ruby's older, slightly plump face and find it hard to imagine her and Mum ever being young. The waiter swings back towards us carrying a tray with two glasses of wine.

'But I'm not old enough,' I mumble to Ruby through gritted teeth, squirming uncomfortably on my chair. The waiter plonks a glass of cold, crisp wine in front of me.

'Course you are. You're old enough to do all sorts of things at 16 and if you can smoke weed you can certainly have a small glass of wine with me, just don't tell your Mum for god's sake.' Ruby laughs.

'I don't ... didn't,' I start to protest.

'Oh chill Cassie, for god's sake. Let's have some fun eh?'

I smile and take a sip of wine from what seems like a very large glass to me. It feels deliciously wrong but right at the same time. The wine is cold and sort of fruity but tart at the same time. I can feel it going down as it hits my empty stomach. I didn't eat any breakfast this morning coz I want to look slim for the party. Not that I'll ever have a figure like Chelsea of course. We nibble on Pintxo and wait for our Pringa and salad to arrive. I'm not really sure what any of the food is that Ruby has ordered but as long as it's nothing rank, like snails or something, I don't really care.

I watch Ruby and notice her eyes following the waiter. As if Ruby. You're like waaaaay too old for him. He'd like never look at you in that way. Oh my actual god I don't believe it. It's like well minging but he's actually smiling at her, and I'm pretty sure it is in that *way*. Urrggghh! That's just rank. I feel a bit embarrassed and look away for a minute. Why is there a painting of a cow above our table?

The waiter leaves again and Ruby looks at me, grinning. 'What?' I ask.

'C'mon then Cas, spill the beans, who are you really getting dressed up for? Who's going to be at this party that you're so desperate to notice you?'

Desperate. I'm not bloody desperate. 'What'd ya mean? I told you, I just wanna look nice for the party.'

'Hmmmmm likely story,' Ruby continues. 'You have plenty of nice outfits hanging up in your wardrobe that would do. You're trying to dress to impress someone. I was 16 too you know.'

Arrggghh! Why are adults always so annoyingly right? I shift uncomfortably on my chair and look up sheepishly from my wine glass.

'Joe,' I finally admit, 'his name is Joe.'

'I knew it,' Ruby replies, triumphantly clapping her hands together. 'And what does Joe look like?'

'Hey Cassie.'

Someone's calling me, and her voice sounds terrifyingly familiar. I look around the restaurant and am absolutely mortified. Pheebs has just sat down at a table nearby. With Joe. My Joe! And just to add insult to injury, Chelsea's with them too. I can't believe it. I just can't believe it. Is it possible to die of embarrassment because I think that's what's happening to me right now? The three, well two at least, most perfect people on the whole entire planet – well, except for Ed Sheeran, Kurt Cobain (but he's dead so I guess he doesn't count) and of course Alex Turner – are sitting together and who am I stuck with? Some old woman. This has to be one of *the* worst moments of my whole entire life. It really couldn't get much worse.

'S'up Cassie?'

'Oh, err, hiya.'

Oh shit, thank you god of chaos. Did you just wake up this morning and decide to piss all over my parade? Now Chelsea's brother, Ollie, the best-looking boy in the whole entire world, has joined them too.

'You ok Cas?' Ruby asks. 'Only I'm guessing that one of those delicious looking young men is Joe?'

I clench my teeth. 'Sssshhhhh,' I reply. 'How do you know?'

'Well, given that you've slumped down in your chair, your hand is now over your face as if trying to hide and the colour of your cheeks perfectly matches the tomatoes on your plate, I'd say it's a bit of a dead giveaway.'

I try to smile but I feel sick inside. This wine has given me a headache. Ruby and I keep talking, in very hushed voices and I try to explain to her who everyone is.

'Hummph,' she says, 'so they're Ronnie Divine's kids eh? Scummy little man.'

'What do you mean? He's still married to their Mum you know, not divorced like my Mum and Dad. I thought they were perfect? They look like the perfect family to me.'

'Yeah well, mark my words Cassie, appearances can be deceiving. Look,' Ruby continues, 'I can see you're eager to get away but just follow my lead, ok?'

'What? What do you mean?' I ask, slightly alarmed. 'What are you going to do?'

'Something that helps, *I hope*; something that raises your kudos with these fake big fish in their little pond.'

'Raises my Q what?' I ask nervously. She calls the waiter over and is talking quietly in his ear. He places his hand gently on her shoulder. She pats his hand and they both laugh.

I sneak a look at Joe and the others and they're all laughing too. Everyone's laughing except me. I look back at Ruby and the waiter. The waiter looks at me, winks again and disappears. Ruby grins at me. I stare at her.

'What then?' I ask, feeling a little uneasy. 'You'll see,' she says mischievously.

# CHAPTER 10

## BO-HO CHIC

**LIZZIE**

*I* can hear laughter before I reach the front door. I throw my bag down under the stairs in the hallway and kick my shoes off. God it feels good to get some air to my poor aching feet. Romeow, our tabby cat, is sitting half way up the stairs, proficiently washing behind his ears. He stops mid lick and looks down at me. His expression is one of contempt and lends itself to the words, "Oh — it's you". He's a temperamental cat to say the least, social but not particularly sociable, his grumpy demeanour the perfect complement to the other teenagers in the house.

'Hey Romeow. Bad day?' I ask. He continues to stare at me before reluctantly managing a small, very lethargic meow.

'I know, I know,' I continue. 'C'mon.' I pat the stair above me. 'Romeow – c'mon, come and say hello.'

Romeow now wears a look of scorn suggesting I really must be as stupid as I appear. Finally, he manages another low meow before promptly completing a one eighty degree turn, whereupon I'm left to look at the backside of a ginger fur ball.

'I'll take that as a no then, shall I, Romeow?' No movement, no sound. 'Thanks,' I exclaim, 'I love you too.'

I open the kitchen door and am greeted by two very giggly teenagers. Well, one real one and one middle aged woman acting like one. Ruby's holding a glass of wine, Cassie a glass of water – I hope? They both turn to look at me. Cassie is actually smiling.

*See, miracles do happen.*

'Oh, hey Mum,' Cassie says, eyes twinkling. 'We've had a great time. Ruby's like aaammaaaaazing. She's so sick and so funny and clever, and like, well, everything really. We have soooooo much to tell you,' she gushes.

'Yes, she is pretty amazing, isn't she,' I reply. Ruby catches the sarcasm in my voice and casts me a look. I feel slightly ashamed at the small stab of jealously running through me.

'And,' Cassie continues, 'here's your money back.' She hands back the crisp notes I'd robbed Peter to pay Paul. I'm confused.

'So you didn't buy anything then?'

'Well, yeah, sort of. Ruby said I need to try it on to show you then you'll understand.' I raise my eyebrows, intrigued. Cassie is grinning like a cat, well, not our cat, but the proverbial Cheshire cat maybe, and disappears upstairs.

'So,' I say, grabbing myself a glass and filling it from the opened bottle of wine next to Ruby. 'It looks as though you two have had a great time?'

'Yeah, we've had fun, and Cassie's a great kid really.'

'Hmmmm,' I reply. 'I suppose she is when she's not screaming and crying and telling me she hates me. Clearly I don't have what it takes to be so bloody ... well ... sick,' I exclaim. Ruby eyes me suspiciously and laughs.

'You're her Mum for god sake; you won't be cool for at least another fifty years!' We both laugh and I feel the tensions of the day start to dwindle. She's right of course. Does there ever come a time when one's parents are cool in the eyes of their children? I think of my own dear Mum and Dad and smile inwardly. They're both mad, in their own unique way, especially Dad, but cool? Yes, I suppose they are.

'Well, what do you think?'

Cassie has breezed back into the kitchen. She is modelling, in the exaggerated style of a catwalk model, a beautiful but very familiar dress. I look from Cassie to Ruby, to Cassie and back to Ruby again.

'Is that –?' I begin to say.

'Indeed it is,' Ruby replies before I can finish my sentence.

The dress opens my dusty box of memories and I'm suddenly transported back to a darkened assembly hall intermittently lit by the flashing lights of the weekly school disco or the more important monthly one held at the local leisure centre. Kisses are stolen in shadowy corners and my stomach flips at the sight of Mark Lyndsey with his fashionable highlighted mullet and white socks. If I'm lucky he'll grab me for the slow dance at the end of the night and we'll probably smooch to Spandau Ballet's *True* or the Jackson Five's *I'll be there*.

*Really? You were that soppy?*

It's the 1980s and I'm a teenager again. This was a time when we really believed Ra Ra skirts and white stilettos were as sophisticated as drinking Pernod and black or Malibu and lemonade; a time when Margaret Thatcher ruled and ruined the country, and a time of yuppies, greed, massive youth unemployment and YTS schemes; of miners strikes, Arthur Scargill and lost industries; the birth of the VDU and VCR's, the Mobile phone and the Walkman; a time of Ska music, the New Romantics, Billy Bragg and Rick Astley; a time when Lionel Richie saw us *Dancing on the Ceiling* after saying *Hello*. This was also the time of Band Aid and Live Aid and a time when we believed, for those of us who cared, we really could make a difference to the starving millions of the world through the union of music.

*God, how naive were we?*

'Oh my god,' I scream, 'I haven't seen that dress in years!' The dress in question is one of a select few designer ones owned by Ruby's Mum. Bought for her during the 1960s (by a famous London gangster, so the story goes), later worn by Ruby and I during the 80s.

The dresses themselves were beautiful but not bo-ho enough for the fashion icons we actually believed we were. So Ruby and I dragged them kicking and screaming (quite mercilessly when I look back at the photos) into the 80s. Leggings, fishnet stockings and lace gloves were added, along with rubber bracelets, layers of beaded necklaces, cropped bolero-style jackets and of course the signature big earrings and big hair with lace ribbons and headbands to finally complete our own street urchin twist.

And yet here was Cassie, another generation on in another century wearing the very same dress I had worn nearly thirty years earlier, and Ruby's Mum twenty years prior to that.

'It's a designer dress, vintage,' Cassie beams as she saunters, hand on hip, around the kitchen. 'Ruby bought me a new pair of shoes and a statement necklace to bring it up to date. But look,' Cassie proceeds to pirouette around the kitchen like a small child playing dress-up, 'doesn't it look good?'

Cassie stops abruptly and turns to look at me, grabbing the back of a chair to steady herself. 'And you should have seen Ruby in action, Mum, with Chelsea. She like so owned her, it was hilarious. Chelsea so thinks she's the knees bees when it comes to fashion, but now, thanks to Ruby, Chelsea thinks I'm friends with a bloody fashion designer for god sake,' she squeals. I look at the young woman standing before me.

'You look lovely Cassie, really beautiful,' I say. She smiles at me. 'Thanks.'

The dress is a tranquil teal in colour and provides the perfect contrast to her lengthy, dark hair and dark eyes. Her legs are slender and unlike mine, long, which is one thing she can thank her Dad for.

*When did your little girl turn into this woman?*

'I don't know,' I suddenly say out loud, still looking admiringly at Cassie.

'Oh for god sake,' Cassie snorts. 'There's always bloody something with you isn't there? What don't you know?'

I sigh inwardly. 'No I didn't mean you Cassie,' I begin to try and explain.

*She may have the body of a woman but the brain is still in the oven – roasting quite nicely, but not yet cooked. What did that article say that Ruby quoted? A work in progress or something? Yes, that's what I see before me, a work in progress.* 'Actually Cassie,' I say looking at her again, 'it is very short isn't it?' Cassie rolls her eyes at me.

*I don't remember it being that short when I wore it?*

'Yes, but my arms are completely covered up.' Cassie states this as if it makes perfect sense but unfortunately makes very little to me.

'And?' I reply.

'Oh my actual god, it's just the bloody rule isn't it?'

'What rule?'

'The bloody fashion rule,' she says, raising her voice. 'Cassie,' Ruby cautions.

'Well,' she replies sulkily, 'did she give birth to me to torture me or is it just that she has absolutely no bloody clue about fashion what so bloody ever? No don't tell me,' she continues, answering her own question, 'it's both.'

Ruby's smile vanishes. 'Cassie, don't talk to your Mum like that, she's given up a lot for you, made sacrifices that you have no idea about and gone without just so you didn't have to.'

Cassie is slightly taken aback at Ruby's rare show of anger.

Her eyes begin to fill up and her bottom lip quivers slightly. 'But it's just a fashion rule that EVERYONE knows,' Cassie shouts defensively. 'Gak Wonk and everyone say it.'

'Well, as I clearly missed that one somewhere, would you care to enlighten me please Cassie?' I feel sorry for her but slightly amused at the same time.

Cassie sighs heavily. 'The rule is,' she continues, her voice breaking a little, 'if you're not showing your arms you HAVE to show your legs.' Cassie stares at me intently, desperate not to blink and let the tears balancing just above her bottom eyelashes, fall. She's sorry but she'll never say it.

'Well then, that makes perfect sense. Now give us another twirl.' I smile at Cassie and she smiles back before quickly turning away to wipe the tears that won't go back to where they came from. Cassie then tries to master her walk in her new, very high heels. Cassie is happy again; I like to see her smile.

'And it's a designer dress,' she repeats, 'I'll definitely fit in at Chelsea's with this dress.'

I wonder at the basic human need to assimilate. The necessity for that badge or uniform that suggests we belong; affirmation that we do fit in, somewhere. With Cassie, for the moment, it's the fake brigade (as Maisy calls them), but then Maisy isn't really any different in her membership of all that appears to be gothic and black. I suppose that's why Facebook and the Twittersphere and whatever the hell else is out there in our computerised, virtual world, works so well. Its confirmation we're not alone.

My thoughts have let me drift for a moment but Cassie's voice is pulling me back, demanding my full and undivided attention.

'Mum. Mum, are you listening to me? Do you want to hear what happened to us or not?'

'I'm all ears,' I respond enthusiastically.

'What?' Cassie screws up her face and frowns at me. 'What are you talking about? I didn't say a bloody thing about your bloody ears.'

'What? No, I meant – oh it doesn't matter. Tell me your story Cassie.'

# CHAPTER 11

MAGNIFIQUE

**LIZZIE**

'Well,' Cassie says thrusting a glossy fashion magazine at me. 'Look at page twenty-two. Who do you see?' I can't see anyone in particular. My eye is temporarily drawn to the opposite page and the advertisement of the exquisitely designed perfume bottle that costs more than a month's wages and a watch that costs more than the house we live in.

I look back at page twenty-two. It's a collage of who's who in the fashion world, a sea of faces, all with their own caption underneath. It's a world so far removed from my own it may just as well be a work of fiction from one of the many books in the Fantasy section of the library; a world of perfect, polished people with unashamedly critical stares and a world quite literally of gross incomes.

I scan the photos several times but I'm still none the wiser. I try to read the tiny writing underneath but am only presented with a mass of blurred words. I reach for the reading glasses in my bag.

'Nope, I don't see anything,' I say, looking up at Cassie and Ruby.

'Oh Mum, look again,' Cassie insists. I ring my slightly sweaty hands nervously and scan the page once more. I can feel Cassie's hot, agitated breath on the back my neck as she leans over me.

*What the hell am I supposed to be looking at?*

'I don't know?' I didn't mean to but I've said my thoughts out loud, again.

'Oh Mum, really?' Cassie sighs. She swipes the magazine from under me and points a very erect, angry finger at one of the photos.

'Looooooooook, just look will you.' I follow her extended digit and, replacing my reading glasses once more, find myself looking at a dark haired woman who bears an uncanny resemblance to Ruby. I pull the magazine closer, then just as quickly pull it away again. I swear my eyes are getting worse. I attempt to read the name under the individual with the slightly obnoxious expression.

'Fr-an-coise Li-bert,' I say, pronouncing it Libert as it is indeed spelt before realising the correct enunciation is Libair. 'Francoise Libair,' I declare. I pull my glasses off and lift my face up to look at Cassie and Ruby. 'Who is she?'

Cassie looks at Ruby and hits the middle of her forehead with the palm of her hand.

'Oh my actual god. Really? You don't know who Francoise Libert is?'

Suddenly the front door swings open and a morose Maisy breezes past looking – if it's at all possible – more gothic than ever.

'S'up loser?' she says to Cassie. She looks straight past me and nods at Ruby. 'Right Ruby?'

'Hey there Maisy,' Ruby replies. Maisy's barely there smile disappears. She scowls at Ruby.

'My name is NOT Maisy, it's Mania.'

'Mais – I mean Mania,' Cassie interrupts like an excitable puppy. 'Who's this?' she petitions Maisy, stabbing the photo on page twenty-two with her finger. 'I bet even YOU know WHO this is?' Maisy refuses to hold the magazine but casts a surly eye at the photo Cassie is pointing to. She is quiet for a moment and I'm secretly hopeful I've found an ally.

'Yeah,' she finally says, 'she's that bloody French designer, Francoise Libert or somink.' My heart sinks. Am I so out of touch with my teenage daughters'?

'There see. *Even* Mais – I mean Mania – knows who she is. God help you Mum. Surely you've heard of Libert shoes and Libert handbags?' Cassie implores. 'She's like, soooooo famous. Don't you know anything?' Cassie rolls her eyes at me again. 'Even Dad knows who she is for god bloody sake.'

*Yes, well, he would wouldn't he!*

I smile, sweetly.

'Okay,' I say, trying to steer the conversation away from my fashion ignorance. 'We've established who this fashion designer is but I still haven't got a clue what she's got to do with you?'

'Ah well,' Cassie says grinning as she runs round to the back of Ruby's chair. She places the photo of the world famous Francoise Libert next to Ruby. I look at Francoise then Ruby, then back to Francoise before finally settling my gaze on Ruby. 'Did you know you actually look a bit like her?' I ask. Cassie groans like she has stomach ache.

'Ov Couse I deed Madame. Are you suggesting zat I am not ze great Francoise Liberccct?' Ruby replies with complete sincerity.

'Riiiigght, I see.' I don't though. 'But isn't she…?' I trail off, trying to find words of diplomacy.

*Oh fuck diplomacy, this is Ruby you're talking to.*

'What?' Ruby asks.

'Well, isn't she a little slimmer than you?'

'Cow,' Ruby replies, laughing. 'But yes, you're right, she is, only slightly though. However, I have a secret weapon every woman should own, unless of course they're stick insects like you two.'

She waves her hand dismissively at Cassie and me and stands up, crossing both hands across her voluptuous breasts before moving them downwards towards her waist. She swings her hips from side to side, Marilyn Monroe style. 'See, don't you think I'm looking rather svelte?' Ruby continues, her voice suddenly hot and breathy.

I study the form of my fine female friend. Her glorious curves remain sumptuously obvious but her profile is … how can I describe it … smooth. In fact, she has less lumps and bumps than me.

'Spanx,' Ruby says simply, 'big fat Bridget Jones knickers. They push everything up and iron everything out. I can't breathe or eat but I look bloody brilliant.'

'You really do,' I reply, but why so dressed up to go shopping with a teenager?'

'Are you kidding?' she says pointing at Cassie, 'just look at her for god sake. Can't have this little minx outdoing me can I?' She winks at Cassie, but the twinkle in her eye doesn't escape me.

'Okay, I still don't understand though?'

Cassie begins her story with great enthusiasm. Her projectile vocabulary spews across my head, splashes around my ears and crashes through my thoughts. Barely pausing for breath she's both vociferous and excitable.

I'm informed that Ruby has been aware of her resemblance to Francoise Libert for some time. She is also very good friends with some of the staff at Catalina's. Especially, and in particular, the waiter serving them, who incidentally also has a brother who works as a chauffeur for a specialist car hire Company.

Cassie's storytelling is intermittently dispersed with a furtive array of strange sounds from her phone that appears to increase tenfold as the story goes on. Apparently news travels fast when you're friends with a fashion designer. Cassie continues with her rapid teenage download of information. She explains that her friends Phoebe and Joe also came into the same restaurant as she and Ruby, along with *the* school queen of celebrity herself, Chelsea Divine and her equally popular brother Ollie.

Cassie, dying of embarrassment and unaware of Ruby's idea, sat nervous and fidgeting as Ruby called Luca, the good looking Italian waiter, over. They talked quietly between themselves, Cassie at this point not privy to the conversation. Several minutes later Luca approached Chelsea's table and spoke to its occupants.

'I didn't know it at the time,' Cassie continues with the child-like enthusiasm of one that has just seen Father Christmas for the first time, 'but he told them he couldn't help but notice that they were looking over at our table, so asked them kindly not to stare at Madame Libert and on no account must they approach her for an autograph or anything as she was out with her goddaughter and she didn't have much time before she flew back to Paris. I don't think they believed him at first coz they just kept looking over at us and laughing.'

Cassie then goes on to explain that after pretending to come off the phone, Luca then delivered a message to Ruby, but addressed her of course as Madame Libert. He spoke in a very loud voice saying that a Ms McCartney, unable to get a reply when ringing Madame Libert's mobile, was now on the restaurant phone for her.

Cassie's face is flushed with excitement. 'You should have seen their faces Mum. Pheebs gave me a look that said "why the hell have you never told me this before?" and Chelsea just looked ... shocked. I swear she didn't close her mouth for like, at least ten minutes.'

Cassie pauses to hurriedly take a gulp of water. 'Then Luca brought the phone to our table and Ruby answered it, speaking English but with like this shamazing French accent. She then like proceeded to have a ten minute conversation with no-one on the other end, laughing and joking and constantly referring to Stella.' Cassie stops for a moment and looks at me. 'You have heard of Stella McCartney right?'

'Yes Cassie,' I reply slightly amused, 'I have heard of Stella McCartney but can *you* tell me who her Dad is?'

'Duh,' she says, 'Paul, that Beatle bloke. Anyway, in the meantime, my phone's like going crazy coz Pheebs is like texting me, and Chelsea and Joe – all of them in fact. I didn't think they'd fall for it, but they did, they really did. Then, while Ruby's talking – but not really of course – to Stella she says something like, "Yes, yes, qui, my goddaughter, she izzzz soooo beautiful, so nat-u-rel. So many of zis girls ere are, ow you say it," and she looks straight at Chelsea and says, "fake".'

Cassie rambles on, desperate to reveal the finale of their devious tale of deceit. 'Then, Luca the waiter declares – again loud enough for everyone to hear – that our car has arrived. I look out of the huge glass window and you'll never guess what pulls up outside for us?'

'No, I probably wouldn't Cassie,' I reply.

'A limousine,' she declares. 'A black stretch limo. For us! Of course it wasn't really for us,' she gushes, 'it was Luca's brother Giovanni driving. He had to pick someone up from the airport or something but as a favour to Ruby,' Cassie nods and smiles at Ruby, 'he picked us up on the way.'

I raise my eyes a little. 'And what pray did Ruby have to do in return for *such* a big favour?' I ask. Judging by the look on Ruby's face the sarcasm in my voice isn't lost on her, but it completely washes over Cassie.

'Then, just as we were leaving Ruby kissed Luca on each cheek and clapped her hands together like well quick, three times and said, "Come Cassee, we ave to leev". Then she like looked across at Chelsea's table and shaking her head and tutting said something like, "Non, non, non, some peepel really ave no dress sense". She was like shamazing Mum.'

Cassie turns to look at Ruby. 'That was like one of the best days of my life, like ever,' she coos. 'Well sick. I still can't believe they all fell for it!'

Ruby smiles at Cassie who then looks down at her phone to address yet another text.

'I'm glad you had fun Cas,' Ruby replies.

I smile at Cassie and Ruby but a tiny current of jealousy ripples across my heart.

Cassie looks up from her phone, half-smiling, and half-frowning. 'Why do they believe it though?' she asks. 'Why do they actually believe that me, a nobody, could possibly be friends with a famous person?'

I'm both angry and saddened at Cassie's opinion of herself. 'Right, let's make this clear Cassie – you are not a "nobody" but a "somebody". We all are and it is people like Chelsea and her brother and their parents that see the world as the Somebodies versus the Nobodies. To them it's all about rank and status. Rank seeks status, and fame and status provides acknowledgement of being someone in a society saturated with rankism. However, in that world, indignities and exclusion abound and it's usually heaped on those considered as nobodies.'

'Here, here,' Ruby says raising her wine glass.

'What?' Cassie replies. I sigh heavily, wondering if I've actually taught my daughter anything of value.

'Emily Dickinson wrote...'

'Oh god no, not more English crap,' Cassie says, rolling her eyes, but I carry on regardless.

'Wrote: *"I'm a nobody! Who are you? Are you a nobody, too? That there's a pair of us – don't tell. They'd banish us, you know."*'

Cassie looks thoughtful for a moment. 'Hmmmmm. Soooo, what you're saying is, Chelsea can only function in a world full of the Somebodies versus the Nobodies, as long as she's a Somebody coz that gives her status and as fame gives you status...'

'And rank,' I add.

'Yeah, that too. So like, it was easier for her to believe than not to believe?'

'Yes, that's exactly it. Fame promises escape from indignity. It quiets those internalised critical voices like classmates, teachers and friends. Having a friend like you – who happens to know someone famous – makes her a quasi-somebody, which, in her eyes, is far better than being a nobody.

'Hmmmmm. Okay. Sick,' Cassie replies. 'I think I understand. She's just shallow, like Dad?'

Ruby and I look at one another.

'Don't keep protecting him Mum. I know it's true and you know it's true.'

*I do know it's true Cassie but how can I put him down in front of you when half the blood that runs through your veins comes from him?*

'Look, all I'm saying is, don't let anyone *ever* put you down. You are, regardless of what anyone else says or thinks, somebody. And the key to killing status and rankism – the source of most of the social dysfunction of human society today

– is recognition of that. We are all somebody and all worthy of recognition and dignity, rich or poor, famous or not. Okay?'

Cassie throws me a slightly annoyed, slightly quizzical look. 'Okay Mum, I get it for god bloody sake.'

Cassie checks the caller ID on her phone and smirks. 'I have to get this,' she says, and gets up to leave the kitchen. Her feet thud heavily on the stairs and she's mumbling some incoherent teenage babble into her phone as she disappears into her bedroom with the usual slam of the door.

I turn to look at Ruby. 'And you said I should have been an actress?'

'Well, it was all just a bit of fun,' she says laughing.

I reach for the bottle of wine and pour us both another glass. 'Now c'mon tell me, you can't kid a kidder, what's the real reason you're all dressed up?'

## CHAPTER 12

TESLA GIRLS

**LIZZIE**

'Oh, I just really don't get it Lizzie, let's just face it I'm too old for this world of technology.'

'Of course you're not Mrs Lambert,' I reply, 'you're never too old to learn anything new.'

'That's easy for you to say,' she replies, 'but I am 84 you know?'

'I know, and just look at you, you're amazing, a real inspiration.'

'Well, thank you dear, that's very kind of you to say so, and please, don't call me Mrs Lambert, call me Beryl, but sometimes I just feel overwhelmed with all this technology. When I look back to when I was a gal I really can't believe how different things are. When you're old, like me, the past is a place I don't recognise, a different world if you like.'

Mrs Beryl Lambert is one the Library's older, long serving customers, recently signed up to one of our computer courses.

She completely vindicates and values the role of Libraries within the community but is thoroughly suspicious of the implementation of new technology. Especially if she feels, as she did with the new self-issue machines, it is technology replacing human beings, which in turn equates to the loss of people's jobs and incomes.

During the library's most recent and third restructure in almost as many years, it was Mrs Lambert that led a petition of some several thousand signatures, against reduced opening hours and more job losses. She then presented it to the local council at the Town Hall. It did cause the council some embarrassment and more than a little unwanted attention but when all was said and done the restructure went ahead anyway.

The petition did help secure the Library an extra two hours a week though. Unfortunately, it is two hours mainly covered by unpaid volunteers. Don't get me wrong, most volunteers are great but their shelf life is short. They come and go in quick succession, using their role of volunteer to gain experience, then – hopefully – paid employment.

'Do you know' Mrs Lambert continues, 'we didn't even *have* a phone in our house when I was a gal? Nowadays it seems as if everyone has a phone, even very young children. I don't know if it's a good or a bad thing?' she continues, shaking her head of very white hair. 'I mean in a way all this technology is making us antisocial isn't it?'

'Hummmph, I'm not sure? I know what you mean though. I have two teenage daughters at home that probably couldn't function without their mobile phones. It's actually quite hard to tell where their hand ends and their phone starts. They're constantly looking down at them too.'

Mrs Lambert clucks and raises her eyes. 'I know all about that,' she states. 'People are constantly bumping into me in the street, and it's *not* to pass the time of day either, it's because they jolly well don't look where they're going.'

Her knowing eyes remain steely but she lets out a small laugh.

'Yes, that does happen, a lot, doesn't it? Annoys the hell out of me too. Although, if I'm completely honest,' I raise my finger, wincing, 'I've probably done it a few times myself.'

Mrs Lambert tuts and shakes her head again but continues to chuckle all the same.

I think of Cassie and Maisy, part of the device dependent generation, heads down, ambidextrous thumbs at the ready, expressions of great disdain or great joy perpetually morphing into one another, their moods dictated by the words and emoticons flashing across portable screens of colourful technology. A huge part of my daughters' daily interaction.

'I'm always amazed how superfast and nimble their fingers are though aren't you?'

'Yes, they do seem to move at lightning speed don't they? Not like these knarly old things,' Mrs Lambert replies, waving slightly deformed arthritic fingers at me. 'So you agree with me then, about technology being anti-social?'

I think back to my recent conversation with Ruby and I'm reminded what an awkward and precarious time one's formative years can be.

'Yes, I suppose so. But then again isn't some of it just, well, being teenagers?'

Mrs Lambert contemplates her reply. She sighs before she speaks again. 'I suppose some of it is.' A hint of reluctant resignation tinges her voice. 'Nothing a good clip round the ear wouldn't sort out though, sometimes. There was much more discipline around when I was young. Never did us any harm either. Taught us to respect our elders. I pity some of the parents and teachers today. Can't even tell a child off without someone ringing social services.'

'Humph, it does feel a bit like that sometimes doesn't it? Children do need boundaries, and guidance. But we live in very precarious times. I want my children to have a voice, even if it is across cyberspace and Twittersphere.'

Mrs Lambert stares at me, her crumpled face bright but mapped and worn with lines of time. 'And as far as technology goes,' I continue, 'I think there always has and always will be, a certain amount of anxiety around technological advances, don't you? It's up to us to put that technology to good use isn't it?'

Mrs Lambert sighs heavily again. 'Yes, I know what you mean dear. What we lose in some things we gain in others I suppose. All this texting, skype thingy, face whotsit and emails do help us stay in contact with everyone more easily. That's why I'm doing this course because I have family and friends abroad. They email me quite a lot but I'm never quite sure how to open my messages properly or how to reply, so I thought it was jolly well time I learned.'

'And so you shall Mrs Lam – I mean Beryl – with my help, so you shall.'

My conversation with Mrs Lambert stays with me. She's certainly made me think, evoked a few memories and I mention it to Simon, as we're getting ready for bed. I like this twilight hour. Dinner is done, packed lunches for the following day are made, and it's a weekday so there are no parties or sleepovers that beckon the girls so I'm slightly more settled, at ease with sleep, which never comes easy when they're out.

The house in the main is quiet, except of course for the faint sounds of technology in one form or another, seeping and bleeping from respective bedrooms, before sleep inevitably – as it always must – wins the battle for peace for a few hours.

'I know what you mean,' Simon says, punching his pillow several times, in the same way he does every night (when he's not working away), before finally settling his head against it. 'Things were different when we were younger. For a start divorce was rare, everyone's parents stayed together. Did couples work at it more though, or were they just stuck with each other?' he asks, his face creased with thought as he considers his own question. 'Anyway,' he continues, 'divorce – just the word itself – was a dirty one. Nowadays it seems like the opposite is true.'

'Hmmm, yeah I suppose,' I reply. 'Ruby and Andy have managed to stick at it though eh?'

*Yes, but why was Ruby so dressed up to go shopping the other day?*

'True, true. And they lost a child so they actually had more of an excuse than most to chuck it all in, so all credit to them.'

Simon's words, unintentionally sharp and jagged, sever my train of thought. I tried – really tried – to keep our family together. Scott's departure, even now, still proves to be painful at times, and never more so than when Cassie is in floods of tears, usually over some occasion or event Scott has once again failed to mark or acknowledge. I struggle with Cassie's grief, struggle to placate her (mostly) justified but extremely emotional outbursts; but to lose a child forever? How does anyone ever manage that pain? How can that possibly ease over time?

'Liz. Lizzie,' Simon's voice is dragging me back to the present. 'Don't you think so?'

'Sorry, what?' I ask, slightly confused.

'That Ruby and Andy are the exception rather than the rule.'

'Maybe,' I say sadly, 'it certainly feels like that doesn't it? Broken Britain eh?

Broken families and broken kids?'

'Hmmmm, I hope not.' His eyes glaze over for a moment, staring into space. I know he's lost in his own thoughts and concerns for Maisy. 'You know what else?' he continues. 'There weren't many fat kids, or adults for that matter, around in our younger days either.'

I throw him a slightly derisive look.

'Don't look at me like that. It's true. You know it is. Too much bloody sugar in everyone's diet these days. We can blame the 80s war on fat for that, and for men wearing white socks and mullet haircuts of course. What on earth were we thinking?'

I look at Simon and raise my eyes. He farts, loudly. I sigh. He laughs; confirmation that, if it were ever needed, the honeymoon period of our relationship is well and truly over.

'Simon for god sake!' I exclaim. He sniggers churlishly like a naughty schoolboy.

*What is it with men and farting anyway?*

I look at him and tut. 'I mean really, I just don't get it, why is farting so bloody funny? Please enlighten me?'

'It's simply because men have a more advanced sense of humour than women.'

'Hummmph, hardly. The truth is you lot just never grow up.'

*At least he doesn't stick your head under the cover like Jodi's husband does.*

I shudder with mild revulsion afraid to divulge such information for fear of giving Simon ideas.

'One of the disadvantages of being with a younger man,' I say out loud.

'Only by a couple of years,' Simon replies.

'You needn't think you're getting a shag now,' I state in mock disgust. He sticks out his bottom lip and folds both his arms defiantly across his chest.

'Oooooohhhhh,' he replies sulkily, 'go on, I'll do that thing you like.'

He glides over towards me and pulls me to him. He kisses my nose and cheek before his hot, wet mouth finds mine, confirmation that – on some level – the honeymoon period is in fact still alive and kicking. His kiss is hard and urgent and I'm safe in the knowledge (at least I think I am) that it's because he wants me. He wants to love, shag, fuck, call it what you will, *me*. He really wants *me*. And it's a very different experience from a pity shag or one of pure physical gratification (not mine), when you know damn well (in their head) the person inside you is fucking anyone (preferably successful and with money) but you.

Simon's tongue expertly finds mine as his hand runs across my breast, hovering gently, playing with my now erect nipple. I pull away from his mouth and look at him as his hand continues to brush across both my breasts. His blue eyes, slightly craggy around the edges, are full of want. I can feel him harden.

'I have to clean my teeth,' I suddenly declare. 'What?' he exclaims, 'you are joking right?'

'Nope. I've been eating garlic. I really need to.'

'Jesus babe, you really know how to kill the moment.'

'Like farting in bed,' I reply. He laughs.

'You're right though,' I attempt to shout through a froth of worked up toothpaste in my mouth, 'there weren't many fat kids around when we were younger. I see loads of them at the library.'

'Yeah, and you know why that is don't you?' he asks, but answers before I get a chance to. 'It's because we played out for hours on end, riding our bikes, fishing, building camps, meeting girls, meeting boys,' he continues. 'I mean, if it was the weekend, or the holidays, we'd be told to bugger off first thing in the morning and we wouldn't be seen again until tea time. By which time we'd be starving and eat every mouthful of whatever was put in front of us.' He pauses for a moment. 'And you know what?' He waves a lone finger with proud authority. 'We were grateful for it.'

I laugh. 'Aye,' I reply, making a very poor attempt at a Yorkshire accent, which actually sounds more like some bizarre mix of Scottish, Irish and Jamaican, 'and yoos try tellin the young kids of today that, and they dunt believe ya.'

Simon grins at me and pulls me into bed, wrapping his arms around me. Holding me. Safe.

We talk about scrumping for apples and blackberries and going home with bellyache and red stained hands and faces. We talk about setting up camps and lighting fires, of racing bikes along the riverbank and swimming in the bower to escape the midday sun. Resurrected childhoods pervading and flickering across our sentimental thoughts.

'And you know what else?' I add. 'We didn't have half the technology our kids have got but ... well ...'

'We survived?' Simon finishes my sentence.

'Yeah, that's just it isn't it? We did survive didn't we? We didn't wear seat belts in cars or helmets on bikes. We only had three TV channels to choose from, not ninety. And if you wanted to turn the channel over you asked permission then got up and clicked the button of the mahogany encased set. We played on grass, we played on concrete, and we fell on both. We climbed trees and fell out of them; we broke teeth, broke bones and split lips. If we got in trouble with the police our parents sided with the law, and if we got in trouble at school we got the cane and our parents merely shrugged their shoulders and told us to make sure it didn't happen again. If we wanted to see friends we walked, or rode our bikes to their house and knocked on their door, walked in and talked to them...'

We are quiet again for a moment; happily tripping, skipping, leap frogging, tigging, tagging and British Bull Dogging down memory lane.

'Memories eh,' I say as the words to the song with the same title run adjacent to my childhood chronicles, iridescent across my psyche like grainy old movie footage. Simon mumbles something but I fail to catch it. 'What?' I say turning to see him grinning at me.

'Don't give up the day job babe,' he says.

I'm horrified. 'Oh god, was I singing out loud?' Simon openly laughs at me, attempting to duck out of the way of the pillow I manage to hit him with. 'Yes, but we had so much more freedom than our kids do didn't we?' I ask. 'Freedom, failure, success and responsibility, and we learned how to deal with it. We survived without mobile phones and computers and tablets, without CCTV and Sunday opening and the bloody government or any other PC body of some sort regulating our lives "for our own good".'

'Yeah, the good old days eh?' Simon continues. 'Everyone always ran to answer the house phone too didn't they? Our house was filled with cries of, "I'll get it, I'll get it". Now, everyone just looks at one another if the bloody landline rings.'

He's right and I savour the moment; re-live the memory of that rush to answer the phone, that feeling of uncertainty about who was on the other end. I could watch that bloody phone for hours if I was expecting a call, constantly walking past it, lifting the receiver to make sure the line was connected then immediately regretting it, convinced my caller had tried to phone at that precise moment but had now given up on finding the line engaged.

'But you know, I don't think I ever imagined then the day when I'd actually be reading my phone.' I pick up my mobile phone and swipe the screen. I've just remembered a work email I meant to do earlier.

'Yeah, we certainly had a kind of freedom I don't think – sadly – our kids will ever experience. But it's difficult not to be amazed by the technology that surrounds our lives now, isn't it?' Simon reaches for his mobile to set his alarm for the morning. 'Pretty mind blowing stuff eh?'

'Hmmm,' I reply, digesting the morsels of this conversation and the one I had with Mrs Lambert this morning. 'Yes, I have to agree, it's hard not to be blinded by science. It's certainly made the world a smaller, more accessible place hasn't it? But is it a scarier place? We can connect with far more people than we've ever been able to but at what price? Surely dominant screen time actually equates to a disconnection with the real world – a disconnection with nature that we had and took for granted? Is the price of all this technology actually our freedom? Well, our children's freedom anyway? Do we have to have one without the other...?'

I suddenly realise Simon is very quiet. I look across at him. His eyes are closed and his lower jaw has relaxed so that his mouth looks slightly open. Catching flies Dad would say.

'Oi,' I say prodding him with my elbow, 'are you listening to me?'

'Ummmm, what, what,' he replies somewhat startled. 'Course I am babe.' Simon reaches for and pats my arm, his eyes closing again. 'S'late and you think too much. The kids'll be fine,' he says.

Maybe I do think too much. Maybe the memories of my childhood have been tainted with misty-eyed nostalgia. Maybe I'll take the kids for a picnic at the weekend, breathe some of that fresh polluted air. I'm sure there's an app you can download to your phone that provides loads of ideas about re-wilding your kids?

*Yeah, like you're ever gonna get Cassie and Maisy on a picnic with you.*

I turn off the light and lay still as the darkness swallows me, my head a hazy mix of childhood memories. I wonder at the staggering speed with which technology has catapulted us into the 21st century. My eyes grow heavy, it's been another long day and sleep is beckoning. Childhood recollections fight fiercely to be a part of my dreams, as do mobile phones and computers.

*Do you remember that really hot summer we had when you were a girl?*

I do remember. It was 1976 and I was brown as a berry – no factor fifty sunscreens then. I can smell the peas I shelled with Mum, fresh from their pods, and taste their crisp, watery sweetness. I can also smell the beautiful bouquet carried from the honeysuckle that seemed to be everywhere and its white petals that provided a mesmerising blanket of snow in temperatures of 90 degrees plus. I can smell freshly cut grass and I remember the straw like scorched patches scored across any remaining lawn caused by the heat of the midday sun. I can hear the hum of bumblebees hovering above the wilting, singed flowers and the revitalising taste of water shared from the hosepipe with my brother. I can taste iron in my mouth from the blood that flowed through it after going straight over the handlebars of my new bike and the feeling of euphoria for beating my fear and getting straight back on after the said incident. I can taste relief in the sweet ice of frozen orange and lemonade lollies rubbed across my sun parched lips and the feeling of liberation from the deadly shades of summer as my friends and I danced around the garden water sprinkler.

Somewhere in this evocative dream a phone is ringing. I answer it but no one replies. Then I realise it isn't ringing; it's actually the sound of a text alert. I read the text:

**The past is an outlandish habitat: things are done differently there.**

## CHAPTER 13

TROUBLE

**LIZZIE**

'Yo, bitch.'

I open the front door confronted by these two words and the back of a tall, dark haired young man.

*Somebody's been watching too many US television dramas.*

A ring of smoke wafts above his head and as he turns to face me I am presented with a cheeky smile and the youthful chiselled features of someone who appears slightly older than Cassie.

'I beg your pardon?' I reply. His expression quickly turns from that of arrogant amusement to sheer horror.

'Oh bloody hell,' he exclaims, 'I'm ... I'm sorry. I thought you were, well, I thought you were Cassie,' he continues.

'Oh? Do you call all girls bitches or just Cassie?'

'What?' he replies, his face beginning to redden slightly.

'Ummm, errrrr, well just Cassie ... well what I mean to say is

'... well it's just ... No.' He coughs to clear a throat that doesn't need clearing. 'It's just that I haven't really made my mind up about Cassie – yet – but if I make her my girlfriend then she'll be my bit...' He trails off, catching the glint of disapproval in my eye. 'It's just a laugh,' he says. 'It doesn't mean I actually think she's a bitch.' He wears an expression of sombre dejection.

The pause between us feels colossal and I can't help feeling slightly amused. I finally break the silence.

'So, what you are saying is – and please correct me here if I'm wrong – if Cassie is *lucky* enough to be your girlfriend then she'll become your bitch and to be your bitch is something good, a term of endearment?' His dark eyes dance with mischief and a broad grin spreads across his face.

'Yo. I mean yeah, that's exactly what I mean Mrs ... Cassie's Mum. You are like, well sick.' Why he feels the need to bend both knees slightly and gesticulate his left hand down towards the ground in the opposite direction as he says this is quite beyond me.

'Wonderful,' I reply. 'Cassie is – potentially anyway – a bitch and I am sick. It's so reassuring to know that men's attitudes towards women have advanced so far. For years now, hundreds in fact, many women, and men, have fought for the equality and rights of women. So, for all those that threw themselves in front of horses, chained themselves to the Houses of Parliament and Downing Street, went on hunger strike and burned their bras, it's so thoroughly heartening to know that despite our progression and the establishment of rights most young women now take for granted, casual, low level sexism still exists. Emmeline Pankhurst and Gloria Steinman would, I'm sure, turn in their graves.'

Oh dear, the glazed, slightly bewildered expression now staring back at me tells me I've gone too far. Cassie is suddenly beside me, anger etched into red lines of embarrassment now spreading across her face. She scurries past, knocking me away from the door, scrunched up jacket in one hand, phone in the other.

'Oh my actual god, really Mum? Really? Joe, just ignore my Mum, she's a librarian. She thinks she knows everything but really she knows nothing. C'mon let's go.' I stifle a laugh.

'I thought you were going to answer the door?' Joe hisses at Cassie as they walk down the drive.

'Your friend's welcome to come in Cassie,' I call after their retreating backs. 'Yo Joe. Bitch,' I shout. Both Cassie and Joe stop walking and turn in unison to look at me, Cassie's face now a deep crimson red. I point two fingers at my eyes then turn them to point at Joe. 'I'm watching you.'

'Mum, really?'

'Did Cassie tell you her Grandfather has his own laboratory?' Cassie glares at me.

'Oh my actual god, Mum. As if!' she shouts back. They quickly turn the corner and are gone, out of sight.

*There. I hope you're pleased with yourself?*

'Well, I couldn't help it,' I respond to myself out loud. 'I, like most mothers, have a built in, primitive urge to defend my children. He called her a bitch for god sake.'

*You call her that – in here, in your head – sometimes. I've heard you.*

'Yes, I know,' I continue out loud, 'but I don't say it out loud (very often) and I don't mean it. Besides, what do young people really know? And what do they know of what we know of the world? C'mon tell me that?'

*Now you really do sound like your Mother! He didn't actually mean it, it's just a few words of a language you're no longer privy to, the language of the young. Remember when everything was 'cool' or 'heavy man' in the 80s or 'fab' and 'groovy' in the 60s?*

*Besides, you've done your best; Cassie can look after herself.* 'Yeah, I suppose you're right,' I reply out loud again.

'Mum?' I turn to see Connor looking at me. '*Who* are you talking to?' he asks.

≶

## CASSIE

Oh my actual god. Why? Why does she do things like that to me? How can Ruby be so sick and Mum be so bloody ... unsick? She's not normal. I think she's like that Sherlock Holmes character, a highly defunctional schitziopath – or whatever it is he calls himself. Still, I'm not going to worry about it coz I'm walking down the street with Joe as my boyfriend. Well sort of, maybe, I think. That's of course if my stupid cow of a mother hasn't blown my chances with him after telling him off like some naughty schoolboy for calling me a bitch. Which he didn't, not really. She's just old and doesn't get it. What is it with old people anyway? I mean really, what do they actually know? And what do they know about the stuff we know about? Zip, zero, nothing, that's what.

'You're Mum's a Don,' Joe says inhaling on the cigarette he's just lit. He draws deeply, before exhaling several impressive smoke rings, making a slightly annoying pap pap sound at the same time. I study his face as we walk. He's beautiful, absolutely gawjuss and I swear I'm in love with him. Even more than I am with Chelsea's brother Ollie. I want to believe he asked to see me coz he likes me but deep down I think it's got something to do with Francoise Libert.

My phone hasn't stopped since mine and Ruby's little stunt. I mean it's literally been Facebook, Twitter, texts, and phone calls galore. Chelsea even phoned me and insisted I go to hers to get ready pre-prinks.

'She's stupid,' I snort, 'that much I do know. I'm so sorry about all that stuff she just said.'

'Nah, it's fine,' he continues, 'she's not stupid, she's sweet, clearly up for a bit a banta. Not like my old lady, moody as fuck. Unless she's shopping of course,' he adds.

'My mum doesn't really like shopping.'

'Yeah, I can see that,' he replies, 'her clothes are a bit shit considering she's friends with a fashion designer and everything.' His words sting, and I'm surprised how defensive I suddenly feel towards Mum. I feel hurt but embarrassed and ashamed at the same time.

I shrug my shoulders. 'She just doesn't buy into materialism and all that label crap.'

'Really?' Joe eyes me suspiciously. 'And yet your Mum's friend, your godmother, is a famous fashion designer – surely she can give her some of her shit?'

I stick my hands into my jacket pockets and screw them into tight fists. This is uncomfortable. I think about telling Joe the truth but then just as quickly swot that stupid idea away. I'm pretty sure Joe would tell Chelsea and once she knew, I'd be finished. It would be like committing social suicide for god sake. 'Nah,' I reply. 'They knew each other long before Rub – I mean Francoise – became a designer. And besides, Mum would look at any free stuff given to her as charity and she won't accept charity from anyone – not when there are people starving in the world, she says.' Joe raises his eyes and smirks at me. 'And, as my Dad has never paid a penny in maintenance for me and Connor,' I continue, 'even though he drives a bloody Beamer, most of any money Mum has had has always been spent on me and my brother.'

'So your Dad's a wanker too then?'

I look at Joe and we both laugh. 'You could say that. Why, what's your Dad like then?'

Joe drops the cigarette he's been smoking and stubs it out with a twist of his foot.

He then reaches into my jacket pocket and takes out one of my hands, curling his fingers around mine.

'I'd rather not talk about that tosser if it's okay with you,' he replies. Joe's hand is warm and feels rougher than mine. I can't believe he's holding my hand in public. We continue just walking and talking.

'She looks good on nothing though,' Joe says. I throw him a quizzical look. 'Your Mum,' he explains. 'For an old woman she's a bit of a MILF.'

'Sicko,' I reply.

Joe laughs and tells me I look like Mum. I pretend to be mortified but secretly I'm pleased coz I think he's actually giving me a jab handed (or is it back handed?) compliment.

He asks me about my piano playing, which makes me a little wary at first coz everyone usually takes the piss of me.

Joe lights another ciggie. 'So are you like gonna play the piano for a living, be a popstar or summit?' Fuck, he IS taking the bloody piss.

'I dunno, maybe,' I snap. 'Haven't really given it much thought.'

Joe looks at me with surprised amusement, dragging heavily on his cigarette again, this time blowing two long streams of smoke from his nostrils.

'Yo, don't be so moody bitch, I was only asking.' He's joking with me, surely he is? But why do I feel like crying and why do I feel so angry too?

'Oh just forget it,' I say turning to walk back in the direction we've just come from. 'Why don't you go back to bloody

Pheebs?' I turn my head to look at Joe. He looks surprised but starts laughing. I turn away again.

'Maybe I will,' he replies to my back. My heart sinks. 'But maybe it's you I'm interested in,' he calls out again, 'not her.' I stop walking and my tummy does a little somersault as my heart floats back up. I remain silent for a moment, still with my back turned, thinking. It's Joe that eventually breaks the silence again.

'Yo, bitch, c'mon, I gave up some important shit to be with you today.' I turn to look at him.

'Please don't call me a bitch.' He smiles at me, a warm, sexy smile, and my tummy flips again.

'Okay,' he replies, 'I take it you haven't got any objections to being called babe though, instead?'

I smile. 'No, babe is fine.'

He walks back up to me and puts his arm around me. 'What kinda music do you play then?'

'All kinds,' I reply, shrugging my shoulders. 'A little classical, some jazz and blues, pop, rock, whatevs really.'

'Sick,' he says, but I'm not sure he really means it. 'So, does your Grandad really have a laboratory?'

I feel an uncomfortable heat crawl up my neck and across my face again. 'No, not really. He has loads of books so it's more like his own private library.'

'Really? Why does he have loads of books?'

'Coz he likes reading.'

'Really?' I can hear surprise in Joe's voice.

'Yeah, really.'

'He's not secretly cooking up Meth then? Or growing pot, or making zombies or something?'

I smirk. 'No, think you've been watching too much TV or playing too many video games.'

Joe laughs, really loud. 'Probably,' he agrees. We're quiet again for a moment.

'So, your Dad drives a BMW does he?'
'What? Oh yeah, he does. Why?'
'Nice cars. Beamers.'
'I s'pose. I wouldn't really know.'
'Anyway,' Joe continues. 'Just how often do you see that Godmother of yours?'

## CHAPTER 14

DIVINE MADNESS

**LIZZIE**

It's fast approaching 10am. The house is quiet. Connor is at school, Cassie at Chelsea's house, Maisy at work – I think – and Simon has been staying away with work for a couple of nights. All I can hear is the gentle hum of the fridge. The dishwasher is loaded, the crumb infested work tops wiped down, and the washing folded and put away. After a manic couple of hours, surely representative of at least half the households in the country, I transcend into absolute peace and quiet. Nirvana, I fear, will never be found but for now I am at one with myself.

I close my eyes and listen to the sound of silence. Unfortunately, I have forgotten to turn my phone off and after mere seconds my peace is sabotaged by a ping from my phone, quickly followed by another, then another. Three texts have interrupted my fleeting moment of concord.

*Oh well, peace and quiet is overrated anyway.*

I pick up my phone, squinting, as I attempt to open my messages whilst simultaneously searching for my reading glasses. The first is from Simon:

*Morning sexy lady. How are u and the kids? Have I told u lately that I love u? Because I do u know? xxxxxxxxxxxxxxxx*

I smile.
*Well, surely that was worth interrupting your Zen?*
The second text, and partly expected, is from my friend Jodi. We have arranged to meet for coffee but unfortunately she lives in what, from the outside looking in, appears to be a whirlwind of torment. Divorced, with a daughter the same age as Cassie and a son slightly older, Jodi met and married Rob, a slightly younger man without children. During one mad night of drunken passion, not long after they were married, Jodi and Rob thought it would be a good idea to have a child of their own. Jodi, despite her advancing years, immediately fell pregnant and the baby turned out to be twins – a boy and a girl, Joshua and Katie.

Their lot in life is now a daily survival route through the perpetual minefield that is the terrible twos and teenage tantrums. Mind you, Jodi did say there is barely any notable difference between the two; it's just that one set of children is more articulate than the other. She's optimistic though, and lives in hope that her teenage children will again – one day – regain the use of comprehensible speech and converse in the same coherent manner as their younger siblings.

*Hi hun, terribly sorry, the dog has just vomited and so have the twins. Been up most of the night, even the bags under my eyes have bags! Can't make coffee but u r welcome here for 4 1? Scuse the smell of vomit & disinfectant. xxx*

As such events occur on a daily basis it's not unusual for Jodi to cancel or change plans at a minute's notice. The third text is from Cassie.

*Are my red shirt and black leggings clean?*

Fingers poised, I tap out my replies.

To Simon: *Sorry, who is this?!!!*

To Jodi: *U sound like a friend in need! Will be there in an hour xxx*

To Cassie: *Good morning Cassie. I have no idea. Why?? Xxx*

From Jodi: *Thanx babe. R u sure u can handle the vomit?!!!! xxx*

To Jodi: *Manage it on a daily basis at work, kids and adults alike! xxx*

From Cassie: *Need em 4 pre pre-prinks 2nite. Am staying at Chelsea's by the way. Can u wash em 4 me pleeeeeaaaassse : ) xxxx*

To Cassie: *I suppose so!! I have nothing better to do with my day off work after all xxx*

From Cassie: *Yay! Sick! Thanku : ) xxxxxxxxxxxxxx*

From Simon: *Oooops sorry, is this u Lizzie? Thought u were sum1 else!! Seriously tho, do love u. Have booked the cottage in Cornwall. Ask your parents to drop by 2 talk about it tonight xxxxxxxxxxxxxxxx*

To Simon: *Will do. Love u2 xxxxxxxxxxxxxxxxxxxxx*

Jodi wasn't exaggerating. The house reeks of an unpleasant fusion of pine disinfectant and vomit. My slightly dishevelled, sleep-deprived friend opens the door with one red faced bawling toddler balancing on her hip, the other fiercely wrapped around her left leg.

'Come in, come in, welcome to Armageddon,' she sighs. Jodi looks exhausted and I'm no sooner in the door when she drops Katie into my unsuspecting arms, who incidentally is still screaming.

'Here, take her for a minute will you,' Jodi says. 'I haven't been able to prise either of them away from me for the last hour and I *really* need some caffeine.'

Jodi walks, dragging her left leg, as Joshua refuses to unfurl himself from it, into the kitchen and flicks the kettle on. 'What was I thinking?' she says, hitting her forehead with the palm of her hand. 'I'm too old for this shit!'

A few nursery rhymes later and both the twins have stopped crying. 'You can come and do that every day if you want,' Jodi says, grateful for the temporary free movement of both arms and legs again.

'I would,' I reply. 'But believe me, Rhyme Time twice a week at the city library, with at least thirty plus kids under five, is more than enough for me.' I glance around Jodi's once immaculate, now toy-strewn kitchen. 'I don't know how you do it?'

'Believe me hun, neither do I.'

'How's Rob?'

Jodi raises her eyes. 'He's okay I suppose. I think he finds these two more of a handful than he imagined they'd be. I'd forgotten what passion killer's babies are. We snatch it where we can these days. It was a quickie across this very kitchen table the other morning,' Jodi laughs, tapping the table with her hand. I laugh with her, lifting my coffee cup off the table in mock disgust.

Joshua starts to grizzle. He stretches out two fat, dimpled arms towards Jodi. She picks him up and bounces him on her knee. Jodi's smile fades 'Do you...' she begins to say but trails off.

'Do I?' I repeat.

'Oh I dunno. Maybe it's just me being oversensitive but ... well ...' Jodi sighs heavily and nods at a couple of photos of her eldest two children, Jack and Emily, 'well, it's just that I know my two can be moody little fuckers. And that's partly down to being teenagers, partly because of the divorce, but I'm convinced Rob loves these two more than them.'

I smile but stay quiet for a moment. Jodi speaks again but her tone is suddenly defensive. 'Don't get me wrong, Rob's pretty good with them and everything, especially when you think he was young, free and single four years ago, and now he's a father of four!'

'Blended families, I think that's what the Americans call us?' I reply. 'They're not easy are they? I rest a reassuring hand on her shoulder. 'Simon and I often lock horns about parenting the kids.'

Jodi looks relieved. 'Do you think you love Maisy differently to Cassie and Connor though?'

I pause for a moment to consider my answer.

'If I'm being honest then, yeah I suppose I do. I carried my two inside me for nine months and there's something special, something amazing about that connection isn't there?'

'Yeah tell me about it,' Jodi replies drolly. 'Indigestion, fat ankles, stretch marks, stitches, sleepless nights – truly fucking amazing. Nothing else quite like it eh?'

I laugh. 'Can't argue with that.'

'But you do admit it's different?'

'Yeah, of course it is. And anyone who says otherwise is a liar. But does that mean because it's different, it's worse or better? Does it mean I don't love and worry about Maisy? Respect her less as a person? Does it mean she pisses me off more, or less than my two? I'd say the answer was a definitive NO. Does it mean that from time to time, subconsciously or perhaps even consciously, Simon and I are slightly biased towards our own children? I'd say yes. Does that make us terrible people? Well, again, I'd say no. It's like any other relationship. If you're willing to work at it, admit when you're wrong and build on all the positive moments, then hopefully you'll get back from it as much as you invest in it.'

Jodi nods her head. 'Yeah I suppose so. It's not easy though is it?' Her reply is more of a statement than it is a question.

A large, hunched over, body enters the kitchen interrupting us. He carries with him a slight smell of body odour intermingled with an overpowering whiff of aftershave. In fact, it smells as though he's poured a whole bottle over himself. He mumbles something completely incomprehensible to my ears, in a voice far too deep for his youthful, acne pustule and pit covered face.

'They're in the conservatory,' Jodi replies, pointing to a pair of large trainers. 'And don't be rude,' she adds. 'Say hello to Lizzie.'

The boy, who appears to carry the weight of the world on his slumped shoulders, throws me a sideways glance. He raises his hand slightly. 'Hi Lizzie,' he mumbles rather reluctantly.

'Hi Jack,' I reply to Jodi's eldest son. 'How are you?'

He shrugs the bent shoulders that appear incapable of carrying his distinctly heavy adolescent head. 'K, I s'pose.'

'Have you had a shower this morning?' Jodi interrupts. 'Yesssssss,' Jack hisses in reply.

'I hope so,' Jodi continues unfazed. 'What is it with boys and washing?' She looks at me and raises her eyes in question.

Jack appears most disgruntled, gathers his things together and mumbles something again. He heads for the front door.

'Don't slam the ...' Jodi begins to say but before she can finish her sentence the front door has crashed shut.

'I can't imagine my Connor being like that. He's still so sweet, still hugs me. He picked some flowers for me on the way home from school the other day.'

'Enjoy it while you still can.'

I smile. 'Yeah I know; he'll be a moody teenager before I know it. But at least I know Connor loves me – well, at the moment anyway – whereas the other two?' I roll my eyes. 'I really think they hate me sometimes.'

'Course they hate you, but they love you too,' Jodi replies. 'They're just bloody teenagers. At least you haven't been compared to Hitler.'

I wrinkle my nose in bemused confusion. 'Sorry, what? What on earth do you mean?'

Jodi explains how she overheard the end of a conversation between Rob and Emily the other morning. 'I walked in on them just as Rob said, "No Emily, unless your Mum is committing genocide, she is not *just like Hitler*". Great eh? Adolf bloody Hitler!' We both laugh.

'Hey, and what about Rosamunde and Sophie?' Jodi continues. 'Did you hear about *that*?'

Jodi, ever the raconteur, starts to tell me of an argument between Rosamunde "Super Mum" Smythe and her "perfect" fifteen-year-old daughter, Sophie.

'It was something to do with texting, at the table I think,' Jodi continues, stroking Joshua's head, now buried between the crook of her left arm and her voluptuous left breast. 'Rosamunde reminded Sophie of the house rule about "no technology at mealtimes" and asked her to put her phone away. Acting defiantly out of character, Sophie refused. So – also quite out of character for the usually calm, "my children slept through the night, only eat organic food, are disciplined through routine (unlike everyone else's feral children) and are limited to several hours of TV and gadget use a day" – Rosamunde totally and utterly lost it.'

'Really?' I ask, finding it both slightly amusing and quite frankly, a relief, to know the normally self-possessed Rosamunde could ever lose it.

'Yeah, well and truly. Apparently. Despite a few tried and tested threats, Sophie stubbornly refused to give up her phone. It's a relief to know the girl is real after all, eh?'

Jodi continued to explain that Rosamunde then proceeded to get up from the table and purposely take some chocolate from the cupboard. She carefully broke the chocolate into pieces and placed it a bowl and then put the bowl into the microwave. She melted the chocolate and then, using a pastry brush, began to paint her hands.

I shoot Jodi a quizzical look. 'Why?'

'Patience my friend, I'm getting there. So, Rosamunde starts to paint her hands, completely covering both palms and all her fingers...' Jodi pauses for a moment to lay a now very sleepy Joshua on the sofa next to his already sleeping sister, rubbing her dead left arm back to life.

'And?' I ask.

Jodi smirks. 'Weee-lllllll,' she continues, 'she then goes upstairs to Sophie's bedroom, where only hours earlier Sophie had proudly made up her bed with a *BRAND NEW*, crisp *WHITE* duvet set purchased with her own birthday money.'

My mind is racing ahead. I gasp, crossing both hands over my mouth. 'No? She didn't?'

Jodi's grin is somewhat triumphant. 'She did. Chocolate

covered handprints *all* over Sophie's new WHITE bedding. Then, get this; Sophie and Rosamunde start fighting, well almost. From what I can gather they exchanged a few blows before Mike intervened and split them both up.

'Really?' I am both appalled and amused at the same time. 'Yeah, poor Rosser, apparently she's having a few problems at work; you know, the usual – budget cuts, talk of redundancy. And Mike hasn't been well either; think they're still waiting to find out if it's cancer or not? I think Sophie was the straw that broke the proverbial camel's back, so to speak.'

'Well, well, well,' I reply, shaking my head. Who'd have thought it, Rosamunde as flawed as the rest of us? I guess there's hope for us yet then eh?' We both laugh.

Jodi walks over to and opens one of the kitchen cupboards. She reaches for a pack of chocolate biscuits, scatters them on a plate and puts the plate in the middle of the table.

'Jaffa cakes, don't you just love em?' She says helping herself. I do, and also reach for a couple. We continue to talk, pausing now and again to cram in more Jaffa cakes.

'It's girls though you know? I say. 'I'm convinced they're more trouble than boys. Talking of which, how's Emily? Did she like the Ed Sheeran concert tickets you bought her for her birthday?'

Jodi rolls her eyes at me and sighs heavily. 'Yes, she liked them.' The intonation in her voice is flat with disappointment. 'She actually hugged me, which was a complete surprise.' She's quiet for a moment, there's a "but" coming.

'But?' I finally say it for her.

'But,' she repeats, 'I couldn't understand why she kept going outside and looking out of the front window. Finally, in the evening, before her ten million friends came round for a sleepover, she asked me if, "that was it, *just* Ed Sheeran tickets". I was slightly thrown and asked her what she'd been expecting. Do you know what her reply was?'

I shrug my shoulders.

'A car!' Jodi shrieks, making me jump. She nervously looks across at the twins and lowers her voice to a whisper. 'A car, like everyone else!' she hisses. 'What the hell is that supposed to mean?' Jodi raises her questioning hands in exasperation. 'Does she think bloody money grows on trees? Of course then she goes off into a major rant about how *her* needs have been sacrificed because of the twins.' Jodi's voice is climaxing again. 'God, I could kill her sometimes.' Her raised voice makes both the twins jump a little; their startled, big brown eyes flickering open in confusion before, thankfully, closing again. Jodi lowers her voice again and attempts a half-hearted laugh. 'I'm thinking of starting a blog for desperate Mum's with teenage daughters,' she says. 'How to Murder Your Teenage Daughters, all ideas welcome. What do you think?'

## CHAPTER 15

PARTY TIME!

**LIZZIE**

How can so few people make so much noise? Simon is just in from work, he looks tired, Cassie and Maisy are upstairs getting ready for separate parties and Connor is downstairs opening the front door to my parents and their dog Freddy.

'There ya go sunshine,' Dad says to Connor passing him a huge slab of chocolate and a £5 note.

'Thanks Grandad,' Connor replies, throwing his arms around Dad, 'you're sick.'

'What? Eh? What'd ya mean? I'm not sick?' Dad replies. 'No Dad,' I begin to explain, 'it's just what the youngsters say. Sick means good, I told you this the other day when you got a bit confused with Cassie – remember?'

'Well, why the hell doesn't he just say "good" then?'

'Stop being so cantankerous,' Mum says, 'and move out the way and let the dog in.' She looks tired, but well.

'You okay Mum?' I ask.

'I'm fine love, fine,' she says. But of course she'd say that even if she wasn't.

'MUM! Mummmmmmm! MUM!' Cassie shouts down the stairs just as the dog spots the cat sitting midway up the stairs. Romeow stares down at Freddy, flicking his tail dismissively. Freddy holds Romeow's stare, barking incessantly. He places a tentative paw on the first step, eager to mount the stairs to seek and make friends with the living, breathing, ginger fur ball, but hardly daring to go any further for fear of being cruelly swiped across the nose as he was on his previous visit.

'Quiet Freddy,' Dad barks. Freddy stops barking, immediately, lowering his head and eyes like a chastised child.

'MUM,' Cassie shouts again, 'is my hair here?'

'What did she say?' Dad asks, looking slightly baffled. 'Is her ear ere?

'No Dad,' I reply, both amused and exasperated. 'She's asking if her hair is here.' Now Dad looks at a complete loss.

'If a here's here?'

'No Dad,' I repeat, 'her hair, she's asking if her hair has come in the post.'

'Hair? In the post? What on earth …?'

'Oh for goodness sake Salocin,' Mum says, her voice clipped and blunt, 'she's talking about a hairpiece, you know, the sort you pin onto your own hair? She was telling us about it the other day.'

'Oh,' Dad replies. 'What's wrong with her own bleedin hair?' Mum looks at me and rolls her eyes.

'There's nothing wrong with her hair Dad, it's just a fashion thing. A lot of young girls wear them. Dad sniffs and tuts and begins to mumble.

'Dunno what's wrong with em all, fake hair, fake eyelashes, fake nails, fake ti...,' he looks at Mum and I and trails off for a moment. 'Blady mad, I reckon, blady mad the blady lot of em. Why can't they just be happy with what they got that's what I say? And madam ere ain't mach betta,' he says pointing to Maisy who has just walked into the kitchen. 'You look like you're in bleedin mournin gal. Why dun cha put a bit o bleedin colour into yer life?' Maisy glares at Dad, forcing her closed, tight lips upwards into a short sarcastic smile.

'I'm going out,' she states.

I tell her briefly of our plans to holiday in Cornwall for a week next month and ask her if she'd like to join us. Her reply is short and to the point, 'Yeah, whatevs,' she says shrugging her shoulders. Then, with a slam of the door, she's gone.

*What's that you say...thank you? For inviting me and arranging it and paying for it. Oh don't mention it. Oh yeah that's right, you didn't!*

Cassie is shouting down the stairs – again – her voice laced with panic.

'STOP Mai ... Mania ... STOP!!' She crashes down the stairs like some crazy bag lady clutching an assortment of large shopping bags, hand bags and what at first glance looks like the recently hacked scalp of some poor, unsuspecting victim but is in fact her hair piece. She looks at Mum and Dad, only just aware of their presence.

'Nan, Grandad,' she exclaims, trying to catch her breath before planting a kiss on each of their cheeks. 'Have to go. Important party you see, and J...' She pauses, her face reddening a little. 'And err important people,' she continues. 'Cornwall sick.' She sticks her thumb up. 'But really have to go.' She blows them both a kiss. 'Mwah Mwah.' She then casts a quick look in my direction. 'I'm going to Chelsea's,' she states before careering out of the door. 'Mai ... I mean Mania ... wait for me,' she shouts.

We watch Cassie struggle towards Maisy's waiting car. One arm waving frantically like a possessed snake, the other arm weighted down by her many bags. Maisy sits, head above the steering wheel, impatiently revving the accelerator, her expression as dark as her black kholed eyes.

The fifty-second whirlwind that is Cassie has left the building. Silence descends and a few stray tumbleweeds roll along the now deserted landscape. Mum, Dad and Freddy all look at one another in disbelief then look across at me.

'Wine anyone?' Simon says.

## CASSIE

The party is full on. The music is like, well loud and there's a constant base line vibrating through every piece of furniture and across every surface in the room. I feel a little woozy and lightheaded, which I don't really understand coz I haven't really drank anything else since 'prinks' earlier.

I never want to do prinks again. I was quite happy sipping my glass of Lambrini but then some stupid idiot suggested shots and drinking games. Eeeuuck, Dirty Pint, Arrogance, Beer Pong, and shots? Yuk, just thinking about the burning sensation down my throat makes me shudder. Joe leans across me.

'Do ya wanna drink?' he asks. I still can't believe he hasn't left my side for most of the night. I feel like I'm on cloud ten, or whatever the saying is.

'Errrmmm, no thanks,' I say, before suddenly changing my mind. 'Actually yes, can I have some water please?' He looks at me and smirks.

'Really?' I nod my head. Then a gawjuss smile spreads across his face. 'Lightweight,' he says as he bends forward to kiss me before heading off in search of drinks.

I look round the huge room that Chelsea's parents call their entertaining area. It's at the back of, slightly set away from, the rest of the house. The house is part of a private housing estate, close to a golf course. Compared to our house it's like, massive. Grand I suppose you would call it, but it all just seems a bit too show-offy to me. It almost feels like the house and the people in it are pretending to be much posher than they really are. I can hear Mum now, if she were here, saying something like "the desperate and soulless trying to impress the deluded and barren with their misguided aspirations" or some dramatic crap like that.

At least Mum doesn't pretend to be something she's not. I look across at Chelsea's Mum and for all her tanned, shiny, wrinkleless face, especially her forehead (fillers and botox probably), she still doesn't look any younger or better than Mum. More glamorous maybe but at least Mum is honest in her dullness. At least Mum smiles. Chelsea's Mum never seems to smile, she always looks pouty and stares at everyone in that sort of critical way that she thinks all her money allows her to. The dance floor is heaving with mad, dancing, bodies and watching everyone is double the fun coz of the mirrored walls everywhere. The atmosphere in the room is buzzing. I look across at Chelsea's Dad who looks like a middle aged idiot, basking in all the female attention that surrounds him while he serves drinks behind his very own life size bar. He looks like a baboon to me. I swear he thinks he's like some bartender character out of the film Cocktail or something. And why girls not much older than me are so ridiculously interested in *such* an *old* man is beyond me. It's like me fancying someone like, hmmm well, like Simon (except of course that would be like incest or something) but EEEEEWWWWW, it's just too gross.

As I continue scanning the room my heart feels like it stops for a moment as I spot Joe. He's talking to someone and I can't see who. He is so gorge, so beautiful. I feel a bit drunk but I think it's love, not alcohol. Yeah that's what it is, I'm drunk on love. Oh god, what's he doing? I can see who he's talking to now and its bloody Pheebs. I feel, well I dunno, my chest feels like it's being squeezed. He's looking right at her, well right at her boobs actually. What are they both laughing at? Why is he moving the hair away from her face? Oh god, now I feel sick. I have to move.

I get up from the expensive but bloody uncomfortable stretched leather sofa we've been sitting on. My bum is numb and the room is swaying a little. I put both my arms out to balance myself. These shoes are like waaaaay tooooooo high. I spot Sophie and Maddy with Luke and a few others. I totter over to where they're all standing.

I also spot Chelsea. How did she end up persuading me to let her wear my dress? Well, Ruby's dress actually. I suppose it looks better on her than me anyway. She is of course, surrounded by boys and they all look ridiculous, prancing and preening around her, arrogant attitudes as big as their ego's, vying for victory, more bothered about being the winner than the prize itself. Still, Chelsea looks happy. She is the centre of the universe and all this attention only confirms that.

My eyes search the room again for Joe but he must have moved because I can't see him anymore. I can't see Pheebs either. My stomach flips. I feel sick.

'Hi Cassie,' Luke says, 'you look errrmm ...,' he stops talking to cough. 'You look nice tonight,' he eventually says.

I frown at Luke. 'Yeah? Thanks Luke.'

I've known Luke like forever and I don't understand why he's being all weird and nervous around me. We usually have good banter together. I like talking to him coz he plays piano too, and guitar. Hopefully Joe will see me talking to him and feel as jel as he just made me feel.

'Have you seen Joe?' I ask him, and everyone else he's

standing with. 'Or Pheebs? Have any of you seen Pheebs?' They shrug their shoulders. My stomach dances with dread.

'I thought Joe was with ...,' Luke begins to say.

'Who?' I reply just a little too quick, a little too snappy. 'You thought Joe was with who?' I demand.

'You,' Luke replies. He looks a bit taken aback. 'I thought Joe was with you,' he repeats.

'What, oh yeah he was, is. He was going to get us some drinks,' I explain, looking round frantically. Still no sign of Joe, or Pheebs. Before I realise it I've pulled out my phone and am thumping out a tweet.

*When you like someone but your best friend insists on flirting with them.*
*#Friend or Foe?*

Suddenly there is a hand running down my back. I turn quickly to see Joe looking down at me and before I can say a word he's kissing me. His mouth is hot and soft and his tongue searches for mine. I can taste alcohol and smell something sweet around him, perfume maybe? It's not mine, it's a different smell to mine but as his hands roam across my back I suddenly don't really care. Joe wants me. He really wants me. I still can't believe he fancies me. I don't know what he sees in me really.

We stop kissing and when I open my eyes I notice Pheebs has joined our little group. She lifts her head up and looks at me. She's been reading her phone and I'm guessing she's seen my tweet. For a split second I regret my quick fingers until I see the way she looks at Joe and the smug way she smiles at me. Something in the pit of my stomach makes me feel uneasy but then Joe grabs my hand and pulls me towards him. How can someone be so perfect, look so fine, smell so good?

'C'mon,' he says. His voice sounds urgent. 'Let's go and find an empty room.' He raises his eyebrows and his piercing blue eyes bore into me.

'What?' I reply slightly alarmed. 'What do you mean a room? Don't you want to stay here at the party?' My mind is racing. It's too early for this; I mean I don't even know if we're properly together? His FB status still says single. My phone pings – Pheebs has posted a tweet.

*CBA!!! Am done with so-called friends. #Get your own life instead of trying to copy someone else's.*

I feel confused, drunk, giddy, nervous and happy all at the same time. Joe's grip on me is tight. He's leading me through a dance floor of hot sweaty bodies but it's surprising how much power his sheer presence seems to radiate. He's a bit like that Moses bloke from the bible who parted the Red Sea, except this is a sea of people, and they're not red. Actually my eyes look a bit red as I catch a glimpse of myself in one of the mirrored walls.

We're in the garden now. The lawn is large and lush and green with all kinds of plants and flowers and garden furniture. It's a warm night but the air is fresh and I feel relieved to be outside. Although most people are inside, a few others have spilled outside like us. There are couples kissing in dark corners and small groups of tired party people sitting cross-legged on the grass or lounging across the fancy garden furniture. Everyone is mostly quiet, mumbling in low voices that are suddenly interrupted now and again by loud, raucous laughter. The air feels heavy with the scent of recently watered flowers, especially roses. I know the smell of roses coz they're Nan's favourite. Every now and then I also catch a whiff of a familiar herbal smell, intermingled with fag smoke.

Joe leads me closer to the main house before leaning against a wall and pulling me towards him. He bends his head towards mine and kisses me again, passionately. I feel tingly inside, especially between my legs and little embarrassed coz I can feel him go hard. I pull away slowly, grateful it's too dark for him to see me blush. He grins at me before taking a packet of fags out of his pocket, lighting one and sucking heavily on it. He lifts his head up to release a stream of smoke from the corner of his mouth. He offers me a drag. I don't really want one but I feel like I should. I inhale as lightly as possible but still manage to cough and nearly choke to death. He laughs at me, takes another drag then stubs it out on the wall before carefully placing it back in its packet.

Before I know it he has quickly guided me into a room in the house. He snaps a switch on the wall and we are suddenly blinded by a bright, glaring light. He looks at me but his hand is fiddling with something on the wall. The light fades. He must have found a dimmer switch or something which I'm like well chuffed about coz I was a bit worried what I look like. I haven't looked at myself properly for at least an hour and I have visions of smudged red lipstick and gunky eyes where make-up and eyeliner collects in the corners of them.

I scan the room quickly, nervously. Despite having slept over at Chelsea's house now several times we're in a room I haven't seen before. It's clearly some sort of guest room. Three of the walls are plain and white, but the fourth has what looks to be expensive (what else would it be) purple and black wallpaper. The furniture is minimal and really modern looking but matches perfectly, not like the mish mashed collection we have at home. There is a black glass sideboard with a few family photos scattered across it and the odd purple, funny shaped ornaments and vases placed between them. There is also a huge flat screen TV on one of the plain walls and a long black sofa with silver metal legs.

To my surprise Joe pushes me down, gently, onto the sofa.

He starts kissing me again. God I hope my breath doesn't smell? He moves from my mouth to my neck, kissing, kissing me softly. His hands are wandering up and down my back, and then, oh god he's moving towards my boobs. Oh no, his hands are on my boobs now. I don't know what to think, what to do. Oh my god he's grabbed my hand with one of his, the other one is still on my boob, and is putting it on his jeans between his legs. I keep kissing him, my eyes tightly closed. A million thoughts race through my head. What if he thinks I'm easy? What if he wants to go further? I'm tingling all over and actually enjoying my physical response to his touch. He's reaching up inside my top now, pulling and tugging at the back of my bra. I hope he doesn't break my bra coz it's new and I really like it.

'Here, let me do it,' I say, pulling away from him for a minute. I really don't want him to break this bra. He smiles a gawjuss smile at me then starts, I am shocked to see, undoing his jeans. He grabs my hand again and thrusts it inside his boxers. I am touching his willy, his hard willy. I'm shocked, really shocked at how hard and big it feels, and wet? Ugghh! Why does it feel wet?'

'Are you on the pill?' he suddenly asks me really casually.

'What?' I reply, slightly taken aback.

'The pill? Are you on the pill?' he repeats. 'Coz I've got something if you're not?'

I don't know if it's the alcohol or because I feel panicky but this suddenly doesn't feel right. I feel sick. I know I'm way behind a lot of the other girls at school. I know a lot of them lost their virginity ages ago but I'm not going to lose it just to be the same as them. Besides, even if I was on the pill, which I'm not, that wouldn't protect me from all the other people he's slept with, would it?

I move away from him. 'I, I don't feel well,' I stutter.

He smiles a big gawjuss smile. 'I'll make ya feel betta,' he says, about to reach for me again.

'No!' I say, 'I don't want ... I can't ... I'm still a ...'

'Oh my god,' he says, surprise in his voice. 'You're not still a fucking virgin are ya?'

'Yeah, I am,' I reply, rather pathetically. Why do I feel ashamed?

'Chels said you were but I thought she was fucking joking.' There's no respect in his voice, 'Oh well, come on,' he says, 'if you're gonna lose it to someone you may as well have the privilege of losing it to me.' He says it as if it's a chore, something I should be grateful for. He stands up and proceeds to pull down his jeans and boxers. My eyes nearly pop out of my head and I can't stop looking at his knob, standing hard and to attention. 'C'mon then,' he says as he takes my hand, 'let's get this over with.' His voice is softer now and I can't tell if he's smiling at me or laughing. I look at him in disbelief. Then suddenly, out of nowhere – and I don't know if it's nerves or the realisation of just how arrogant Joe actually is – I start laughing and I can't stop.

'What the fuck are you laughing at?' he says, now pulling his jeans up again. I can't reply because I'm still laughing. 'Can't be arsed with stupid, immature...' he continues, fumbling with the zip of his jeans.

'I'm sorry,' I stutter. My laughter drains away as I realise he's going to leave me, doesn't like me, even. 'Don't go,' I plead, 'can't we just kiss and stuff?'

He strides towards me and leans in close. He looks angry.

'I'm sorry,' he says, 'but I'm not into silly little girls.' He starts to walk towards the door when suddenly, out of nowhere, vomit projects from my mouth all across (thankfully) the tiled floor of the room. I feel awful.

'Oh no, help me Joe, please help me,' I beg through a mouthful of sick. He looks repulsed.

'Uuugghh, that's bloody disgusting Cassie,' he says, before disappearing back out of the door we came in.

Oh god, I had such high hopes for tonight. It was all going so well, how did it end up like this? Joe storming out, and me, sitting in my own sick? I start to cry, huge heavy sobs.

'Mum,' I call out to no-one. 'I want my Mum.'

# CHAPTER 16

## THE OPPRESSED

**LIZZIE**

I balance on one leg using my left hand to pull my sock onto my left foot and my right hand to clean my teeth whilst simultaneously looking for my reading glasses. I'm running late. Simon looks at me and laughs. I attempt to talk to him through the white froth that has built up around my mouth but give up when I see the quizzical look on his face.

'Found them,' I shout, finally locating my reading glasses. 'I was thinking of investing in a chain to put round my neck for these little suckers,' I say, my mouth now froth-free.

Simon raises his eyes in mock disapproval. 'You're really going for that dowdy librarian look then?' He looks me up and down and I recoil a little, not really sure whether to laugh or feel offended.

*Well, you heard what Cassie thinks of your fashion sense – that's right, you have none!*

I pull my red and grey striped jumper over my head and smooth it across my grey fitted trousers, before slipping on every librarian's basic requirement, sensible shoes.

'Smart casual,' I say defensively, smoothing my hands across my thighs, as I turn from left to right, slowly moving both hands across my reasonably flat stomach.

Simon comes up behind me and envelopes me in his strong arms.

'You look great babe,' he says, kissing the top of my head.

I turn and wrap my arms around his neck, and smile. We rub noses.

'So, what's happening with Cassie today?' he suddenly asks.

'What do you mean?' I reply somewhat confused.

'Well, it's been a few weeks now since she finished school. She starts sixth form in September which actually means fewer subjects to study which equates to more time ...'

'And?' I ask, pretty sure I know where this is going.

'Well, isn't it about time Cassie got herself a part time job? You know, so she can help out a bit, buy a few of her own things? Money is a bit tight at the moment. Besides, the work experience will do her good.'

My good mood has swiftly disappeared. And not because I disagree with a word Simon has just said but because of the hypocrisy of those words.

*Here we go again.*

As a blended family (*who the hell came up with that ridiculous label anyway – sounds like one of those bloody coffee adverts?*) we're still on a learning curve. The boundaries for the kids are discussed, agreed and set, and then moved, usually by Simon and often without my knowledge.

'Oh I see,' I snap. 'You mean you don't want Cassie swanning around doing sod all for the summer like your daughter did last year? The same daughter that freeloaded and contributed nothing? The very one who started college for a couple of months only to drop out without telling us? The one that *I*, me,' I emphasise with a raised finger and raised voice, 'had to threaten with the withdrawal of all privileges and any financial help until she started to look for work with barely any back-up from you.'

Simon frowns defensively. 'I did back you up. When I could. I can't help it that I work away a lot.'

'Yes! Leaving me to do all the disciplining on issues *we've* agreed on. Only to find because Maisy, or Cassie for that matter, have phoned you in floods of tears, *you* change the bloody rules.' He smiles a wry smile, as if I've just given him a compliment, which only serves to infuriate me more. 'You do realise Maisy blames me for everything?' I yell. 'And I mean, everything!' I cross my arms defiantly.

'Yeah, well, she's been a bit lost,' Simon replies.

'Ohhhhhhh okay,' I hiss, feeling the anger rise within me. 'Your daughter is permitted to, to, just drift, because bless her, she's a bit lost but my daughter has to knuckle down does she?'

It isn't what Simon means and I know it but I'm really pissed off now.

Simon wears an expression of irritation. 'Keep your voice down please,' he hisses back.

'Why?' I snap, 'so the kids don't hear what an absolute prick you are? Well perhaps they should hear what you've got to say eh? See the other side of good old Simon?'

'No,' he replies through gritted teeth, 'it's just we always said if we had any problems with the kids we'd talk about it – together – and agree a solution – together. Maisy did, if you remember, try and get some work, eventually, after some persuasion.'

I shoot him a look that screams disbelief. 'There is no problem with *my* daughter,' I reply, 'and persuasion you call it? It was a huge kick up the backside, mainly from me,' I reply, jabbing my finger hard into my chest.

*Ouch, don't be so rough!*

'Meeeeeeee,' I repeat, 'you know, the big bad stepmonster!!!!'

'Look,' Simon replies clearly exasperated, 'you've got me all wrong. This has all come out ... well ... wrong. It's just that well ...'

'Well? What?'

Simon sighs heavily. 'I dunno. It just seemed easier to give in to Maisy sometimes than deal with her moods.'

'Oh, okay! You mean the moods I deal with on a daily basis because you're not here most of the time?'

'Fair enough,' he replies attempting a laugh until he sees my stony expression. 'I'm not laughing,' I say chastising him in the same way I so often do the school children that visit the library and think it's fun to throw the books around.

There's an awkward silence between us before Simon eventually breaks it. 'Look,' he says, slightly deflated. 'I just don't think it's a good idea for Cassie to mooch around the house all summer is all I'm saying.' He attempts to put his arm around me but I shrug it off.

'Then you tell Cassie,' I say, struggling to keep my voice down. 'I'm sick to death of playing the bad cop and you always coming across as the good cop all the time. You stay at home and deal with the fall out and I'll piss off for a change.' Simon looks hurt but I'm too angry to care right now. 'I'm late for work, I have to go.'

Simon's face hardens. 'Yeah, well, don't forget it's my works do tonight.' His response is palpable and now equally cold. He throws several notes of mixed currency on the bed. 'And for god sake,' he continues, looking me up and down again. 'Get yourself something decent to wear will you.' Then with a slam of the bedroom door he's gone.

*Arrggghh!!! Self-righteous bastard.*

I grab the money, throw my jacket on and leave the house in the same manner as everyone else, with a SLAM of the door.

৯

I'm seething and muttering madly to myself all the way to work. I stab a text message on my phone to Ruby.

**Can you meet me at lunch today? Urgently need to buy something new for this stupid do tonight? Xxxx**

I've got a good bloody mind not to bother.

*How dare he? And going on about Cassie like that; one bloody rule for his daughter, a complete bloody nother for mine. He's right though, you know that? It's not good for Cassie to be mooching around day after day.*

'I know, I know,' I say out loud.

I don't know what happened at that party Cassie went to but she hasn't been the same since? Hasn't left the house, hasn't seen Chelsea, or Pheebs for that matter?

And that Joe boy hasn't been round anymore.

*Maybe you scared him off?*

'Maybe,' I say bumping into a woman in the street.

'Yes?' she replies, stopping and looking at me, slightly confused.

'I'm sorry, what?' I ask her.

'Mary,' she says, 'you just said my name – Mary – but I don't think I know you?' She looks at me suspiciously.

'Did I?'

*You really must stop talking to yourself out loud.*

'First sign of madness!'

'I beg your pardon?'

'What no,' I reply, 'not you. I was talking to myself out loud.' I try and explain that I actually said *maybe,* not *Mary*. The woman continues to look at me warily before shaking her head and moving on.

*Oh well.*

I cross the road and head for the library. Once inside I swipe my security card at the door marked "staff only" and let myself into the staff room, proceeding straight to my locker to put my bag away. Joan is in, quietly sipping a cup of tea, attempting to read. She looks at me, smiles and nods her head towards Raj, who is pacing the long thin room like a rabid dog. Joan raises her eyes, her expression one of resigned exasperation.

Raj looks at me. 'Has you heard?' he says. 'Heard what?'

'They're bloody bastards innit.'

'Who are?'

Raj thrusts an angry finger upwards. 'They are innit. They're doing it again, another bloody restructure.'

My heart sinks. Not another one. 'How do you know?'

'We got a meeting today innit, at 12 and let's just say a little bird from the HR Office. Actually she's a bit of a big birdie.' Raj winks at me. 'Fond of cake, if yoos get my drift? Anyway, yeah, she said there's a meeting planned.'

There is indeed a meeting at 12pm and it takes place upstairs in the unfinished Shark Aquarium above the library. The very same aquarium that some bright spark had the idea for in the first place and the council budget actually approved. The same budget used to erode and continually hack away at what little library service we have left, including its hacked off employees. The objective of building such an exhibit was to bring something new and exciting to the city – apparently. Thousands of pounds were found and spent before the logistics of an inner city Shark Aquarium – above a library – were properly considered. The idea was thus abandoned part way through construction and we are now left with a half completed room of glass devoid of any and all aquatic life. All our meetings now take place in this eerily strange and sharkless wall-to-wall chamber of glass while the rest of the time the Council tries to rent it out as a Function Room.

Our irksome MD delivers, yet again, another artificially heartfelt speech. His voice is loud and full of conviction but the content of his speech is purposefully vague. The council have asked for savings without reducing the library opening hours. The savings will, yet again, come in the form of a reduction of posts, five in this instance. We are asked once again; to study the new timetables and indicate which roles we would like to be considered for. They have however, we're told we'll be pleased to know, managed to create a couple of posts with zero hour contracts.

Why for one moment does this buffoon of a man think this news is pleasing? Whom exactly does it please? It certainly isn't those of us who have partners who already work in unstable industries. It certainly isn't the mortgage or credit companies or even those wishing to rent a property.

To say the mood amongst all is sombre would perhaps be an understatement. Raj is incensed and voices his anger back in the staff room.

'What,' he says, slapping the back of one hand onto the palm of his other, 'is wrong with wanting decent, secure employment?' Mumbles of empathy with his statement ricochet across the staff room walls.

Raj raises is hands questioningly, too furious to sit, prowling amongst us, restless, looking for solace but finding none amongst his workmates today.

'Arrggghh man,' he says, anger permeating his every pore, 'this aint right. We need to fight or somink innit.' He pauses for a moment; the low disposition among the library collective has now plunged to new depths. I personally welcome this hiatus and judging by the faces of my colleagues, so do they. No one disagrees with Raj but his angry, passionate words are merely rubbing salt into a very raw, open wound.

'Cornish pasty anyone?' Trevor says attempting to bring a semblance of normality back to the rundown staffroom and it's equally dejected occupants. 'They're homemade,' he begins to say before Raj cuts him off.

'And...' *Oh god he's off again*. 'Don't even get me started on these zero hour contracts,' he continues, 'and yoos all know I'm right.'

I look at my watch. I need to meet Ruby in five minutes. Raj is in his stride, rallying support among his oppressed work colleagues. Slipping away isn't going to be easy.

'You know what those contracts encourage?' Raj continues, his ranting becoming more animated by the minute. 'I'll tell yoos,' he persists, waving his right index finger at no-one in particular. I can hear the inward sighs of everyone willing him to stop, and yet at the same time, compelled to listen to this angry young man. 'It means a disposable, throwaway workforce. This is the future of the yoof of today innit. And that's exactly where they want us, cap in hand, subservient and grateful. Master and servant eh? Master and servant.'

'Depeche Mode I think you'll find,' Trevor says leaning across to whisper in my ear.

'Sorry?' I reply, completely thrown.

'Oh come on,' Trevor continues, grinning. 'I know your charming face has aged far better than my craggy old one but I can't believe you don't remember the 80s?' I laugh, for what feels the first time in hours. Raj catches sight of us both and stares, sternly.

'Anyway, where was I? Oh yeah, those greedy bastards,' Raj says pointing skywards, 'want everyone back in the good old days innit? Oppressed, working for fuck all and grateful. Well, everyone except them of course, with their expenses and their second homes and their annual bonuses. Bonuses that, may I add, would probably feed the entire African continent. Everyfing, I means everyfing,' Raj rallies, slapping the palm of his hand again, 'good, honest, hardworking people has fought for in this country is gradually being eroded away – yeah? If they keep this up I'll never get away from my bloody family innit? Can you imagine me?' Raj asks, pointing at himself. 'A little grey haired Indian still living with his elderly parents?' The room is filled with slight ripples of laughter. 'They'll be generations of kids never being able to afford to leave home.'

I gasp inwardly; Raj's words fill me with cold terror.

*Oh my god, can you imagine a lifetime of Cassie and Maisy, never leaving home?*

'Now that is madness,' I say out loud.

'Yes my friend, madness indeed,' Raj replies, seeing another opportunity to speak.

*You have to stop him.*

'Yes, but ...' I interject at lightning speed. 'Do not forget the words of Charles William Day;

*"Madness is an excited mind, indulging in the dreams of imagination, until the heated fancy makes chimeras appear real."*

Raj scratches his head and looks suitably thrown for a moment. 'Err yeah,' he replies, 'that err...' he trails off and scratches his head again. 'That too,' he adds. His expression is one of amused bewilderment as he continues to scratch his head, quietly repeating my words to himself.

It's done the trick. I see my opportunity to escape and grasp it, along with – so it appears – half the staff room.

## CHAPTER 17

LETHARGY

**CASSIE**

Oh my god, this must be what it feels like to die of a broken heart. That's what's happening to me. I'm dying and wasting away to nothing. I run my hands across my stomach and hips. Yep, there are definitely two bony bits that weren't there before. I don't understand why I still have a muffin top though?

Joe has broken my heart and I'll never recover from this. I can't eat, I can't sleep.

I'm mortified when I remember Chelsea's party. My phone's pings, I have a text. I lift my head out of my duvet to check it. Wow its 11am. I obviously did manage to sleep for a while. It's only been for about an hour though. That's why I have to lay in every day coz I just can't sleep. I can't eat either, although maybe some ice cream would help, just a bit.

I make my way downstairs. The house is deathly quiet. And perfectly tidy, just as Mum likes it. Worse than Monica from

Friends she is. A complete and utter neat freak. Has a complete bloody eppy over a few bloody crumbs on the worktops. She really should just chill, get a life or something. I check who my text is from. Ah bless, it's Sophie. She's been like, shaaammazing since the party. A real friend; not like bloody Pheebs. Bloody cow.

*Hey Babe. WAKE UP!! Job vacancies at the shop where I work. Lingerie Dept!*
*Whoo Hoo! Have arranged an interview 4u 4 2moz 10.30.*
*Loads a fit hotties. Money in your pocket. Be there xxxxxxxxx*

A job eh? I'm not really sure if I want one at the moment. I do really deserve the whole summer off considering how hard I worked for my GCSEs. I'll think about it. I suppose it'll get Mum off my back. She keeps nagging me to get a job. I told her I'd sort it. She said it's not easy given the current climate (god knows what the weather's got to do with getting a job?). I mean, really though? How easy was that? The job's virtually mine. Oh shit I have to have an interview though. What do I say? Oh well, I'll ask Mum, she'll tell me. I suppose she is good for some things.

I sit my phone in its docking station and play the Artic Monkeys *R U Mine* at full volume, purely to drown my sorrows of course, and dance away all my heartache. I love the Arctic Monkeys, especially Alex Turner – even more than Joe actually – and I'm going to marry him one day. He doesn't know it yet though of course.

It's a beautiful day; the sun is streaming through the kitchen window; another perfect reason to eat ice cream. Well, that and I really need to eat to keep my strength up. I really can't let my depression affect my appetite. I am virtually wasting away after all, even though the bathroom scales don't indicate it. I think they must be broken.

Oh my god, someone's knocking at the door. My heart beats really fast. What if it's Joe? Please let it be Joe. Oh god no! On second thoughts don't let it be Joe. I look a complete mess. I'm only wearing a skanky pair of shorts and an old tee shirt, and, oh my god, no make-up! I rush up the stairs, three steps at a time, narrowly missing kicking Romeow, who is, was, sleeping on his usual favourite step, about half way up.

'For god bloody sake Romeow,' I shout, 'are you trying to bloody kill me?' He looks completely terrified and flees to the bottom step before looking up and scowling at me. He then saunters away, very slowly, in search of a new sleeping place. Why do we have to have such an anti-social cat? He hasn't sat with me once through my recent trauma. Selfish cat.

Oh god the doorbell is ringing again. I grab my false eyelashes and, squeezing out too much glue, attempt to put them on. Only problem is I now have glue all over my fingers and the lashes are sticking to them instead of my eyes. Arrrrrrgggghh! After several desperate attempts I manage, somehow, to get the falsies on top of my own lashes. I pinch some colour into my cheeks, slap some lip-gloss on my lips and run my hands through my limp hair. I grab Maisy's huge square brush and desperately try to give my hair some body by back combing it. Only, now I look like I have limp hair with a bird's nest on top.

Oh bloody hell; whoever's at the door is now knocking – loudly. Whoever it is, they are clearly desperate to see me. Unless it's the bloody postman of course? I look out of the upstairs hallway window, squinting and shielding my eyes from the sun with my hand but I can't make out who it is. Oh well, this will just have to do, birds nest and all.

I make my way back to the top of the stairs. Be still my beating heart. I smooth my hands across my stomach (why do I still have a muffin top?) then down across my legs. Shit! I don't have a bra on. He, whoever it is, will see my odd sized boobs. I reach for my bargain Primark padded, ultra-lift, electric blue bra. I must be ambernextplus or something coz somehow whilst running down the stairs I manage to slip my bra on under my tee shirt. I reach the front door, take a deep breath and clear my throat. I'm planning to open the door and speak in my best sexy voice – soft, low and slightly husky, like Ruby was with that waiter. I press the handle downwards, my heart beating loudly in my chest.

'Yes,' I say, all hot and breathy. My heart drops. I feel it thump into my stomach. 'Oh, it's you,' I say to Luke. Why does he keep coming round to see me? Although, he does appear to be holding a tub of ice cream in his hand, so maybe I will let him in, even if it is the third time this week.

Luke flinches slightly and looks positively perplexed. 'Umm, you seem to have something crawling down your face,' he says pointing to my cheek.

'Eek, what the hell is it?' I scream, waving my head and my hands simultaneously. Luke takes hold of my hands and pulls me towards him. He looks at me and smirks then brushes something from my cheek.

'Here,' he says holding it in his hand, 'I'm not really sure what it is?' I look at the black, many legged thing sitting in the palm of Luke's hand and realise it's one of my falsies.

'Oh, it's just my eyelashes,' I explain. 'And, err,' he says grinning.

'What now?' I snap.

'Your top seems to be twisted in your …' he coughs and turns slightly pink. 'Your um, bra,' he continues.

I look down and see I'm clearly not as amberdextplus as I thought I was. 'Oh whatevs,' I reply, genuinely not bothered. It's only Luke, no-one important, no-one to impress. 'Come in then,' I say.

'I thought you might like this?' Luke says holding up a huge tub of cookie dough ice cream as he follows me into the kitchen. 'I know it's your favourite and I thought it might cheer you up, what with Joe and his Facebook status and everything.'

I swing round to look at him. 'His FB status, what do you mean?' He suddenly looks very sheepish.

'Shit,' Luke says, squirming. 'I just assumed with you being so upset about him and everything. Well, I thought you probably followed him and ...'

I grab my phone and jab my finger at the Facebook icon. I click onto Friends and find Joe. I hunt for his profile, my eyes rapidly scanning and searching for information. Then I see it, his status, in huge black letters, for the entire world to see, and screaming at me:

*IN A RELATIONSHIP!!!!!!!!*

Oh my god. This is serious. Since the party and up until the early hours of this morning his status was single. I'd hoped beyond stupid hope that if he was having some fling with Pheebs (I still can't believe she'd do that to me?), it wasn't anything important; a meaningless, temporary, physical release that would leave him empty and in no doubt that I was the one. But now he's in a fully-fledged relationship, my hope as crushed as my poor fractured heart. I look from my phone to Luke then back to my phone again, speechless. I click off Joe's profile and onto Pheebs's. A recent selfie of her smiles back at me.

'Arrggghh, I want to claw her eyes out,' I yell. Luke jumps back, slightly alarmed.

I look at her status and there it is, bold as brass as Grandad would say:

*IN A RELATIONSHIP!!!!!!!!*

'I saw Pheebs the other day,' Luke says. 'She said she's been trying to get hold of you, to explain...'

'Don't,' I reply, 'ever mention her name to me again, okay?' Luke's expression is like Connor's when I tell him to shut up. 'Okay,' he replies. 'Oh god, I feel sick,' I say pacing the kitchen, 'I'll never eat again.'

'So you don't want this ice cream then?'

'Don't be an idiot,' I say grabbing two spoons from the cutlery draw, 'do you think I'm going to let a tub of perfectly good ice cream go to waste?'

Between the two of us, Luke and I manage to polish off the whole tub. Well, Luke eats more of it than me, if I'm truthful, but the very small amount I did eat has made me feel a bit better. He's brought his guitar with him. He sets it up next to my piano and we practice a few songs together.

He's actually a really good friend and one of the only people from school that thinks playing the piano isn't weird. He asks me if I've seen Chelsea and did I know she was in New York? Who the hell doesn't know from her zillions of tweets every three seconds?

***Chelsea Divine is looking from the top of the Empire State Building #Awesome!***
***Chelsea Divine having Breakfast at Tiffany's #Charming***

And so it continues, Chelsea Divine, blah, blah blah, hash tag more blah. Not that I'm jealous. I nearly could have gone to New York too, if we had the money. Chelsea wanted me to go with her, she asked her Mum when they found me and my sick in the guest room that Joe left me in. Oh god, my face flushes up at the mere morose memory of it all. Why did Chelsea have to ask her Mum then? When I'd vomited over her very expensive tiled flooring? I couldn't look at Chelsea or her Mum but I could see Chelsea's Mum, using my profiterole vision. She was all stern faced and glaring, mouthing a definite NO to Chelsea. I don't care. Chelsea's only friends with me coz she thinks my godmother is Francious Libert. As if. I can't believe she honestly believes that. I don't think she does really. She's just hedging her bets in case. She'll drop me like a ton of bricks when she finds out the truth. And she will find out, sooner or later, and then I'll have to face her and Joe and Pheebs at Sixth Form in September. 'Oh god, I don't want to go to Sixth Form,' I wail at Luke, just as we finish playing *Rolling in the Deep* by Adele.

'Why don't you study music at College with me. I mean, like me?'

'What,' I reply, 'I didn't know you were going to college?'

He smiles. 'I did tell you, about six months ago. You obviously weren't listening.'

'I've never really thought about it,' I reply, suddenly filled with excitement. 'It's just my Mum puts all this pressure on me to get my A Levels so I can go to Uni and ...'

Luke cuts me off. 'You can go to Uni if you complete this course, it's equivalent to three A Levels, 180 UCAS points.'

'Really? That would be like so aammaaazing to study music, and we could like help each other out, and like perform together. Oh my god,' I gasp. 'Would we have to perform to like real live people? That would be sooooooooooo like scary, but way better than A Levels.' Luke laughs at me.

'You do know you're slightly insane right?' he asks.

'Of course,' I reply, 'it runs in the family.'

I'm absolutely convinced and I've made up my mind. I *am* going to study music at college. Persuading Mum is going to be the real problem.

## LIZZIE

I sigh heavily as I pull up the drive of the house in my car. It's 3pm, twenty-eight degrees outside, and all the curtains are closed. The wheelie bin, now empty, still stands where it did this morning and if I find the house in the same state as it was yesterday I swear I am going to lose it.

Simon's right, it's not good for Cassie to be mooching around doing nothing. It's a breeding ground for hedonistic melancholy. I reach for the door handle, and then step back for a moment. It's been a bad day, my head hurts, my feet ache and I can feel the resentment rising within me.

*Take a deep breath and count to ten.*

I rub the back of my neck with my hand then suddenly have the urge to look round. It feels as though someone is behind me but when I look I don't see anyone. I walk towards the end of the driveway then stop to look left and right but see nothing or no one of interest. I shrug my shoulders and continue rubbing the back of my neck as I head back up the drive towards the front door.

I take another deep breath, open the door and walk in. The stifled air hits me. It feels like a bloody sauna.

*Keep calm Lizzie – keep calm.*

I immediately start pulling apart curtains, releasing blinds and flinging open windows to let in some much needed fresh air. I notice cups and plates dispersed at will or at random around the kitchen, as are various tea or coffee stained spoons. Knives with remnants of butter also lay littered amongst crumb-infested worktops. My anger is rising like bile in my throat.

I walk into the darkened living room to find Cassie ensconced on the sofa. The TV is blaring. She is oblivious to my presence, clearly mesmerised by the threatening looking individual talking, on whichever ridiculously melodramatic soap opera she appears to be watching. She is still wearing the same tee shirt and shorts she slept in and appears to have one false eyelash on and one off. The tightly wound coil suppressing my anger is about to unfurl.

A voice on the TV speaks. *"I'll give you everything you need* (dramatic pause) *to put him away for a very long time".* The delivery of his words is more pantomime menacing than bona fide villain.

'Cassie,' I say rather loudly. No response. 'Cassie,' I say again. 'Shhhhhhhhhh,' she hisses at me, 'I'm trying to watch.'

*What's to watch? Surely it's the same storyline used again and again, just on a different day with different characters?*

'Don't tell me,' I say, 'he's her long lost son who's come to her rescue because she is being abused by her new partner and that woman there is his sister, who didn't know she had a brother, which is ironic because she had an affair with an older, married man when she was a bit younger resulting in a son that also had to be given away. Oh, and she's just the nosy neighbour.'

I'm being flippant of course; making it up as I go along, but Cassie looks at me in utter disbelief, screwing up her nose and opening her mouth – wide.

'You bloody cow,' she says quite mortified, 'why would you do that? Why would you spoil the plot like that?'

'Don't call me a cow,' I reply, trying to stop myself from laughing. 'I didn't spoil the plot. I was mocking it, making it up for goodness sake. You know my thoughts about these ridiculous soap operas. Drama for drama's sake.'

'Oh whatever,' Cassie states. 'I'm going for a bloody shower.'

'Now just a minute young lady,' I say drawing on the simmering anger that so far I've managed to keep in check. 'We need to discuss the possibility of you getting a job and your plans for Sixth Form.'

'I've got a job,' Cassie replies very blasé. 'Well, I've got an interview for a job. Tomorrow. And I'm not going to Sixth Form anymore ...'

I raise my eyes. 'Oh...?' I reply.

*This had better be good.*

Cassie takes a deep breath. 'I'm going to college, to study music,' she says.

*Do I detect a hint of fear in her voice?*

'With Luke,' she continues. 'And yes – before you ask – it does carry enough UCAS points to go to Uni.'

I'm impressed. I expected her case against going to Sixth Form to be a quixotic one and the tone she takes with me is not surly or sulky but intrepid.

'Now if you don't mind,' she continues. 'I need to have a shower.'

※

'Wow, you look amazing babe,' Simon says. His eyes run roguishly across me from head to foot in obvious admiration. I am secretly chuffed to bits and my inner voice is whooping and singing in my ear.

*Work it girl, work that body.*

However, I am, rather childishly, still miffed about our minor heated exchange of words this morning.

'Thanks,' I reply.

'And your hair,' Simon continues. 'It looks, well, it looks great.'

'Thanks, Maisy did it for me.'

And wasn't that a bolt out of the blue, Maisy offering to do my hair after Cassie refused on the grounds of being "too depressed to help". I must admit I was a little hesitant at first, thought it was some kind of trick, a way for Maisy to avenge herself on me for my mere presence in her life, but I was pleasantly surprised. She blowdried, back combed and curled my hair to within an inch of its life but the end result was amazing. It was a sort of mother-daughter bonding moment. Well, when I say bonding, what I actually mean is Maisy spoke six words to me instead of the usual three. It was nice though.

The atmosphere between Simon and I in the car is frosty to say the least. He's driving and continues to look straight ahead; I look out of the passenger window.

'Look,' he says, turning to look at me briefly. 'I'm sorry about this morning, I didn't mean anything by it.'

'S'fine,' I respond.

*Child.*

He runs an exasperated hand through his hair. 'Well clearly it isn't.'

'Let's not talk about it now eh,' I say snapping on the radio, providing an excuse not to talk.

We drive for a while just listening – or at least pretending to – the radio. 'You okay to drive home if I have drink tonight?' I ask, knowing damn well Simon will concede to my wishes in return for a pleasant facade in front of his sleazy, sybarite boss. And I don't mean Andy, who's actually the other MD of the company *and* the only reason Simon puts up with Dean's bullshit. Well, that and the mortgage and three kids to support of course.

'What? Oh yeah, I suppose so.' I can hear the disappointment in his voice. These work events are always more palatable when one is very inebriated.

*Yes!* My inner voice says, punching the air with a fist.

As soon as we arrive I spot Ruby and Andy and make a beeline for them. Thank god they're here. We're probably the four most unpretentious people in the room. Maybe I'm just getting cynical as I get older but I really can't concern myself with bothering about who went where and in what villa on their holidays, what new car they are in extreme debt for and their oh so marvellous recent shopping trips to New York and Milan. *It's all just bollocks, complete and utter bollocks. Consumed with consumerism, pretending to be something they're not just to please Dean, the fat cat boss who espouses morals and virtue but would slit his own mother's throat just to make a profit.*

'Wow, look at you,' Andy says genuinely impressed, 'you look the best I've seen you look in years.' It's a back-handed compliment but appreciated all the same.

'Thanks Andy,' I say grinning.

'Come on,' he continues, 'give us a twirl.' I am slightly embarrassed but concede attempting a half-hearted pirouette.

'Leave it to me to bring out your inner goddess,' Ruby says, looking equally, if not more stunning than usual.

'She does look good doesn't she?' Simon says behind me, placing his hand on my shoulder. My petrified heart softens a little and I look at him and smile.

'Get the drinks in then,' I say.

The meal is over. The epochal bullshit speech about mutual respect and regard for his company and its employees by Dean is done and half the room now seem to be on a mission to get sloshed, including me.

'Ooooh K C & The Sunshine Band,' I say as one of their songs bellows out across the dance floor. 'C'mon Rubes, les dans,' I suggest but I'm off before she replies. 'I love this song,' I shout across the dance floor towards our table. Ruby has joined me. Simon and Andy look on in amusement. I attempt to sing the words to *Give it up*, yelling from the top of my lungs whilst pointing at Simon. He looks round the room nervously then puts his head into his hands. I thrust, gyrate and grind my body whilst my arms flail around at will. I'm pretty confident the stares befalling me throughout the room are indeed looks of admiration at my skilful dance moves.

*Eat your heart out Beyoncé!*

Then, I catch sight of myself in a mirror. I stop dancing for a moment – shocked at what I've just witnessed.

*When did you start dancing like a parent? These moves looked so cool in the 1980s.*

'C'monnnn,' Ruby hollers when she realises I've stopped moving.

*Oh sod it.*

I begin thrusting my booty and propelling my arms in unison with hers. I turn to look at Simon giving him my best, lips puckered, smouldering gaze that, again, when I catch sight of in the mirror, actually looks more like I'm suffering with constipation. I shuffle across the dance floor towards Simon, one hand resting on my swivelling hip, the other outstretched, beckoning him in my best sexy come-hither fashion.

Simon raises his eyebrows and shrugs his shoulders. I continue serenading him.

*Well we certainly know where Cassie gets her musical ability from don't we?*

'Yep,' I reply out loud. 'S'meeee!!!' Suddenly Simon is by my side. Clearly, my sensual, rhythmic love dance has won him over.

'Whooaa, steady there,' he says, grabbing me by the waist before one of my raunchy moves is a move too far and almost sees me colliding with the floor. 'Who's had too much to drink then?' he continues, holding me safe and strong in his arms as he's always done.

'Me!' I reply giggling. 'Haf I tol u laylee that I love you?'

'I love you too babe,' he replies.

'I'm sorree if I've erm, hiccup, embaress iss you.'

Simon looks across at Dean who has also hit the dance floor and appears to be as equally deluded as me in what he clearly believes are his own proficient dance moves. He has the substantial build of a rugby player and his violent foot stamping, rhythmic body slapping and strange tongue protrusion suggest he is suitably involved in some kind of pre-match, Maori tribal war dance than at some, slightly upmarket, works do. Simon looks back at me.

'Oh well,' he laughs and begins grinding his body against mine. 'If you can't beat em, join em eh?'

## CHAPTER 18

SUMMER HOLIDAY

**CASSIE**

It's early morning and the sun is shining through a slit in the old fashioned flowery curtains. The first smell to hit my nose is the musty, fusty pong of the bedding. I need a wee but I can't be bothered to move. Plus the toilet here is rank. It has the same mouldy smell as these sheets. Mum said it's just because the cottage we've hired has been locked up for a few months, but I'm not so sure. It just smells rank to me. So does the tap water, so asking if it was safe to drink was a perfectly illegitimate question. It certainly didn't warrant Grandads reply of:

'For fack, facking sake Cassie, this is bleedin Cornwall, not the back of bleedin beyond! Of course the blady tap water's safe to drink. Who does she think she is? Lady bleedin Muck?'

And, I'm pretty sure that *was* a spider that ran across my bum last night too when I sat on the loo. If it'd happened to anyone else they would have screamed out as well, so there was no need for Mum to have a complete eppy like she did. Idiot. And I certainly did not wake the whole bloody house up like she said. It was only her, and Simon and Nan, oh yeah and Grandad coz I remember him calling me Foghorn Lil, and Freddy. So it wasn't the whole house. God she exaggerates so bloody much.

I still can't believe her reaction though when I told her I was going to college instead of Sixth Form. I thought she'd go bloody mad, but she just looked really pleased and said she was well-chuffed coz she always hoped I'd do something with music. I thought she was going to have like some major rant about it. Bloody adults. Don't make any bloody sense at all.

Talking of which I wonder if Dad has got to Florida yet. I still can't believe he wouldn't take me and Connor with him. Oh god, now I feel like crying again. He said it's because Harriet is so young they don't have to pay for her. But coz we're older and bigger he'd have to pay for me and Connor and coz he doesn't have a job we can't expect Sharon to pay. Why though? We are Dad's children too so why, if Sharon is the one earning the money, won't she include us as well?

I tried to tell Dad how hurt I felt but he wouldn't listen. So then I started shouting at him. Then he told me not to be so selfish coz we are going on holiday with our Mum and Harriet is doing exactly the same and going on holiday with her Mum. The only difference is that he'll be there with them. Why does he do that? Why does he twist things like that, like I'm the one in the wrong? Why doesn't Sharon like us? I just don't get it. Bitch. Don't want to go to stupid Florida anyway. Cornwall is just as good.

I can't see him but I can hear him. Freddy has just nudged my door open and is sniffing round the room. God he is so nosy. I can see him now; he stops sniffing, looks up at me and barks. I pat the bed and call him to me. He cocks his head to one side, sits down and proceeds to scratch his ear with his back leg. After a vigorous rubbing, he stops then lowers his head downwards and starts to lick his gonads. Eeeewww! He's like sooooo bloody disgusting.

'Freddy! Bloody stop it,' I shout, but he completely ignores me. The licking sound is making me feel sick. 'Freddy!' I shout louder, but this time I throw one of the revolting crocheted cushions from the bed at him. He stops immediately and looks at me, shocked. Then he jumps onto the bed, pounces on me and pins me down whilst proceeding to lick my face. Bloody disgusting dog. Licking his balls one minute then licking my face the next.

'Freddy! Stooooooooop-iiiiiiiitttt!' I try to shout in between his slobbering tongue all over my face. I can't help thinking about what Zoe Price from school, and what she said she does with her boyfriend, which is as equally, if not more so, repulsive. I shudder. I don't care what anyone says, I will never – ever – lick anyone's balls. Not even Joe's. Well, maybe I would lick Joe's. I wonder what they taste of? I shiver in disgust. Yuk. It's just too rank. No. I will not lick anyone's balls. Ever.

Joe has texted me a couple of times. He said he was sorry for leaving me at Chelsea's that night. He said he likes me, a lot – but he just needs some time to think at the moment. I asked him why his Facebook status said he was in a relationship. He said he'd explain when he sees me at school in September. I told him I wasn't going. He seemed shocked. Still didn't ask to meet up with me though. Idiot. Think as much as you want Joe. Take as much time as you need, I won't be waiting for you. Except, I know that's not true. I'll probably wait until the end of time for Joe. Well, at least until I meet and marry Alex Turner from the Arctic Monkeys anyway.

The smell of cooked bacon is wafting up the stairs and has interrupted my thoughts. Clearly Freddy has smelled it too coz he's stopped licking my face and is running full pelt down the stairs. I decide to stay in bed for a bit longer so I won't get roped into helping out. If I leave it long enough everything will probably be ready when I go down. Anyway I deserve a rest coz I worked really hard for my GCSEs. And I start my new job next week in the lingerie department of Ashford & Bloom. Blooming 12 hours a bloody week I have to work! More at Christmas! As well as going to college in September. Besides, Mum likes cooking and cleaning.

## LIZZIE

I'm so glad we're here. I really needed a break. There is so much upset and unrest at work about further job losses; I feel as though I'm working in a cocoon of cacophony. I know a week in Perranporth isn't particularly grand and doesn't have the same ring to it as St. Moritz, Monaco or Florida for that matter. Bastard. Why? Why even tell the kids he was going there if he had no intention of taking them? I close my eyes, switch the pause button on my thoughts and take a deep breath. My mind is working overtime.

I inhale a familiar fusion of moist sand and brackish seawater. The sun is warm but it's still quite early so there's no real intensity to its heat. An ocean breeze dances around my ears and brings with it the sound of laughter and dogs barking. Childhood holidays are evoked and Scott is washed away by a tsunami of juvenile memories.

Connor shouts. 'Mu-um. Mum! Can you hear me?' His voice carries across a seasonally temperate Cornish wind.

'C'mmmoon,' he beckons, waiving excitedly. 'Grandad says we might find treasure – real *pirate* treasure.'

Of course they will, if Dad has anything to do with. Well, fake, real pirate treasure anyway. Doubloons – gold preferred but silver is acceptable – will have been purchased from the local gift shop "Little Gems". Authentic replicas, ensconced carefully somewhere about Dad's person away from small prying eyes only to be magically discovered by eager hands when trawling among ancient Cornish caves.

We are heading around the headland of Halzephron towards Dollar Cove on Lizard Peninsula. Apparently the Cove derived its name from folklore surrounding the wreck of the Spanish ship, San Salvador, which was lost sometime during the 17th century and supposedly laden with silver dollars. A number of which, it's claimed, are still washed up from time to time after some of the more majestic storms pummel this rugged but beautiful, exposed coast.

At high tide the beach here is generally comprised of shingle and stone but as the tide drops, as it has this morning, a breathtaking sandy bay is revealed, broken up by a scattering of contorted granite protrusions.

Mum and Dad are en-route towards the dark open mouths of a few of the caves up ahead with Connor and Summer – my 7 year old niece, dreadlocks and all – in tow. Freddy and Simon are running along the expanse of golden sand, although who is leading who is a little confusing.

'Penny for them,' Sean, my brother asks. I look up skywards and feel the promise of another fine day bathe my face. 'Your thoughts,' he continues. 'A penny for your thoughts. Or maybe that should be dollar,' he adds as an afterthought.

'Oh I don't know,' I reply sighing. 'I was just thinking about when we were kids.

I'm so glad Mum and Dad used to bring us here. I don't think

I ever really fully appreciated just how beautiful this place was ... is. I can see why you came to live here.'

Sean smiles. Our conversation is interrupted by delighted squeals emanating from one of the caves up ahead. The body of a child, followed by a smaller one emerge. They wave their hands ferociously.

'Treasure Mum,' Connor shouts. 'We've found treasure,' he continues before they both disappear again. I turn to look at Sean's sun kissed face and we both laugh. The buzzing voice of a sand martin catches my attention and I look up again. Several of them fly together above our heads, their white bellies and brown breast band clearly visible. They are social creatures and head towards their colony of burrowed nests in the eroding cliffs.

'God it's so good to be here,' I say. It's just so, how can I put it...'

'Spiritual?' Sean suggests.

'Yes, that's exactly what it is. Spritual.'

We stop walking and perch amongst the rocks. I look around, in awe of the view that meets my eye. Except for the technology in my pocket and the clothes worn by ourselves and a few others on the beach. There is no other visible sign of what century we are living in. We are on the edge of the world, amongst it all, the sea, the beach, the land, the flora and fauna.

'You should just drop out Sis. Give up the rat race and join us.'

'Hummmmph – yeah. It's a nice thought but not that easy Sean. Connor's still at school...'

'Home school him like we do Summer,' Sean interrupts. 'And Cassie wants to go to college,' I continue, 'possibly university. Then there's Simon's job and my job, although that's in doubt. Again. And, as much as I'd love to live your slightly beatnik way of life I'm not sure everyone else in our household would. But it's good to be here. Good to see you.'

I look towards the mouth of the cave again, watching as two excited treasure hunters dance at its entrance.

'Summer's certainly growing and she's just beautiful, you know.' Sean smiles again.

'Yeah, she is isn't she, just like her Mum.'

'And her Dad,' I say, elbowing him playfully. 'Where is Natasha this morning anyway?'

'Nat? She's getting a few things ready for tonight. Picking some veggies from the garden, making sure we have enough homebrew and stuff. You are all coming, right? It'd be great to see Cassie, and Maisy of course. Does she still dress like a vampire?'

I sigh. 'Yes. Well no, not a vampire. At least I hope that's not what she's trying to be?'

*She does like the Twilight movies and books though?*

'Hmmmmm, note to self, check Maisy's teeth next time you speak to her,' I say out loud.

Sean laughs. 'Maisy the vampire,' he declares. 'It does have a certain ring to it doesn't it?' His expression becomes one of concern. He places one of his rough, work-wearied hands on mine. 'How are you Sis? You and the kids?'

'Ahhh well, yes, me and the kids?' I reply, running my free hand through my hair. 'What can I tell you about the kids? Connor's great, a bit forgetful, a bit too laid back for his own good sometimes, but otherwise great.'

'And the girls?'

I raise my eyes and smile. 'The girls ... let me see. For a start they're girls, but not just any girls, they're *teenage* girls. Add to that fact they are slightly damaged teenage girls with an abundance of raging hormones, which in turn makes me, in their eyes anyway, both the devil incarnate and the wicked step-monster. Does that give you some idea?' My intonation is one of exasperated amusement. 'So, bearing all that in mind, then yeah, I'd pretty much say the girls are fine.'

'Fi-ne?' Sean repeats slowly. I look at him and laugh. 'Fucked up. Insecure. Neurotic and Emotional,' we both say in unison. Sean winks at me. 'And you? How are you Sis. And Si?'

'Simon's great. We have our moments, usually about the kids,' I say rolling my eyes. 'But otherwise yeah, he's a keeper I think the saying is.' I linger for a moment. 'It doesn't stop...' I pause.

'It doesn't stop what?' Sean asks.

I pull my hand away from his. 'The fear,' I reply, washing both my hands in dumb show. 'I still feel so vulnerable at times and I still don't understand Scott, and why he left. Well no, actually that's not true. I know exactly why he left. Money, of course – his first and last love – but why, why, why has he virtually abandoned the kids? I don't get that? How many times do I have to keep picking up the shattered pieces he leaves behind?'

Anger clips my voice. Sean takes both my hands in his, the manual labour of an outdoor life evident in their course, jagged texture. He looks straight at me.

'Simon's not Scott. He won't leave you.'

'How do you know?' I protest.

Sean raises a finger and puts it to my mouth. 'Si won't leave you,' he repeats. 'And the girls, and Connor, will be just fine.'

I stare back at Sean and grimace. 'You think so?'

'Absolutely. Connor's smart, like his Mum of course, and both the girls are far brighter than you give them credit for.'

I raise my eyes and guffaw. 'Hmmmm. You think so? I'm not so sure. Did I tell you I overheard them talking the other day? They were discussing the Prime minister and couldn't remember his name. Do you know what name they finally settled on?'

Sean is already laughing. 'Go on then, what?' he asks.

'Cameron Diaz,' I declare. 'Cameron blinking Diaz.'

'Oh well, give em some credit, they got half the name right. Right?'

I hold my hands out in hopeless question. 'I suppose so.'

'Where are they anyway? Didn't they want to come to the beach this morning?' I grin mischievously.

'Let's just say they had a few things to do,' I reply.

## CASSIE

I'm still fuming. I can't bloody believe what they did. "We cooked, so you clean." Bloody cheek. And I wanted to go to Dollar Cove. Snot fair.

'Arrggghh I'm so bloody angry,' I say to Maisy, as she continues to wash the dishes and I dry them. 'I mean, what kind of godforsaken place doesn't have a dishwasher anyway? Standing here, drying bloody dishes for god bloody sake. This is supposed to be *my* bloody holiday. And yours too of course,' I add.

'So?' Maisy replies, loudly chewing on the gum that never seems to leave her mouth.

'So – duh – the clue is in the word, *holiday*. Here look.' I throw down my damp tea towel to extract my phone from my bra. 'I'll look up the meaning of the word on my phone.'

'Why do you keep your phone in your bra?' Maisy asks, grinning at me.

'Duh! Same reason you keep your fags there. So Mum can't

get at it when she's having an eppy at me and threatening to ban me from using it of course.' Stupid bloody question.

I click on my internet browser and tap in the word *holiday*. I scroll down the list of meanings that have appeared. 'Ah-ha, see, here it is. *Holiday – a period of time when one does not have to work.* See, I told you. And what are we both doing here, right now, on our first day...'

'Oh fuck off Cassie. You and I both know we virtually do fuck all most of the time.'

'Speak for your bloody self. I do the dishwasher at home and I put the washing machine on and I cook...'

'Yeah, once in a blue bloody moon, and then don't we all have to hear about it for days on end.'

Maisy laughs. I laugh back and flick her with the tea towel that is now so damp I swear it's actually making the dishes wetter, not drier. It'd be just as well to let them dry by themselves really. 'Besides,' Maisy continues. 'If helping out here scores me a few brownie points then I'm happy to do it.'

'Why?' I ask suspiciously.

'No reason.' Maisy shrugs her shoulders. 'I just think Lizzie does well loads and there's nothing wrong with us returning the favour.'

'What?' I reply, nearly choking on the whole jammie biscuit I've just stuffed in my mouth. 'You're usually moaning what a bitch she is.'

Maisy scowls at me. 'No I'm not.' She pauses for a moment then swaps her scowl for a grin. 'Well ok, yeah, maybe I do – sometimes – when she is being one. I don't always mean it though.'

We're quiet for a minute. Then, spookily, as if our thoughts are telepathetically linked – soul sisters rather than step-sisters – we both say together, at the same time, 'We're worse!'

We piss ourselves laughing, but I still don't trust Maisy.

I look her straight in the eyes. She looks away. 'You're up to something.'

'Not.'

'You are.'

'Am NOT,' Maisy says through gritted teeth. 'Now finish drying this lot while I have a shower.' She flicks my face with water and runs off.

Just coz she's a year older than me she always thinks she's the boss when Mum and Simon aren't around. Well, she's not. And she's not the bloody boss of me either. I'm drying these dishes coz *I* want to. Not coz *she* said so.

My suspicions are aroused though. Something doesn't add up here. She's being too nice about everything. I wait until I hear her turn the shower on then I creep up the stairs and into the bedroom she bagsied. I'm actually a bit pissed off coz her room's like way bigger than mine, and she doesn't have gross, disgusting curtains and bedding like me. They're actually a nice pink colour, which is wasted on her coz she only likes black.

I wander around the room, opening cupboards, lifting her duvet cover up and stepping over yesterday's clothes, already thrown across the floor, including her knickers. Eeeeewwww. Nothing looks dodgy or seems out of place though.

'Arrrrrrggghhhh.' Maisy suddenly screams from the bathroom. 'Fuck, fuck, fuckity fuck,' she hollers. I run, panicking, into the hallway. She flings the bathroom door open and looks shocked.

'What?' I ask bewildered. 'What is it?'

'The bloody shower's freezing!' she screams, shivering. 'There's no bloody hot water left. They must have all used it this morning.'

She looks really grumpy as she hovers in the doorway, her jet-black hair dripping down her shoulders. The small towel she wears barely covers her.

Maisy looks at me warily. 'Have you been in my room?'

'No!'

'What'd ya want then?'

'Nothing. I rushed up to see why you were screaming.'

'Okay, well, you can go back downstairs now,' she orders.

She seems agitated but rooted to the spot. 'What are you up to?'

Maisy looks straight at me, as if she's thinking about what to say, almost turning blue now coz she's shivering so much.

She sighs heavily. 'Oh whatevs,' she finally says. 'You can know.' There's a sound of resignation in her voice. I'm becoming more and more confused.

'Know what?'

Maisy stares at me again, unsmiling. She really is quite pretty without all that black crap on her face.

'I swear to god though,' she says in a voice laced with threat. 'If you breathe one word about this to Dad or Lizzie, you'll be a dead fucking bitch. Right?' Maisy walks towards me waving a blue finger with a black painted nail in my face.

I step back from her, annoyed that she seems to be threatening me. 'O bloody K, I s'pose!'

Maisy takes a deep breath. 'Right,' she says again. And with that she turns and heads for her bedroom. I watch her walk away from me. I'm confused. I thought she was going to tell me something?

My eyes follow and examine her body. I'm curious and secretly compare her body to mine. She has quite a thin neck and a back that seems way too small to carry the boulder holders she has to wear. Bitch. She certainly doesn't qualify for the Itsy Bitsy Booby Committee like me. Lucky cow. My eyes continue to wander, down her back and past the tiny towel covering her booty. Yes! She has cellulite too, at the top of her legs, just like me. And then I spot it.

'Aaaarrrrrrgggghhhh,' I scream. 'Oh my good fucking god. Is that for real? O M G!!!!'

Maisy turns back to look at me, grinning. 'Pretty sick eh?' She looks really pleased with herself. My mouth falls open, and I don't seem to be able to close it again. Either she's really, really brave or really, really stupid. The smile on her face quickly disappears though and she suddenly becomes serious again.

'NOT. A. FUCKING. WORD. THOUGH. Right?'

CHAPTER 19

SURPRISE!!

LIZZIE

Perhaps it's the perfect English summer night that is making me feel warm and contented inside. It's the kind of balmy evening that feels a rarity; especially after the disastrous summer we had last year. Then again, perhaps it's too much home-made wine and my rose tinted reading glasses, that I have decided, at least for the time being, not to put on a chain around my neck in the style of stuffy old librarian. Which leads me to observe that all is well with the world.

*I could live like this.*

Dad is dozing in his chair, waking from time to time, laughing on cue, assuring everyone he is only *resting* his eyes. Mum, who looks a little tired to me, is also merrily drinking and people watching. Connor, who I fear is plotting something, is ensconced in a corner of the garden, whispering and chuckling with Summer and, as my eyes drink everything in, I notice that even the girls are pleasantly amiable and unusually chatty.

Maisy in particular appears to be very fond of one of Sean's friends. Australian I think he is, given his accent. I haven't seen either of the girls on their phones for several hours now, which is indeed a minor miracle of sorts.

I sigh contentedly. Didn't someone say it's the moments that count? Well right here, right now, I'm drunk on the contentment of this moment. Sipping my wine I look up at the old farmhouse that is home to Sean, Natasha and Summer. Although slightly dilapidated and in need of major repair work, it does look particularly charming on this warm summer night. Tell-tale cracks of subsidence have all but disappeared under the veil of the night sky and the flaking paint only adds to its rustic charm. We are all outside, gathered around the solid wooden table hand-crafted by Sean himself. A table that only an hour earlier beheld a banquet fit for a king; a feast of home grown produce including, of course, sumptuous English strawberries with a generous helping of clotted Cornish cream. Home-made paper lanterns rock gently in the tepid breeze and the waves of the sea, although a couple of miles away ripple and break gently in the distance.

I look towards the end of the table and Simon, who I fear is slightly more inebriated than me, is deep in conversation with Sean and his friends. Sean has grown a small beard since I last saw him. Its dirty blonde in colour and perfectly matches the dreadlocks that fall down his back. His face, set against his simple white shirt, appears more tanned than it actually is and the vivid colours of his tattooed arms flicker and dance in the subdued candlelight. They say first impressions count and anyone would be forgiven for thinking that someone of Sean's appearance, lifestyle and as one that introduces his nearest and dearest friends as Radical Rick, Dangerous Dave and Crazee, was perhaps of limited intelligence. This really couldn't be further from the truth and once again our hospitable host proves to be a salient, well-informed raconteur who carries himself with great aplomb.

Natasha wanders over with more wine and pulls up a chair next to Mum and myself. She has a very earthy, yet ethereal presence. Perpetually calm, I don't think I've ever seen her lose her temper; then again she doesn't have to live with two tortuous teenagers. Her white dress, seasonally floaty, is elegant yet simple, and her long blonde hair hangs freely down her back. Her barely-there make-up is minimalist. A dab of lip-gloss and one coat of mascara at the most.

'Hey Ellie,' Natasha says to Mum, 'you okay? You look tired?'

'I'm fine Natasha, really I am,' Mum replies in her no-nonsense tone.

'Well, you know if the radiotherapy hasn't … doesn't work,' Nat continues. 'You should think about taking Cannabis oil. It's supposed to cure cancer you know? Mind you it isn't cheap,' she says frowning, 'and this bloody place is a money pit.' She looks up at the house. 'Bloody freezing in the winter it was, and leaks? I think the whole house was one big leak. We had buckets everywhere,' she exclaims. 'So anyway, unfortunately we couldn't afford to buy it for you, the cannabis oil that is, but Sean has, shall we say an eclectic group of friends.' She laughs and nods her head in the direction of Dangerous Dave; an intriguing name for one of such slight, almost boyish physique. 'I'm sure he could help us out if you wanted some. You know, mates' rates and all that.' Natasha laughs again. It's a soft, alluring laugh that flows like warm honey and is pleasantly contagious. Mum giggles and I follow suit.

'Why's he called Dangerous Dave anyway?' Mum asks, her furrowed brow marked with curiosity. 'To tell you the truth, I wasn't entirely sure if he was a she if you know what I mean.' Nat and I laugh and Dad opens one eye and smirks.

Mum's tone is suddenly defensive. 'Well,' she continues. 'It just seems like anything goes these days. Boys want to be girls, girls want to be boys. Then there are those men, I forget what you call them, the kind that seem to be both?'

'He-shes,' Dad exclaims, now opening both eyes.

Mum shoots him a look of alarm. 'How do you know?' Dad smirks and closes both eyes again.

Natasha raises her hand slightly and waves it from left to right. 'Swings both ways,' she whispers.

Mum looks a little taken aback for a second. 'Well, live and let live I say. It all just gets very confusing though sometimes. Things seemed a lot simpler when I was younger. Anyway, you still haven't explained why he's dangerous?'

'Well,' Natasha lowers her voice to a whisper again. 'You see that rucksack that never leaves his side? Let's just say it contains a number of legal and illegal substances. He's dangerous because there's nothing the man can't get hold of.' Mum looks suitably shocked. 'Sooooo...' Natasha pauses, nodding in Mum's direction, 'if we need some cannabis oil, Dave's your man.'

Mum purses her lips, her expression suddenly severe. Is she offended? 'I've never tried weed,' she suddenly blurts out. I look across at her, surprised.

'Put it on your bucket list,' Dad says opening one eye again.

'I've tried it,' I confess.

'When?' Mum asks.

'When Ruby took me to Amsterdam not long after Scott left, remember? You and Dad looked after the kids for me.'

'Yes, I remember. Well? What was it like?'

I think back for a moment. My memories of that trip are mixed. I weighed nothing and looked terrible, my appetite completely suppressed by the great weight of sadness I carried with me. Ruby was just another brick in my wall of support. I was grateful to have her and she knew what I needed. We went shopping, avoided men, drank wine and smoked a little pot.

I smile at Mum. 'It made me laugh – a lot – which was good because I never thought I'd laugh again,' I reply. Mum smiles back but she wears a look of concern. 'Then we got the munchies,' I continue, 'we ate far too much and then the paranoia set in, for me anyway. I was convinced everyone in the restaurant we were seated in was staring at us, which, with hindsight, they probably were because we'd both been laughing like drains for the previous two hours. Anyway, we then decided we should go back to our hotel. We headed straight for the bar; ordered two strong, black coffees and found a quiet corner to sit in until I stopped thinking I was a film director in the middle of a live film shoot, which only made Ruby laugh more.'

Nat bursts into loud fits of laughter, as does Dad who has now sat bolt upright, eyes wide open. Mum just looks confused.

'Why did you think you were a film director?' she asks. 'God knows? I kept standing up and randomly shouting, "Cut!" every ten minutes or so. I'm sure a psychologist would have a field day with that one.'

Nat's now laughing so hard she has to hold her stomach. Mum continues to look dumbfounded. 'It was just part of the reaction to the pot Mum,' I try to explain.

Mum's face is a picture and I can't help joining the laughter. Her expression is one of unease as she shifts uncomfortably, trying to understand.

'Well then,' she finally replies. 'I've clearly led a very sheltered life. Sod the cannabis oil, bring out the pot.'

The image of Mum smoking pot makes me laugh so hard it brings tears to my eyes.

'Well, the offer's always there ...' Nat begins to say but doesn't finish her sentence due to the extreme shouting taking place at the other end of the table. I'm not sure what all the fuss is about but all hell appears to have broken loose.

Simon's voice is exploding with expletives. My serene

interior is replaced by a confused foreboding as my stomach lurches into my mouth. For one dreadful moment I'm terrified that Simon's slightly conservative views have collided with Sean's radical socialist ones. However, I'm rather shocked to see, Simon's barrage of abuse is aimed at Maisy. She is hovering nervously behind Sean's friend Crazee, the Australian, who is standing with his arms outstretched protectively in front of her. 'Why Maisy? Why?' Simon shouts. 'Why would you do that to me?'

'I didn't do it to you did I?' Maisy shouts back. 'I did it to me, to my body, not yours.'

Sean is standing behind Simon, a strong arm held across his chest, restraining him. I rush forward and all my irrational thoughts come with me.

*Is she pregnant? Injecting drugs? Or maybe she's cutting herself, self-harming?* I play her words over again in my head, "I did it to my body, not yours". *Oh my god, what if she's caught up with some pimp and is prostituting herself?*

'What?' I exclaim. 'What the hell is it?'

Simon's face is flushed with anger. 'Go on then show her,' he shouts at Maisy. 'Show Lizzie what an absolute bloody idiot you are.'

'Calm down mate,' Crazee says, his Aussie twang highly audible. 'It's not actually that bad.'

Simon turns and glares at Crazee. 'I'm not your bloody mate, mate,' he states through gritted teeth. 'And don't tell me to calm down when my 17-year-old daughter has mutilated herself. For life,' he adds.

Connor and Summer are sniggering and Cassie is wearing an amused smile.

'I haven't mutilated myself,' Maisy shouts back. She starts crying. 'I hate you,' she says between great gulps of tears. 'I bloody hate you.'

*Well, at least it's not you she hates for a change.*

'True, true,' I respond to myself out loud.

'What do you mean true?' Simon looks at me, confused. 'Have you bloody seen it?'

Connor and Summer, who have now crouched down next to Maisy, have caught my attention. They are pointing and staring intently to the side of Maisy's left leg. Freddy has joined them and is barking incessantly. Maisy is wearing tiny shorts, which throws me for a moment. She must have changed at some point during the evening because I swear she was wearing leggings earlier. Suddenly I spot what the commotion is all about. I get a little closer, bend down towards the side of Maisy's leg and put my reading glasses on. Although god only knows why I do this? They're for reading.

'Oh my god,' I say, swiftly standing upright. 'Is that real?' I look at Maisy's tear sodden face. I can't quite believe what I've seen so I bend down again for another, closer inspection. 'Is it permanent?' I ask.

'Of course it bloody is,' Simon shouts at me.

'It's err, well, it's um ... very colourful,' I continue, unsure how to handle this. I am slightly shocked and slightly mesmerised by the artwork of a tree that has been permanently tattooed onto Maisy's leg. It starts at her ankle and winds its way right up and into her shorts. And beyond for all I know? I attempt a half-hearted laugh. 'I see you got over your fear of needles then?'

Sean cajoles a reluctant Simon over to where Mum and Dad are still sitting and Crazee wraps a consoling arm around Maisy's shoulders leading her away, towards the end of the garden. I catch a quick glimpse of Maisy's retreating face. She's upset, but not that upset. She appears to be enjoying the attention of Sean's Aussie friend.

*If I didn't know any better...?*

'Oh shut up,' I reply out loud.

'Well how would you feel if it was Cassie?' Simon responds to my outburst. I laugh inwardly.

*You'd have, as Cassie puts it, a flippin eppy.*

I summon a kindly, reassuring voice. 'I know, we do need to speak to her, but not now. We all need to just calm down tonight and talk about it tomorrow.'

*At the end of the day it is only a tattoo, isn't it? No big deal really.*

'Ca'mon you lot,' Dad suddenly pipes up. 'It's not that bleedin bad. Just remember – it's not a life, it's an adventure!'

## CHAPTER 20

WIPEOUT

**CASSIE**

*I* can't believe the holiday is nearly over and I've like barely used my phone at all. Well, once in the morning, a couple of times in the afternoon and about ten times in the evening, which is like nothing really. I keep turning it off coz Dad keeps posting pictures of himself and Sharon and Harriet in Florida, on Facebook. I feel well chocked up when I see them. But I don't care; I've had a great holiday here.

Except when Freddy tripped me up on the beach of course, and I fell into the water, fully clothed in front of all the good-looking surfers Uncle Sean was teaching. Stupid dog.

I look across at Maisy who is tapping away on her phone again, grinning like a stupid person. I'm sure she's talking to Crazee – again! She always smiles when she's with him or talking to him. I think she loves him and I'm pretty sure she's done it with him. I didn't realise he was only two years older than her, he looks like well older, like 21 or something. His accent is well funny too.

I'm pretty pissed off actually coz Mum and Simple Simon hardly said anything to her about that bloody tattoo. Well, I'm not actually sure what they said coz they talked to her in private but they've let her keep it. Bloody favouritism. If that was me they would have made me get rid of it. It can be done. I've seen it on TV but it costs like, well loads. I don't want a bloody tattoo anyway; what's so great about someone slamming a needle into you for hours on end?

It's stopped raining and Uncle Sean is calling over to me and Connor to join him for one last surf together before we help pack up to go home.

'C'mon you couple of groms. The wind's blowing offshore so it's perfect,' he shouts. For god bloody sake, I wish he wouldn't call me that, I'm a bloody adult now. Almost.

'Coming,' Connor and I both shout. Connor is wearing one of Uncle Sean's rash guards and a pair of shorts but even though the sun is shining I know I wouldn't be warm enough wearing just that so I've nabbed Nat's sleeveless vest to go over my tee-shirt and shorts.

Uncle Sean makes sure our leashes are in place whilst screaming The Doors song *Break on Through (To the Other side)* from the top of his lungs. It's like dead embarrassing but nobody on the beach seems to mind. Uncle Sean seems to know everyone anyway and most people just wave and smile.

Suddenly we're in the water and for a few seconds I feel as though I can't catch my breath. It is bloody freezing! Then we're off, immersed in the great big blue. Connor and I stick with the mushy waves coz we're generally new to this whilst uncle Sean rides the more high energy ones, the groundswells further out, generally amazing us with his ripping, slashes and layback's. He is actually like sooooooo bloody amazing, and doesn't wipe out once, unlike me and Connor, much to his amusement. I don't care though; I'm loving every minute.

I didn't think I'd enjoy surfing coz I can't really wear my hair extensions or my false eyelashes but it's actually well sick, well loads of fun. I get lost in the moment of it and don't care what I look like, a bit like when I'm playing piano.

Everyone thinks it's great that I'm going to study music at college. Uncle Sean even got his guitar out in the evenings and everyone sat round singing and stuff, like from the olden days.

I quite liked helping Natasha on her allotment too. Picking fruit and veggies and stuff is like well sick, especially the strawberries, although Nat said I actually ate more than I picked. The bugs and worms were a bit freaky though and the chickens were well vicious when I went into their coupe to collect some eggs. They like, well attacked my hands, pecking them and everything. Connor didn't seem to mind though. I think the chickens actually preferred him to me. Nat wouldn't let me collect any more eggs after my first attempt coz she said my screaming was scaring the chickens. What she didn't know though, was I did it on purpose to make Connor feel like he was good at something.

It's started to rain again. 'Four seasons in one day eh Cassie?' uncle Sean says to me as we wander back up the beach. I know what he means. The weather today is like well freaky. First thing this morning it was a bit cool and breezy, then the sun came out and it was like, well hot, and now it's raining, again. Must be something to do with that ouzo layer, glowball warming crap. I wonder what a glowball actually is?

Well that's it then, holiday over. Goodbye scenic Perrenporth, hello boring home. Both cars are packed and sloppy goodbyes have been said. Connor is travelling with Nan, Grandad and Freddy and I'm stuck with Mum, Simple Si and the moody cow in the corner.

It's a good job Maisy didn't bring her own car coz I don't think she would have actually left if she had. She's like, well loved up, absolutely crazy about Crazee, and he is about her I think. His Facebook status says "Crazee in love with Maisy", which is kind of cute I suppose, but a bit obsessive. They've only like known each other for a week. I'd never get that besotted about someone after just one week for god sake.

I look over at Maisy. She's all huddled up against the car door with her back to me, flicking through the pictures on her phone and sniffing. I don't think I've ever seen her like this about someone. I didn't even realise she actually had real feelings, until now.

Oh god, Mum and Simon have put the Radio on, Oldies FM or something – boooooorrrrrrriiiinnnggg! Why do they listen to music stations where idiots just talk all the time? I grab the earphones from my bag. Time to put on some real music. Arctic Monkeys me thinks and Alex Turner telling me *I Bet You Look Good on the Dance Floor*. When I become a famous performer I *will* marry Alex Turner.

Time to make a tweet I think. I scroll through all the photos of the holiday on my phone. Me at the cottage in Perranporth. Me at the bar on the beach in Perranporth. Me running on the beach in Perranporth. Connor, and me eating strawberries. Me surfing. Mum and Simple Simon. Me at St.Ives eating a Cornish cream tea. Grandad with cream on his nose. Me surfing again. Freddy barking. Connor rocking the peace sign above my head – idiot. Me at Lands End (I don't think it was stupid to ask if that was where the end of the world is?). Maisy and Crazee snogging – again! Ah ha here it is, me and all the good looking surfers. I begin to tap out my tweet.

**Holiday at an end, sad to say goodbye to plenty of sun, sea and #you guess the rest!!**

See what you think of that, Joe. Oh god, why did I have to think of him. Now I feel sad. I tap on the Facebook icon on my phone and pull up Joe's profile. My heart sinks. He's *still* in a relationship? Oh, hold on I've got some likes for the photos I've just added. I tap onto them excitedly. My heart sinks again. Four likes. One each from Sophie, Pheebs and Luke and oh god – sooooo embarrassing – Nan! I tap onto Pheebs's profile, also *still* in a relationship. Arrggghh, I'm getting angry now. Although, to be fair, she has tried to contact me loads. Said she has stuff to explain and hates not having me as a friend. I do actually miss her like, loads too. Maybe I will meet up with her when we get home.

I tap onto Dad's profile and, oh great, he's changed his profile picture to one of him, Sharon and Harriet with some of their favourite film characters standing behind them.

'Arrggghh, I pissing hate the pissing lot of you,' I scream.

Before I know it Mum has swung round from her seat and is glaring at me. Simple Simon is watching me in his rear view mirror, scowling and Maisy, well, that's the first time I've seen a smile on her face since we left.

'Oooooppps. Sor-ry,' I smirk, sinking down in my seat. 'Forgot I was wearing my headphones.'

# CHAPTER 21

## AND THE RESULTS ARE AS FOLLOWS ...

**CASSIE**

*H*oney and I are flicking through the cards at the local newsagents. We're looking for a birthday card for Lorenzo. Honey is my lesbian friend from college. She's like so tall and willowy, a bit like a model really with long, dark flowing hair. I thought Mum and Simon would be like well gayest when I brought her home for a sleepover but they were fine, treated her like normal, which she is of course; except she is a bit dumb sometimes. She's like well sick though coz she plays the saxophone and sings. All the boys fancy her coz she's a lesbian. I'm thinking of becoming a lesbian but it's a bit difficult at the moment coz I'm seeing Joe again. Sort of.

He came to see me when we got back from Perranporth and we talked a lot. He said he likes me a lot and he even still liked me when I told him I wasn't the goddaughter of a famous fashion designer. He said he'd kind of guessed that wasn't true but he wouldn't tell if I didn't. He said he set his Facebook status to "In a Relationship" coz he wanted to take some time out without being hassled by loads of girls to think about me. Me! There were rumours he was seeing a rich girl from one of the schools in the city during the summer and then she dumped him. He says not. I believe him – I think. My phone pings. I tap on it.

'Oh my god,' I shout. Honey leans over me to look at my screen. 'It's a dick pic, from Joe.' We laugh like idiots, much to the annoyance of Mr Dunmore who owns the shop. I stare at the image on my screen and zoom in. It disappears after ... five, four, three, two, one seconds and I laugh, really loud, when I realise it's not actually real. It's one of those freaky pictures from the internet of misshaped fruit that looks like a willy. I'm a little relieved if I'm honest, I don't really want to see Joe's willy — well, not on my phone anyway.

'I might turn straight if I can find a cock like that,' Honey suddenly says embarrassingly loud. Mr Dunmore raises his eyebrows and tuts at us. I feel slightly mortified and look away, pretending to stare intently at the cards again.

I smile as my eyes fall on the "congratulations" section coz they remind me of the cards everyone gave me when we got back from Cornwall. Well everyone except my knob head Dad again. My GCSE and piano exam results came through. I was well chuffed with three A's, nine B's and one C for my GCSEs. But the best, most unbelievable result was my Grade Eight Piano exam. I got ninety-five percent, upper distinction.

Mum was like well pleased and like nearly hugged me to death and everything. Which I actually didn't mind. I haven't let her hold me for a while and she smelled warm and homely, sort of like fruit and garlic and hairspray and some of that looovvly Jean Paul Gaultier (isn't he a singer too?) perfume Simon bought her. She stroked my hair like she did when I was little and kept saying it had all been worth it, all the hard work had been worth it, whatever that meant? Then she ordered takeaway pizza and let me have a bit of a gathering, which was well sweet.

Simple Simon was well sick too coz he gave me twenty quid, which I know isn't New York like Chelsea (I still can't believe her Dad's run off with a 21 year old) but it felt like it meant as much, to me anyway.

I felt like I was walking on the moon for days. Nan and Grandad gave me a card and a necklace with a piano on it and Maisy (still can't believe the bloody Emo freak got off so lightly with that bloody tattoo) bought me a sick photo frame with musical notes on. Connor made me a photo to put in the frame. It was a picture of me playing the piano with Alex Turner superimposed onto it to make it look like he's sitting next to me. He said he knows how much I love him and when I'm a famous superstar I can show him.

I feel like well emotional when I think about how sick everyone was. Oh and of course, Sean, Nat and Summer skyped me when Mum texted them with the good news. Summer told me she had made a new best friend called Stardust and it was like amazing coz they became best friends within seconds of meeting each other. She said they had so much in common coz they were both half-princess and half-rebel. Then, bless her, she burst out singing a song she had written for me to congratulate me. It was called *Cassie My Sassy Cousin:*

*Cassie my sassy cousin got her exam results today... Oooh oooh, yeah, yeah.*
*Cassie my sassy cousin, it's the piano she can narf play Cassie's so clever, it's so true.*
*Cassie I wanna be just like you – oooh oooh oooh. Cassie my sassy cousin, that's all I have to say!!*

And what did that sperm donor unfortunate enough to be

my father get me? Nothing, zero, zilch, naff all, that's what. As usual. He said my piano exam result was good but he was quite disappointed with my GCSEs coz he thought I was set to get straight A's. Really? Like you ever helped me with any revision, ever? And as for saying studying music was a bit arty farty – really? Let's see if you're calling me arty farty when I become the next Adele or Beyoncé, or ... or ... arrrggghhh! Idiot, bellend, twat, dickhead. Why is it so hard for you to acknowledge anything I do? Why will I never be good enough for you? What have I done that's so bloody bad?

'Cas! Cassie babe. Where are you?' I look up to see Honey staring at me and clicking her fingers in my face.

'Oooops – sorry. Drifted off there for a minute.'

'I should say,' she replies, smiling. 'In a right little world of your own there weren't you hun? Was it Luke or Joe you were dreaming of shagging, maybe both?' Mr Dunmore tuts again. 'C'mon,' Honey continues. 'This shop's rubbish. We'll get Lorenzo a card when we go into the city for college this afternoon.'

We move away from the cards and head for the door. 'Did I tell you Ikram was seen finger blasting that girl from the Dance and Drama group at the back of the supermarket the other day?' Honey says. I cringe, coz I know Simon knows Mr Dunmore really well and Honey only talks on one level – loud. 'Personally, I dunno what he sees in her,' she finishes, before smiling sweetly at Mr Dunmore and striding model-like out of the shop.

Mr Dunmore shakes his head at me as I follow. I smile and put my head down. I must remember not to come back here for a few weeks.

'It's quite a nice little town you live in isn't it? A bit boring, but nice.'

Honey lives in the centre of the city, right near college. I never really gave it much thought until I went to college but

Great Tosson is quite different to the city, more cliquey and gossipy somehow. Nan and Grandad moved here from London years and years ago when Mum and Uncle Sean were little. When they grew up, Mum and Uncle Sean moved away. Then Mum came back with me and Connor when Dad left. We moved into a really small house in Honeypot Lane for a while then when Mum and Simon met we moved to a bigger house in Old Sodom Lane. So I live in Great Tosson down Old Sodom Lane – couldn't make that up if I tried. Dad still lives in the city but you'd think it was a thousand miles away; the fuss he makes about how much trouble and inconvenience it is to see us.

'It's okay I suppose,' I continue, 'everyone sort of knows everyone and yeah it is a bit boring. Except in January.'

'What happens in January?'

'We have a whole weekend dedicated to the Straw Bear. It's like a pagan festival where we burn the Straw Bear.'

Honey looks dumbfounded 'What? Burning Bears and nut festivals?'

'Eh? What do you mean nut festival?'

'You said Pecan Festival? I like pecans, but what exactly is a pecan festival?'

'No, you idiot,' I reply laughing, 'I said pagan, a pagan festival. It takes place every January, a couple of weeks after New Year. There's like loads of street dancing and stories and a man dressed as a huge straw bear is followed around the streets that are all closed off to cars and traffic. It also involves lots of drinking; lots and lots of drinking actually. People come from all over the country. Some people even travel from abroad, Germany and stuff. The whole town is heaving with people. Then on Sunday afternoon we burn the bear.' Honey looks shocked.

'Really? You burn the man dressed up as a straw bear? Isn't

that like murder or illegal or something?' I slap my forehead with the palm of my hand – ouch, a little too hard.

'No Honey,' I begin to say, 'we burn the straw of the bear, like the costume, not the man who wears it.' Honey looks confused. 'Oh never mind.'

For a brief moment I suddenly realise what it might be like for Mum when she's talking to me sometimes.

## LIZZIE

It's fairly quiet today in the library so Amira has assigned me with the challenging task of making an eye catching display to draw more young adults to our non-fiction books. Thankfully I'm still here and have managed to hold onto my job – this time. The idea of trying to snare teenagers, disposed to and distracted by an array of technological gadgets, to a book display, seemed a little daunting at first but I've actually been inspired by my own young adults at home.

The first couple of books to sit on my display are about tattoos. One is a vivid and fascinating illustrative guide to a selection of some of the many thousands of designs available; the other is a history of permanent inking.

To say I was slightly shocked when I first saw Maisy's indelible inking would be an understatement. However, it has grown on me over the last couple of months. I've become used to seeing the full length of the side of one leg marked with the delicate but definite etching of the trunk of a tree. Subtle browns and dark greens climb the length of her leg and culminate into an explosion of pinky reds and whites as the full bloom of a cherry blossom tree spills across her thigh and up across her waist. It's both beautifully designed and executed but if I were totally honest I'd have preferred it if she'd had something much smaller.

Simon, for once, actually came out of this particular ruckus in a much less favourable light than usual and was quickly demoted to bad cop for a change. I on the other hand was promoted, albeit very briefly, from wicked step monster to understanding parent, at least in Maisy's eyes. To Cassie I was just the cow that let the Emo freak off *again*. It wasn't so much that Simon was pissed off, he'd said, but more that he was disappointed she hadn't discussed it with us first. And of course he's worried about future implications it might have with jobs and people's attitudes towards her. I reminded him times have changed and whereas tattoos maintain a largely homologous relationship with deviant behaviour for older generations, people from a variety of backgrounds now choose to modify their bodies through permanent body art.

I reminded him of the many major not to mention minor celebrities that display their body art with pride. 'Many of them, strong, independent women,' I said.

'Hmmmph,' Simon responded unconvinced. 'Tattoos certainly seem to disseminate across all racial groups but I'm not so sure about class. I don't think we'll ever see the day Royal Family members have "his n hers" matching tattoos do you?'

'Stuff class,' I replied. 'Anyway I hate to break this to you but as much as we all like to believe in fairy tales, I don't think Maisy or Cassie will be meeting and setting up home with a prince anytime soon, at least not the blue blooded variety.'

I was hardly in a position to criticise Maisy. The night we discovered her inking Sean had sat for at least an hour beforehand explaining the story of his life marked out in intricate artwork across both arms. Sadly though, I quietly agree with Simon and think the social costs are still greater for women. Hopefully that will change over time. Maisy said she doesn't care what people think and won't conform to bigotry. Good for her.

She's still crazy in love with Crazee (I still don't know why he's called Crazee?) mostly via Skype and text as he's had to go back to Australia. But he seems to have had a positive effect on her as she is now simultaneously studying Art at college whilst working as many hours as she can fit in at Goth Shock.

We haven't told Simon yet but she confided in me that she's saving to go to Australia. I'm so torn as to how I feel about this. On the one hand I'm completely full of admiration for her and want her to spread her wings, but on the other there's a part of me that doesn't want to let go, even though biologically she isn't mine, in every other sense she is. And I wonder if I've done enough. I'm reminded of some of the words from the letters written by Mary Wollstonecraft about Fanny (I can hear all the kids laughing at that name), her infant, illegitimate daughter and companion during her travels around the Nordic countries during the late eighteenth-century.

*"You know that as a female I am particularly attached to her – I feel more than a mother's fondness and anxiety, when I reflect on the dependent and oppressed state of her sex. I dread lest she be forced to sacrifice her heart to her principles, or her principles to her heart...I dread to unfold her mind, lest it should render her unfit for the world she is to inhabit – Hapless woman! What fate is thine!"*

Of course we live in different times; things have changed, even since my younger years during the 1980's. There's more freedom and opportunity for women than there has ever been. However, those calm, vast waters are still infested with vicious predators. I only have to look at Amber and I'm soberly reminded of the outlook for the new, younger generation. One of dead end jobs, working (if they're lucky) well below their qualifications or potential, the promise of property-owning democracy dead and always at the mercy of private landlords or the state. The Bleak House generation?

*Aren't we full of doom and gloom?*

Oh god, maybe I should stop reading the news. The girls will be just fine.

Encouragement and guidance is all they need.

I smile to myself. I must have done something right because although Maisy's slightly gothic look and tattoos can be unnerving, to some anyway, I admire her confidence to buck the trend; refuse the dictates of conformity and fashion and just be free to be. Anyway, as Dad is always rightly saying, "It's not a life, it's an adventure".

'Looking good, Lizzie, innit,' Raj says behind me, staring at my now half-filled display. He's also managed to hold onto his job.

'Me or the display?'

'You always look good Lizzie,' he says. 'You is a MIL...' he trails off, hints of red permeating his bronzed cheeks. 'Ahem,' he coughs and clears his throat. 'You could do with some real crime stories,' he suggests. 'Young lads love reading that sort of shit. And cars,' he adds. 'Mix it up with the health and beauty girlie stuff. I'll go and grab a few for you,' he says, and disappears upstairs.

Inspired by my own dear Cassie I also throw in a few books about music to the display, including an assortment of biographies about various rock and pop legends. Cassie seems to be settling in at college. She seems to have, thankfully, slightly more confidence than she did at school. Unlike school, the playing field at college has levelled somewhat. Status and acceptance isn't limited to the thin, rich, pretty girls doing their thin, rich, pretty thing. Mutual respect is based more on ability, not size, race, gender, sexual preference or money. Although judging by some of the heated discussions that take place at our house during band rehearsals once a week, artistic temperament is definitely alive and kicking. There are certainly a few divas in the making.

Starting the music course with Luke by her side has helped Cassie too, I think.

Bless him, I still remember him as the quiet, rather serious little boy in the same class as Cassie at Primary school. I can't quite believe, despite following her around like a love sick puppy, it actually took me to point out to Cassie just how smitten the lovely Luke is with her. Cassie seemed genuinely shocked when I suggested it.

'I've bloody known Luke for bloody years,' she'd shouted in disbelief. 'Course he doesn't bloody fancy me.'

His guitar strummed serenade (following a drunken walk home from a late night party), alongside the dawn chorus of birds one morning, finally convinced her, I think. He was, despite Simon's grumpy demeanour at being woken up at the crack of dawn, actually very good, sort of Ed Sheerenish.

Cassie is now of course, despite only being at college for seven weeks, a bona fide music expert, which finds me constantly being chastised for listening to, "that crap" which is nearly always "waaaaayyyy too poppy", or "ridiculously commercial", or "unforgivably predictable".

I laugh to myself. I'm still, for the most part, the devil incarnate, the nagging old cow and wicked step-monster that has nothing better to do than interfere and ruin the lives of my teenage daughters. But maybe, just maybe, things are moving in the right direction. The girls are, to a point, maturing. I see light at the end of this tunnel that has at times felt like a perpetual teenage cyclone of raging hormones. I've even managed to convince Amber to apply for work. Maybe, just maybe life is becoming…easier?

I sneak a quick look at my phone ensconced in my pocket to see if Ruby has replied to my text about meeting for coffee later. She has. And she's blown me out, again. She has a meeting, apparently. Sounds like a perfectly plausible explanation, but then again so were all the others of late.

'Lizzie! Lizzie,' a breathless Amira is scurrying over and calling out to me. 'We've just had a call from the hospital asking if you can please go there as quickly as possible – something to do with Cassie your daughter and an accident with her ear?'

CHAPTER 22

HOSPITAL

**CASSIE**

For god bloody sake why does Mum have to make like such a psycho fuss about everything? I can't bloody help it if I had to go to hospital and it's not my fault I didn't know it wasn't bloody serious. You'd think she'd want to be at hospital with her own daughter for god sake. I admit I like overreacted a bit but I didn't want to end up bloody deaf did I? It was all the ear piercer man's fault anyway. He's the one that like dropped the bloody silver ball from my tragus piercing into my ear. Idiot. And he kept my bloody money. Knob head. I daren't tell Mum that though coz she's bound to go into the shop and make like a bloody scene. It's full of pumped up, bearded tattooists for god sake.

Honey thinks it's like well funny. She thinks Mum's like well cute for caring. It's dead funny watching Mum's confused expression every time Mum sees Honey coz Honey like, always wraps her arms around her and kisses her on the cheek. At first I thought it was coz Mum was like gayest, but that didn't make sense coz Mum's not prejudice about anyone, except me of course, and maybe Tabitha, our nosy next-door neighbour. I think Mum feels a bit embarrassed coz I don't even hug her like that, and Mai – I mean Mania – definitely doesn't. I suppose Connor does though, little creep. That's just Honey though; she's just like, well affectionate with everyone.

Anyway, I suppose I did have a bit of a fit coz I had no bloody idea what that suction thing was that the stupid bloody doctor woman was waving next to my ear. Actually, she was well nice, better than Mum about it all. She just laughed at me, whereas Mum just gave me one of her scowly looks that makes her frown lines look even deeper and told me to stop being so childish. How would she like a huge hoover thing in her ear? Actually it wasn't that big but it was like, well noisy. I reckon anyone would scream, even though the doctor woman said her previous patient – a 5-year-old who had pushed sweets in her ear – didn't. I don't believe her. It came out pretty quick though, but uggghh, no way did I want to keep it when the doctor asked me if I did. Why would I want to keep something that's been rolling around the inside of my ear for god sake?

Mum was sort of nice afterwards though, and has taken me and Honey for a coffee. I'm having a large iced caramel frapp with extra cream on the top. Sorted. Mum is dead embarrassing though and has started asking Honey loads of questions. Honey doesn't seem to mind though, and I was like well shocked when she said her Dad and all his family had disowned her coz she was a lesbian. I didn't think that kind of prejudice existed anymore and had only ever happened in the olden days, like when Mum was young. Mum was well nice to Honey about it all.

She can be pretty sick, sometimes.

We've talked well loads about college too. I fessed up to Mum that I was actually well nervous when I started. I felt like the little kid starting big school all over again, so it was pretty sick having Luke there with me. I still can't believe he fancies me though. And, like oh my god, serenading me under my bedroom window with his guitar, singing a song he wrote about me was like well cringe, but – I have to secretly admit – kind of sick too. Joe would *never* do anything like that for me. I can see him now, smirking and ridiculing Luke. He's not even really that much into music. In fact, most of the time it feels like he's not really that much into me. So why do I fancy him and not Luke?

I still can't believe what happened to Chelsea. Joe seems to think her Dad has taken all their money and left Chelsea and her Mum and brother without a penny. They've gone up north or something to stay with family. I can't imagine Chelsea living a life without money. It'll be like a well major culture shock for her. I suppose I do feel a little bit sorry for her though, even though she was a complete bitch, coz I found out that she actually got off with Joe a couple of times during the summer. Joe says nothing really happened between them, that he was with her more as a favour, coz she seemed vulnerable, and that the whole time he was with her he couldn't stop thinking about me (a part of me, a really bad part, can't help wondering if he doesn't want to be with her now coz she's not rich anymore?).

And here I was all this time thinking it was Pheebs that had got off with Joe, when she had actually got off with Charlie Carmichael. He is a good friend of Joe's, which was why she was talking to and hanging out with Joe, to get closer to Charlie. He is like well quiet, nothing like Pheebs, and yet she seems to be like madly in love with him? She said she didn't want to tell me about Charlie coz she was afraid I'd laugh at her coz he's not that good looking or clever. She thought I'd be all-judgemental. I was well insulted and told her best friends don't ever judge. I'm glad we've made up.

I do feel happier at college. Especially being on the music

course coz there's like such a mad mix of people and everyone's like reeeaaalllly really talented and they all love music like me. It's like soooo different to school. The girls couldn't be any different. Instead of the verbal put downs and bitchy comments that were an absolute must of the fake brigade who ruled the school with their ridiculous code that despised different, my music friends actually celebrate diversity. No one is punished for not being thin enough or side lined for not having enough money or ridiculed for still having pubic hair. Focus is on the talent of the individual, and stuff all the other shit.

Honey and Louisa are the main singers on the course, and they're like well funny when they talk coz Honey's dead common (or street innit she says) and Louisa's dead posh and all her yeah's sound like yah's and her really's sound like rarely's.

Me and Luke play keyboards and there are well loads of guitar players, but I think Sam and Justas are particularly brilliant. Justas is from Poland. He seems like well grown up compared to me. He's travelled like loads and never seems to get upset when people shout out things like "go home you Polski bastards". His nickname is Useless but that's like a joke coz he really is like such an amazing guitar player.

Dannisha is an awesome bass player and is like well stunning, probably more so than Honey actually, but I'm really not sure about the blonde weave and blue contact lenses. Her afro – which I have only seen once or twice coz it's kept tightly braided under her blonde wigs most of the time – is like truly striking just like her hazelnut eyes.

Jack is an excellent drummer, as is Simone but I felt well sorry for her when the drum stool she sat on the other day actually collapsed under her weight. Every week she's on a different diet that never seems to work. She said she was bullied at school because of her weight. They said the only diet she was any good at was the see-food (see food and eat it) diet. I've seen her come alive on this course though, and she has sooooooo much more confidence than when she started, and it's like well mesmerising to watch her play the drums. Now, whenever she sees anyone from her old school that thinks they have a right to shout mean things at her, she laughs at them. She told one boy that he talks so much crap his face is actually starting to look like the arsehole he is and she asked another one "who made you the fucking body police?" Then she threatened to wrestle him to the floor and sit on his gobby face, which did a pretty good job of shutting him up, actually.

Tansy plays the trumpet. She dyes her ginger hair black, and spray-tans her pale, vampire white skin. I think she wishes she was black, or mixed race at least. She's a good dancer too, always shaking her booty – or twerking her badonadonk as she says – every chance she gets. When she talks she says things like, "whaddu yooz talkin bout bruva" or "diz iz inglish innit", which is well different to how she speaks to her Mum. She doesn't know I do, but sometimes I follow her when she sneaks off to speak to her Mum on the phone, and she has a really soft Irish accent. Some of the other idiot boys around college call her a Wigger behind her back, which is like, well out of order and well derogatory. She just isn't sure who she is right now, like me. Can't everyone just try out being whoever they want to be? Knob heads. Thankfully, all the boys on the Music Course are like well chilled (although that may be coz they're stoned most of the time?). Anyway, whatevs college is waaaaayyyyy better than school.

We don't just sit round playing our instruments all day though. There's like well loads of other stuff to learn. We all have to have singing lessons and then there's the theory stuff, which is like boooooooring. We also learn composition and have to use like well-complicated software and computers for that. Then there's the finance side of the business, and freelancing, which is like selling ourselves, but not in the prostitute type of way. We also have jazz lessons and performance workshops and lunch time concerts three times a week. On top of all that we're doing like a major big performance in the evening in a couple of weeks' time, which all our families can come to. I'm like dead nervous. Of course, Mum and Simon and Mai – I mean Mania — and Connor and Nan and Grandad are coming. Even Joe said he'd come, but Dad still hasn't replied to my text to let me know if he's coming or not. Knob.

My phone pings. I've got a message. I hope its Joe. Mum and Honey are still jabbering away, which is sick coz Honey is like well talkative and she's keeping Mum occupied while I check my phone coz Mum gets like well lame if I get my phone out when we're eating and drinking. I look up to check Mum hasn't seen me when someone catches my eye. It's Ruby, a couple of tables behind ours. She's laughing and joking with a man sitting opposite her. The back of his head looks familiar. I'm pretty sure it's Luca, from the Catalina restaurant. I tell Mum and she turns round to look while I shout out to her.

'Ruby. Hey, over here,' I say waving.

Ruby looks up, she seems surprised. She pulls back from the man opposite her and sits up straight.

I stand up from my chair and point to the top of Honey's head. 'Come and meet my friend,' I ask. Ruby smiles, then gets up and walks over to us.

'Hello ladies,' she says.

I introduce her to Honey and of course Honey stands up and hugs and kisses Ruby. Ruby looks a bit taken aback and laughs. Then we all laugh, except Mum. Mum seems moody? She looks at Ruby then looks at her watch then looks back to Ruby again.

'I thought you had a meeting?' Mum says.

Ruby waves her hand dismissively. 'Cancelled,' she replies. 'So you didn't think to call me, meet for that coffee after all?'

Mum makes a point of looking over at the table Ruby has just left. Ruby swings round to look too. The man that was sitting opposite her still sits. Ruby looks back at Mum again. She fiddles with her hands and seems nervous.

'Didn't want to mess you around,' Ruby replies. 'Thought I'd do a spot of retail therapy instead. Then who should I bump into but Luca. Cassie, you remember Luca?'

'Yeah, course I do.' I explain to Mum and Honey who Luca is, giving Honey a shortened version of mine and Ruby's celebrity shopping trip.

'Hmmm, really?' Mum says.

Ruby raises one of her arched eyebrows then says she has to go. What the hell was that all about? I shrug my shoulders and go back to looking at my phone under the table. It's another message from Pheebs. She wants to meet up coz she has something she wants to tell me. She said I'll never believe it?

Friends are weird.

## CHAPTER 23

## DANGEROUS LIAISONS

**LIZZIE**

*I* squirm uncomfortably in my seat.
*Why in god's name did I choose to wear these knickers?*

'God bloody knows?' I suddenly shout out. Tabitha my specious, gossipy, neighbour glares at me. She is, rather surprisingly, a friend of Raj's and has joined him and a few of us from work for his birthday celebration meal. When I try to explain that I was actually talking about my choice of underwear and *not* responding to her question as to why men find her *so* attractive, I don't think she actually believes me. I don't, however, give a shit.

Why did I pick these knickers though? I've worked all day at the library, made a quick pit stop here and then have to dash off to Cassie's concert in an hour. I tried to pick an outfit to suit all three obligations. God knows why I went for the sexy underwear? What the hell was I thinking? I should have stuck with function over fashion in that department.

*Note to self – keep sexy undies for the bedroom only.*

I rock awkwardly in my seat, swapping butt cheeks in a pointless bid to prevent the black lacy thong, positively beautiful on the hanger in the shop, from being eaten by my arse. Twelve hours wearing this bloody thing is tantamount to torture.

Simon is picking me up from the restaurant so I make the most of it and order a large glass of wine. If I have to endure two hours of song and dance from First Year Music and Dance students at least the wine might help, perhaps even improve, the performance. If the strange noises emanating from the garage at our house during recent rehearsals are anything to go by I don't actually hold much hope.

'Tut, tut. Too much wine doesn't help anything, Lizzie,' Tabitha says.

'Nope, but neither does water eh? Cheers,' I say raising my glass. She looks at me in the same way someone does when they stumble across a bad smell. I take a large swig of my wine and much to Tabitha's amusement nearly choke to death when I spot a familiar face across the restaurant.

*What the fuck is Ruby doing?*

My best friend looks as though she's enjoying a romantic dinner for two, only it's not with Andy. I swear the young man enjoying her full and undivided attention is Luca, again, the waiter from Catalina's. I grab my phone from my bag and use a combination of index fingers and thumbs, squinting without my reading glasses, to stab out a text message to her.

'Ah ah ahhhhhh,' Tabitha says wagging her finger and nodding her head from side to side like some defiant child.

*With a bit of luck her head will spin right round and off in a minute.*

'Didn't Raj tell you?' Tabitha continues. 'Didn't you tell them all?' she says turning to Raj, before turning back to look at me.

'Errrrr...ummmmm,' Raj replies, his tone uncharacteristically obtuse.

*Either Tabitha has something on him or there's history between these two. Raj is acting like a bloody idiot.*

'Raj and I agreed,' she continues, with smug satisfaction. 'No mobile phones at the table. They really are killing the art of conversation you know.'

*Yes and some people are only alive because it's illegal to shoot them.*

I'm pissed off because I actually agree with Tabitha. I can't normally abide the use of mobile phones at the table. It's a sad but common occurrence to see a table full of adults and children alike, heads down, zombified and hypnotised by that little device in their hands. Simon and I have banned them at mealtimes, much to the annoyance of the girls.

'You are *so* right Tabitha,' I reply with as much conviviality I can muster, which frankly isn't much. I'm grateful though. She has, albeit unwittingly, given me some thinking time. I need to hold fire, gather my facts; god knows how many relationships have been irretrievably broken by text.

I look across at Ruby again. She throws her head back and laughs. I feel obliged to look away. Why do I feel like I'm intruding?

My feet feel like blocks of ice and I stamp them under the table. My choice of footwear has proved to be about as practical as my choice of underwear tonight, given the bloody weather outside. Strappy heels and snow are never a good combination. 'Bloody hells bells, is it cold in here or is it me?' I ask no one in particular. Ruby runs her finger across the cheek of the young man opposite her again.

'Cold? You think this is cold?' Raj says, 'try living in my

house innit. My bloody parents won't put the heating on until December 25th.'

'Really? I've *had* to put ours on, even though it is only October.'

I look out of the window. It's still snowing. Great white flakes of the stuff, falling in abundance, marked out against an inky black sky. God knows what the gas bill will be this quarter if this weather keeps up for too long.

'Yeah I'm serious innit. It's their Christmas present,' Raj continues. He wears an expression of animated disbelief. 'Until then we all have to huddle together in one room like some Dickensian Workhouse just to keep bloody warm.'

'Your hair is sitting in your curry darling,' the overtly camp waiter says to me as he leans across the table with yet another bottle of wine. He looks at Raj and winks. His pouty lips are full, the intonation of the words that fall from them, suggestive.

'*Enjoy,* my lovelies!' he says.

'Whoa, you've pulled there Raj,' I mock. Raj looks embarrassed, his laugh nervous. My eyes flit capriciously from Raj to Tabitha, from Tabitha to Ruby. Why is Ruby stroking her friend's face? Why are Raj's cheeks flushed? Shit, my hair really is in the curry. I love Thai red curry, but not in my hair.

I grab a paper napkin and drag it across a section of hair to soak up the spicy red sauce. Satisfied I've done the best I can for now I look up again at Raj and Tabitha. Raj looks rattled. I smile at him, try and put him at ease. Suddenly I see it, a flicker of disappointment across Tabitha's eyes. I know something – or at least she thinks I do – that only she thought she was privy to. I look over towards Ruby's table again. Is Ruby cheating on Andy? Surely not? Is Raj gay? Fuck, my head's spinning and the wine hasn't even kicked in yet.

The meal passes pleasantly enough and I even manage to remain only slightly offensive in the face of Tabitha's highly offensive presence. I have other, far more pressing concerns. I need the loo (way too much wine) but going would mean Ruby seeing me, as she hasn't yet. I'd have to pass her table to get to the loo. Empty plates are adiosed away by various waiting staff before once again our very own darling waiter returns with menus.

'Dessert anyone?' he says, holding a small notepad in one hand and a poised pencil in the other. Menus are once again perused and a brief discussion ensues as to whether dessert really is just too much of an indulgence.

'Ooooh goo on,' the waiter says throwing his limp-wristed, pencil-holding hand forward. He looks at us expectantly but his eye is drawn frequently and noticeably towards Raj. 'May as well go alllll the way eh?' he continues, playfully. His laugh is course and throaty.

It's no good. I really do need the loo. I order something called Death by Chocolate (there could be worse ways to die) and excuse myself. I manage, somehow I think, to slip by Ruby unnoticed and it's such a relief to pee but more of a relief to pull these bloody knickers off. I consider taking them off altogether. I laugh. I can't remember the last time I flew solo. Simon really would think it's his lucky night. I decide, for better or worse, to keep them on. I check my reflection in the mirror whilst washing my hands. God where did all these wrinkles come from? I re-apply some lip gloss then use both hands to smooth down my dress before taking a deep breath. My thoughts have turned back to Ruby. If she didn't see me going into the loo, she'll definitely see me coming out.

*Just act normal.*

'Yeah, good idea,' I say out loud.

*Why the fuck am I so nervous? Oh bollocks to this. Here I come, ready or not.*

I pull open the heavy door and stride out confidently.

They've gone. The table for two that Ruby and her friend had been sitting at is vacant and all that remains is a flickering tea-light and two empty wine glasses. I look round in confusion before grabbing the attention of the flamboyant waiter from our table.

'Err excuse me. Where are the couple that were sitting at this table?'

He tuts and raises an eyebrow. 'Oh them? They've gone darling. Couldn't keep their hands off each other. Told em to bugger off and get a room.' His laugh is loud as he executes a dance turn before deliberately mincing his walk. And, just like Ruby and her companion, he vanishes from sight.

## CASSIE

OMG! Oh my actual bloody god. I could cry. No, actually I am crying. And now I look like Maisy – I mean Maniac, or whatever the fuck her bloody name is – coz my make-up's running all down my bloody face. Could this night get any worse? Half the equipment's not working, including one of the keyboards, there's problems with the lighting and once again, once *a fucking gain* that knob head, dickweed, idiot, stupid, moron wanking excuse of a father of mine is not coming to see me. AGAIN! Add to that the fact Joe – who is supposed to be my boyfriend (although we're not actually official) – is also now not coming. Even though he bloody prooooomised me he would. And, just to finish me off completely, to add insult to injury, Mum and Simon may not be coming either. Take me out the oven. Stick a fork in me. I'm sooooo bloody done.

Simon text to say Mum slipped over in the snow and now her ankle has like completely swollen up like a balloon or something and she can barely walk. What idiot wears heels in the snow for god sake? Simon thinks she may have a concussion too, coz apparently she keeps saying it's a good job she kept her knickers on or something?

Luke and Useless have been like well sick and told me not to get too upset. Useless even made me laugh and said he could probably speak to some Polish gangsters and get a hit out on Dad and Joe if I want. He was only joking of course, at least I think he was? Honey is like soooooo sweet and is going to completely reapply my make-up for me. Pheebs has also texted me back (I'm like so glad we're friends again), after my major meltdown text to her and she's promised to come and support me, despite like throwing up every ten minutes.

I still can't believe she's pregnant. I know it's the last thing Mum would want for me but Pheebs seems well happy. I don't envy her and I don't wish it was me but I wish Joe would love me the way Charlie loves her. He's bought them a house and everything. Apparently he was left some money by a dead relative or something, which he's used as a deposit. God, Pheebs is actually going to be like a real live Mum to a real live baby! Freaky!

## CHAPTER 24

### THERE'S A FUNKY PURPLE HAZE AROUND THE MOON

**LIZZIE**

'Simon I'm fine,' I snap as I try to hobble up the stairs to the seating area for tonight's college performance. I'm not of course. The pain, caused by the rather unsightly, bruised and battered purple cankle of my left leg is intense. I tripped, as Dad would say "arse over tit" and fell, twisting and landing with all my weight on my ankle whilst leaving the restaurant earlier this evening. Luckily Mum was on hand to give me one of her horse pill painkillers which, when consumed with large amounts of alcohol, doesn't exactly get rid of the pain but has left me with an interesting woozy feeling.

'You're a bladdy idiot encha,' Dad scolds me; 'you need to get to a bleeding hospital. That leg looks like it needs seeing to.'

'I can't let Cassie down Dad. Scott's not coming – again.' Dad rolls his eyes and shakes his head, muttering expletives under his breath.

'When have you ever let that gal down?' he continues. 'Besides, we're here for her, me and yer mum. She'll be fine.'

'No Dad,' I reply, grimacing as I try to move my leg to get comfortable. 'I need to be here for her.'

*Only because you're afraid of her.*

I look down at my purple throbbing ankle. The swelling, at first the size of a tennis ball now appears to be the size and shape of a rugby ball.

'Independent little bagger,' Dad grumbles. 'Always were and still bladdy is.'

Suddenly the lights dim, large stage curtains swish open and through an explosion of stage lights we, the audience, are suddenly exposed to an eruption of dance and sound. An inordinate combination of gyrating bodies moves this way and that, merging with rhythmic sounds pulsating across the stage and beyond.

'Look, there's Cassie,' Connor shouts excitedly, waving his outstretched arm towards the left of the stage.

'Where?' says Dad, squinting and putting his glasses on for a better look. 'There, there!' Connor continues, pointing excitedly. My ankle throbs in time with the base line of the pumping music as my eyes search frantically for Cassie amongst the throng of performing bodies. I spot her, one of two keyboard players. She is in a standing position, head down, hands spread-eagled and fingers moving with lightning speed across the black and white keys of the red Nord she's playing. She looks up from time to time laughing, the movement of her head metrically modest. I stare incredulously at the woman before me; my daughter, bane of my life, jewel in my crown.

'She looks good, doesn't she?' Simon says squeezing my hand.

I look up at him and smile.

The intro song finishes and the stage quickly clears. For the next hour-and-a-half we are entertained by an array of interesting dance and musical acts. Some are, shall we say, *different*, especially a number of the contemporary dance interpretations of classical ballet.

'Gawd "n" Bennett, fat girls in tutu's? What's that all about then?' is I believe how Dad phrased it.

Some of the student rap songs also prove to be rather interesting, particularly one called *Suspect* performed by Marcus otherwise known as Mar Cus a.k.a Straight Trip. I'm not even going to attempt to ask Cassie what that's supposed to mean. Wearing trackie's that fall below his boxers and a snap back cap, circumspectly balanced on a rigid quiff; Mar Cus a.k.a Straight Trip covets the microphone handed to him and virtually eats the black spongy muffler as he begins his rapid recital:

*Everybody say yeaaaah Oh oh oh... Hey eh eh eh... Oooooh yeaaaah...*
*Yooos my mumber one SUSPECT My baby girl RESPECT Heart like an eight track Makes me go EEERECT Oh oh oh...*
*Hey eh eh eh... Oooooh yeaaaah...*
*Yooos my number one SUSPECT So you is so RUSTIC Don't you see? I is your number one GANGSTA*
*...Not a HAMPSTER Who ain't free*
*You do me Up, I do you down Yooos in luck So don't leave town*
*Yooos my SUSPECT, but trust it Yooos gonna love it when I THRUST it In the place yooos wanna be, WITH ME*
*Yooos my mumber one SUSPECT My baby girl – RESPECT*
*Heart like an eight track Makes me go EEERECT Oh oh oh...*
*Hey eh eh eh... Oooooh yeaaaah...*

Although actually quite awful the *Suspect* Rap and its Rapper prove to be entertainingly compelling. He finishes to a rapturous applause and one very confused looking audience member – namely Dad.

'What the bleedin hell was that all a-bleedin-bout?' he says, turning to look at me.

I shrug my shoulders and smile. 'Who knows Dad?'

All is hush, the hall once again quiet and bathed in darkness. Two spotlights then interrupt the shadows and shine across the stage but their contents are empty?

Clearly the technicians have missed the mark. After dancing around the stage for several seconds the spots finally locate two patiently waiting individuals. Standing in one circle of light is Cassie and in the other the talented Miss Ripley, or as she is simply known to all and sundry, Honey.

Cassie begins to play and I well up; not just from the pain of my ever-growing cankle but from the beautiful melodic waves of sound dispersed from expertly played black and white keys scattering a rainbow of familiar resonance. After Cassie's brief solo performance Honey joins in, and between them they hypnotise the audience with their version of Bob Dylan's *'To Make You Feel My Love,'* recently covered by the lovely Adele of course.

'See, I told you she was good didn't I?' Mum says as she always does; the pride in her eyes as evident as my own. And clearly we're not the only ones to think so. The applause is thunderous. Connor whistles his appreciation through four fingers (as taught by Uncle Sean), whilst Dad yells, 'Gow on gal.' Mum claps with such vigour I'm reminded of an over enthusiastic seal dancing for fish. I swear her hands have actually turned red. Maisy, who never claps for anyone, is also demonstrating her appreciation through applause, albeit rather lethargic and in time with the constant movement of her gum chewing jaw.

'She's good Lizzie, really good,' Simon says turning to look at me. 'But then we always knew that didn't we? I couldn't be more proud you know?'

'Thanks babe.' I smile. 'It's just a pity that ... well, you know ... that he ...' I stumble to get the words out but we both know who I'm talking about.

'Fuck him, his loss.' Simon waves his arm dismissively but in doing so inadvertently knocks my leg and throbbing ankle.

'Ooouuuch,' I wince in pain.

'Told ya,' Dad says with smug satisfaction. 'You need to go the bleedin hospital.'

'Here, have another pill,' Mum offers, as she begins rifling through her oversized handbag. 'Keys? No. Hand-cream? Nope. Mints? No.'

Mum passes these and other various items to Dad who sits patiently with open arms, receiving what appears to be the entire content of her bag as she continues her search for the horse pills she'd given me earlier. Dad's look is one of resignation until he spots the half eaten roll of mints.

'Mmmmm, mints. I'll have one of those,' he says.

'Tissues? No,' Mum continues. 'Lipstick? No. Sausage? Uggghh! Oh dear, so that's where it went,' she says sniffing the contents of a sinister looking napkin. 'I brought that home for Freddy the other week. Purse? No. Light bulb? No.'

'Light bulb?' Dad exclaims, now balancing the booty from Mum's bag precariously on his knee, including – and without packaging – a forty-watt light bulb. 'What the fu...?'

'Ah hah! Here we go,' Mum says rattling a white plastic bottle. 'Painkillers!'

I tilt my head back and greedily chuck another pill down my throat.

When I look up again, Cassie is once more poised at her keyboard but is now joined by several recognisable college friends including Simone on drums, Sam and Justas on guitar and Jake on vocals. Honey, who has now swapped the microphone for her instrument of choice, cavorts provocatively across the stage with a saxophone that proves to be longer than the tiny dress she wears. They are all members of The Incandescent Adolescents, the band they formed at college. The only member I don't recognise is a slightly older looking boy playing bass? As the band start to play I recognise the sound. It's an original song Cassie and The Incandescent Adolescents have practised, re-practised, fought and shed tears over during the last few weeks of rehearsal at our house.

The song, like the band (according to Cassie) has a gritty, indie feel about it, but it's also full of humour. It was decided that Jake, a tall, gangly boy with blue eyes, black hair and a cheeky dimpled smile, had the energy and attitude to deliver the vocals. A front man with ... well, front.

As Jake swaggers across the stage and assertively grabs the mike, I have to agree, he definitely has the preposterous stage presence required to deliver such a song. Guitars are strummed; drums banged and keyboards struck, to form a veritable cadenced jamboree. Jake cracks a huge smile. It's a mischievous smile and far too knowing for his young years. He bounces on the spot, once, twice, three times then begins to sing. His voice is raspy and raw, compelling to listen to:

*Woke up this morning Feeling rather crap Mamma said, son*
*Where d'you get that cap?*
*Coz there's a funky purple haze around the moon Yeah, there's a funky*
*purple haze around the moon Funky purple haaaze*
*Funky purple haaaze*
*Yeah, there's a funky purple haze around the moo ooo oon*
*My Father said,*
*Hey boy get your hair cut, And I said get outta here Kiss my Butt*
*Coz there's a funky purple haze around the moon Yes, there's a funky*
*purple haze around the moon Funky purple haaaze*
*Funky purple haaaze*

*Yes, there's a funky purple haze around the moo ooo oon*
*Sped off to work,*
*In the Bro's white car When all I wanna do Is smoke a cigar*
*Coz there's a funky purple haze around the moon Yes, there's a funky purple haze around the moon Funky purple haaaze*
*Funky purple haaaze*
*Yeah, there's a funky purple haze around the moo ooo oon*
*Fags and a Lighter And the skanky git Mix em together*
*What the hell d'ya get?*
*Coz there's a funky purple haze around the moon Yes, there's a funky purple haze around the moon Funky purple haaaze*
*Funky purple haaaze*
*Yes, there's a funky purple haze around the moo ooo oon.*

Is it the pills Mum's given me or was that actually as good as my ears supposed?

Have I just witnessed the birth of something *special*, both a visual and sound extravaganza or has my heady cocktail of drugs and booze messed with my senses? Judging by the standing ovation for The Incandescent Adolescents I suspect it's the former. 'Boody hell,' Simon says turning to look at me. 'You'd pay to see them wouldn't you? Not a lot, not, you know, Coldplay or the Rolling Stones kind of money, but decent money.'

*Funky Purple Haze* is the finale of the show and a breathless Cassie rushes off stage towards us.

'What d'ya think?' she asks, wide eyed and buzzing. 'Amazing Cassie,' says Simon.

'Sick,' Connor says.

'Yeah,' Maisy says nodding. 'Whatevs. I thought you said Blue Horizon was gonna make an appearance though?'

'Blue Horizon? What the bleedin hell is Blue-bleedin-Horizon?' Dad interrupts.

Cassie sighs and rolls her eyes. 'She's an upcoming singer, Grandad, I told you about her the other week. She's got a massive following and is gonna be huge!'

Dad scratches his head and Cassie turns her attention back to Maisy. 'Nah,' she replies pointing in the direction of the young man I didn't recognise, now expertly fingering his bass guitar. 'She was too busy in the end so she sent her bass player Ralph, he's just got back from touring with her in Australia. You should speak to him.'

Maisy breaks into a smile. 'Okay,' she says and she wanders off towards the stage. Cassie turns to look at Mum and Mum grabs her by the shoulders.

'Told you you were good didn't I? Told you she was good didn't I?' she repeats turning to look at me.

'Whooo hoo Cas,' Dad says. 'There's a Fancky Purple aze arhen the Moon. What d'ya think?' he asks, gyrating and swinging his hips Mick Jagger (he thinks) style.

Cassie laughs. Then she looks at me and her smile vanishes. 'How's your ankle?'

'Sore,' I reply pointing downwards. Her eyes widen in surprise.

'Shit. You'd better get that seen to.'

'I think you may be right but I wouldn't have missed it for the world Cassie – you were brilliant.'

'Huuummph thanks. I'm not as good as some of the others,' she replies, shrugging her shoulders. 'But yeah, thanks.' Her doe- eyes lock with mine. She's trying not to cry. 'He didn't come Mum,' she says. Small darts of pain splinter my heart. I swallow hard.

'I know love.' I pull Cassie gently towards me and hold her. 'It's his loss. It's your Dad's loss.'

'What?' Cassie retorts, pulling away. 'I'm not talking about

Dad. Bloody idiot never comes to see me in anything I do. I'm talking about Joe. You know ... Joe? My boyfriend?'

'Oh,' I reply slightly confused, 'right. But he's not ... well I didn't think he was ...? Oh Cassie he's not worth it. Your happiness doesn't depend on the permission of others you know? And ...well, besides...'

Cassie's eyes narrow. 'Besides *what*?' she asks.

'Well ... I just think you could do so much better for yourself than someone like Joe. C'mon, don't let him spoil ...'

'Arrrggghhh. I knew you'd say that. This is soooo bloody typical of you. You don't have a bloody clue do you? He loves me you know? I mean reallllly loves me.'

*Is she trying to convince herself or me?*

'Look! Look,' Cassie continues, thrusting her phone at my face. I screw my eyes up in an attempt to try and read the screen without my reading glasses. I can just about make out the words *luv* and *gawjus* before Cassie snatches it away again. 'Oh just leave it,' she shouts. 'You never support me in anything.'

## CHAPTER 25

DON'T SHOOT THE MESSENGER

**LIZZIE**

She knows I know. Although quite what it is I know I can't really say, but I'm pretty sure she's being unfaithful, having an affair, call it what the fuck you will but I know she's cheating on Andy. That's why she's avoided all my texts and then, after finally agreeing to meet me, chooses to pay for us both at Catalina's to soften the blow. Unless – god forbid – Ruby actually wants to introduce me to the recipient of her affection? He does work here, after all. My eyes dance capriciously amongst Catalina's young male waiting staff and I'm relieved not to see Luca among them. The restaurant isn't particularly big and with its eclectic mix of dark, wooden tables and odd chairs, soft sage painted panelled walls and crisp, white linen tablecloths, it carries an air of casual chic, almost restaurant-cum-cafè. No wonder Cassie enjoyed coming here when the two of them went shopping together. I smile to myself. At least Cassie's happy again. It's amazing how a cheap bunch of supermarket flowers and huge slab of chocolate can melt a girl's heart. I didn't think Joe had it in him if I'm honest, didn't think he possessed a single romantic bone in his skinny body.

I strain my neck looking towards the heavy glass door, nervously searching out Ruby but there's still no sign of her. I look away again and observe ladies clutching big designer handbags arriving to lunch and businessmen and women in designer suits talking shop. If you were, are, anyone of significance this is most definitely where you'd choose to eat, mainly because the extortionate prices keep riff raff like me out.

I hate to admit it but I feel slightly uncomfortable. Although I think of myself as a people person, adept at adapting to all kinds of situations and individuals on all levels, equally at home with Ruby as my fidus achates or simply my BFF, I never really move in the circles that frequent Catalina's. The staff are all friendly enough though, and don't appear to be particularly phased by my cheap dress or sensible shoes. Knee high boots would have been better, especially as this snow looks like it's here to stay, but I couldn't get the left boot over my still fat, still sprained ankle.

I stare up at the huge painting of a cow just above our table. The waiter (not Luca), white-jacketed and bow-tied, drifts over casually, advising me it's the work of a local artist if I'm at all interested? I smile politely and shake my head. Despite the fact Ruby is now twenty minutes late (I wonder if she's bailed on me?) there's no urgency to move me on. He asks me if I'd like something else to accompany my complimentary water. I'm tempted to order a glass of house white, but if Ruby fails to turn up the cost of this one item alone will eat into a significant chunk of this week's food budget. As I consider this slight dilemma, Ruby strides confidently, purposely up to the table.

'Oh god, I'm exhausted,' she states, almost throwing herself onto the chair opposite me. She looks at the water I'm drinking, scrunches up her nose in disgust and orders two large glasses of white wine.

'Hey,' Ruby smiles, 'how's you?' Despite their evident wealth, Ruby and Andy have always remained pretty grounded. They are however, at ease with their money and although never brazen about their financial good fortune there is no doubt whatsoever that they enjoy spending what they have. 'C'mon let's order,' Ruby continues, perusing the menu. 'I'm bloody famished.'

I, on the other hand, am not. I'm nervous and as usual my anxiety has squashed my appetite. My leg begins to move involuntarily up and down under the table. I'm sure the other leg would join in if my ankle weren't injured. Ruby orders prawns with romesco sauce and a selection of cold tapas including jamon serrano, queso manchego and olives. I order pan-fried hake with white bean and chorizo broth.

I look at Ruby and wonder what the fuck I'm doing here. So what if she's having an affair, is it really any of my business anyway? Perhaps Andy knows? Perhaps he's impotent or they're swingers or have an open marriage or … god knows?

'Yes it was me you saw the other night,' Ruby suddenly blurts out, as if reading my mind 'and yes I'm having an affair.' She takes a large slurp of wine, as do I.

I knew it but I'm still a little taken aback. There is a long pause between us as I try to find my response.

'Okay,' I eventually manage to say.

Ruby sinks her glass of wine and orders another one. She looks at me through narrow eyes. 'Don't judge me,' she says waving a finger at me. 'Don't you dare judge me!'

'I wasn't … I'm not,' I protest. 'Does … Andy know?' Ruby shrugs her shoulders and I can't help but smile. She wears the same sullen expression of petulance that Maisy does when I catch her smoking in her bedroom.

'I dunno ... yeah ... no ... maybe?'

'Why?' I ask. Ruby shrugs her shoulders again. 'It's complicated. You wouldn't understand.'

'Try me?'

We both look up and smile fallaciously at the waiter who places two plates of gastronomic artwork in front of us. We both eat too little and drink too much.

'I think I'm trying to hurt him,' Ruby says, after several moments of silently pushing a glossy orange prawn around her plate.

'Hurt him? But why? Don't you love Andy anymore?'

Ruby smirks at me and shakes her head. 'Of course I love him. We've been together like forever, and I've never *stopped* loving him – despite his fat belly and weird hobbies.'

I take a few moments to digest Ruby's words alongside the food I'm struggling to eat. Reluctantly resurrected, I'm reminded of Scott's infidelity. Minor flushes of anger colour my cheeks. Or is it the wine?

'How can you cheat on someone you claim to love?'

Ruby bangs her fork down on her plate. 'I wondered when this was going to get back to you' she hisses. Her intonation is derisive and I feel deeply wounded. 'Oh don't give me that stupid look,' she goads. 'We can't all be fucking perfect like *you* Lizzie.'

'Whhooaa, just a bloody minute now Ruby,' I reply, using my hand as a stop sign.

'Waiter,' Ruby shouts. She is uncharacteristically obnoxious, waving her arm in the air and clicking her fingers. 'Nother glass of wine please.' I put my hand over my glass to reject the refill the waiter offers me. Ruby scoffs, angry and drunk, but one of us has to stay sober.

'S'alright for you,' Ruby continues. 'With yerr perfect lil famlee and perfect lil life.'

I laugh but I'm incensed. 'Perfect life? Perfect bloody life? Are you fucking kidding me? Cheated on, left high and dry with two kids ... then what Ruby? Three damaged people ...'

'Huuuummmpph! *Damaged* – why *do* people love to bandy that bloody word around?'

I'm ready to erupt but I ignore the sarcasm in Ruby's voice. 'Three damaged people meet two other damaged people,' I continue. 'Add to that an ex-husband who doesn't give a shit, a job – thanks to an endless round of cuts – I can barely hold onto, a mortgage we can barely afford and two out of those three kids can scarcely stand the sight of me. Yeah, perfect fucking life eh Ruby?'

Ruby slumps forward and puts her head in her hands. After a moment she looks up at me, blinking heavily, supporting her chin with her right arm now resting on the table.

'Yoos have three, I only want one. Not greedy. Jus' one to call my – NO – *our* own. He wouldn't though see, said he couldn't stan to love an looooose like that again. Said he'd leave me if I gor pregnant. So!! Wos a girl to do eh?'

My head is slightly fuddled, never was very good at drinking during the day. It takes me a minute to catch up. Although Ruby and Andy are generally of gregarious character they were both extremely private about their loss of Lilly. As the years passed it was generally accepted that the mere mention of her name was taboo and most definitely not a subject open for discussion. I accepted and respected that. How was I supposed to know that secretly Ruby still yearned for another child?

I asked her if she'd spoken to Andy, explained to him how unhappy she was? She said no. She said he'd made his mind up years ago and she knew he'd never change it. I told her people do change and can change their minds. I said it wasn't too late, that more and more women were having children later in life. I told her she *must* speak to Andy. After all, didn't she owe it to Andy and most of all herself to explain how unhappy she was.

'Yoos sanctimonious bi *hiiccuupp* chhhh,' Ruby eventually replies. 'I don nee your fuckin pity and I defnee don nee your bloody judgement.'

Despite her unpleasant outburst I remain surprisingly calm. I'm just about to respond but Ruby beats me to it. More words spill from her mouth but these words are heavy, and they hit me like a sledgehammer to the stomach. I become paralysed and rooted to the spot. Although Ruby is drunk and slurring her words, these words are different, these words are crystal clear. I stare at her in disbelief, barely able to take in what I've just heard. Ruby shrugs her shoulders again and merely smirks back at me.

'Ooooppppps! Let the cat outta the bag there eh?' And with that Ruby attempts to stand up, placing both hands on the table to steady her. She heaves her drunken self up, and leaves.

Her words are still playing in my head, rattling around like marbles in a metal dish. Glass against metal, crashing and colliding with one another, spinning faster and faster until the whole sound translates into one continuous white noise. I am stunned. Surely Ruby didn't mean it? Surely I heard her wrong? Ruby was drunk for god sake. That's what it is, Ruby was drunk and got confused and I heard her wrong. She wouldn't – couldn't – do that to me. Could she? At least, that's what I try and tell myself. But I know, deep down, in the sick pit of my agitated stomach that every damning word playing over and over again in my head is true.

I remain in my seat, too horrified to move, eventually aware of someone standing next to me.

'Err excuse me Madam,' one of the waiters is saying. 'Ere is zi bill.'

*Oh fuck – she's left me with the bloody bill! I'm screwed.*

I smile weakly and cough to clear my throat. 'Ahem. Do you take credit cards?'

## CASSIE

I keep looking at the flowers Joe bought me and smile. Orange roses and yellow lilies, to say sorry for not coming to my college performance. He said he was shy, didn't want to do the "family" thing. I don't blame him. I wouldn't want to sit with my family either, but he could have come and sat somewhere else. Personally I think he was getting chonged with his friends again. Off his head and forgot all about me. Don't know why he has to do that stuff all the time? It's okay I suppose, now and again.

I look at the flowers again, bend over and sniff them. I sneeze. They smell sort of sweet, like Nan. It's the first time anyone has bought me flowers. Simon buys them for Mum all the time. I used to think it was like well soppy, rank even, but it's different when the person you love buys them for you. Joe still won't make us official on Facebook though, and he hasn't actually said he loves me, but why would he buy me flowers if he didn't love me?

Mum's in a well bad mood. She went to meet Ruby for dinner at Catalina's I think, but came home like, well angry. Not shouting and storming round the house like when we don't tidy up angry. I can still answer her back and get away with it when she's that sort of angry. This was a different angry. I don't think I've seen this angry side to her before, sort of quiet and seething, a black, blank angry. Everything about her, her voice, her body language, her death stare, everything told me not to mess with her. So I didn't.

I was going to ask her if I could borrow some money but I

swear Mum's eyes went black – like in the Twilight movies – so I changed my mind. I'd been talking about Ruby and when I looked at Mum's face she looked like she was going to burst into tears one minute then kill someone the next? I think Mum and Ruby have fallen out, which is weird, coz in all the years I've known Ruby I've never known her and Mum fall out.

I love Ruby. I hope Mum and Ruby make friends again soon.

## CHAPTER 26

### IT'S BEGINNING TO LOOK A LOT LIKE CHRISTMAS

**LIZZIE**

*E*very year I swear my cynical, socialist views will not be temporarily disabled and blindsided by some over sentimental, mawkish, consumer driven, drivelling TV advert. I will not be moved by a Christmas campaign designed to pull at the heartstrings whilst inadvertently directing the purse strings. I will not be moved, in any way, shape or form by advertising that has now become as much a part of the yuletide season as turkey, absurdly silly knitwear and mistletoe and woe in soapland. And yet, once again, this year like every other year finds me in the kitchen, after making excuses to absent myself, blubbing like a baby. I am, I have to admit, stirred by the genius of the Christmas advert.

Everyone has caught onto it. TV advertising with an emotional connection; nostalgia poked and provoked. So, here I sit, quite innocently minding my own business, watching the usual Saturday night TV when out of nowhere, during the commercial breaks, I am dragged, like poor old Ebenezer Scrooge, back through the memories of my Christmases past.

First there are the Christmases of long past – my own childhood. A childhood where my parents struggled but stayed together nonetheless; money was tight, carpets and wallpaper were a distasteful mix of browns and olive greens and always had some sort of flowery design. Flares, long hair and platform shoes were the order of the day for men as well as women, and life seemed a little more ... simple. We didn't have a lot but we were grateful for what we did have and filled the gaps with love. Then of course we are reminded of the big man himself; Christmas past but not so long ago. Depictions of a round, jolly, seventy something year old in a bright red, fur trimmed suit to match his beard with black shiny boots and the all-important sack of toys. Father Christmas doesn't live at our house anymore but through the power of advertising, I grieve his loss. I am reminded of those magical moments I created with Cassie and Connor – later Maisy and Simon too. Carrots left out for Rudolph and a mince pie and glass of sherry for Santa; decorating the tree to Christmas songs, then worn out and huddled together on the sofa, cup of hot chocolate in hand, watching something seasonal; and of course the squeals of delight at some ridiculous ungodly hour. And not a care in the world that I had nothing or very little to open, the giving far more enjoyable than the receiving.

Then of course there's Christmas present. Sulky, surly teenagers; the *yoof* of today aggrieved and embarrassed at their parents, grandparents or younger siblings' best efforts to include them in the festive seasons activities, only to be drawn in at the last minute under mock protest and duress. I sigh out loud, lost in an abyss of memories.

*Where has it gone? Where have all the years gone?*

'You okay babe?' Simon has sneaked up behind me. He

wraps his arms around my waist and holds me tight. I lay my hands on top of his and hold on for dear life. I don't reply. Simon thinks I'm mourning sentimental memories of Christmases past – which I am – but I'm also grieving the loss of my friend. My best friend.

'Christmas adverts eh? They get me every time too.' I swing round and look at Simon as he folds me into his chest. He strokes my hair and I can smell him, fresh, familiar and safe. I eventually look up.

'The kids are growing up fast eh?'

Simon tilts my chin up towards him and looks at me. 'Just remember the words of one very wise old man,' he replies. I frown – confused. 'It's not a life, it's an adventure!' Simon declares in his best cockney accent, which is in fact very poor. But it's done the trick and I'm smiling again. He bends down and kisses me. His lips are warm and hot on mine. He loves me but he also wants me. His passion is hard and evident, to me anyway, and for a moment I'm lost.

'Urrggghh, for god sake get a bloody room will you? That's like well gross,' Cassie, who has now joined us, says. A look of horror flicks across her face.

I laugh.

'You're just jealous,' Simon smirks.

'As if.'

'She's right Dad. It's really not right, get a bloody room.' Maisy has now joined us too, and trailing just behind her is Connor. He looks slightly puzzled.

'Why do Mum and Simon have to get a room?' he asks.

Everyone starts to laugh.

'Who wants hot chocolate?' Simon shouts.

## CASSIE

Perverts! Perverts! Perverts! It's Christmas Eve and that's what I'm surrounded by. A bunch of peodo pervs who left it to the last minute to buy their wives, girlfriends or whoever, their Christmas presents from the lingerie department. I wouldn't mind but the idiots don't even know the sizes they need. Really? How can you not know the size of the woman you're with? And saying things like, "about your size" or "like you but fatter" or "like you but thinner" really doesn't help. Neither does showing me a picture of her on your phone thank you very much. And stop picking all the pervy crotchless knickers and bras with removable nipple tassels. Women want class not crass. At least that's what Maria says.

Maria's dead sweet. She's a bit old like Mum, but she took a bit of a liking to me when I started working here and looks after me. She's dead funny too coz she keeps telling all the men off for leaving their Christmas shopping to the last minute. She says that saying they've had to work is not an excuse coz women work too, and they don't leave it to the last minute. I feel a bit sorry for some of them coz they look a bit sad after Maria's laid into them. They have that same look on their faces that Freddy – Nan and Grandad's dog – does when he's been told off.

Still, it's not been too bad today, although it really is a crime that people have to work on Christmas Eve. It should actually be illegal. It's Christmas Eve for god sake! All the chocolates are good though. We keep being given them as gifts by some of the customers and we put them in the fitting rooms and all the staff in the lingerie department sneak in and gorge on them. I actually think I've had too many today, though. Maybe that's why I feel sick. And oh my god, if I hear *Frosty The Snowman* one more time I think I'll bloody scream. The same six Christmas songs played on a continual loop is absolute torture. And just to add insult to injury Mum keeps playing the same bloody songs at home. I caught her dancing to them in the kitchen the other day. She didn't know I was there and I felt a bit sad when I watched her coz it reminded me of the Christmases when I was little. Mum would just randomly put Christmas songs on and me and her and Connor would dance round like idiots. It brought a lump to my throat as I watched her throw her moves. Why do adults dance so badly? I wish I'd danced with her.

'S'cuse me love,' someone says behind me. I turn to see a customer, a man, and he's ancient, at least 50 years old. 'You look like a lovely young lady,' he says. Oh god, not another perv. 'I wondered if you could help me choose some underwear for my daughter, she's about your age?'

'Your daughter?' I exclaim, before I can stop myself. Surely this man is a perv of the highest order. Why would a dad buy his daughter underwear? It's just too wrong. I try to be okay with him, but he's turned my stomach a bit. and I know my voice comes out all prim and huffy. 'Do you have her sizes?' I ask. He hands me a piece of paper.

'Wrote em down,' he says, smiling.

'Follow me,' I say a bit too snottily. We pass the crotchless knickers and the detachable nipple tassels. I shudder. I definitely need to get him away from this section. I'll take him to the pretty stuff then I'm leaving this pervert to it. I bet Joe would like crotchless knickers and nipples tassels. I suddenly blush at the thought. No, I couldn't, wouldn't dare wear them for him, even though we've done it, twice now. And he still won't make us official. My thoughts are rudely interrupted by the perv again.

'She could do with some of those bras that have a bit of padding,' he says, attempting to laugh. 'Bless her, there's not much to her.' Oh my god this man is a creep. I swing round to look at him. He looks embarrassed and steps back from me. 'Well that's what her Mum said,' he explains. He can clearly see the disgust I feel in my face coz his voice is like really nervous sounding now. 'My wife said to ask for the padded bras because it'll make her feel more grown up,' he gushes. 'It's the chemo you see. It makes her lose her appetite. It's her 16th birthday the day after Boxing Day, and we decided – my wife and I – to throw her a bit of a party. She's been so brave but missed out on so much. So we just wanted to make her feel special, and you know, grown up.'

Oh no, now I feel really bad.

'We've got her a dress and shoes and my wife was going to come and get her the underwear today but, but …' He trails off. He doesn't cry but his eyes start to fill up. 'Well, it's just that Mia, my daughter, wasn't well again today and she wanted her Mum. Kids always seem to want their Mum when they're ill don't they?'

I nod rapidly in agreement. It's true, when I came home drunk the other week and met up with Hughie and Ralph in the toilet (that's what Uncle Sean said it sounds like when you're throwing up) it was Mum I shouted for. Although, she didn't have to be so bloody moody coz I'm pretty convinced I did NOT wake the whole house up. I do remember Romeow sitting outside the bathroom scowling at me though.

'So I said I'd sort it,' the man continues. 'I was a bit worried because I thought everyone would think I was some sort of pervert,' he says, laughing. I kind of flinch and cringe inside. 'But I'll do anything for my girl. And I thought you looked really kind,' he says, looking straight into my eyes.

I squirm. Now it's my turn to be embarrassed. Yeah, lovely, kind, wonderful me who only moments ago was thinking what a huge, sick, perv you were. What's that saying – never judge a picture by its book or something? I feel so awful, I try to be extra nice.

The customer gets his phone out and shows me photos of

Mia with hair and photos of Mia without hair. He tells me she's been sick with leukaemia for two years and the outlook isn't good. He says both he and his wife have planned this big 16th birthday for Mia at home coz they're not sure she'll be around for her 17th. I suppose this man, this stranger could be telling me a pack of lies, could actually be a perv but something tells me he's not. There's something really genuine about him and I feel well bad for his sad, sad smiley face.

I help him pick out two lovely knickers and bra sets that I really like. I tell him about Nan having cancer and then I tell him what a lovely dad he is, not a complete knobhead like mine. He thanks me like tons and then wishes me a happy Christmas. I wish him one too, then, as I watch him walk away from the till, I have an amazing idea. I run after him and ask him if Mia would like a real live band to play at her party.

'We're not very good,' I tell him. 'In fact we're crap but we might make Mia laugh.'

The man smiles a really big smile but his eyes fill up again. He looks a bit embarrassed before he finally says, 'That would be wonderful, really lovely, but ... erm well, the thing is, we can't really afford to pay you.'

'You don't have to pay us! And anyway, we're that bloody bad you'd want your money back if you did,' I snort.

He says he's sure that's not true. I'm not, but I take his details and watch him walk away a happy man.

Oh my god I've just booked the band's first live, albeit unpaid, gig. OMG! What have I done?

## CHAPTER 27

T'WAS THE NIGHT BEFORE CHRISTMAS

**LIZZIE**

*I* almost enjoy Christmas Eve more than I do Christmas day. All is calm, all is quiet, the dinner to feed the five thousand tomorrow is prepped and the girls have been at work all day. Simon is out doing his Christmas shopping, which in truth means present buying for me left, as usual, to the last minute, and Connor and I have been lounging together, ensconced at either end of the sofa, watching an array of festive films, including my all-time favourite, *It's a Wonderful Life.*

'Mum,' Connor says wearing a quizzical look, 'so does the moral of that story mean that even when everything looks like it's going wrong or seems really bad, if you look at it from a different angle, it's still a wonderful life?'

'Erm, yeah I guess so,' I reply, relishing this one to one time without interruption from sulky, surly teenagers. 'I suppose it's also reminding us that good friends and family touch and influence our lives, more often than not in a good way, but that we don't always appreciate it at the time.' I think of Ruby as I finish saying this. I think of all the times she was there for me.

*Or they can ruin everything you ever believed about them.*

Connor looks thoughtful. He never really says much, always happy to go with the flow, never one to make waves like his sisters'.

'Soooo, you mean like how Simon has been good with me and Cassie and you have with Mai ... I mean Mania?' he asks. I flush a little, almost embarrassed to accept my son's obvious compliment.

*Clearly you've done something right.*

'It doesn't always feel like it,' I reply out loud.

'Nah, I know,' Connor replies, before I have time to explain that I was actually talking to myself, again. 'Cas and Mai – I mean Mania – both call you a bit ...' Connor trails off mid-word covering his mouth with both hands. He looks positively mortified if albeit a little amused at the same time.

I raise my eyes and examine him above my reading glasses. 'Yeah well,' he continues. 'They do call you *that word* sometimes, but only when they're angry.'

*Which is all of the time then.*

'But most of the time they only say good stuff about you.'

'Really?'

*That's a bloody revelation.*

'And funny. They think you're funny coz you dance sort of stupid.' Now it's my turn to look mortified. 'Not stupid stupid, but you know, weird, like grown-ups do.' His intonation carries with it a reassurance that I might understand this explanation.

Suddenly the door bursts open bringing in a waft of cold air and Cassie.

'Waz up losers?' she says throwing herself onto the sofa. 'Hey Cas,' Connor replies. 'I was just telling Mum that you and Mai –

I mean Mania – think Mum's well funny when she dances.' A huge grin spreads across Cassie's face.

'She is. You are,' she says looking at me. 'What is it with old people not being able to dance anyways?' Cassie then jumps up and does an alarmingly good impression of me dancing. Connor tries, for at least two seconds, to contain his laughter before rolling around the floor in hysterics. I love the sound of Connor laughing. His voice hasn't broken yet and it's still wonderfully childlike. Before I know it the room is filled with raucous laughter.

'Thank god I'll never embarrass my children with my dancing,' Cassie blurts out in between our collective guffaws.

'What makes you so sure?' I ask.

'Because err, duh? Unlike your generation, my generation can actually dance.' As our laughter subsides Connor wanders off into the kitchen in search of food.

'How was work?' Cassie shrugs her shoulders. She looks so like Scott when she frowns.

'S'okay I s'pose. Full of perverts.'

'Perverts?'

'Yeah, perverts,' Cassie repeats, as if what she's saying makes perfect sense. 'I got the band a gig with one of them though.' I raise my eyes in alarm. 'Well like actually he turned out *not* to be a perv, he was just buying underwear for his daughter.'

*Oh yes, I can see that makes perfect sense.*

'And it's like well sad and everything coz she – the perv who's not a perv's daughter – has cancer. So we're doing the gig for free.'

'Well, that's lovely Cassie,' I say, my heart swelling with pride. 'Very commendable, very spirit of Christmas and all that.' Cassie smiles at me. 'Yeah,' she replies, 'it is, isn't it? Makes you think though, doesn't it?' She looks lost in thought for a moment. 'Anyway, we sound bloody awful, so if nothing else we'll make her laugh.'

The door opens again and Maisy walks in. Despite her thick black make-up I spot her red puffy eyes. Cassie looks at her then rolls her eyes at me.

'Right,' she declares, standing up. 'I need to get ready coz I'm going out in an hour.'

'Where are you going?'

'To Pheebs.'

'Not the Old Shuck then?'

'Yeah, maybe later, for a bit, to meet Joe and everyone. It is his uncle's pub after all.'

'Careful,' I warn her. 'No alcohol and not home too late. It's a big day tomorrow. Everyone's coming to dinner and I want you sociable and awake.' Cassie scrunches her nose up and rolls her eyes at me again.

'For god bloody sake Mum, it's Christmas bloody Eeeeeeve.' I look at her with pursed lips. Cassie slumps forward. 'Kay, o bloody kay.'

I'm sure I hear her mumble the words "fun sucker" before she slams the door and disappears up the stairs faster than her normally work-wearied legs carry her. I hear a loud thud.

'For god bloody sake Romeow,' she yells out. 'Are you trying to bloody kill me? Stupid bloody cat. It's all your bloody fault Mum,' Cassie shouts down the stairs. 'I bet you train him to try and kill me don't you?'

*What a good idea.*

Much to my relief Cassie laughs, before I hear her disappear into the bathroom and turn on the shower.

Maisy shakes her head and grins. 'Psycho,' she says.

'What me or Cassie?' I reply smiling.

Maisy crosses both her arms across her chest and shrugs her shoulders. 'Both,' she states.

*Well that's two words she's said to you, one more and she's said her quota for the day.*

'How was work?'

Maisy shrugs her shoulders again. 'S' okay.'

'Not full of perverts then?'

Maisy looks at me, positively dumbfounded. 'What?'

'Never mind,' I laugh. 'It was just something Cassie said earlier.'

*She really does think you're a psycho.*

I sigh inwardly. This step-parenting malarkey doesn't get any easier, even after all these years. Come to think of it, parenting in any form is bloody difficult – full stop.

'It's already Christmas day in Australia,' Maisy suddenly blurts out before bursting into tears. I walk over to her and sit down next to her. I know if this were Cassie I'd pull her into my arms and hold her, but it's still not that easy with Maisy. She's never been particularly demonstrative with her affections, even with Simon.

I don't think Simon and I were ever particularly unrealistic in our expectations of closeness and intimacy with each other's children. We knew it would take time, but how much time?

*Oh sod it, trust your instincts and just hug the girl already.*

*Can't you see how upset she is?*

I reach into Maisy's personal space and pull her next to me; rocking her softly, reassuring her everything will be okay. I'm pleasantly surprised to find she lets me. We sit like this for several minutes before I gently pull away and suggest a nice cup of hot chocolate with marshmallow and cream. Maisy looks at me through black mascara stained eyes and smiles. Then something amazing happens.

Two words.

'Thanks Mum,' she says.

Up to this point I've always been known as "you're not my

Mum" or "Lizzie" and clearly as Connor pointed out earlier also an assortment of other less flattering names including "bitch" and "psycho" but never, in all these years, "Mum". I'm a little flustered and overwhelmed.

It's true then, miracles really do happen at Christmas.

&

## CASSIE

'Cassie, Cassie, get up, get up, its Christmas morning!'

'What, who, where ...' I croak. 'Is that you Dad?' Uggghhh god why is the room moving?

'No stupid, course it's not Dad. It's me, Connor.' Obviously it's Connor, why would I think it's Dad? We haven't spent Christmas with Dad for years. 'C'mon Cas,' Connor continues excitedly. 'Get uuuuppp! It's Christmas morning! Everyone's here. Well, Nan and Grandad, and Uncle Sean and Natasha and Summer. Even Maisy's up. We're all waiting for you!'

'Oh god, I really don't feel well,' I mumble. My mouth is drier than hot sand and my tongue is sticking to the roof of my mouth. I try to lift my head off the pillow but I swear the bed starts to move.

'What's wrong with you?'

'Don't shout,' I plead.

'I'm not,' Connor replies. 'I'm just talking normally but I reckon you're hanging.'

I'll tell Mum,' he says bouncing back off the bed.

'No!' I shout. Ouch, I lower my voice again coz shouting hurts. 'Its fine, I'm fine. Just give me two minutes and I'll be there.'

'Okay,' Connor replies, leaving my room, snapping on the light on his way out. Arrrrrggghhh, I feel as though I've just been blinded. The bright light bores into my eyes and forces me to take cover under the duvet. O M G. How much did I drink last night? I thought I only had two drinks? I can't let Mum know I'm hanging; she'll kill me what with it being Christmas bloody day and everything.

I count to ten, take a deep breath then attempt to get out of bed. Slowly. Even the sound of my bare feet on the carpet is too loud and ugh ... oh god, I think I'm going to be sick. A wave of cold sweat runs through me and I swear I can feel the blood from my head drain into my feet. I hold onto anything and everything as I try and navigate my way to the bathroom. My stomach feels as though it's folding in on itself and the hot burning taste of sick is rising in my throat.

I make it just in time to meet Hughie and Ralph at the bottom of the white porcelain loo bowl. I spit out the pieces of sick that are trapped around my teeth and use the sleeve of my dressing gown to wipe the dribbles of vomit sitting around my mouth. I'm well chuffed though, coz I feel surprisingly better, except for the pneumatic drill in my head, that is. I try to clean my teeth to get rid of my skanky breath but even that's too noisy.

I look up at myself in the mirror as the toothpaste foams around my mouth. My eyes are all bloodshot, framed by black smudged mascara and my face is a disgusting chalky white colour. I turn my head and look at my side profile. Yep, still have my downright bloody offensive nose with its humongous bump. Thanks Mum. Am defo gonna get a nose job when I get enough money.

I stop mid-brush as the memory of last night comes flooding back to me. That's right; I was drinking some alcohol but not much. I was only going to have one or two but then I stupidly tried to keep up with that girl Joe was flirting with. Why does he do that to me? Why does he do all that crap and tell me I'm like special and everything but then not make it official and flirt with other girls? And why, when he treats me like shit, do I still fancy him soooo much? And why, when Luke treats me like a princess and is into music like me, do I not in any way whatsoever fancy him?

Oh god I can hear Mum calling me. And now the bloody dog is barking, which is like well bloody loud. Each and every yap and woof crashes into my ears. I swear my ears are going to split open in a minute. I can't even shout at Freddy to stop coz the sound of my voice is too loud for my thumping head.

I walk down the stairs, slowly. I use one hand to hold the banister and the other to hold my forehead as the thud of each step sounds much louder than it probably is. I walk into the living room to thunderous applause and shouting. Oh god. Now I think my head's actually going to explode.

'Bout bloody time, gal,' Grandad shouts.

'At last!' Connor declares.

'Someone's hanging a bit heavy, eh Cas?' Uncle Sean says, grinning. Mum shoots me what looks like a look of disapproval. Thanks Uncle Sean, I was hoping to get away with it.

Mum disappears for a minute. God knows what she's doing but I'm probably well and truly in for it now. Nan looks at me over her reading glasses and smiles, a sort of knowing look. Maisy and Nat are talking. They both smirk when they look across at me. Summer runs up to me and flings her arms around my waist. Was I really that small once?

'Happy Christmas Cassie!' she shouts, nearly squeezing me to death.

'He's been, you know? Father Christmas I mean, he's been,' Summer continues excitedly. She's all wide eyed and full of wonder. She makes me smile but my throat tightens and I suddenly feel a bit sad. I kinda get that Dad doesn't like me much at the moment, especially when I cry and yell at him. But how could he not have wanted me when I was little, like

Summer? I'm trying so hard to hold back my tears but one stupid one manages to escape and is running down my cheek. I lower my head and quickly put my hand up to my face to wipe it away. When I look up again, Simon is standing next to me.

'Happy Christmas Cas,' he says, with his warm, smiley face. I can't reply, so I look at him and nod my head up and down in response, just in case any more tears escape. I think he gets it coz he smiles and winks at me.

'Happy Christmas, trouble.' I turn to see Mum standing behind me with tea, toast and paracetamol. I laugh and the tears fall now anyway.

'Thanks Mum,' I manage to say. 'Happy Christmas.'

## CHAPTER 28

LOVE IS ALL AROUND

**LIZZIE**

*I* scan our living room and take in the mass of bodies that are now very quiet but up until an hour ago were as riotous and strident as any football or rugby match. Such is the eclectic gathering of our family Christmas dinner.

Has it been stressful?

*Yes.*

Am I exhausted? *Abso-bloody-lutely.* Is it worth it?

*Without a doubt.*

Life is so hectic. Christmas is the one time of the year that forces us to remember each other for a while; even if it just to remind us, in some instances, seeing each other once a year is enough.

Some of the bodies that made up the Christmas jamboree have disappeared for one reason or another and the sounds now filling the room with the remaining few are not silence but contented exhaustion. Dad and Uncle Teddy are almost mirror images of each other. Sat on one of the two cat clawed sofas, legs outstretched displaying compulsory Christmas socks and hands locked across full stomachs as if guarding an item of superlative and priceless value, leant back, eyes closed and open mouthed as if catching flies.

Connor, still going, is ensconced in one of the four corners of the room with Summer. His laptop perches precisely on crossed legs and he is clearly in his element, beating his younger cousin at one or other of his many amusing computer games. Mum, with one eye closed, the other focussed on the flickering images of the TV nods, mostly out of politeness, to the muffled ramblings of Aunt Marie sat next to her.

Sean is sat outside the living room via the patio door leading to the garden. He has pulled up an old plastic garden chair that has seen better days and, with his back to us, is smoking. Maisy has joined him and is, I'm pretty convinced, smoking too.

Simon, sprawled across the floor, is talking to his cousin, Mike. Andy would have been with them if he were here. Their heads are leant against fully occupied sofas, sipping whiskey and talking inebriated bullshit. I feel sad that Andy isn't here. Every now and then Simon looks up at me, and smiles. I smile back at my lovely man. The only people missing are Ruby and Andy. I miss them both dreadfully, but seeing them is not an option. I feel lost without Ruby in my life, like I've lost a sister – except a sister wouldn't betray and hurt me like Ruby did. I still can't quite believe what she did. I wake up some mornings thinking it was all a bad dream, which it is in a way. I haven't told Simon why I'm not talking to Ruby, he just thinks we've had a bit of a falling out and we'll make it up. We won't though. How can I?

Ruby did try to contact me. Bombarded me with messages via phone and every form of social media known to man, woman and child, for a couple of weeks, imploring me to speak to her, to let her explain. I wanted to, but when I remembered what she told me, what she'd done, I couldn't, I just couldn't. I can't see her because ... I can't forgive her. I've tried, really tried, to find forgiveness in my heart, but I can't.

Cassie, who, surprisingly out of choice, is sat next to me on our other cat ravaged sofa, is both equally engrossed in the film (*Love Actually,* one of our favourites) I am half watching and her phone. She stares intently at the TV, smiling or frowning depending on what particular emotion is evoked with each scene but her viewing is constantly interrupted throughout. A continuous stream of various dinging, ringing, swishing, swooshing and tweeting sounds emanate from the small device that is as much a physical part of her as her hand itself.

Cassie doesn't know I am, but I'm watching her. Quietly laughing to myself as she holds her phone out in front of her – at arm's length – pulling several strange faces, using her free hand to bouffant the back of her hair. She tilts her head to one side and puckering her lips – the most worked out muscle in Cassie's entire body, Simon says – takes yet *another* selfie. One of several million, I assume.

I'm slightly drunk, but happy-ish. It hasn't been a particularly easy year, financially and otherwise but, whether it's through blood or friendship, I'm very rich in the love that surrounds me tonight. As if on cue Hugh Grant's voice reminds me – like the song – that *Love Is All Around.* Cassie and I look at each other and laugh realising, we've both said the words out loud and in unison.

'Mu-m,' Cassie says.

'Yes Cassie?'

'Well, I just wanted to say – thanks.'

'For what?'

'Ummmm ... everything.'

# CHAPTER 29

## NOW IS THE WINTER OF OUR DISCONTENT

**LIZZIE**

Maybe it's the short days and the long nights responsible for my current malaise. Christmas was nice but hectic as usual and as we left behind another year and saluted a new one, I experienced an overwhelming sense of gloom. My Christmas good cheer was I fear packed away and assigned to the loft with the tree and decorations.

Maybe I'm just not genetically programmed to cope with the cold and never ending winters this one already is. Snow for a couple of days can be wonderful. Especially when it settles and one is observing it behind a cosy, centrally heated window. I hope to god Raj's parents have put the heating on by now. Watching large flakes of the white stuff float down featherlike against an inky black sky is mesmerising. Falling faster and thicker, swabs of cotton wool cover and conjoin everything in its path. Nothing escapes its descent. Soft and soundless, its assault is ruthless, concealing everything in its wake. The discernible quickly becomes the indiscernible. All is a whitewash of white, regardless. All is one, for a while.

But then it melts and turns to slush or worse, it freezes and mastering mobility becomes purgatory. Fifteen layers of clothing are required before leaving the house along with obligatory hat, scarf and gloves. What was crisp and bright and white is now grey and dark and damp. Murky mornings travelling into work melt into bleak evening's returning home from work. I have a bloody Roman nose for god sake. I'm just not built for this crap. I sigh inwardly and examine my nose in the bathroom mirror. I hated it at school, used to dream of the perfect little ski jump nose that plastic surgery would achieve. Why are we never happy with what we've got? Why do we always compare ourselves to others instead of keeping the comparisons within? I still can't believe Ruby looked at my fraught and complicated life and saw something preferable to her own. But then, I still can't believe Ruby, full stop. She wished me a happy new year via text. I didn't reply of course, and I haven't heard anything since.

I take in a side profile of my face. Nope, am still okay with the nose. I'm happy to say I grew into it. I am however a lot less happy about the visible march of time across my face, especially the crow's feet and wrinkles and in particular the ones around my eyes. Oh god, what could I achieve with a face from twenty years ago and all this knowledge? Youth is most definitely wasted on the young.

Cassie is calling me.

*What now? What has your unpaid skivvy not done now eh?*

Oh god. Is this actually as good as it gets? Shackled and weighed down by a duty of caring for others but at the same time no sense of anchorage, no sense of self.

Maybe I'm having a break-down or a mid-life crisis or worse still maybe it's the onset of the menopause?

Happy bloody New Year! My phone pings. I swipe the screen and am told that one of my friends has made a status. It's Jodi.

*Is it Wine O' Clock yet???!!!*

I smile. What a jolly good idea.

I must find a way to impede this on-going trepidation, void of hope for my future. Oh well, the Straw Bear festival is imminent. Always a good excuse for a bloody good knees up, and who knows, the snow may even disappear?

CASSIE

I think Mum has that SAD disease. The one where winter makes you depressed or something coz she's like dead moody at the moment. It's funny coz they're the same letters I've got Dad stored under in my phone. SAD coz he is, SAD coz that's how he makes me feel and SAD for Stupid Arsehole Dickhead.

Anyway, Mum didn't have to bloody snap my head off like she did. I only asked her if my pink dress was washed ... and if she could give me a lift to town. Oh yeah and if she could lend me thirty quid till the end of the month ... and if I could have the Band round for pizza before practise next week ... and if Honey was okay to sleep over for the Straw Bear, oh and of course if she could give a few of us a lift to the band's gig on Friday, and a lift home of course. It's only eighty miles away for god bloody sake. What's the big bloody deal? Psycho. You'd think she'd be happy to help me. She doesn't exactly lead the most interesting life in the world. That's why I don't understand her being such a stress head. I mean, really, what does she have to stress about? Try being me I say, then you'll really understand what stress is. I have work stress, college stress, Band stress, Joe Stress, Luke stress, Pheeb stress, Honey stress, piano stress *and* of course DAD stress. And then, *please*, don't even get me started on my fat arse, small boobs and Roman nose stress. Stress, stress, stress. My life is like, well, one long ... STRESS!

Honey is jabbering away at a hundred miles an hour as usual and is now trying on her fiftieth outfit for the Straw Bear. She's like dead excited about it, thinks it's quaint. She says she's never been to anything like this coz she's just lived in the city all her life and this is like a traditional small town event, a pagan festival celebrated for as long as I can remember. Although there are a few locals who think of it more as one long pub-crawl. Connor's even doing a Morris dance at twelve o' clock in the market square. Cringe. I officially disown him, do not know him, am in no way related to him until it's done and his ribbons and hankies and bells are removed.

I like that Honey just rambles on and on coz it means as long as I fix my gaze on her yappy mouth and keep up a constant stream of listening noises I can actually just drift off for a while and think of Joe. Why did he tell me he loved me the other day and then deny it? I know he was drunk but don't people – boys I mean – don't boys tell the truth when they're drunk? Uncle Sean says not. Uncle Sean says boys say whatever they need to say to get whatever they want to get when they're drunk. Harsh. I think he's wrong though. He's just old – although not as old as Mum – and cynical. He's just forgotten what it's like to be young.

So, does that mean Joe does really love me? Even though he still won't make us official? I've got butterflies just thinking about him. Mum doesn't like him; I know she doesn't, even though she acts all friendly in front of him. It's all false, all just an act.

'Hello Joe. How are you?' she says. 'Would you like a cuppa?'

I've heard her though, moaning to Simple when she thinks

no-one can hear, usually about me and Maisy, never about the perfect child. She says she's fed up with Maisy's surly face and bad attitude. I suppose, to be fair to Mum, Mai – I mean Mania – does look like she's going to murder you sometimes if you ask her about Crazee. And she gets dead moody if she doesn't hear from him for a couple of days. And she blamed Mum when Simon and Mum said they didn't have enough money to lend her for the flight to Oz. I do feel sorry for Maisy though, and I get it. She's in love and desperately missing her boy. Why do old people not understand that?

Mum definitely doesn't like Joe. She thinks he's using me, said she doesn't understand why I can't fall for someone like the lovely Luke. Poor Luke, he is lovely but you can't help who you bloody love, Mum. Look at you with Simple for god's sake. Or worse than that, Dad, once! Why don't I fancy Luke though? He is quite good looking, although not quite as much as Joe, he likes music, he likes me for god sake. He always answers my texts and calls and is never too busy with his stone head friends to see me, and yet, I've put him well and truly in the friend zone.

'Cas, Cassie, are you listening to me?'

I look up to see Honey strutting catwalk style across my bedroom.

'Well? What do you think?' she says running her hand across the tiniest, shortest dress in all of history.

'Ammmmazing. You look gaw-jus Honey. All the boys will be wishing they were girls, or at least spend most of the day thinking they have what it takes to convert you.' Her laugh is as loud, as usual. 'Won't you be cold though?'

'Nah,' she replies covering her tiny dress with the tiniest jacket and biggest scarf I've ever seen.

'Oh well, that's okay then. And at least it's stopped snowing.'

## CHAPTER 30

### THE BURNING OF THE BEAR

**LIZZIE**

Oh my god. Is that banging sound the noise of real drums or just the rhythm of my thumping head? I lay very still. I'm pretty convinced if I move, my head will explode. Somewhere beyond this bedroom, life is unfolding. My ears pick up familiar sounds. Toilets flush, showers run and hairdryers blow. Muffled conversations are diffused with guttural guffaws and raucous screams. I can hear the dishwasher being loaded. It must be Simon. God forbid one of the kids actually noticed it needed doing. Just another Saturday morning and yet, not far from my bedroom window in the outside world, I also detect the foreign sounds of flutes, bells, whistles and the periodic clash of metal and wooden swords. The festival is already in full flow.

Unfortunately, I partook in a little too much festival spirit at the barn dance last night. As is custom the Straw Bear began in earnest yesterday evening and will continue throughout the whole of today, culminating in the Burning of the Bear tomorrow. Originally taking place on Plough Tuesday, the Straw Bear is a long standing local tradition going back at least a couple of hundred years. Every year a man is covered from head to foot in straw and where once was led from house to house in exchange for gifts of food, money or beer, now leads a procession of street entertainment.

A good night was had by all – I think? I wonder if Jodi's as hung over as me. That apple and raspberry cider was potent, went down far too easily, hence the hammer in my head this morning.

'Mum,' Connor says breathlessly, bursting into my room. 'Have you seen my sword? Oh...you're not even up yet? What's wrong? You don't look so good? Are you hung over? Are you going to miss me dancing on the Market Square?' He sounds worried. 'Coz I was really hoping you'd be there, to see me?'

*Bloody hell, he's turning into Cassie.*

'I'm fine love,' I lie. 'Just a bit of a headache. I'll be there, don't you worry. Not going to miss my boy and his sword fighting.'

Connor sighs. 'It's not sword fighting Mum, it's dancing with swords.'

Suddenly the door crashes open. 'Mum!' Cassie shouts. 'Oh, you're not even up yet?' She looks at Connor with disgust. 'What you doing in here, loser? I thought you had some stupid hankie waving, bell ringing, Morrissey dance to do?' Connor rolls his eyes and sighs heavily.

'It's a sword dance Cassie, a Long Sword dance. Not Morris dancing.'

'Yeah, whatevs. It's bloody ridiculous is what it is. Just don't talk to me while you're wearing that stupid costume okay?'

Connor lowers his head. 'I'm going to look for my sword.'

'Oh dear,' Cassie says turning back to me. 'Who had a little too much bragget last night then eh?'

*Only to drown out your incessant whinging about Joe. Again!*

'Who's hanging this morning then?' Cassie continues, grinning. 'I have some great news though.'

*What? You've finally seen the light and dumped Joe?*

'You're never gonna believe this?'

*Probably not ... but then again?*

'Try me,' I say forcing a smile.

'Well, I've just been speaking to Joe...'

*Oh god here we go again.*

'And guess what?'

'I couldn't if I tried.'

'He's only gonna go and make us official, on Facebook, with a picture and everything!'

'Wow!'

'Isn't it! I think it's coz I was so upset last night?'

*You don't say.*

'And I finally told him, gave him an ultimatum. Said I was sick of this casual shit and if he didn't make it official I'm done with him.'

*Like you were done with him on Wednesday, and last week, and the week before that?*

'Anyway I was talking to him, just now on the phone. Oh yeah, Honey said thanks for letting her stay by the way. She's dead excited. Anyway, where was I? Oh yeah, so I was just talking to Joe on the phone and he said like he'd given some thought to everything I said to him last night.'

*Screamed at him you mean.*

'And he said he's prepared to take it – us – to the next level. Isn't that aammaazinng?'

I resist the urge to laugh, or do I mean cry? Maybe both?

'I know like it's the Straw Bear and he's probably drunk already but ... well, people tell the truth when they're drunk. Don't they?'

Does she really want me to answer that? Whatever I say will be wrong.

*Yep, you're fucked.*

Cassie looks at me, waiting for my reply. 'Well?' she asks. I attempt a smile but remain silent.

'Cas? Cassie babe?' Honey calls out. 'You ready?' Thank god for that. Saved by the bell or in this case, the Honey.

To my slight embarrassment Honey wanders into my room. I try to sit up and press my hair down with the palms of my hands.

'Hey Lizzie,' she says. 'Hello Honey,' I reply.

'God, you look like, well rough,' she continues, perching on the end of the bed.

'Thanks.'

'S'okay, don't worry, we all look crap without our make-up on. I could do yours if you want? I'm quite good at doing old people. I might even be able to make you look a bit younger?'

I decline her very generous offer and tell the girls I'll look for them both at the festival later.

*Yeah, see em and run you mean.*

They leave my room and I breathe a sigh of relief, throwing the duvet back over my throbbing head.

'Oh by the way,' Cassie says. She has come back into my room again. 'I'm going with Honey to the STD clinic on Monday.'

'WHAT?' I exclaim throwing the duvet off again.

'Yeah, she thinks one of her exes might have Chlamydia so I'm gonna go with her – you know, for support.'

I open my mouth to speak then close it again. Then open it again and close it again. Cassie laughs.

'Okay,' I eventually reply.

'Sees ya later.'

'Yeah. See you later.'

I'm flattered Cassie feels she can talk to me, tell me things, intimate things, but can there be too much honesty between a mother and her daughter? I sigh. Oh well, at least they're being sensible.

## CASSIE

For once in her life Honey is quiet, mesmerised by the colour and noise of a heaving town that only days ago was quiet and boring. The Straw Bear dances in the main street and a procession of people follow him, cheering, banging drums and waving sticks with bells on.

Honey spots Joe up ahead disappearing into the pub with the usual crowd so we follow them. My phone pings, it's a text from Mia – she says she's too ill to come today which is like, a real shame coz I think she would have loved all this madness. But it is bloody cold. Freezing actually. I feel as though my bloody face is gonna crack like an ice cube in a minute, so it's probably just as well she didn't come.

I love Mia. I'm so glad she liked the underwear I helped her Dad Clive (the perv who isn't a perv) pick out for her. She is brave too. Mostly for fighting cancer but also for letting The Incandescent Adolescents play at her birthday party. She said we were brilliant and is like, our number one fan. Everyone did seem to really like us despite the fact we went wrong a couple of times. And of course Honey tripped over one of the amps, her skinny, long legs flapping open and her short, short skirt riding up showing her tiny black thong. I swear she almost gave some of the Dads watching us heart attacks (some of the Mums too, actually). Some of the Dads were like, actually drooling at the mouth. Pervs. Oh well, it gained us a few more fans.

I still can't believe Blue Horizon turned up to sing a couple of songs too. Maisy asked her bass player Ralph, who she's been a friend with since our first college performance (and, as it turns out, is also friends with Crazee) to ask her. I didn't think she'd like, actually turn up, coz she's becoming like well famous now, but I think she was like well moved by Mia's cancer and stuff. Blue Horizon whose real name is Jessica (I prefer Blue Horizon) and is sooo sick and sooo talented said we, the band, were amazing and she's gonna like our Facebook page. I don't think we are that good – we're not bad – just okay. At the moment anyway. But we're getting better and thanks to Mia and her friends we're starting to get a real following now.

I don't know what's up with Mum not being up and ready this morning. That's so not like her. She's been acting weird for months now, ever since her and Ruby fell out. I still can't believe they're not speaking. They've been the bestest of friends for like, forever – surely whatever the problem is they can sort it out? Mum won't tell anyone, not even Simon, why they've fallen out. I mean really, like for god sake, it's just so bloody childish. I actually think it's Mum just being a complete bitch coz Ruby keeps trying to arrange to meet up with Mum but Mum just ignores her. I know, coz I've seen some of the texts Ruby sent Mum, except Mum doesn't know I know.

Oh shit, Joe's just come out of the pub. With some bloody girl draped all over him! Why? Why does he bloody do this to me?

## LIZZIE

Simon brings me a much-needed cup of coffee. He tells me Connor found his sword and has gone off to practice with the other members of the team before their big performance at the Market Square.

'You will be there to watch him?' Simon asks.

'Course I will.'

'You okay babe? You don't seem yourself lately?'

'In what way?'

'Dunno, just sort of ... distracted?'

I look at Simon's concerned face. *If only you knew!*

'I'm fine, honest.'

He smiles. 'Really?'

'Really. Now go on, bugger off and let me get ready. I heard Andy's voice downstairs so I know you're itching to go.'

'You sure, because I'll wait if you want?'

'Bugger off!!!'

'Okay,' he says, kissing the top of my head. 'We're taking Maisy with us because she's pleading poverty, again.' I roll my eyes. 'And, well ...' Simon pauses at the door, 'are you sure you don't want me to ask Andy to ask Ruby to come ...?'

I shake my head. 'No!'

Simon sighs. 'I wish you two would bloody work this – whatever it is – out. You've been friends for years, since you were kids. Surely...'

'Leave it Simon,' I snap. 'Not now, okay?'

Simon shrugs his shoulders and holds his hands up in surrender. 'Okay, okay. You're the boss.'

And with that he is gone. The house is quiet.

The truth is I'm happy to let Simon go for a while. I need

time to apply my mask, and I'm not just talking about make-up. And it's still cold out. The snow's cleared but its bitter, which only adds to my misery. Besides, it won't be the same without Ruby. Mum and Dad will be about but they'll probably watch Connor then go home. There'll be plenty of other people for me to join in with though, to follow the procession of the bear; stopping off at most of the town's drinking houses along the way, but I'm not feeling it this year.

I feel so betrayed by Ruby. Why? How could she do that to me? The anger that has fuelled me over the last few months has subsided and I'm now left with a desperate pain that won't heal. Why did Ruby tell me? She'd kept it quiet for all those years, so why tell me at all? Ignorance is bliss. I've been through enough. So why? WHY hurt me like that? Was it to ease her conscience, make herself feel better? But look at the cost, look at the devastation she's caused me! Sometimes honesty is NOT the best policy. She should have kept her fat mouth shut. I loved and trusted her and now that's all gone. Ruined. Forever.

My thoughts are spiralling out of control. I need to get out of here. Me and my thoughts are not a good combination. I need Simon. Not that he'll even notice if I'm there or not today. It's the one time of year Simon becomes quite blokeish. There's something about a group of men, real ale and a pagan festival. It's like watching a load of bullocks, talking bollocks. And where, or why for that matter, do they find the smut in everything? But, when the herd convenes, rules and codes must be adhered to – apparently.

I drag my malaise and myself to the bathroom and shower. Thank god I'm not working today. I felt totally deflated after Amber's outburst yesterday afternoon. It's not that enough both my daughters appear to blame me for everything wrong in their lives, but Amber does too.

'That's what yoos gets for helping,' Raj had said, rather unhelpfully.

That's all very well, but don't those of us who can help ourselves have a duty to help those who can't? Amber is part of a system set up to fail her. What a sad indictment for one so deprived, born and raised in the thirteenth globally prosperous country in the world.

Temporarily employed for Christmas, Amber was thriving. I saw a change in her, we all did. She worked hard and enjoyed earning her own money. She knuckled down, gracefully accepting any training or criticism, the first to accept extra hours to cover the Christmas rush. She worked her bloody butt off. And, what did she get, after Christmas, in return for her positive work ethic? The offer of a nine-hour a week contract, that's what. How in god's name is anyone supposed to support themselves on nine bloody hours spread across the week? And, not even the same days from week to week.

She wasn't deterred though and with a little help from yours truly, used her experience to apply for other jobs. And what is her reward for her diligence and application? Zero hour contracts that's what. I can't blame the girl for exploding.

'You lied,' she screamed. 'I did everything you told me, everything I was supposed to and it's all just gone to rat shit. Why? Why would you get my hopes up like that? Don't you realise there's no hope for losers like me?'

It's just a pity Amber felt the need to share her distress with not only me, but every other patron in the library, and then consequently thrown out. Thankfully I pleaded Amber's corner – again – and managed to persuade Amira not to ban her completely. I hope Amber didn't mean what she said about getting pregnant?

I step into the shower. The water feels good. More grey hair discovered, including pubes – not good. Must make an appointment with the hairdressers. I step out of the shower and dress in a hurry. I give my hair a few blasts of the hairdryer then stick it under a woolly hat; at least it'll cover the grey.

With twenty minutes to spare before Connor's performance, I step outside. The snow's gone but there's still a painful chill in the air. Grey hair or no, the hat, which I pull further down, is staying on regardless. A cold tremor shoots up the back of my spine causing me to shudder. I instinctively spin round almost expecting to see someone watching me. Ruby maybe? The street is overflowing with people but I don't notice anyone in particular. I shrug it off. Must just be the cold weather.

I stick my gloved hands into my coat pockets and make my way towards the centre of town. The sky is dirty dishwater grey and a slight wind nips on contact carrying an unwelcome sting. I've only been out the house for a couple of minutes and, despite my many winter-proof layers (thank god for thermal vests), I'm already cold. Slowly but surely the warm blood running through my veins begins to cool and harden like ice. It's one of those red nosed, runny eyed, straight to the core, bone cold days.

I think of Connor and instantly feel bad. Hello guilt my old friend. Why is it some of us are pre-disposed to carry tons of the stuff yet others like Scott, and even Ruby for that matter, are blissfully unaware of its existence? I should have got up earlier, made sure Connor was warm enough, wished him luck. God, I hope he wore his vest.

Poor Connor, he never really gets a look in with the girls. I wonder if he'll hate me as much as they do, one day. Must give him lots of praise today.

My self-indulgent melancholy is temporarily hindered as I push my way through swarms of people gathered along every street. Our small and usually quiet town is bustling and bursting at the seams. An infestation of locals and visitors alike follow the bear made of straw, enthusiastically entertained by an entourage of story tellers and street acts. Musicians provide a melodic din across an eclectic sound of instruments. Bagpipes, harmonicas, mandolins and hurdy-gurdys intertwine with the heartbeat of base and side drums to well-known songs such as the *The Curly Headed Ploughboy* and the *Old Drove Road*. Flamboyant costumes of the Morris, Molly, Rapper and Long Sword dancers inject a welcome relief of colour into the drab and dreary backdrop. Technicolor tatter-coats dazzle the eye, as do some of the more eccentric waistcoats, rosettes and neckerchiefs. Others sport flashing, neon armbands and some wear straw hats; while others show off black bowlers or top hats. Women predominately fashion layered, ankle length skirts that rustle with every twist and turn whilst men prefer knee- length breeches. White handkerchiefs are waved ceremoniously and whoops and cries of varying voice are thrown up and caught on the wind. There is rhythmic clash of metal from the Long Swords complimenting the hollow collision of clay pipe wielding Morris dancers.

'Liz, Lizzie love, over here.' I look across a flock of faces and pick out Dad's. I continue to push my way through the throng of good spirits, hoping some of it may actually rub off. Enticing smells of mulled wine and roasting hog hangs heavy amongst the atmosphere of pagan abandonment. Joyous escape from fuel bills, job losses and pay cuts. A brief but hedonistic trip into carnival and Mardi Gras.

I surreptitiously snake my way around a team of Molly dancers in the full throes of the Molly Broom. Clog dancers in wooden soled shoes provide percussion to the jangle of Morris bells and sweet echo of whistles and flutes.

Dad stretches out a hand. We're within touching distance of each other now. I reach out to grab him but out of nowhere a Molly dancer with his blacked out face snatches both my hands and spins me violently. His laugh is low and jolly. He pulls me towards him and cat-like rubs his cheek against mine, his voice booming as he wishes me health and happiness. He spins me once more before finally releasing his grip and moving on to his next victim. I stick one arm out to regain my balance whilst the other instinctively reaches for and begins to rub at my one black cheek.

'Whoa ho! Steady there gal,' Dad says, his strong arm securing me from my dizzy tryst.

Laughing, he leads me over to our waiting gaggle. Connor looks up and spots me, waving his sword enthusiastically. His face beams with pride. Simon and Andy, engrossed in conversation, are chewing the cud with a couple of other bullocks, clutching plastic pint glasses of something, no doubt, piquant and intoxicating. And, despite her alleged embarrassment, I spot Cassie with Honey and a few other familiar faces, ensconced in a corner with a clear view of Connor. Maisy's gothic aspect doesn't look out of place with the Molly dancers. She pretends to listen to Mum who is jabbering at her side, nodding politely here and there, but every now and again checks her phone and smiles.

My phone vibrates in my pocket. I pull it out and clumsily attempt to swipe the screen but it doesn't work with gloved, fat fingers. Reluctantly I pull my glove off. The cold air immediately wraps itself around my hand; joyful in its discovery of yet more exposed flesh to attack. Frozen fingers stab at my phone screen to reveal a text from Jodi.

*Hey hun. Sorry I missed you. Twins were freezing so had to go. You up for the cinema next week? 12 years a slave looks good? Xxxx*

Twelve years a slave – he's lucky, I've spent the last 17 years a slave to kids! I text her back and Dad nudges me. Connor is poised and ready to begin.

'This is what it's all about, ain't it, gal?' Dad says. I turn towards him, the exposed parts of my face now uncomfortably numb as the cold continues to gnaw its way down to my bones.

I smile and wish I meant it. 'Yeah, I guess it is Dad. I guess it is.'

## CHAPTER 31

### EPHEMERAL THOUGHTS

**CASSIE**

It's April 17th, 2014 and Nan's first official year free of cancer. Yay! Four more to go then we can breathe a proper sigh of relief. Today is also, I'm like well sad to say, the day the world lost a musical legend – Cheo Feliciano, a Puerto Rican composer of salsa and bolero. After successfully fighting and beating liver cancer last year, he died in a car crash this morning. It's like soooo sad and just goes to show how freaky life (or death) can be.

I know he was like one of the biggest, most influential singers of Latin music ever but I was like well chuffed when I discovered him for myself. He had a sick baritone voice and like so owned Salsa and Bolero but he was also an amazing sonero singer too. That's the great thing about studying music at college; it's teaching me things I didn't know. I just thought singers were just ... well ... singers. And studying music also challenges us all to seek out different sounds. One minute I can be playing Beethoven's *Moonlight Sonata*, the next it could be the Arctic Monkeys *I Bet You Look Good on the Dance Floor* and the next Cheo's *Anacaona*. It's sick. College is waaaaaayyyyy better than school.

I love music. Nearly as much as I love Joe. In fact, I think I'd die without music.

I'd definitely die without Joe. I suppose I get my love of music from Mum. She's always dancing round the kitchen (although not so much lately?) to something, has done for as long as I can remember. Simple Simon thinks he's a bit of a musical expert too. He does have a huge vinyl collection (including a lot of 80s stuff – eeeek!). And even though they're like *really* old I swear Nan and Grandad know more about music than me.

Joe's not really into music, neither is Dad. In fact, what exactly is Dad into? I give it some thought for a minute. The only things I can think of are expensive cars, his big house (that doesn't have room enough for two more) and designer clothes and furniture. Knob. He traded me and Connor for that shit. Oh great, now I feel angry again. Time to write another song.

Mai ... I mean Mania, is saving to go to Australia in a couple of months. I still can't believe she's going. She's nearly finished her Art course (which she's like well sick at) and recently started working for free a couple of hours a week at a Tattooist's called Rebel Yell. Maisy says the name of the shop reminds her of us coz she's the rebel and I yell – a lot. Idiot. She says she wants to be a tattooist in Oz. No worries there then eh, Simple Si, about work and tattoos? She can bloody have as many tattoos as she bloody wants.

Mum's not right lately. I thought it was coz she had that SAD thing but Spring is here and she still seems zoned out, somehow. I can't believe she's still not talking to Ruby. I caught her standing and staring at the cherry blossom tree in front of Nan and Grandad's house the other day. She just stood there for ages. I'm not really a naturist and stuff but even I have to say it was like, amazing; "a breathtaking, beautiful pink cataract of bloom" – I think that's the way Mum described it?

Actually I need to write that down. I write all the time now when I'm inspired – scribbles and nonsense that become songs for the band. Joe inspires me a lot, and Dad. It's been two months now since Dad last contacted me. Dickhead. Everyone keeps saying I have to stop writing sad shit all the time though. I can't believe Pheeb's baby is due any week now. She's like well big – in a nice, pregnant sort of way. I still don't understand why she's having a baby so young though? Sometimes I think its coz she thinks there was nothing else for her to do. She wasn't very clever at school, but then again neither was Maisy. I haven't seen her like forever now but Chelsea's still being a complete bitch coz even though she's miles away – up north with no money apparently – she made like a well derogatory comment about the picture Pheebs posted showing off her baby bump. Said she was fat. Pheebs was like well upset so I messaged back.

***You're not pretty if you're mean to people. That's #UGGGGLLLLLYYYY!***

I'm pleased to say lots of people agreed. Stick that up your fake arse Chelsea!

Joe's just text me. He wants to see me again tonight. I look at his photo on my phone – he's just like so perfect and sooooo fit, almost even more so than Alex from Arctic Monkeys actually. And he told me he loved me last night. He hadn't even been drinking, so I know he meant it. So why does he act like I'm invisible when he's with his friends?

Arrrrrggghhh! Whatevs! Why are people so complicated?

## LIZZIE

Spring has well and truly sprung but winter still resides deep within me. Although not particularly large or fierce, the black dog has been my constant companion these past months. I try my best not to feed him but I'm sure he gets bigger and grows stronger every day. I have so much to be grateful for, so it's wrong on so many levels to allow this blackness to engulf me.

Mum has been given her first year clear of cancer, both the girls are doing exceptionally well at college, Connor is settling in at Secondary school and Dean has offered Simon a promotion at work, although it's meant him having to work away from home a lot more.

Dean has assigned some of Andy's work to Simon because Andy is cutting down his workload to spend more time with Ruby apparently. God I miss her, but I still can't forgive her so that, as they say, is that. I never knew I had it in me to be so unforgiving. It doesn't sit comfortably though. That's why I won't explain my estrangement from Ruby with anyone else. I don't want to corrupt their thoughts with my pain, make the kids or Simon or Mum and Dad for that matter feel obliged to choose a side.

Ruby still texts me from time to time. Less lately, usually one or two sentences, pleading to be heard. I still ignore them. However, I can't quite bring myself to delete her number from my phone, not just yet anyway.

Despite my good fortune though, Maisy is back to hating me and hasn't called me "Mum" in months. She blames me and solely me for the fact we're not able to give her some money towards her trip to Australia. Cassie thinks I'm a complete bitch to abandon my best friend, and my lovely Connor appears to be morphing into a teenager – only very gradually, but it's happening nonetheless. He is still very demonstrative in his affection towards me, however he does lose patience with me from time to time, telling me to "Do one Mum – just do one" when I misunderstand him. I still haven't worked out what "doing one" entails?

Amber looks terrible and just scowls at me when she comes into the library, usually to make trouble. And there are also rumblings of further job losses at work. On top of all that I'm still trying to come to terms with Raj's suicide attempt.

Tabitha was most upset when she found out I was the one who discovered Raj and got him to hospital to have his stomach pumped. His family were away on holiday and something about his demeanour at work unsettled me. He went home early saying he felt unwell. All my primal instincts were screaming at me to check on him. His door, thank god, was unlocked, and I found him face down in his own vomit, surrounded by empty pill bottles and packets.

It was shocking, truly shocking, and not least because I had no idea Raj had been feeling so desperate. I was not best pleased to see my neighbour Tabitha at the hospital. However, I was pleasantly surprised to see a softer side to her when Raj came round. She seemed genuinely concerned for her friend. She still enjoyed gossiping about it to all and sundry though, but thankfully had the good sense not to reveal his identity.

It turns out Raj is gay and is struggling to reconcile his love for a man he has known for some time and bringing shame on his family. If he chooses the man he loves, he loses his family, and if he chooses his family, he loses the man he loves. I said he must speak with his family – that perhaps he underestimates them. Surely they loved him and wouldn't just abandon him? He told me I was naive and I was the one who underestimated just what people were capable of. I thought of Scott and the way he is – or should I say isn't – with Cassie and Connor. And then I thought of Ruby and what she had done to me. I realised, sadly, that Raj was right.

## CASSIE

Thank god, Mum seems to be back to normal. Well, as normal as she's ever likely to be anyway. She really scared me the other day. I came home from college early coz the tutor for our afternoon lesson went home sick, so we were all allowed home. A few members of the band stayed and practised but I had this like strange urge to go home. Good bloody job I did coz I found Mum in the kitchen drunk out of her head. She'd bunked off work, which she like *never* does, and was dancing round the kitchen to Bob Dylan's *I Want You* (I'm sure I remember that song playing a lot when I was little, before Mum and Dad split up). It was playing full blast on repeat. Mum was wearing her jammie shorts and T-shirt, empty bottle of wine in one hand and empty wine glass in the other. She was laughing and dancing barefoot round the kitchen. She barely even noticed me when I came in, and even laughed when I shook her and asked her what the hell she was doing.

I tried to turn Bob Dylan off but she just turned him back on again, then grabbed another bottle of wine and screamed at me when I tried to take it off her. I told her she was scaring me and I was going to get Nan or Ruby. Then she went mad and grabbed me. She told me to NEVER EVER bring that fucking bitch anywhere near her. I think she meant Ruby, not Nan! I said I didn't understand what the problem was, that she and Ruby had been friends for years and surely whatever their stupid problem was they could work it out?

Then Mum crumpled to the floor, really sobbing and crying, tears and snot everywhere. I really wanted to ring Ruby but something inside told me not to. I knew there was a line and I couldn't cross it, even though I wanted to. Then Mum suddenly started heaving, like Romeow sometimes does when he has a fur ball in his throat. Then she like, threw up everywhere. It was like well gross coz her hair and everything got covered in sick.

I don't know how I did it but I managed to get Mum upstairs and in the shower, then I went back downstairs and cleared up all the sick on the kitchen floor, which was like sooooo disgusting. When I went back up to check on Mum, she'd crashed into bed and left the shower running. I laid a towel over her and put a bucket next to her and sat with her for a while until she properly fell asleep. Then I spent the rest of the afternoon watching crap TV and checking on Mum in between.

I got rid of the empty wine bottles and when Simon got home I just told him, and Connor and Maisy, that Mum had a tummy bug. She slept all afternoon and all night and mostly all of the next day and night. But today she's fine and acting like nothing happened. She did look at me across the dinner table and mouth the word "thanks", but that's it. I know she won't say anymore, and I'm too scared to ask coz I don't want to see her like that again. I think it's got something to do with Maisy though, coz when I was dragging her upstairs to the shower all she kept saying was "ask that fucking bitch about your sister".

CHAPTER 32

COMPLACENCY

**LIZZIE**

Tired. Why am I so tired? I open Maisy's bedroom door and stare at the carnage before me and feel my mood deflating as fast as my sanity. What's that saying about kids? Something along the lines of *"they break your back when they're young, your hearts when they've grown"*. Admittedly things were difficult when Scott left. Trying to balance a job to pay the mortgage and getting the children to school and childcare felt like a never-ending whirlwind. Most of it passed in a haze of constant exhaustion. A continuous round of school runs, collections from after school clubs and childminders, trips to the dentist and doctors, hospital appointments, ballet classes, swimming lessons, piano and guitar lessons, football, karate and dance classes. I'm sure I met myself coming most days.

Still, those hazy years – years that passed in a weary blur – were somehow better than the lull I find myself in at the moment. Admittedly there were times spent mopping up tears (especially Cassie's), trying to explain why Scott had let both her and Connor down *again*. Nonetheless we had fun. Our cosy home of three oozed with love and affection. I loved my children, and they loved me back.

Then we met Simon and Maisy and life became – if it was at all possible – a little more hectic. But it was good, it worked. So how did I get here, a place of sulky, surly indifference – at least on the part of the girls (although Connor is fast catching them up)? A place where I love, but most of the time dislike, my daughters? Why must everything be a battle, every request ignored and every rule broken? Why do we have to live in such disharmony?

*They're teenagers, it's their job to hate, disrespect, and ignore you. Nobody said it'd be easy.*

'I know, I know,' I reply out loud.

*And you can stop doing that.*

'Doing what?' I ask no-one in particular.

*Talking to yourself out loud. They'll take you away.*

'Hmmmm ...' I snort. 'I should be so lucky; *they* won't take anyone anywhere these days. Government cuts are leaving most services at breaking point. My advice if you are going to have a breakdown? Be sure to do it during the day because the crisis teams are closed outside office hours. I should know because a number of those poor individuals most in need of help – but not qualifying for one stupid reason or another – often seek sanctuary within the library. Raving, tumultuous half-people left to their own devices, wandering aimlessly amongst the fiction and non-fiction, desperate to find relief from the inclement British weather and their troubled thoughts.

I step into Maisy's room and sigh. How many glasses does she have in here for god sake? There must be at least twenty. And they all appear to have their own flourishing growths. How difficult is it to pick the bloody glass up, carry it downstairs and put it into the dishwasher?

I can feel the resentment rising within me. As usual, Simon's not here to help. I know he's working harder than ever – for us – but there's a part of me that firmly believes he's happy to be away from the day-to-day shit.

Posters of ominous looking individuals adorned across Maisy's bedroom walls stare at me – some in various states of undress, others hidden by menacing masks or disturbing make-up, not a smile in sight. Her carpet is a polluted sea of chocolate wrappers, dirty underwear, clean underwear, empty coke cans, cigarette packets, an assortment of nail polish bottles (mostly shades of black), make-up (mostly black), old clothes, new clothes, clean clothes, dirty clothes (mostly black) all intermingled with plates containing half eaten food in various states of decay.

I scream – Arrggghh! – but only I can hear it in my head. I refuse to deal with this. I walk out and close the door behind me.

I open Cassie's door and hover reluctantly. It's the antithesis of Maisy's room and I am greeted by the aroma of recently burned incense sticks and sweet smelling candles. An array of cerise pinks and hedonistic purples clash with Laura Ashley bed linen and an eclectic mix of rock and pop stars watch me as I tentatively scan the usual hiding places. Although on first sight Cassie's room is far tidier than Maisy's, she too appears to be completely incapable of transferring mugs, cups and plates back to the kitchen. And, as expected, a hotchpotch of culinary devices and utensils, including a whisk of all things, have been shoved under her bed or neatly stacked behind her curtains.

I'm suddenly filled with a feeling of deep resentment and decide to abandon ship. There's still a dishwasher to empty, washing to hang out, bins to bring in, the cat litter tray to empty, rubbish to take out (don't forget to separate the recycling) and a food shop to do. A heavy cloud is descending and I'm struggling to shake it.

Is this it? Is this really my lot in life; a meagre paid job, servitude and ingratitude from kids that hate me and betrayed by loved one's and friends? What? What the hell is in it for me? Why the fuck am I so angry and why do I feel so bloody guilty for feeling so angry?

Turning the bathroom and hallway lights off, that have – yet again – been left on, I descend the stairs in a manner far more controlled than I feel. The lights in the kitchen also burn brightly, despite the daylight that pours through its windows. The worktops are strewn with crumbs, cereals and god knows what else, and mugs, bowls and plates have been abandoned at will.

'Hey Mum, what's for dinner tonight?' Connor suddenly asks behind me.

'Mum, did you wash my white top?' Cassie demands to know, shoving Connor out of the way.

'Lend us a fiver will ya?' Maisy asks.

*Please!! What's wrong with the fucking word please?*

A fuse is shorting in my head. If I didn't know better I'd have said there was smoke wafting from my ears.

'I am a person you know!' I yell. The kids look stunned and just stare at me. 'I had a life once, before kids. I smoked and drank and danced naked in the moonlight, and I dreamed. I was, wanted to be, someone – once! But look at me now, just some robot bloody skivvy here to serve you lot. Make your own bloody dinner, wash your own bloody top, and stop smoking and save your own bloody money. I'm off.'

## CASSIE

'Stop Mum, stop!' I yell running out the door after her. 'I need a lift, you said you'd give me a lift.' Mum's car window is open so I know she can hear me but she continues pulling out of the drive away from me. Stupid moody cow. I really need a lift, it's like sooooo important.

I stamp my foot as Mum pulls away. 'Arrrggghhh,' I yell after her. 'Sometimes I wish ... oh why don't you just piss off and don't bother coming back.' I don't know if she hears me.

What the hell was that all about? What does she mean she smoked? Hypo-bloody-crite. And what does she mean she had dreams once? Doesn't everyone dream at night, when they're asleep? Or does that stop when you get old? Why is she making such a bloody fuss about everything? And as for dancing naked in the moonlight – I knew she was bloody mad! She promised me a lift to college, and now I'll be bloody late for bloody rehearsal for the first part of our major bloody project, which is like well bloody important and well bloody stressful.

'She's having a breakdown or mid-life crisis I think,' Maisy says. 'Or maybe it's the menopause?'

'Tell me about it, Mania.'

'Don't call me Mania. My name is Maisy.'

I look at Maisy, baffled. Is everyone losing it today? 'But you always say you hate the name Maisy?'

'Yeah, well, I've changed my mind.'

'Why?'

'Because Crazee researched its meaning and ...'

Maisy pauses for a moment and I grin at her. 'And what?'

'Well, Crazee said the name Maisy comes from the Latin 'Margarita' which means 'Pearl' and that Ancient Persians believed pearls were formed when oysters came to the water's surface to look at the moon. A drop of dew formed in the shell of the oyster, which was then turned to pearl by the moon. So Crazee says, no matter how far apart we are or how many miles separate us, when he looks up at the moon every night he thinks of me, Maisy – his beautiful pearl.' Maisy's cheeks flush up and she looks down, fidgeting with her hands. I continue to stare at her and smile.

It's nice to see her so happy. She looks back up at me and runs her hand through her hair. 'Or some shit like that,' she adds, shrugging her shoulders. 'Until we can be together again.'

'Oh my god, that's like weeeeeellllll romantic. He like, well loves you.'

'I know,' Maisy replies, grinning.

Maisy actually smiles well loads since meeting Crazee. I study her face and didn't realise, coz it's happened so gradually, but she actually wears loads less make-up now too. Well a lot less black stuff anyway.

'C'mon,' Maisy says to me and Connor. 'Let's tidy up quick so Mum doesn't have another meltdown when she gets home. Then I'll give you both a lift.'

'Thank god for that,' I say relieved. 'We have like major rehearsals today at college.'

'Yeah well, don't get too used to me bailing you out. A couple more months and this car will be sold and I'll be on my way to the land down under.'

'What's a lay-down-under?' Connor asks. Maisy and I just look at him and laugh.

'That too!' Maisy says winking at me.

Connor looks even more confused so I just tell him to shut up and turn to Maisy again. 'That's like such a scary thought. I still can't believe you're actually going to leave?'

'Yeah it is scary but exciting too – I think?'

It'll only be another year for me then I'll also be leaving too to go to Uni, thank bloody god. What will Mum do then eh, with barely anything to do and only Connor to look after? She'll be sorry then that she shouted at us.

❦

## LIZZIE

'Well, well, well, I'd recognise that gorgeous derriere anywhere, and it still looks as good as it did thirty years ago.'

I'm bent over by the shelves in General Fiction, shelf tidying and unable to see the speaker of the voice behind me. I attempt to stand up quickly, dropping several hardback editions of *Gone With The Wind* in the process. Unsure whether to feel completely insulted or if I'm honest, a little bit thrilled, I turn and am greeted by a handsome but slightly craggy middle-aged face. His smile is broad and the hair on his head thick and dark with a good sprinkling of grey. It's the eyes that give it away though, eyes that coruscate; grey and mischievous, eyes of years gone by that bore into me and finally force the penny to drop.

'Oh my god Nigel! Nigel Fogerty,' I say, shocked to see a real blast from the past.

I impulsively throw my arms around him – sod protocol. 'You look just the same.'

'I wish,' he replies patting a rather rotund belly. I laugh. 'And these,' he continues, pointing to the lines around his face.

'Ah well, yes. Unfortunately, we all have those,' I reply cupping my face.

Dear, lovely Nigel. How wonderful to see him. He always had a bit of a crush on me at school but unfortunately I didn't feel the same. I loved him as a friend, just never fancied him. He was to me what Luke is to Cassie I suppose? I laugh to myself because I can actually hear Mum's voice in my head, "Why don't you go out with Nigel? Such a lovely lad".

'So, you work here then?' Nigel asks turning his head from left to right surveying all that is the city library.

I feel my face redden a little. 'Yep, I certainly do. Worked for the library service in some capacity or other for oooh, err ... let's just say for longer than I care to remember.'

'Okay, sick. Shit, must stop saying that. Got into the bad habit of talking like my daughter.' Nigel laughs.

'Oh great, you have a daughter?'

Nigel's face flushes a little. 'Yeah, Rio.' He winces, his face creasing with embarrassment. 'I was, as you may remember, a big Duran Duran fan? And so was – as it turned out – my wife Claire, and Rio, as a name, just seemed like a good idea at the time.'

'I think it's a beautiful name. How old is she?'

'Eighteen.'

'Oh that lovely age then?' My intonation is acerbic. Nigel raises bemused eyes and nods.

'How about you? Do you have any kids?'

I tell him all about Cassie, Connor and Maisy. I also tell him about Scott and the divorce and of course I tell him all about Simon. He tells me he's sorry about my divorce. I tell him I'm sorry to hear his wife has Multiple Sclerosis.

He waves his hand dismissively. 'It is what it is. We're still mad about each other, even after all these years. You have to be happy with what you've got. I'm glad we managed to have Rio though,' he adds. 'We'd always hoped to have a big family but you never quite know what life is going to throw at you do you? You're lucky to have three Liz. I bet you're a good Mum too?'

I think about my earlier behaviour and cringe. 'Hummmph, I'm not so sure about that.' Poor Connor, his little face looked so upset. So did the girls come to think of it. Must make it up to them all later.

'They're still alive if that's what you mean!' I laugh. 'I try to be a good Mum I suppose, but I don't always feel very good at it. I swear both the girls hate me.'

I'm being serious now but Nigel just cocks his head to one side and laughs at me. 'They're just being teenagers. It's their job to keep you on your toes.'

I ask him what he's doing here and to my surprise he explains that he's checking in with us reference arrangements for his book reading at the library tomorrow afternoon. My lower jaw lapses suitably enough to show my shock.

'Oh my god! You mean you're Jules J. Clarke, the science fiction writer?' Currents of unease surge through me infused with small sparks of envy.

'Yeah,' he blushes. 'Prefer to use a pseudonym. Not really into all that fame malarkey.' Nigel pauses and casts another spurious eye on our tired surroundings. It's been a while since the Library last had a makeover. 'I always imagined you as a writer Liz, what with your love of books and everything. Not that there's anything wrong with this of course.' He runs a hand through his hair. His intonation is apologetic. 'You are working with books after all. But, well, you should give it a go sometime. Writing, I mean. If I can do it anyone can. I was a plumber before I started writing, and I swear to god my first book – if you deconstruct it – is all about plumbing in a science fiction setting. Give it a go sometime, Liz. Just put pen to paper and see what happens.'

We exchange contact details and I agree to meet him tomorrow for lunch after his book reading. As he leaves I experience yet another hot flush and sense of unease and disappointment. His imprint on the world is notable and worthy. What – if indeed I have made any impression at all – is mine?

# CHAPTER 33

## THE LAST SHELTER OF THE INCOMPETENT

**LIZZIE**

God, it's been such a busy morning but there she is again. That must be the fifth time Amber has come in today. She looks awful. Her hair is limp and greasy, her complexion pale and her tired eyes are bloodshot. She hovers nervously, watching me like a hawk, waiting for an opportunity to swoop down on me. I don't think I can deal with her today; I've had more than my fair share of awkward customers and I'm still upset about the way I left the kids this morning. I do love them all but why do I have to become a raving lunatic before anyone listens to me?

'Oi, scuse me Miss.' I turn to see a man, one of our customers, talking to me. 'Do you know that bloody machine isn't working again?' He's clearly as irritated as I feel.

'Yes, we are aware,' the exasperation rather too evident in my voice. 'If you see my colleague Raj over there, he'll be able to help you.'

Raj took a couple of weeks off work citing gastric flu as the reason for his absence. He seems okay, but who knows what's really going on inside someone else's head? The irritated customer picks up the irascibility in my voice and intuitively backs down.

'Bloody technology eh?' he replies half laughing.

'Great when it works?' I respond with a nod and a tight-lipped smile as he wanders off towards Raj.

Amber has seen her opportunity and seizes it.

'Lizzie,' she pleads. 'You ave to help me.' She cradles both arms around her now very noticeable bump. 'He said he's gonna take my baby from me when it's born and sell it for god sake.' I sigh heavily and look at Amber's pasty, almost alabaster face and deadbeat eyes. She reeks of cigarette smoke.

*What kind of home are you going to provide for that baby Amber?*

'Who is, Amber?' I reply.

'Travis, my boyfriend.' Her eyes bore into mine, racked with desperation. 'Look,' she continues. 'He just wants some money. So, I was finking if maybe you could lend me some and I give it to him, then he'll leave me and the baby alone.'

'How much were you thinking?'

Amber is quiet for a moment then lowers her eyes and slumps towards me. 'Dunno.' She shrugs her shoulders. 'A couple of thousand?'

'Pounds?' I ask in disbelief. 'I'm sorry Amber, we just don't have that sort of money.'

'Liar,' she shouts. 'I've seen where you live.'

'Sorry? What? What do you mean?' I ask, slightly taken aback. 'How do you know where I live?'

'Oh forget it,' she snaps, before starting to cry, visibly shaking. 'Look, I've told you before. I know someone who works in a Women's Shelter, a refuge …'

Amber cuts me off before I can finish. 'Just leave it,' she

hisses. 'I thought you cared; I thought you'd bloody understand? Why am I always on my own?' Amber turns on her heel and within a few strides has left the building again. I feel wretched.

※

What a day. I feel both mentally and physically exhausted. I pull my car into our drive, relieved to turn the engine off. The exhaust is blowing and the tinny rasping noise has made my head hurt. It'll never pass the MOT sounding like that.

*More bloody expense.*

I look up at our house and think about my earlier conversation with Amber. The exterior is looking as shabby and tired as I feel, but it's a reasonably average sized house in a pleasant enough area away from the city. We are however mortgaged up to the hilt and still have three kids to support. Appearances can therefore be deceiving. However, compared to the Victory Housing Estate I believe Amber lives on in the city, my home is positively charming.

Amber's less than humble abode is one of the many concrete buildings that forms part of the estate originally erected for the social housing project to accommodate London's overspill started in the early 1970's. Unique in design, it was declared a planning success with promises of a modern day spectacle upon completion.

Unfortunately, this particular urban development, with its square maisonette blocks and many small, under lit, dark passages – perfect for performing and hiding bad deeds – proved to be desperately unimaginative. And now, thanks to high local unemployment, political disenfranchisement and crime, the Victory Housing Estate is more urban blight than delight on the city landscape. A modern day dystopia rather than utopia.

I sigh and rest my hands and head on the steering wheel. Simon and I work hard to keep this modest roof above our heads but I don't take any of it for granted. A couple of major mishaps could so easily find us living very different lives. I think of the poor homeless guy I see most mornings on my way into work; camped up between the job centre and the now empty and boarded up building that used to be the local theatre.

I lift my head up again.

*What you need is a nice cup of coffee.*

That's exactly what I need. I'm not expecting anyone home for at least another hour, so despite whatever mess awaits me inside, a cup of coffee with a good book and my feet up is precisely what I need right now. I'll apologise to the kids for being a grumpy old cow when they get home, and we'll have takeaway pizza for tea. My phone pings – it's a text message from Ruby. I pause for a moment deciding whether to read it or not. I miss her. I miss the stupid cow so much. I decide I will read it, my frozen heart is thawing a little.

**Lizzie, PLEASE FORGIVE ME!!!! I love you and I'm so, so SORRY. Xxxxxxxxxxxxxxxxxxxxxxxxxxxxxxxxxxxxxxxxxxxx xxxxxxxxxxxxxxxxxxxxxx**

Maybe I can forgive her? Maybe I should allow her the time to explain? I'll think about it some more later.

I clamber out of my faithful, yellow car and notice rust building up around the door seal. I make a mental note to get it checked.

'Lizzie,' a familiar voice calls out. I'm both surprised and a little unnerved to see Amber standing on my drive. 'Did you think any more about what I said earlier?'

I'm thrown by her presence and a little bewildered by her question. 'Sorry? What ...?' I reply. 'What are you talking about Amber?' She seems nervous. I replay our earlier conversation in my head. 'Is it the money you asked for? Because if it is, I told you, I ... we ... just don't have that sort of ready cash.'

Amber stares at me, anxious and annoyingly picking at her non-existent fingernails. I feel sorry for her but irritated at the same time.

'Just give us your fucking money bitch.'

I jump as a tall, stocky man appears from nowhere to stand behind Amber. Amber opens her mouth to speak. 'I'm sorry,' she mouths.

The menacing looking individual places a heavy hand on Amber's shoulder and exposes a fistful of chunky gold rings. Maybe it's the way they catch the light from the sun but each ring appears to be tinged with spots of red. His shaved head, with its noticeable V shape, is absent of any hair he may have had and his designer tee shirt is tucked into the jeans he wears below his waist. The trainers he sports, well out of our monthly budget, appear barely worn.

'Travis I presume?' I ask in a voice far more restrained than I feel. He looks confused.

'What ya tell her my name for you stupid fucking bitch,' he says, gruffly using the palm of his extensively bejewelled hand to slap Amber around the head. I flinch.

'Ouch,' she calls out, cupping then rubbing her now bright red ear. My stomach flips. I'm starting to feel very uncomfortable.

'Don't hurt Amber please,' I state. He grins at me.

'Or you're gonna do what about it bitch?' he replies, slapping Amber again. She yells out in pain. He laughs.

'Please,' I continue. My inner voice is silent and has temporarily abandoned me. 'There really is no need for any of this. Here ...' I open my bag to look for my purse. 'I don't have much on me but just take whatever I have and let's forget about all this nonsense eh?'

'Fuck off bitch. You think coz I'm not fucking rich like you, I must be fucking stupid?'

I look at his angry face. He's a bully and for the briefest of moments my confidence has returned. I step towards him.

'Rich?' I ask incredulously. 'I don't know what gives you that impression but yes, you most definitely are stupid to even consider that.'

Amber closes her eyes and I see the dread that flickers across them as she opens them again.

Travis steps forward, glaring at me and cracking fingers. The hairs at the back of my neck stand on end and I can't help staring at his fat fingers now morphing into huge fists. Something tells me this man carries little or no regard for the poor souls unfortunate enough to find themselves at the end of those fists. Adrenalin pumps through me – fast and furious – and my heart beats loud in my ears. My need to fly is far more compelling than any fleeting thoughts of standing to fight.

'Look,' I say, my tongue sticking to the roof of my now very dry mouth. 'I honestly have nothing to give to you. I'd give you my debit card but the account is probably overdrawn.' I try to laugh in the vague hope of diffusing the air of violence that sits so comfortably with this aggressive individual.

He draws in close, hovering with intent. I notice several small scars below one eye and numerous small brown circular patches intermittently dispersed across his neck. His teeth are stained and his breath has the same sickly sweet aroma that lingers heavily around some of the poor, less salubrious looking individuals that often visit the library, especially during the colder months of the year.

'Shut up. You fucking stuck up bitch.' He leans in and lowers his face towards mine. My sense of smell is overpowered by the toxicity of his breath. 'You!' he yells. 'In yer big fancy ouse.'

*But it's not big, or fancy! The furniture's old, the decor dated...*

Travis lifts a shiny, silver blade from his pocket and runs the blunt edge with considerable force down the side of my cheek. 'Now,' he orders, 'just do as I fucking say and no-one gets hurt. Understand?' I nod my head in affirmation, pure terror having snatched my voice away.

I hate to admit it but I'm now truly, truly frightened. The strength in my legs has disappeared and they feel as though they are about to buckle beneath me. I catch sight of my reflection in the front-room window of the house. It's terrifying to see the panic etched into my features in all its transparency. My apprehensive mind runs wild and the 'what if's' bounce off all my rational and irrational thoughts. Can I get to a phone? Can I get into the house without him? Should I call for help? Should I attempt to run? Are the neighbours in?

Amber's troubled voice interrupts my thoughts.

'Just leave her alone Travis. I bloody told ya she don't have nuffink,' she yells, pounding her fists on his very broad back.

Travis turns so quickly I barely have time to see what he does. Amber falls to the ground clearly recoiling from the full force of his fist. As Travis steps to one side I see Amber cradling her face. She looks a mess, her face a red explosion as blood pumps rapidly from her nose. Impulsively I run towards her but am stopped in my tracks by an excruciating pain at the back of my head. I feel violently sick and my head has started to spin. I have no idea if I'm standing or falling. No, I'm falling, I'm definitely falling. I can see the moon. I'm sure I can see the moon, and there's a funky purple haze around it? Oh god why did I yell at the kids this morning? Why can't I hear? Why is there no sound? Why is it so dark...?

## CHAPTER 34

### WITH OR WITHOUT YOU?

**CASSIE**

Oh my god, oh my god, oh my god. I can't breathe. I really can't breathe. My chest hurts, my stomach hurts and my head hurts. My legs feel too weak to carry my body but I can't sit down. The lights are too bright and that disinfectant smell is making me feel sick. All I can do is pace the corridor and wring my hands over and over again. My trainers keep making a ridiculous squeaking noise. Sometimes it sounds like I'm farting. And I look really skanky coz I was at a Zula, Zimba, whatever the bloody name is, fitness class and my arse looks huge in these bloody leggings. And I have sweat stains under my arms. Oh my actual god, am I really thinking about farts and my arse? Oh god I feel sick again.

Connor looks so sad. I can't normally stand the little shit but he looks so sad. I'll give him another hug. Oh my actual god, Maisy's hugging him. I've never seen Maisy hug anyone, except the cat.

I check my phone again. More messages from Pheebs and Luke, nothing from Dad. You fucking idiot. We need you. Connor and I need you. This is sooooo important. Where are you?

The hospital is filled with people and noise. Curtains are swished open and quickly shut again. Men and women in white coats and green onesies roam up and down and in and out of various rooms and cubicles. Sometimes they walk quite slowly, at others times they rush off like Olympic runners.

Different sized trolleys clack along the corridors; some with people on, others with strange looking machines and my ears recognise familiar sounds; sirens, screaming, shouting, even laughing at times but I also hear less familiar things like voices talking across radios, bleeping sounds that remind me of a slow heartbeat, the stretching and snapping of rubber gloves and the clanging of metal waste bins. My nose also picks up a strange mix of bleach, soap, expensive perfumes and cheap body sprays as well as the more repulsive smell of sweat, blood and vomit.

I don't believe in you but thanks god. When I asked you to make Joe my boyfriend proper, I meant it. When I wished Mum would piss off and never come back I didn't.

My phone is vibrating like crazy. Using my thumb I scroll down my screen quickly, skipping all the other names, desperate to see if Dad has responded, but no, nothing. I've heard from everyone except Dad. Even Joe has sent me a message. I'd normally be well chuffed to get a message from him but I can't even be bothered. I just want my Dad and as usual he's not here.

## CONNOR

I feel quite scared. Everyone keeps telling me not to be but I know they are, so I can't help it. Simon keeps walking in and out of different doors then walking back to where we're sitting. He doesn't really say much but he does keep shaking his head like he's saying no to something.

Cassie just keeps looking at me then her phone, then gets really angry.

She doesn't shout like she does at home but I can hear her whispering the same words she uses in a really angry voice.

Maisy's make-up is all smudged round her eyes from crying and she's hugged me twice now. Maisy never normally hugs anyone, except the cat. She smells quite nice actually. I think she's wearing some perfume like Mum's and her hair smells of strawberries.

Grandad keeps trying to make me laugh but then it's like he forgets I'm here and keeps going really quiet until he looks up and sees me again. Nan just keeps rubbing my hands – I'm not really sure why – and buying me drinks. I'm not normally allowed fizzy drinks, except at Christmas or on my birthday coz Mum says they're bad for me, but Nan says I can have as much as I like today. I kinda don't want to drink the second one Nan's just bought me though coz I've sort of made a pact with myself, promising not to drink it in return for Mum to be okay.

Uh oh, Cassie is standing in the middle of the corridor shouting really loud at her phone. I can't really understand her words coz they're all jumbled up with her crying and shouting. The only one I can understand is "why" – she keeps saying that word a lot.

Oh no, she's done it now, I reckon. Simon is walking up to her really fast and his face looks really angry. Thought so, he's grabbed her phone off her and – oh – he's hugging her. And she's letting him. That's a miracle coz she never normally lets Simon (or Simple as she calls him) anywhere near her. She's put her arms around him and he's holding her really tight, and stroking her hair, kinda like the way I stroke Freddy.

Nan has bought me some chocolate. I think she's put all her money in that vending machine. I open the packet and put one of the chocolates in my mouth. I normally love chocolate but my tummy feels like it's going round and round and the chocolate feels like it's stuck in my throat coz it's hard to swallow. I fold the packet up and put it in my pocket. I think I'll eat the chocolate later. I'll share it with Mum coz I know she likes chocolate, a lot.

I don't say it out loud but I actually feel really scared.

**MAISY**

Please don't go.

## CHAPTER 35

LOSING CONTROL

**SIMON**

I still can't believe I'm doing this. Lizzie is desperately hanging onto life and I've left her to speak to this idiot. I should have punched his lights out years ago. I can't stand to see Cassie so upset though. I love her, I love all the kids. I've done my best to fill the colossal gaps this prick's left in his children's lives but Cassie needs her Dad. I get it. So why the fuck doesn't he?

A wild fusion of fury and fear is building and bubbling just below my civilized surface. I'm seething and fuck political correctness. It's moments like this that social etiquette evaporates. The moments every man fears; the unleashing of the beast within; that crass, almost base animal just waiting for its moment to break free, to cut loose the reins of social politeness and moral decency and run unrestrained from the nuisance of reason. In short I want to pulverize his fucking face in.

How dare you take me away from the woman I love, the

mother of your children? Oh god, I should have been there for her. That's my job, to protect my woman, my family. And fuck this equality shit, she is *my* woman, it is *my* job.

I think of Lizzie's face. Was she frightened? I laugh a little, if she were she wouldn't have shown it. She may be slight but she's a proud, feisty woman. She would never have given whatever ruthless pig attacked her, the pleasure of seeing how frightened she was. But then again, how the fuck do I know? I wasn't there. Even if she did successfully conceal the terror of the situation she would have felt it. And she was alone with that fear.

I feel sick. I pull over and stop the car. I should have been there for her. What kind of fucking man am I? Oh God what if she…dies? Life without Lizzie would be unbearable. And what about the kids? What about Cassie and Connor? And Maisy, she can't lose another mother. Fuck, fuck, fuck it all to fucking hell. Why didn't I tell Lizzie – every day – just how much I love her? I place my hands on the steering wheel and squeeze them until my knuckles turn white before head butting it with full force.

'I should have been there. It should have been me,' I shout. My head hurts but I don't really feel it. I leave my head resting on the wheel as thoughts I don't want to think plague my mind. After a few moments I look up and inhale deeply before exhaling slowly. I can't do this. I can't think like this. Salocin reckons we're all interconnected and vibrate across different dimensions or something. He says projected negative thinking only brings negative results. He said we have to stay positive, send out positive thoughts. Sounds like a load of bollocks to me but right now I'll hold onto anything that keeps my Lizzie with me.

I pull my reasonably priced car onto the large drive of Scott's almost stately home, next to the brand new Range Rover and BMW. Spirituality doesn't reside at this address, only spirits of a material world. I shake my head in amusement. This man pays nothing towards the upkeep of his children and gets away with it, by law. I walk tentatively towards his mock something or other front door, constantly repeating the words *I will not punch his smug face in* to myself.

I knock loudly and a rather harsh looking woman half opens the door.

'Yes?' she says.

'Can I speak to Scott please?'

'Mr Lloyd,' she turns and shouts through the house. 'There is a man here for you.' She turns her attention back to me again and frowns. 'What is your name?' she asks, in a thick Eastern European accent.

'Just tell him it's Simon.'

'Is Mr Simon,' she turns and shouts again.

I hear footsteps along the hallway and a man muttering loudly. 'Who?' He sounds irritated and impatient. 'Bloody immigrant workers. Waste of bloody time ... Oh Simon ... mate,' Scott says pulling the door wide open and stepping in front of the now very disgruntled looking woman still hovering. 'Yes thank you Agnieszka,' he orders, his tone arrogant and dismissive. He looks a little thrown and runs a hand through his floppy brown hair. 'Bloody housekeepers.' He rolls his eyes. 'Can't get a decent one if you try.'

'I wouldn't know.'

'No, well . . .' he falters for a moment and hides behind his throat clearing silence that whiffs of embarrassment. 'God. Anyway how's Lizzie?' he eventually asks. I laugh inwardly, wishing I could believe the concern in his voice.

'Not good. *Really* not good.'

'No,' Scott replies shaking his head. 'Terrible. Shocking in fact. Any idea who did it? Cassie did phone me. In floods of tears she was. I could barely make out what she was saying.'

'That's why I've come, because the kids want you to come to the hospital.'

'Ahhh mate, I would if I could. But ...' He trails off and shrugs his shoulders. I look at him dumbfounded.

'But what?'

'Well, I've got Harriet to look after and...'

'Bring her with you.'

'I can't mate, really.'

'She might die,' I blurt out. 'Lizzie may actually not make it. The kids need you.' I'm pleading with him but at the same time desperately trying to control the red mist now descending upon me.

'Yeah I know,' Scott replies, visibly squirming. 'It's shocking. And sad, it really is very sad and everything, but it's not ...' I look at him, gobsmacked.

'Not what?'

'Liz isn't ... well, isn't ...' He pauses to sigh. 'Look,' he continues. 'Liz isn't really any of my concern. Sharon wouldn't like it if ...'

'Not any of your fucking concern?' I shout, interrupting him. 'They are *your* fucking kids for god sake. Their mother is lying in hospital in a coma and there's every possibility she won't make it, and it's no fucking concern of yours?' My voice, raised from the pit of my stomach, is demonic. I grab Scott forcefully by the neck. 'Don't you care at all?' I spit into his face. 'I don't fucking understand you. What the hell's wrong with you man. Cassie and Connor have your blood – are part of you for fuck's sake. Doesn't that mean anything?'

Scott just stares at me, wordless and open mouthed. The rage that has almost consumed me is simmering dangerously below my thin veneer of rationality, threatening to boil over at the next tiniest provocation. I release my hand from his throat and stare into his empty eyes.

'Tell me, because I'm really keen to know. Why not abandon the kids completely? Surely abandonment would have been far kinder than this barely there, barely caring relationship you persist with? Have you any idea how much heartache you cause? How much destruction you leave in your wake?'

Scott doesn't reply.

'You know what?' I ask without waiting for a reply. 'I can see it in his eyes; Connor gave up on you a long time ago. He may be younger than Cassie but he's an old soul in a young body, more worldly, somehow. God knows how but he seems to manage your rejection. Cassie on the other hand is far more vulnerable. She's desperate to be Daddy's girl, constantly trying to make sense of your blasé dismissal of her. And it doesn't matter how many times we tell her it's not her, she still doesn't get it. And frankly neither do I – *mate*.'

I spit the last word out as I lean in towards him again. 'Cassie's your daughter – *your* little girl for fuck sake. True she's a bloody pain the arse at times, but she's also innocent and trusting; touchingly grateful for any attention, especially the negative kind you seem to be so fucking good at dishing out.'

Scott continues to stare at me, speechless and quivering like the spineless excuse of a man he is. 'Seriously, would it be so very hard to throw Cassie one tiny crumb of affection, one morsel of love and support?' I wait for his response, but nothing comes. 'Well?' I demand.

'They can't live with us – if Lizzie dies – they can't live with us.' Finally, the bastard speaks and this is his pathetic response. 'We … we can't afford it,' he stutters. At any other time, I'd laugh at this low life. Ridicule his moral code – or lack of. But today the woman I love is as close to death as it gets and today I'm not the person I was yesterday. Scott flinches as I raise my fist above his head. He puts two arms up to defend his face.

'Dooonnnt …' he shouts.

Something inside me has snapped and I lash out in a way that is primeval and instinctive. The beast within me has awoken and possess me now, body and soul. My right fist propels hard into his left cheek. I'm done with talking. I need to act. He moves, I follow with speed and catch him hard on the chin with my left fist. Punching someone hurts, more than I remembered, but my adrenalin-fuelled body cares little for the pain I feel, and even less for the recipient of my inflictions.

I pummel Scott, blow after blow; my normally dormant beast keen to make the most of this rare appearance before being yanked back and restrained by the shackles of civility. I slam into him with my full body weight and knock him to the floor. Blood as red as my rage splatters and gurgles from somewhere and the taste of hot, liquefied metal fills my mouth. This isn't just about Scott though. I'm not just beating him, I'm pulverising the cunt that hurt my Lizzie too. Blood squelches between my fist and Scott's face and I can hear the cracking of bone. Is it his nose? His cheek? His neck? I don't give a fuck. The beast is free and can't be stopped.

'STOOOOOOOOOOOOOOP IIIIIIIIIIITTTTTTTTT.'

Mid-punch, I'm suddenly alerted to someone screaming behind me. I look at the bloody face below me and feel the beast reluctantly begin its retreat. I stand up and stagger away from Scott turning to look in the direction of the screaming. I stare straight at Cassie's tear-soaked face. Scott has clearly caught me a blinder because my blurred vision runs red across my left eye.

'I'm ... so ... sorry ... Cas ... ee,' I say bending over, holding both knees. My body is coming down from its adrenalin rush and I'm surprisingly out of breath. Clearly I'm not as fit as I thought I was. Cassie's shoulders shudder in time with her pitiful wailing. She looks from me to Scott then back to me again.

'You shouldn't have done this Simon,' she cries. 'Mum

always says violence solves nothing. Look what violence has done to her. You're both pathetic.'

I raise one of my hands; I'm still trying to catch my breath. 'S'all my fault Cassie,' I admit. 'I started it, not your Dad.'

'No Simon,' she replies, her face marked with pain. 'I heard every single word you said and every single one of them is entirely true.' She turns to look at Scott, her outstretched arm pointing at him. 'If he even *tried* to be some sort of Dad you wouldn't be here beating him up.'

Cassie walks straight past me towards Scott, tears flowing freely down her cheeks.

'Mum might die,' she says in a voice that is now calm but filled with heartache. 'Mum might die and I just wanted my Dad, it's that simple. After all this time, all the disappointment you've put me through, I still wanted you. You! I don't want your money or to live with you, I just needed to know that somewhere there is a place for me with you. But there isn't is there? You never were and never will be there for me, will you? And for the first time in my life, I actually understand – it's not me, it's you. I'm done, Dad. Finished. Simon's my real dad. I don't ever want to see you again.'

# CHAPTER 36

REMORSE

**CASSIE**

'I'm sorry Cassie,' Simon says again, briefly looking at me before turning back to concentrate on the road ahead. He has one hand on the steering wheel, the other holding a manky tissue I found in the bottom of my bag, which he holds on the cut above his eye.

'It's fine, Simon, honest.' I know he feels well bad but I don't want him to. The truth is, Dad deserved everything he just got.

'I didn't plan to go there and beat your Dad up you know?' Simon continues explaining, as if he hasn't heard me. 'I was hoping ... well, I thought if I talked to him, he'd come to the hospital for you and Connor ...'

'I know, Simon, I understand, really I do. It's fine. I don't love you any less or anything.' Simon turns to look at me again and smiles. It's a lovely, familiar smile but his eyes don't follow suit. Like mine, they're so, so sad.

'How did you get to your dad's anyway?'

'I followed you in a taxi. I had a suspicion you were going to Dad's.' Simon sort of laughs and shakes his head.

'You're just like your mum,' he says. 'No flies on you eh?'

Flies? I'm confused. Why would I, or Mum for that matter, have flies on us?

Somehow it doesn't feel right to ask, so I decide not to right now. 'Yeah,' I say, also sort of laughing. 'No flies on me.'

※

When we get back to the hospital Nan, Grandad and Connor are still waiting where we left them but Maisy has gone out for some fresh air, apparently. More like nicotine laced air. Grandad looks at the cut above Simon's eye. He raises his hand as if to point and opens his mouth to speak. Nan steps forward and places her hand on Grandads arm and squeezes it. Grandad closes his mouth again.

'She's still in surgery,' Nan says. 'The doctors said they would come and speak to us again in a while. Oh and I phoned Ruby and she's on her way over too,' she adds.

Mum and Ruby are still not speaking but I've still been texting and Facebooking with her. I knew she'd come. I'm glad she is coming. She can take up some of the slack from Nan and Simon for a while. They're trying to keep it all together for the rest of us but they both look shattered.

My phone hasn't stopped – some calls but mostly texts. Some telling me to keep my chin up, or stay strong or be positive, others just asking me how I am. Pheebs has even offered to get on the bus with Nancy and come to the hospital, which was like well sweet of her but I said no coz Nancy, the baby, is only two weeks old. I really thought Joe would come to support me and everything, but he just said to call him when I get home. Which was sweet – sort of – I suppose?

Maisy is back, reeking, as I suspected, of fags.

'Look who I found skulking about outside,' she says. As she moves away Luke hovers reluctantly behind her.

'I ... erm ... I ... ummm,' he says looking nervously at me. 'I thought I could perhaps ... ummm ... be of some help? But maybe I shouldn't have ...' He pauses.

I'm disappointed it's not Joe but touched nonetheless. I walk towards Luke and hug him. 'Thanks,' I mumble burying my head into his leather jacket.

I love the smell of Luke's jacket, it's so familiar. There have been so many times I've lent my head on Luke's shoulder when he's wearing that jacket. Usually when I feel down, usually about Joe.

When I eventually pull myself away from Luke I notice two familiar faces in green onesies walking towards us. My stomach lurches forward and I'm suddenly full of dread again. I try to read the faces of the two surgeons that have been operating on Mum but their faces give nothing away. Someone else, a man, is walking just behind them. He has a small child walking at the side of him and they are holding hands.

'Okay,' one of the surgeons says. 'Can you all take a seat please? We need to talk to you.'

I follow their faces, still trying to read them. I feel sick, really sick. Luke squeezes my hand and someone else squeezes the other.

'Hello Cassie,' the other person says.

'Hello Dad,' I reply.

# CHAPTER 37

TRYING TO COPE ...

**CASSIE**

'But Mum doesn't make them like that.'

'For god bloody sake Connor stop moaning will you,' I say for at least the hundredth time. 'I don't bloody care if she doesn't make your sandwiches like this. I do and right now that'll bloody have to do.'

'But you've made them all weird,' he says, his unbroken voice getting higher and louder with each word.

'Then you bloody make em,' I shout, throwing the knife down. Connor's bottom lip starts to quiver and his eyes fill up. 'What if ...' He begins to say. He pauses and quickly rubs his eyes with his fists. 'Where will we live if Mum dies, Cassie?' he finally blurts out.

I'm floored by his question and just look into his big brown eyes. He like so has Dad's eyes. I know Mum's in a coma and it's been two weeks but I can't allow myself to think of her not being here. Can't and won't. Connor just keeps staring at me waiting for a reply. I stand in stunned silence, also waiting for a reply to come. Words of wisdom to comfort and make us both feel better. Nothing comes though.

'We can't live with Dad. And Nan and Grandad are too old and Uncle Sean is too poor ...'

'We'll stay here with Simon, stupid.'

'Really?' he replies, his eyes suddenly huge like Romeow's become when he's about to pounce on something. 'Even if Mum dies?'

How can Connor keep saying that word die? I want to punch him in the face but I know he's just frightened. Nan says where there's life there's hope though. So that's what I carry with me each and every day – hope.

'Of course, you idiot. Simon says we're as much his as Maisy is and besides, Mum will be fine, I'm sure of it.' I'm not really sure though. The truth is, I've never felt so unsure about anything, ever. 'Anyway, hasn't Grandad asked you to help him make a special lotion or potion or something in his lab to help Mum?' I remind him. Connor's sad face morphs into a huge grin. I'm not really sure what I think of Grandad putting silly ideas into Connor's head but if it gives him hope I suppose it is okay. 'Right then. Let's finish getting this pack-up made or you'll be late for school.'

Connor continues smiling at me before he throws both his arms around my waist and hugs me. I hug him back, for a few seconds. I can feel my chest tighten with uncertainty and all I really want to do is start screaming and shouting and tell anyone who'll listen it's not fucking fair! But I can't.

'C'mon loser,' I say, pulling myself away from Connor. 'I'll finish making the sandwiches and you get the rest of the stuff. And not just crisps and chocolate,' I add, as he heads towards the snack cupboard. 'Put some bloody fruit in there too.'

I see Connor off to school then spend half an hour

wandering aimlessly around the house. It's been two weeks since Mum was attacked and she's still in a coma. The police are still appealing for witnesses and it's been on the news and in the papers and everything. It sort of doesn't feel real, kind of like it's happening to someone else. I feel like I'm wandering around in a thick foggy haze, my vision smudged, my ears stuffed full of cotton wool balls. I'm trying to act normal, especially in front of Connor, but the truth is I've never felt more abnormal in my whole entire life.

Uncle Sean came up as soon as he found out. After a week and no sign of Mum waking up we had a bit of a family gathering and it was agreed that someone would visit Mum everyday on like a rota basis but in the meantime everyone should try and get back into some kind of normal routine. Normal? How can anything ever be normal again?

Based on all the medical evidence and blood on the drive it's believed Mum suffered a severe blow to the head. A punch delivered within close range, so brutal and so quick she didn't even stand a chance to defend herself. I feel sick when I think about it. Like *really* sick. Why would someone do that to Mum? Why would anyone want to hurt her like that? I keep picturing her face and how frightened she must have been, and the last words I shouted at her.

Oh my god! Oh my god! I can't breathe. I grab my throat with both my hands and open my mouth, trying to force air in or out – anything to stop me from gasping. My heart beats so loud I swear I can hear every beat and my chest feels heavy, like it's crushing me from the inside out. I'm sure my heart is going to burst through my ribcage in a minute like in those alien films. I want to die. It should be me in a coma coz I'm such a complete and utter bitch.

They say you hurt the one's you love the most and it's true. For as long as I can remember I've tiptoed around Dad, desperate to get his love and approval. And all this time Mum gave me more love and support than any one person deserves, especially me. And all I ever did was take my shit out on her.

'I'm so sorry Mum,' I whisper. My legs aren't strong enough to hold me and I fall to the floor like a crumpled piece of sheet music. I haven't cried since the first day Mum was admitted to hospital but now, my tears fall easily. Hot salty water stings my eyes and snot runs from my nose into my mouth. As I sit on the floor, eyes closed and sobbing I feel something soft against my skin. When I open my eyes I see Romeow. He looks at me and meows and then an actual miracle happens. Without any persuasion from me, Romeow climbs onto my lap, curls into a ball and begins to purr. I stroke his soft fur and he meows again. My breathing starts to slow right down. I immediately feel calm again.

※

I make my way onto the Intensive Care Unit where Mum is. Simon's here. He seems surprised to see me.

'Hello trouble, thought you were going to college today?' I shrug my shoulders. 'Needed to see Mum,' I reply.

He smiles. 'Okay. You have a chat with her and I'll go and grab a coffee.'

I sit in the chair Simon was in and stare at Mum. I'm glad he's left the room coz I can be more honest with her. She still looks kind of freaky coz her neck's supported by a brace and there's a web of intravenous lines, feeding tubes, suction pumps and drains connected to some part of her body, not to mention mechanical ventilators and a whole load of other tubes that do god knows what. Still, she doesn't look as bad as she did on that first day when they took her down to surgery. They drilled like a proper hole in her head so they could insert a device called an intracranial pressure monitor to check for bleeding and swelling inside her skull. That was the worst forty-eight hours of my life. 'I really thought we were going to lose you Mum,' I tell her.

I wonder if she *can* hear me?

I've Googled everything I can on the subject of impaired consciousness (coma to everyone else) and they all advise the same as the doctors – coma patients should be spoken to as if they are awake. There are hundreds of stories of people who were in comas and they all claim they could hear family and friends talking to them.

Course it's dangerous looking at stuff on the net coz you get to read all the bad shit too, those that didn't make it ... or worse. Is it bad not to want Mum to live if she's like so badly brain damaged she doesn't even know me? Oh god, how bad am I? I'm such a bad person to think that. The lump in my throat makes it hard for me to talk. If Mum can hear me talking to her I don't want her to hear me crying.

I ring my hands and shift uncomfortably in the chair, listening to the constant clunk of the ventilator pushing oxygen in and out of Mum's lungs. I get up again and walk towards the bed that cradles Mum. The noise of the machines maintaining her life hurt my head. I put my earphones in and touch the music icon on my phone.

Suddenly the haunting voice of Kate Bush fills my ears. The song is *This Woman's Work*, one of Mum's favourites.

I run my hand across Mum's warm but lifeless arm and lift her heavy, limp fingers, holding them in mine. My fingers, made by her – her, my Mum.

Why didn't I tell you how much I love you? You gave me everything and all I gave you in return was shit. I let Mum's hand drop gently back onto the stiff sheets and look at her sleeping face. Her skin, normally sun kissed and flushed from all her woman's work is too white. I run my shaking finger across Mum's nose and laugh when I find her bump. Then, using the finger from my other hand I trace the bump on my nose too, before bending down and kissing the tip of Mum's beautiful nose.

'Please don't give up, Mum,' I whisper. 'Please.' My tears fall silently down my face.

'I'm so sorry, Mum. I never meant to hurt you. You're strong Mum, you have to come back. You never give up. You have to make it, eh?'

Shit. Did I really see that? Did Mum's eyes flicker or am I just imagining it? 'Simon! Nurse! Someone! I think Mum's eyes just opened!'

## CHAPTER 38

GRANDAD

**CONNOR**

'You alright love?' Nan says to me.

'I'm fine Nan,' I reply.

'Because you mustn't worry you know? I mean, I know you are worried but we all have to stray strong and positive. You know that's what Mum would want, right?'

'I know Nan.'

'But you know I'm always here for you?'

'I know Nan.'

'You can tell me if you're worried, and we'll sort it out together?'

'I know Nan, thanks Nan.'

'Leave the bleedin boy alone Ellie,' Grandad says, ruffling my hair (why do old people always ruffle kids' hair?). 'He's alright encha lad?' I smile at Grandad and nod my head. 'Besides,' he continues. 'We've got important work to do aint we Connor?' He winks at me but Nan just sighs and rolls her eyes at Grandad. We take our mugs of hot chocolate that Nan has just made us, and head out to Grandads laboratory. It's not really a proper laboratory. It used to be an old garage that Grandad converted but it actually looks more like a Library coz it's filled with hundreds and hundreds of books. I recognise some of the writers like J R R Tolkien, Ian Fleming, Roald Dahl and J K Rowling, but others, wearing old brown or red leather jackets, I've never heard of or can't even pronounce. Some of Grandad's books are so rare and so precious he actually has them locked up in glass display cases. They are a bit old and tattered but you can tell from some of the amazing pictures and the yellowy, brown pages they really are from the old, old, olden days.

Grandad pulls a stool out for me to sit on and he slowly lowers himself into his black leather swivel chair. We take a loud sip of hot chocolate then look at each other and laugh coz we both know if Mum were in here with us she'd shout at us for slurping.

'Anymore trouble with that Warraner kid?' Grandad asks.
'Jason? A bit,' I reply.

'What kinda trouble?' Grandad asks, raising his bushy grey eyebrows.

I shrug my shoulders. 'He said Mum's as good as dead and even if she does wake up she'll be like a vegetable; a dribbling retard that has to wear nappies and will be shagged by the polski carers who will have to look after her – when no one's looking.'

'Did he now?' Grandad replies. One of his eyes begins to twitch and his nostrils flare ever so slightly. He looks angry. 'That bigoted ass of a father of his is teaching him well then. And what else?' he continues in a voice that unlike his face is much calmer.

'And I punched his lights out,' I reply. Grandad's face breaks into a huge smile and he begins to chuckle so loud I can't help but join in.

'That's my boy,' he finally says after we stop laughing.

We sit quietly for a moment, only breaking the silence from time to time with the odd slurping and gulping noises we both make as we finish our hot chocolates.

'Aaaaahhhh,' Grandad finally says as he slams his cup down on the side using his hand to wipe away any of the drink left on his lips. I do the same then we grin at each other. 'C'mon then yang Connor, look lively, let's get this elixir made eh?'

'Okay Grandad, let's do it. Let's get this lixar made for Mum.'

Although most of Grandad's room is crammed with books there is one small corner filled with laboratory equipment. A Bunsen burner, clamp stand and test tube holder all sit on an old wooden bench along with other weird instruments like forceps, crucible tongs and dropper pipets. There is other stuff but they're the ones I can remember the names of. There are also a couple of shelves with neatly stacked glass beakers and flasks as well as watch glasses and test tubes. Hanging from a few rusty nails banged into the wall are some protection goggles and on another, higher up shelf there are lots of different coloured glass bottles with lids, some containing what look like powders, others have liquids. Some have labels with writing on and some have no labels at all, whilst others have a yellow triangle with skull and crossbones and the words DANGER, TOXIC HAZARD underneath.

Grandad reaches for a mortar and pestle at the back of the bench. Then he pulls out a small set of stepladders, and slowly, taking one step at a time, huffing and puffing, he reaches for some of the bottles on the high up shelf and passes them to me to put on the wooden bench. I don't know if any of the stuff Grandad does is real – "playing at being a bloody alchemist or wizard or what bloody ever" – Mum (when she was awake) and

Nan would mutter to each other when they'd think I wasn't listening. But I don't really care. I love that Grandad's a bit mad, a bit eccentric. It's better than golf or football.

Grandad puts what looks like a few leaves and some different coloured powders into the mortar and tells me to start grinding them up with the pestle whilst he looks his two, oldest and favourite books, both locked separately in their own glass display cases. He very carefully takes out the first book. I watch him as I continue grinding, suddenly sneezing as some of the powder rises up my nose. It's a big, black leather bound book full of strange pictures. There are absolutely no words whatsoever in this first book, that's why it's called *Mutus Liber* which means *The Wordless or Silent book* – at least that's what Grandad tells me.

Grandad holds the book really carefully, like you would a new-born baby or something. After making a few grunting noises he finally places it onto the lectern that sits next to the wooden bench. He carefully opens the book to a page he has bookmarked and places one hand, moving it around in a circular motion, above the picture on the page. He looks up and closes his eyes, his hand still hovering and muttering a few words I don't understand. All of a sudden he opens his eyes and turns quickly to look at me.

'Ow's that grinding coming on then yang Connor?'

'Alright I think Grandad.'

'Good, good,' he says, but he sounds sort of distracted. He then reaches across me for a clear bottle containing what looks like some sort of white cream or lotion. He takes the mortar from me and pours some of the white stuff in. 'Right,' he says handing it back to me, 'nar give that a bit of a stir.'

I start to mix it up and notice the white stuff has the same smell as the moisturiser Nan uses. 'Gow on boy,' Grandad says, 'put some blady elbow into it.'

I continue stirring whilst Grandad puts the *Silent Book* back into its glass case and takes out his next other favourite book. This one is slightly smaller than the last one with a very old binding – of worked copper Grandad says. And unlike the last book (Grandad also tells me) that had pages made of parchment, the pages of this book are made from the bark of trees. He treats it with the same care as the last book. He also places this one on the lectern and again opens it to a bookmarked page. This book is called *Abraham The Jew* and like the last book this book also has lots of pictures and diagrams but unlike the last one this book also has lots of writing.

Grandad starts to read the pages of the book he's opened, whispering words to himself. I stop stirring and watch him, suddenly feeling like I'm in a Harry Potter movie or something. He turns his head towards me and looks at me over his reading glasses.

'Right then yang Connor, put that mortar down and repeat after me – *Om Mani Padmi Hum*.'

I do as Grandad asks and start chanting. 'Armani Padmee Hummm,' I say.

Grandad laughs and repeats the words slowly until I begin saying them the same way as him. Grandad explains that the words are from a Tibetan Buddhism mantra and that saying them out loud brings blessings of compassion, or something like that. I feel a bit stupid chanting out loud, but I carry on anyway. '*Om Mani Padmi Hum, Om Mani Padmi Hum*.' We repeat the words over and over again. I keep my eyes closed and after about five minutes I start to feel really calm. As I continue saying the words, I can see Mum awake and happy and back to normal. It's a bit freaky actually coz it's like I can actually feel her and smell her. And every now and again, when I see her face really clearly, she looks like she's frowning at me and Grandad – but in a good way.

'Right then,' Grandad suddenly shouts, making me jump and sorry to see Mum disappear again. 'That should just about do it. Talking to the universe we were Connor. Now then,' he continues. 'You put that mixture into this plastic bottle.' He passes me a clear, empty bottle and points to the contents of the mortar. 'I'll just put this book away.'

'Okay Grandad,' I reply, feeling a little bit sad but happy at the same time.

I pour the lotion into the plastic bottle using a funnel. Grandad then takes it from me and screws a lid on. He hands it back to me with a big smiling, craggy old face.

'Nar, you make sure you rub this into ya Mum's hands every time you visit her in hospital and we'll see what happens eh?' Grandad smiles at me again and winks.

'Okay Grandad,' I say, winking back.

I felt a bit sad when I first got here. My legs felt too tired to walk properly and my shoulders hurt and felt heavy, like they were pushing me down. But doing this with Grandad has made me feel better, lighter in a way and happier – a bit happier anyway. I know some lotion, potion whatever it is won't make Mum better. But you never know – and I can hope. I really, really can hope.

# CHAPTER 39

KNOCKIN' ON HEAVEN'S DOOR

**CASSIE**

Oh god I can't do this, not today. No one can deny Dylan's *Knockin' on Heaven's Door* is like an ammmmazing song and Honey's rendition is hauntingly beautiful but Luke will have to play keyboards for the upcoming gig coz every time I play it I literally feel myself falling apart. It's been months now since Mum's attack and she's *still* in a coma and of course the longer it goes on the less chance there is of her ever waking up.

I could swear Mum moved her eyes that day I went to visit her when Simon was there and had gone off to get coffee. The Doctors said it was just an involuntary spasm or something, but I swear it wasn't. I think Mum heard me talking to her.

I'm fine most of the time and the rota system we've got going seems to work. Basically Simon is back at work, sort of part-time for now and Maisy has put off going to Oz – she said she won't go until Mum wakes up. Crazee said he'd wait for her, which is like well sweet. So Maisy is still working and Connor's still going to school and I'm trying to keep going to college as well as still working part-time in the lingerie department. So between us lot, Nan and Grandad, Ruby and Andy, Jodi and her brood (god knows how Mum doesn't wake up with those bloody twins running around – noisy little buggers!) we all take it in turns to visit and talk with Mum each day. Uncle Sean travels up to visit when he can.

Sometimes we – me and Maisy and Nan – help the nurses wash Mum. I don't mind washing her, even though it can be a bit intimate sometimes coz her boobs and wanny have to be washed (I usually get the nurse to do those bits). It's strange though coz it feels like our roles have reversed and now I'm the one taking care of Mum, which is like so weird and just goes against the natural order of things.

Nan says as long as Mum is still alive there's hope. Nan also said we mustn't get down and always remember that hope is the Aunt Hissy Fit of despair – I didn't have a bloody clue what that was supposed to mean until Maisy explained that Nan had said antithesis. Antithesis – Aunt Hissy Fit – all sounds the bloody same to me. At least I made everyone laugh though. Grandad says laughter is the best medicine.

Nan is right though; we do have to have hope. I try to, and I try and carry that hope with me every single day. But sometimes my heart is so full of the stuff it's just too heavy to carry. Today is one of those days. I want to be numb, to not feel, to not think. To wake up one morning without desperately searching for my hope that I know I lose during the night; especially during the small, dark hours after midnight. That's the time Grandad calls the witching hour, when witches, ghosts and demons are at their most powerful and black magic at its most effective. I don't know how he knows all this stuff – read too many books I think – but there are definitely demons playing with my head in the middle of the night sometimes.

People are cruel too. I'm not sure they actually mean to be but everyone stares at me in the college corridors. I've taken to wearing sunglasses all the time but as a music student they don't actually look too out of place. People whisper too, in their little groups and I hear them. My ears are so sensitive they twitch and swivel like Romeow's, detecting every word they think I can't hear. *Sucker punch* and *king hit* are the worst. My stomach physically flips when I hear those words. And sometimes – I'm a bit ashamed to say – my stomach isn't the only thing to flip. Sometimes I do too.

'It wasn't a fucking King hit,' I shout. 'It was a huge, fucked-up COWARD punch. Only a fucking COWARD would throw a punch like that. Not Sucker, not King but C O W A R D!!!!!'

Without a word Luke takes my place at the keyboard. He knows my struggle with this song and once again he comes to my rescue. Luke always seems to be there just when I need it. Useless watches me move discreetly away from the keyboard. He places his guitar back in its case and sidles up to me.

'Lap?' he says.

'Yeah lap,' I reply.

I walk over to Marcus, our tutor, who is helping Louisa with her arpeggios. 'Going on a loo brake Marcus,' I say. He smiles, nods at me and turns his attention back to Louisa.

I wander along the corridor, away from the Music Department. The sounds of rehearsal grow faint and I'm swallowed up by the eerie quiet of the college as life inside this huge warren continues behind its many closed doors. Even before I reach the exit I'm already fumbling for the fags and lighter in my bag. I swipe my ID card in front of the electronic thingy whatsit and wait as the double doors slowly open.

I'm relieved to feel fresh air on my face. I lean against the brick wall next to the door and light the fag in my hand. I suck on it hard. I look up and close my eyes blowing smoke through the triangular shape I've made at the corner of my mouth. Mum would hate to see me smoking. I keep my eyes closed but I'm aware someone is now standing next to me and I know it's Useless.

Useless takes the fag from my hand and also inhales deeply before exhaling through his nostrils. Ever since Mum was admitted into hospital me and Useless have got into this routine of sneaking out whenever I've had enough and walking a complete lap of the college. We smoke, talk shit or sometimes just don't talk at all. That's the great thing about Useless. There's nothing sexual about our relationship. He just gets me. We get each other.

'How iz your Mum?' Useless asks, his polish accent as strong as ever.

'Still breathing – just,' I reply laughing. I tell him about our recent police visit.

'They got him,' I tell Useless. 'They got the scumbag that attacked my Mum.'

I'm glad they've found him. I've been like dead frightened he might come back for the rest of us, which I know is really selfish of me. Sometimes though, late at night, when I'm in bed and can stop pretending to be okay in front of everyone – especially Connor – I imagine Mum's attacker coming to the house and me shooting him. I don't know how I'd shoot him coz we don't have a gun but I want him to die for killing me, little by little, every day.

*"To be, or not to be: that is the question"*. I get that now. Mum loves Shakespeare and I always said I didn't understand what the hell Shakespeare was going on about in most of his plays but now I see it all so clearly. Well, I see Hamlet's grief anyway and it matches mine perfectly ...

> "Whether 'tis nobler in the mind to suffer The slings and arrows of Outrageous fortune, Or take arms against a sea
> Of troubles,
> And by opposing end them? To die: to sleep; No more; and by a sleep to Say we end
> The heart-ache and the Thousand natural shocks That flesh is heir to"

'Apparently Mum's attacker was connected with that bloody Amber girl who came into the Library a lot,' I continue explaining to Useless. 'The one Mum actually helped well loads.'

Useless shakes his head but says nothing. Which is fine, no words are needed.

Useless lights another fag and passes it to me, and yeah I know they could give me cancer one day but right now, I don't give a shit. For now, these cancer sticks are helping me through this. Even John Lennon said, *Whatever Gets You Through The Night*.

I take another long drag and exhale, really slowly. It makes me feel kind of woozy. Mum would hate it if she knew I was smoking. Maybe that's why I'm doing it, hoping in some stupid way she'll know and be so angry she'll wake up.

Dad hates me smoking too. Maybe that's the real reason I'm doing it, to piss him off. To push him and test his new found interest in me and Connor. To be fair though, he has been quite good with us since Simon beat him up. He's changed a bit. Nothing drastic though. It's not like some fairy-tale ending to our dire situation with Mum. We still don't have a room at his house and Sharon still doesn't really like us going there. She says what she thinks people expect her to say to us but she doesn't really mean it, there's no warmth in her words. It's all for show, especially if she has guests – then we really see the actress in her come alive. That's when the hugs and the crocodile tear good advice and words of comfort are dished out, but it's all an act. A huge, big, fat fucking lie. I want to scream at her, 'STOP IT YOU LYING BITCH,' but I don't want to jeopardise what little bit of something we have with Dad right now, coz I don't know if it'll last.

Over the last few weeks Dad's got into the habit of taking me and Connor out instead of meeting at his house. I know it's coz Sharon doesn't want us there but that's fine by me coz I don't want to be anywhere I'm not wanted anyway. We only meet Dad for a coffee (or milkshake for Connor) and a chat but he tries to do it once a week. So things are slightly better, I suppose. Sometimes Dad brings Harriet with him. Harriet is 4 years old and despite being half Sharon is actually dead cute. Well, most of the time. We had one meeting the other week that did like really upset me. I was talking to Dad and obviously calling him Dad. The more I talked to Dad the more I noticed Harriet's face become all twisted up, like she was confused. She watched me for a while then suddenly started screaming, 'He's not *your* Daddy, he's *mine*.'

I tried to explain that her Daddy was also mine and Connor's daddy – we just had different Mummies – but she just kept shouting it over and over again. What hurt the most though was the smirk she had on her little face as she said it. Did she know she was hurting me? Dad didn't say much to stop her but he did intervene when I explained to Harriet that I was her sister and Connor was her brother. I said that she was our sister and we were all family but she didn't seem to like me saying that. She just kept screaming and shouting, telling me that I'll never be a part of her family. Dad did actually tell her off then, sort of. 'Just ignore her,' Dad said. 'She's only little, she doesn't really know what she's saying.'

'Really?' I asked. 'Did she hear that from someone else

then?' Dad's cheeks flushed up really red and he seemed embarrassed. 'Why does Sharon call you Scottie?' I also asked him. 'It makes you sound more like a dog than a person.'

Dad looked and me and sighed. He seemed tired and – what else? Sad? Yeah I could see something in his eyes and it wasn't happiness. I wanted to grab Dad and shake him, to tell him I felt sorry for him, that I hate the way Sharon orders him around, that he should stand up for himself and tell her his name is Scott not Scottie and also tell her that we are his children as much as Harriet is. I wanted to scream at him and tell him he sold out, gave up me and Connor and Mum for money and possessions. All the things that make up life's unnecessities and that while he may have all the lovely playthings any man could want; it came at a price. I decided (in the end) to keep those thoughts to myself though.

Dad squirmed uncomfortably and didn't answer my question and as usual tried to change the subject. He pretended to ask about college and I pretended he cared. Harriet hopped onto Dad's knee and wrapped her arms around his neck, staring at me – all the time smirking and saying, 'My Daddy, *not* yours.'

I actually hated Harriet at that moment, believed she was some sort of devil child, like *Damien* from *The Omen*. I swore to myself I'd never forgive her – and I meant it – until I found myself doing the same thing to Maisy a week later.

I'd decided to pay Mum a surprise visit at the hospital. It wasn't my turn that day and I couldn't remember whose it was but I'd had a shit day and an overwhelming urge just to be with her. When I walked into her room Maisy was there, sitting on a chair next to Mum's bed. She was reading out loud. Maisy didn't hear me come in and as I got closer I realised Maisy was reading Shakespeare. I know how much Mum loves Shakespeare and out of nowhere my body filled with rage and jealousy. Why hadn't I thought of doing that for Mum? I was her daughter, her *real* daughter and it should have been me reading that crap to her, not Maisy. I'm not really sure what happened next except my angry words quickly turned into an eruption of screaming and yelling followed by a real physical fight. I hadn't had a real fight since I was about 11 years old. I forgot how much it hurts.

'She's not your Mum,' I'd screamed at Maisy. 'She's mine. She'll never love you like she loves me. NEVER!'

It was only when we were separated by a couple of nurses and I replayed my words back in my head, I realised what a bitch I'd been. At least Harriet, at the age of 4 years old, had an excuse – I, now 17 years old, should have known better. The atmosphere at home was horrible for a couple of days. I finally got the guts up to apologise to Maisy then we both collapsed into each other's arms in floods of tears. In a stupid sort of way it's made us closer though.

I ask Useless how things are going with Rae Rae (her real name is Rachel) a girl on the Dance course at college he secretly loves and has done now for the last two years.

'She doesn't know I exzeest,' he says. 'Well no, actually that's a lie she does, but only as a friend.'

'She's friend-zoned you then?'

'Ahhhh Cazzie, I am so far in the friend zone she actually sends me photos of her in her underwear asking me what I think her boyfriend will think!'

'Shit, no way?' We both sigh. 'Unrequited love eh?'

'Yezzz, obsolutely. Gives me plenty of song writing material though – mostly sad. A bit like Luke with you I think?'

I swing round to look at Useless. 'You think?'

'You know so Cazzie. The boy iz crazy about you.'

'But he's seeing Nicole. I didn't think ...'

'You think every time you lay your head on his shoulder, or you text him or call him when you're feeling down, it means nothing more than friendship to him?'

'I ... I do love Luke but ... but ...'

'As a friend?' Useless laughs. I shrug my shoulders.

'What is it about love anyway? I *should* love Luke, but I love Joe. And I'm not actually that convinced he really loves me. He's always so worried about what his friends think all the time. He won't come to the hospital with me you know? He said he doesn't do hospitals!'

Useless just looks at me and shrugs his shoulders. 'I don't know Cazzie, it's a crazy world huh?'

'It certainly is Useless. You do know I love you though right?'

He grins at me and opens his arms wide. 'Of course, what's not to love?'

We complete our lap of the college. I slip back into class and Useless follows five minutes later. Marcus, thankfully, doesn't seem to notice how long I've been gone. My phone vibrates. It's a text from Simon confirming he's picking me up from college today. He usually works away a lot but since Mum's attack Andy has made sure he stays local, which is good, coz having Simon around makes me feel safe.

Unfortunately, it's taken all this shit to happen to make me realise Simon is actually my real Dad.

'Hi,' I say climbing into the car. Simon smiles but his eyes never do.

'Hello trouble,' he replies. 'How was college?'

'S'okay I suppose.' I tell him about rehearsals and *Knockin' on Heaven's Door*. He looks sad but tries to hide it, sad and tired. Acting is draining, I should know.

Simon tells me a bit about work then we talk about Mum. 'Do you know Guns and Roses did a cover of *Knockin' on Heaven's Door*? Early 90s I think it was,' Simon says. 'I saw them perform it live, at Wembley. Turns out your Mum did as well. We were both actually at the same concert.'

I smile. I can't imagine Mum being into heavy rock and the outspoken ranting of Axle Rose.

'Course we didn't know each other then ...'

Simon pauses for a moment, looks lost in thought, then smiles again. He looks at me. 'Wish I had known your Mum then. She's made me Cassie, made me a better man.' He looks back towards the road in front of us. I squeeze his arm. He coughs and clears his throat. 'Course, if I had known her then and we'd got together there'd have been no you or Connor or Maisy. And life would certainly have been a lot less interesting then eh?' We both laugh.

'Hmmmmm, it certainly would have been a lot quieter I reckon.'

We carry on talking about Mum for a while. I ask Simon if he washes her too sometimes. He says he does. I want to ask him if he does her boobs and wanny but then change my mind. I turn the radio on even though I have a thumping headache and Bob Marley's voice blares out the song *Three Little Birds*. Simon looks across at me and we smile, like properly smile at each other. As Bob's warm, soulful voice continues to fill our ears I have an overwhelming feeling – or is it still just desperate hope – that everything really is going to be okay. Before I know it me and Simon are singing and laughing hysterically. Maybe Mum is going be all right, maybe this song coming on the radio just at this moment is a sign?

I feel my phone vibrate in my pocket and choose to ignore it, preferring to continue listening to Bob and his Wailers. Simon looks the happiest I've seen him in ages. The song comes to an end and my phone is vibrating again. I pull it from my pocket, a bit annoyed if I'm honest. I answer it and its Nan but I can't understand her for crying. I tell her to slow down coz I can't make out what she's saying. She's quiet for a moment then repeats what she's just said, this time more slowly. I let the words sink in but I feel sick and can't talk. I can actually feel the blood drain from my face. Simon looks at me, confused.

'What? What is it?' he asks.

'Kay, okay Nan,' I eventually manage to say. 'I'll tell Simon, yes, yeah we'll come straight there.'

I stare at my phone, not believing the words that just came from it.

'What? Tell me what?' Simon says again. I slowly look across at him.

'Oh my god Simon ... we ... we have to go to the hospital.'

My head is spinning. I feel like I've drunk too much or smoked too much weed.

'STOP THE CAR SIMON – PLEASE STOP THE CAR!' I yell but it's too late. The food in my stomach has climbed into my throat and before I know it I vomit across the dashboard.

Clearly everything is *not* going be okay.

# CHAPTER 40

## GONE ... BUT NOT FORGOTTEN

**CASSIE**

*I* feel numb. Why is it raining? Why is the sky grey? And why is the wind blowing? Connor says heaven is crying. I'm not crying. I just feel numb. Simon is crying – no sound, just silent tears running down his cheeks. He's got his arm around Ruby who is crying uncontrollably. Great sobs of bare, naked grief; all gaping and exposed for everyone to see. Her tears are black from the mascara running down her face.

No one is wearing black, we weren't allowed to. Bright, bold colours, that was the request. A celebration of life is what today is supposed to be. But how can we celebrate life when death is so final? The end – the full stop – of all vital functions of the body including the heartbeat. That's what I read when I looked up the definition of death.

Oh god, I think Ruby has collapsed. Simon and Maisy are helping her up. They sit her down on the sofa. People are rushing over to her. Someone is giving her a glass of water. I laugh to myself coz I can hear Mum in my head and what she would have said,

"Water? What good is water? Have we no wine here?"

Connor looks up at me. It's strange because I hadn't noticed it before but he doesn't look up at me very much at all these days. He's grown so much, and Mum missed it. Connor tugs my jacket. His lips quiver and his eyes are glassy reflecting my grief. But like me, he doesn't cry. It's as if we're both afraid to. No words spoken, we hug each other.

'I'm so glad I have you,' I whisper in his ear. He doesn't reply, just nods his head up and down in agreement. I feel a big strong arm fold around me. I'm so glad Dad is here. He doesn't say anything either, just looks down at me, and smiles. I manage to smile back. I look across the room and catch Simon watching us. He smiles at me too, and winks, but his eyes are not smiling, just his mouth. Poor Simon, he looks so tired and worn out.

Joe isn't here. "I don't do funerals babe", he said.

People keep coming up to me and saying things but thankfully no one seems to expect me to reply, which is just as well really coz I think my numbness has affected my hearing coz I can't really hear what they say. I catch odd words or phrases from time to time like "so sorry", or "lovely person", or "so young", or "here if you need us". But it's all just noise to me.

I look around the room amazed at all the people here, all in their bright, colourful clothes. I watch them, fascinated how they manage to talk about the weather and the economy and even laugh a little. Not loud, belly laughter. It's sort of restrained, polite laughter; but laughter all the same.

Someone has gone; the world will never be the same again. Everyone, everything should just stop, at least for a moment – shouldn't it?

My numbness is changing to a weird tingling sensation as the hearse pulls up outside the house. The room is starting to sway. I didn't want breakfast this morning but Simon said I had to try and eat something and now I can feel toast in my throat coz I can't control the tummy spasms forcing it back upwards. I manage, somehow, to swallow my marmalade-flavoured sick back down, repulsed at myself. Connor grabs my hand and holds it in his and I'm surprised at its rough texture; Connor the man-child. I feel Dad's hand in my back, gently pushing us towards the door.

Most of the people in the room step back politely; it looks like the parting of a sea of people, paving the way for close family and friends. Simon is up ahead, still supporting Ruby. Who's supporting Simon though? Nan and Grandad are here too, of course. They look small and frail today. Grandad is unusually quiet. It wouldn't be respectful or right but I wish he'd shout out his usual,

"It's not a life, it's an adventure!!!"

This doesn't feel like an adventure though. It's not a life anymore. Death is the full stop; the punctuation mark that brings everything that was alive and touchable to a standstill.

I can't remember how I got from the house to the car or the journey for that matter. I remember looking out of the window and faces, serious and sombre, staring back. I remember trembling and my teeth chattering. Am I just cold, or frightened, or both? I remember the rain, each and every drop crashing onto the roof, colliding with the windows. And then suddenly we are at the church – the final destination.

The church, probably really beautiful in sunlight, is fearful today, as dark and gothic as my heart. Even the colours of the huge stained glass windows seem washed out. Dad has guided me and Connor to one of the long, dark benches at the front. We sit, listening to the church fill up behind us. There is a gentle hum of voices, whispered conversations, quiet crying and polite coughing, until eventually the heavy, wooden doors bang to a close. Silence reigns, before the wind rasps and rattles every sealed window and door, demanding to be let in, eventually finding its own way through. It salsa's around my feet and hands, my big nose and my small ears. I want to stamp some life back into my feet, but I feel rooted to the spot, frozen and unable to move.

The vicar, priest man person is talking. He welcomes everyone on this sad day, I think. I can hear the droning of his voice vibrate high up into the arches of the ceiling – I can even see his lips moving but everything seems muffled as if I'm underwater. I stand up when we're supposed to sing hymns and sit down again when we finish singing. Who's laughing? I can hear laughing. Death isn't funny. I look up, relieved to see Simon is now speaking. He probably said something funny. He continues to talk and I can hear again. I've surfaced for air and the mute button is deactivated. Simon's voice is warm and familiar. Simon's voice is home. He reads something by Samuel Butler.

> "*I fall asleep in the full and certain hope That my slumber shall not be broken; And that, though I be all-forgetting, Yet shall I not be all-forgotten,*
>
> *But continue that life in the thoughts and deeds Of those I have loved"*

Simon has to stop from time to time, his voice gripped by grief, before taking a deep breath and soldiering on. It's all too much for Ruby though, who now seems to be wailing. It's a terrifying sound and I wish she would stop. My throat tightens and hot salty water bathes my eyes and blurs my vision. I purse my lips and use every ounce of strength not to blink. I will not cry. I will not cry.

The service is at an end. The coffin bearers, including Simon, pick the coffin up and very carefully balance it on their shoulders. They then walk, very slowly, down the aisle, to the haunting voice of Richard Hawley singing *Long Black Train*. It's a beautiful song but too, too sad.

The words linger in my head as we follow the coffin. It's good to get back outside, even though it's started raining again. The coffin is lowered into the ground and flowers and earth are thrown onto it. Final goodbyes are said.

'Goodbye Andy,' I whisper. 'Safe journey on your long black train.'

# CHAPTER 41

NEW BEGINNINGS

**CASSIE**

I'm sitting with Ruby in her huge kitchen. She stayed for a while at the wake-celebration thing, but then she told Simon she had to leave coz she felt unwell. Simon asked me if I'd go home with Ruby while he looked after the other guests along with Maisy and Connor.

Ruby has changed out of her funeral dress and now has grey trackies and a sweatshirt on. Poor Ruby, her face looks so pale. She's sitting crouched over, hugging one knee and staring into space.

'Cup of tea?' I ask. 'Rosie Lee Grandad calls it.'

Ruby starts to rock back and forth, still holding one knee, her eyes filling up again. I'm surprised she still has tears to cry; she's shed so many. 'I didn't deserve him,' Ruby says. 'It should be me dead, not him.'

I make my voice soft. 'Don't be silly,' I reply. I pull out one of her funky orange chairs and sit opposite Ruby. I hold her hand.

'It was an accident Ruby, a stupid, stupid car crash. No one's fault.'

'I'm being punished,' she replies. 'For being such a bitch. This is my penance for being unfaithful.'

I look at Ruby, confused. 'What? What do you mean?'

Ruby covers her face with both hands and makes a weird groaning noise. 'It's all such a fucking mess,' she mumbles, then screams so loud I actually jump. I don't really know what to say so I decide nothing is best. We sit in silence. All I can hear is the hum of the huge fridge. I feel nervous and rub marks off my hands that are not there. Eventually, after what feels like forever but is probably only a few minutes, Ruby speaks again.

'I had an affair Cassie, with Luca.'

I'm shocked, mainly that someone so young could fancy someone so old. And again I don't really know what to say.

'Oh,' is about all I can manage. I feel hurt for Andy (even though he is dead).

Everything is quiet again and I'm lost in thought.

'Why?' I eventually blurt out. 'Why would you do that to Andy?'

'Because I'm a stupid fucking bitch.'

God this is so awkward. I wish Mum were here. I laugh nervously.

'I was drowning, Cassie. Drowning and desperate for Andy to see me. He was so wrapped up with work, with the company, he didn't see how unhappy I was. I really didn't care if I got caught, I was trying to get his attention.'

Ruby explains how devastated both she and Andy had been when Lilly died, how she wanted another child but Andy didn't. How they both loved each other but how empty Ruby felt without Lilly. I asked Ruby why she didn't just get pregnant anyway coz surely Andy would have come round in the end? But

Ruby said no, Andy had made it quite clear, he said if she got pregnant again, he'd leave her.

'The affair with Luca, is that why Mum fell out with you? She knew didn't she?'

Ruby laughs and shakes her head. 'Yes, she knew – well, had her suspicions – but no,' she says. 'Your mum wouldn't fall out with me over that. Don't get me wrong, she was angry, told me off. Said I had to get my shit sorted.' I have a mental image of Mum doing just that and it makes me laugh out loud. 'Told me it was wrong, that I needed to speak to Andy. Good advice of course, the right thing to do, but then my stupid drunken spite fucked it all up completely.'

I'm confused again.

'I don't know why I said it,' Ruby continues. 'After all these years I carried that fucking guilt with me, silently suffering but always keeping my fat gob shut. And then out it all came, like some sort of pent up poison, desperate to escape. But then I lost her, Cassie. I lost your mum, and now I've lost Andy. Forever.' Ruby bursts into tears again. 'It's all my fault,' she says in between great sobbing gulps. 'It's all my fault and now I'm being punished.'

I feel sorry for Ruby but also confused and if I'm honest, a little bit annoyed. 'You know that's just not true,' I reply very matter-of-fact. I am trying to copy Mum's annoyingly reassuring tone. 'You were a bit of a cow for having an affair but Andy dying was an accident. Pure and simple.'

'But ... but,' Ruby stutters. I pass her some of the crumpled but unused tissues from my pocket. 'What if he was thinking about me – us – thinking about what I'd done? What if he was so busy thinking, he stopped concentrating on his driving for a second and lost control of the car?'

'What, you mean the affair? What if Andy was thinking about your affair with Luca?'

I look at Ruby's tired, worn out face. She dabs her red, sore eyes and equally red nose. My heart sinks. The truth is I know exactly how Ruby feels; the guilt she carries. That god-awful day Mum was admitted into hospital never leaves me. From the minute my eyes open in the morning right through and into the night my thoughts are always haunted. Why did I say that? Why did I choose those words to yell at Mum's disappearing back? *"Why don't you just piss off and don't bother coming back"*. Each and every single one of those words feels like a ball of splinters in my throat or drops of acid on my tongue. I don't deserve a voice or the power of speech. Sticks and stones may break my bones but words will never hurt me. What a load of bollocks. Words can hurt – really hurt.

I do have a voice though and I manage to find it again. 'Coz if that is true – that you believe Andy's accident is your fault for being a bitch – then what you said to me that day Mum was rushed into hospital, you know, about it not being my fault and that I wasn't getting what I'd asked for? Well, then that isn't true either is it? If you're being punished then surely that means I am too, for also being such a bitch.'

Ruby looks up at me. She frowns then smiles and not just with her mouth, her eyes smile too.

'You're far too clever for your own good young lady,' she says. I smile back.

Ruby opens her mouth as if she's about to say something else but clearly changes her mind and closes it again.

'Why ...?' I start to ask before pausing for a moment. I know Ruby's close to telling me why she and Mum fell out and although I desperately need to know, I'm not sure I actually want to. I take a deep breath and go for it. 'Why did you and Mum fall out Ruby?'

Ruby's expression changes again. She looks like someone has just slapped her. She dips her head back into her hands again and rubs her face really hard. She rocks backwards and forwards and won't look at me.

'Ruby, please,' I plead.

Ruby takes her head out of her hands and stops rocking. She looks straight at me, her eyes filling up again. 'Oh god, if I tell you Cassie, I'll lose you too and I couldn't stand it. I can't lose anyone else, not now.'

I'm starting to feel scared, scared shitless if I'm honest. What could be so bad that Ruby actually believes I'd abandon her, especially now?

'You won't lose me Ruby I promise – on Mum's life.'

Ruby stares at me, eyes wide. 'Don't say that. Take that back,' she yells. 'You can't swear on Lizzie's life because *you will* hate me. *You will* want nothing to do with me, like your mum did.'

I laugh – sort of. 'For god sake, Ruby, whatever it is it can't be that bloody bad?'

Ruby's eyes darken and she just stares at me. 'I slept with your dad, Cassie – years ago – I slept with your dad. Scott.'

I feel as though I've just been punched in the stomach, winded and unable to talk.

'What ... what do you mean?' I eventually manage to stutter.

I don't know if its relief or fear or grief but now she's started Ruby doesn't seem to be able to stop, the whole story comes pouring out of her mouth. Waves made up of words, one after the other crash so quick and violently into my head I can barely keep up with her. Ruby explains about another time her and Andy were going through a bad patch in their marriage, years ago when they were much younger.

They were arguing, mostly about having children. Ruby wanted them but Andy didn't. Things got so bad they even stopped sleeping together for a while and Ruby thought about leaving Andy. She said she bumped into Dad on a night out. I was a baby, only a couple of months old, and Mum was at home looking after me. Ruby said that she and Dad were both really drunk and Dad was like being really attentive towards her, complaining that Mum didn't understand him. Ruby said she slept with Dad out of spite towards Andy and didn't give Mum a second thought – until afterwards.

Ruby said it was one night, not an affair – a drunken, stupid, stupid mistake. And she stayed well and truly out of Dad's way after that.

Shit, now I understand why Mum was so hurt. Her best friend had slept with her scumbag husband – who happens to also be my wanker of a Dad. I feel numb. How could they? Isn't that like a cardinal sin or whatever the bloody saying is?

Ruby is still talking but I feel sick, not realising the best is yet to bloody come. What Ruby tells me next completely floors me, totally and utterly head fucks me. Ruby confesses that Lilly was my sister – well, half-sister. She explains that she fell pregnant after sleeping with Dad, but she didn't realise until months later, by which time her and Andy were getting on much better. When she worked it out she knew though, from the dates of the pregnancy, that the baby she was carrying was Dad's and not Andy's. She took a chance and told Andy about the pregnancy but lied about the dates. Andy wasn't too happy at first but he eventually accepted the pregnancy and Lilly as his. Ruby said Andy was a brilliant Dad to Lilly. But when Lilly died, Andy told Ruby no more, no more children – he couldn't and wouldn't do it again. It was only after Ruby spilled her story to Mum (Ruby said she envied Mum coz Mum has me and Connor and Maisy) she went home and confessed to Andy that Lilly had been Dad's. There's another mad twist to this story though. After Ruby confessed to Andy what had happened with Dad, Andy confessed to Ruby that he'd had a vasectomy just after they'd married (he'd been abused as a child or something and was afraid to be a parent, in case he fucked it up) and he knew, for all those years, Lilly wasn't his. He didn't know at the time and didn't want to know who the real father was, he just knew it was important to Ruby to have a child and he surprised himself how much he loved Lilly and how easy it was to be her Dad. What shocked him the most was the terrible sadness he felt when Lilly died.

Ruby and Andy had deceived each other big time.

Ruby stops talking but my head is spinning. My emotions are all over the place and I'm not sure how I feel about anyone.

I reach inside my bag for my purse and pull out the crumpled photo of Lilly. I stare at her sweet little face. Lilly, my sister. I pass the photo to Ruby.

'Here, look. I carry this photo of Lilly with me everywhere.'

Ruby looks surprised and stares at the crumpled picture, stroking it with her finger. We both burst into tears but this time Ruby rescues me, hugging and holding onto me for dear life.

'I'm so, so sorry, Cassie. Please forgive me,' Ruby says. I can't tell whose snot and tears is whose anymore. Everything tells me I should be fuming with Ruby, that I should hate her guts. But I don't. I'm angry but I feel sorry for her and I still love her. I need to forgive her, but I also need to forgive myself for being human, for being flawed – like everyone else it seems.

Ruby pulls away from me, still holding onto my shoulders, tilting her head to one side, studying my face. 'God you look so like your Mum,' she says. 'I miss her sooooo much Cassie.'

'Yeah, me too,' I whisper.

Ruby grabs my hand and holds it tight. 'Well then,' she says. 'Where's there's life there's hope eh? So we mustn't give up on her. Now, what do I have to do to get a bloody cup of tea round here?'

I wander around Ruby's beautiful kitchen (slightly dazed). My hands fall across her gorgeous granite worktops. I open cupboard doors and release gently gliding draws, searching out cups and spoons. I flick the switch of her orange, high tech kettle – just one of the many well sick gadgets she has, including a juicer, an espresso maker and a wine station, not to mention the copper sink, the wood fired pizza oven and the warming drawer. It's an amazing kitchen just like something you'd find in those expensive glossy magazines. It's the antithesis (I like that word now) of our dated kitchen with its un-matching appliances and worn out, well used look.

Ruby wanders up behind me.

'I love your kitchen,' I say.

Ruby looks around her. 'I'd rather have Andy,' she sighs. 'Cassie, I have something else to tell you.'

'Oh god, what? I'm not sure I can handle anything else Ruby.' I laugh but I'm not joking.

'I'm pregnant?'

'What?' I reply, almost scalding myself with hot water from the kettle I'm now holding. 'But, but I thought you said Andy had had a hysterectomy?'

Ruby laughs. 'Vasectomy, Cassie, but yes, yes he did. But he had it reversed and ... well it worked. She looks at me and attempts a smile.

'Really? The baby is Andy's this time? Not Luca's or someone else's?' I cringe as I finish asking. 'Sorry,' I add.

Ruby shakes her head. 'No, you're right to ask. No more deceit, no more lies. But yes, the baby really is Andy's. I'm 12 weeks.'

'Did Andy know?'

'Yeah. He did, and he was chuffed to bits. We talked it all through and we agreed it was something we should try. He forgave me my affair with Luca and said it probably wouldn't have happened if he hadn't been so selfish. He said he was frightened but he was really pleased when I fell. Not acting for my benefit or anything. He was genuinely really happy for us.'

Ruby starts to cry *again*. I grab her and hug her.

'That's like, well sick. Ooh ooh it might even be a little boy?' I continue excitedly.

'Yeah, it'd be nice wouldn't it?'

My head feels fucked and wanders off with my thoughts for a minute. OMG, like oh my actual god, life is like, so fucked up – so complicated. Like, this crazy, crazy shit is real, it's all actually real.

Ruby's voice interrupts my thinking. 'I've got a scan next week,' she says. 'Will you come with me? I mean, you don't have to or anything. I just thought, if you wanted to...?'

'Of course I will' I reply. I feel overwhelmed and flattered. 'I'd love to Ruby.'

'Really?'

'Yeah, really.'

'Thanks Cassie, it means a lot to me.'

I shrug my shoulders. 'S'kay. And anyway, where there's life there's hope eh? Oh my god, you so have to go to the hospital and tell Mum. If that doesn't wake her up nothing will!'

# CHAPTER 42

## PEOPLE ARE STRANGE

**CASSIE**

'But I do love you Cassie, honest babe, I do.'

I look at Joe. I've heard it all before. 'Really Joe. And what exactly is it that you love about me?'

Joe shrugs his shoulders. 'Everything?'

He puts his arm around me and pulls me to him. God he smells so good. I love him, I really do, and this is breaking my heart but I can't do this anymore.

I push Joe away from me. 'Then surely if you love someone Joe, you support them, when they need you?'

Joe's face darkens and his eyes narrow, he looks moody. 'Oh like that tosser Luke I suppose?'

'He's not a tosser Joe, Luke's a good friend.'

'Yeah, only coz he wants to shag you.'

I roll my eyes and shake my head. I feel exhausted. 'Well at least he doesn't come up with excuses when I ask him to visit Mum with me.'

'Yeah, well, I don't do hospitals babe, you know that.'

'Or funerals, or gigs or just about anything else I ask you to in fact, eh Joe?'

'Yeah, so, I can't help that I'm a busy man.'

'Busy doing nothing with your stoner mates you mean.'

Joe looks wounded. 'I'm sorry babe, I love you, I really do, but if you're not with me 100 percent I can't carry you – us – anymore. My Mum's seriously ill, then there's the band and Connor. Do I go to Uni or don't I go to Uni? Ruby's having a baby. I can't keep trying to fit in with you when I have so much other serious shit going on.'

Joe pulls me to him and kisses me, really soft but strong at the same time. 'I love you Cas.'

I feel myself melting, giving in again. It takes all my strength to push myself away from Joe.

I shake my head. 'No Joe, you're not going to talk me out of it this time. This really is goodbye.'

Joe's eyes actually start to fill up. 'But I will change, Cassie, I promise. I'll go to the hospital with you. I'll even come to your next gig. When is it?'

I sigh. 'I already told you, it's tomorrow. Mia's Dad Clive asked us to play at her wake.' Joe looks confused. 'Mia – remember? I met her at Christmas, she had leukaemia. She died Joe. She was only 16 years old. I told you this.' Joe still looks confused. 'Oh for god sake, Joe! Anyway, The Incandescent Adolescents are playing tomorrow for Mia, to say goodbye. It'd be great if you could come and support me?'

'Ahhhhhh, right, tomorrow is actually a bit short notice …'

I shake my head and start to walk away. 'You'll regret it,' Joe shouts after me. 'Loads of girls fancy me.'

My heart is breaking. I know I'm doing the right thing, for me anyway – but it hurts so, so bad. Oh god I wish Mum was awake.

I walk, very slowly up our drive, getting my Connor face ready. I have to stay strong and act normal for Connor, and Simon and Maisy for that matter.

Mark, Tabitha's husband from next door, is on his drive cleaning his car. 'Hey Cassie,' he shouts out. 'How's your Mum?'

I shrug my shoulders. 'Much the same,' I reply.

I walk towards Mark. He looks embarrassed. 'I'm sorry about Tabitha, the other week,' he says holding a bucketful of water in one hand, running his other one through his hair. I'm not sure what he means. I frown at him, tipping my head to the side. 'You know,' he continues, 'when the reporters were camped out and Tabitha was giving them all interviews about what a great friend she is of your Mum's.'

I laugh. 'I don't think we all thought anything of it, or expected anything less from Tabitha if I'm being honest.'

Now it's Mark's turn to laugh.

He asks me if I'm okay. He says I don't look so good. I tell him about Joe, and having to put on my Connor face before I go in the house every night. I tell Mark I'm exhausted, and sad. So, so sad and afraid that Mum is never going to wake up.

'Have you got half an hour?' Mark asks. 'I've got an idea.' I nod. 'Follow me,' he says.

Mark puts down his bucket of water and walks down the side of his house towards his back garden. I follow him, slightly unnerved.

'Is Tabitha in?' I ask.

'Yeah, she's bathing Fortuna. Getting her ready for bed.'

We walk through their immaculate garden that perfectly matches their immaculate house, down towards their shed house at the bottom of the garden – also immaculate – decked out with beautiful furniture and a cinema style movie screen.

'My bolt hole,' Mark says turning to me and smiling. 'Now, take a pew,' he says patting the plump, brightly coloured cushion forming the seat of one of six rather expensive looking chairs. He pulls a chair out for himself opposite me, plucking something from his pocket before he sits down. 'Ta dah,' he says holding up a ready-made spliff between his fingers.

'Really?' I say, more than a little surprised. 'Does Tabitha know?' Mark laughs. 'Maybe, maybe not. Who gives a shit?'

He puts the spliff in his mouth and holds a lighter beneath it, sucking hard. Mark pulls the spliff away from his mouth and exhales, offering it to me.

'I don't know if I should?' I look nervously towards the door. 'Don't worry about Tabs, her bark is much worse than her bite you know?' I open my eyes wide in disbelief. 'Now, come on,' Mark continues. 'Just a couple of tokes and you'll feel okay again.'

I take the spliff from his outstretched hand and put it to my mouth. 'Shouldn't do it all the time though mind,' Mark says waving his finger at me. 'But every now and again is fine.'

And it is fine, mighty fine. My knotted body is unravelling and for the first time in a long time I feel calm.

Mark and I talk loads – shit mostly. I tell him about Joe and my broken heart and about how much I want to play for Mia tomorrow but also how much I don't. I've had enough of death. Mark tells me about Tabitha. About what he sees in her that others don't – that she is actually very kind and very loving (yeah, right!). Her biggest downfall is just that she loves to bloody gossip. We both agree love is a strange thing, whoever it was you happened to love.

My cares of the last few months are drifting up and away when the door to the shed house abruptly swings opens. A fake tanned Tabitha stands in the doorway, fluorescent pink manicured nails of both hands resting on both hips. She looks like thunder.

'Mark, what the hell are you doing?' she screeches.

Me and Mark both look at each other and burst out laughing. 'Fuck off Tabitha,' we both say at the same time, both looking rather surprised at each other. Tabitha hovers for a moment – her face still like thunder – tapping one of her claws on her bony hip before pirouetting back out of the door.

Mark takes another long drag from the spliff. 'Oh well,' he says, blowing the smoke from a corner of his mouth. 'I definitely won't be getting a shag tonight.'

We both laugh again and continue talking crap when the door bangs open once more. It's Tabitha again, balancing a plate of fancy looking sandwiches in one hand and a baby monitor in the other. She places the sandwiches down gently on the expensive looking glass table that matches the expensive looking chairs, then snatches the spliff from Mark's hand taking a long, hard drag herself. Tabitha hands the spliff back to me and that's the first and last drag she takes. She does sit with us though, for a bit longer. She dominates the conversation but I don't actually mind coz she's bigging up Mum, telling me what a wonderful person she is and not a gossipy bitch like herself. It's a side of Tabitha I've never seen before and it's nice, really nice. After about ten minutes Tabitha gets up to leave – the snuffly baby noises on the baby monitor seem to concern her. She tells Mark not to be too long and she tells me to look after myself and she hopes Mum wakes up soon.

'Oh, and if you ever want your hair doing,' she adds. 'I'll give you a discount.' She puts one hand on her hip and cocks her head to the side to look at me. 'Your hair is not actually too bad but god, that sister of yours, she'd look so much better as a blonde.'

And with that Tabitha disappears.

I've had to grow up so fast these past months. I think of Ruby, of Dad and Joe – I think of Tabitha. I realise people never stop surprising you.

## CHAPTER 43

ACCEPTANCE OF THE INEVITABLE

**CASSIE**

It's funny how life changes. And despite every effort not to accept those changes – no matter how hard we fight them – before we know it they've become part of everyday life. It's been six months now since Mum was admitted to hospital. Studying at college, going to work and visiting Mum are just part of my usual routine. I know almost everyone at the hospital by name, including the doctors and nurses and even the cleaning staff.

The terrifying thing is I'm adapting to Mum not being around. I know – we all know – the longer she's in a coma the worse the outlook is. I've read everything there is to read at least fifty times over. I probably know more than the bloody Doctors actually. That's why I know it's important to keep talking to Mum when I visit. Lots of ex-coma patients that did recover say they could hear friends and family talking to them when they visited.

I also know if Mum does come out of her coma she could be brain damaged. I'm ashamed to admit it, but I actually think that'd be worse than if she died. She would be dead in a way. I know everyone else thinks the same thing but none of us has the guts to say it.

If someone had told me six months ago though, that I'd be capable of contemplating life without Mum I'd have punched their lights out. I still miss her though, so much, every single day. I'm constantly getting my phone out to text Mum. Or I'll sprint up the drive and burst through the front door to tell her something, then I remember she's not there. Sometimes, when I'm scared shitless that I'm forgetting Mum altogether, I ring her phone just to listen to her voice on her answer phone message. I keep Mum's phone constantly charged just so I can hear her, remember the sound of her voice.

I tell Mum everything when I visit her but it's not the same coz she can't give me one of her funny looks. And even though I know she's proud of the good stuff, I can't see it in her face, or hear it in her voice. I took Mum for granted, I know I did. I just didn't realise how much.

I always thought Mum never understood me. Now I know that's so not true. I love how she seemed to steer me, without me even realising it, somehow in the right direction. I miss how a text would come through just when I needed it. Sometimes it was only two or three words but it was always just when I needed something or someone. It was like Mum was psychic or something. I miss her honesty too, even though I didn't always want to hear it.

I wonder if Mum does hear me talking all my crap on my visits with her.

I walk towards the main hospital entrance (it's my turn to visit Mum today) the one I've passed through at least a million times. I catch my reflection in one of the huge glass windows. I stop for a minute, turning my head from left to right, examining my profile. I touch my nose and smile. I *do* like my Roman nose. It's got character.

A man on the other side of the window distracts me from my thinking. For god bloody sake he's smiling and waving at me. He thinks I'm bloody flirting with him! Eeewwww! What a bloody perv. He's like well old, at least 30 years old. Why are all men pervs?

The automatic doors open, then close again before I have chance to walk through them. Something's caught my eye. I could be wrong but I'm pretty sure I've just spotted Nan and Grandad's car in the car park. It looks like their car and it has the same ManGenie air freshener I bought for them, hanging from the rear view mirror.

I smile, remembering the day I bought that air freshener. I chose that one mainly to cheer up Connor coz I know the ManGenie is a character from one of his favourite computer games. A half man, half genie thing that has magical, mystical powers, I think? And coz Connor often visits Mum with Nan and Grandad when they drive to the hospital in their car, I thought he could hang it up and it would be something else for him to focus on. But it smelled so good I was actually thinking about keeping it for myself.

On the day I bought it I went to visit Mum at the hospital as usual, and rather unusually everyone was there coz it was Uncle Sean's birthday. I burst through the doors of Mum's room shouting,

'Oh like my actual god, you lot *so* have to smell my ManGenie.'

I couldn't understand why everyone fell into hysterics, at least not until I thought about what I'd said and how rude it actually sounded. Oh well, at least it made everyone laugh. I wish Grandad would stop shouting out, "Oi Cassie, smell my ManGenie" at every opportunity though. It's like soooo embarrassing.

I wonder why Nan and Grandad are visiting today? They must have decided to drop by too. Unless ... oh my god. What if it's nothing to do with Mum? What if it's Nan again? Or no, my mind is racing now – what if it's something bad to do with Mum? What if ...? What if ...?

I suddenly feel a bit panicky. I start to breathe really fast and I swear I can hear the blood pumping through my veins. My phone rings and I jump. I reach into my jacket pocket for it but stupidly drop it coz my hands are all sweaty.

'Arrrrggghhh!' I shout out loud. It stops ringing. I've missed the call. I scramble to pick my phone up from the floor thanking god it's not broken. I check who it was. Oh, it was only Luke. I check my texts but don't have any new ones. Okay, so no news is good news then?

'Hey Cassie,' someone shouts. I look up and see Zack and Linda, two of the nurses from Mums ward passing into the opposite corridor. 'Great gig the other night,' Zack says.

'Really?' I reply. I'm never really sure if people are being honest or just kind when they say good things about the band.

'Yeah, really,' he says. 'Well sick. I've put some feedback on the band's Facebook page. I'll defo be at the next one.'

I smile. 'Thanks,' I say and feel myself puffing up with pride. 'I'll tell Mum.' Zack and Linda both look at each other.

'Haven't you seen your Mum today?' Linda asks.

I can't read the expressions on their faces. 'No,' I reply cautiously. 'Why?' They both look at each other again. They're acting weird and suddenly seem in a hurry to go.

'Okay,' Linda simply says. 'We'll see ya later.' And with that Linda grabs Zack's arm and drags him off down the corridor.

Zack turns back to look at me. I can't read his expression. What is it I can't read in his eyes? I watch them get further away until they are gone.

The hairs on the back of my neck stand on end and my stomach is twisting into tight knots. I feel nervous, like I'm about to perform on stage. I don't understand why. Why do I feel like this? I have a really, really bad feeling and my fear suddenly turns into anger.

I never gave up on you Mum; a voice screams inside my head, not once, not ever did I give up hope. So don't you dare give up on me?

I'm rubbish at running but my feet are carrying me so fast I'm at the entrance to Mum's ward before I know it. I stop, staring at the doors that are now as familiar to me as my own front door. People are coming and going, a sea of faces, some recognisable, some not – but still I stand, frozen to the spot. Tony the Italian cleaner swings through the doors that hold me mesmerised.

'Cassie,' he calls. I look at him but don't respond. 'You going to see your Mamma, yes?' he asks. I hardly dare breathe, never mind speak. I nod my head as he reaches across to me and squeezes my arm. Then he's gone.

What? What was that supposed to mean, the voice inside my head screams? Oh my god, I know Mum has only been with us in body these last months but her spirit's been here, I know it has. I've felt her. No one else believes me but I know her eyes flickered that morning I came to see her all those months ago, when Simon left me to talk to her while he got a coffee. I told Mum I was sorry and I know she heard me coz her eyes moved. It was only for a split second but they opened, I know her eyes opened. I've managed without you Mum but you can't leave us. You just can't. We've got too much to talk about, too much to do.

I don't remember walking through the doors but now I'm

walking along the corridor towards Mum's room. Everyone's staring at me. I can feel eyes on me from everywhere but I can't face looking at them all. If this is bad why didn't anyone call me?

Oh no! No, no, no! Someone's sitting on a chair outside Mum's room. It's a man and he's hunched forward with his head down. As I get closer I realise it's Simon. He doesn't make a sound but he's crying. I know he's crying coz his shoulders are moving up and down. Oh my god, I want to scream but I can't. I physically can't find my voice for a minute. If Simon is crying then this really is bad news coz I've never seen him cry – well, only once, sort of, at Andy's funeral. But not once for Mum. I kneel down next to Simon and lift his face to look at mine. His features are all screwed up and he won't look at me but his face is stained with tears. I grab him by the arms and shake him really hard.

'What?' I yell, 'What is it Simon?'

He takes a deep breath before exhaling really slowly. He turns away from me, placing his head in his hands again, hunched over like Ossie Moto or whatever the bloody name of the Hunchback of Notre Dame is. Oh my god, I swear I'm going to throw up right here, right now. I can manage without you Mum but I don't want to. Oh no, please no. Why was I such a bitch to her? Mum will never, ever know how much I love her.

I try to stand up but my legs feel really weak and my head's like all fuzzy. This can't be it, can it? Why? Why give me six months of hope and nothing to show for it? My chest is starting to hurt. I swear my heart is breaking. I suddenly think of Ruby. Poor, poor Ruby, so this is how she feels.

I don't know how but I manage to stagger up. My head falls forward, suddenly too heavy for my shoulders and my hands are trembling. I place my shaky hand on the silver door handle and push it down to open the door. My heart is beating so fast and so loud it drowns out all the other sounds around me. Please Mum, I still have hope. Please don't leave me, we still have too much to do together. I take a deep breath, lift my head back up and walk in.

I stand and stare in complete and utter silence, amazed that my legs are still holding me up. I can't believe it; I can't believe my eyes. There isn't a part of my body that isn't shaking as my tears fall freely and silently. Connor, who is sitting on the bed with Nan and Grandad turns to look at me.

'Cassie,' he yells. 'It worked, it worked! Grandad's special lotion, it actually worked. Look, Mum's awake.'

Mum turns to look at me. She smiles. She really smiles. It's such a wonderful thing to see. I know, whatever happens, I'll always hold that smile in my heart forever.

Connor has jumped off the bed and is standing beside me. 'Don't cry Cas,' he says. 'It's okay. Mum's awake; you won't have to worry so much about me now.'

Through my tears and snot I somehow manage to smile at Connor. He takes my hand and leads me really gently over to the bed, over to Mum.

'Cassie,' is all she says, but what a beautiful sound. I wrap my arms around Mum and hold onto her. I can't, won't ever, be able to explain to anyone how I feel right now. Nothing, not even the words of a song, will ever explain how I feel at this moment in time; the – by far – best moment of my whole entire life.

I eventually pull myself away from Mum and look at her. 'SHIT, BUGGER, FUCK and ARSEHOLE,' she shouts.

'Oh, okay!' I reply, slightly confused.

To my astonishment everyone starts laughing. Nan then goes on to explain that Mum has actually been coming out of her coma for the last couple of days and at the moment she is suffering from PTA which means post-traumatic amnesia.

Inappropriate behaviour like swearing and shouting is not unusual and it will stop – eventually.

I don't really care. Swear as much as you like Mum, just don't ever leave us again.

# CHAPTER 44

## HOME AGAIN, HOME AGAIN JIGGETY JIG

**CASSIE**

*I* feel like some whirling dervish, half-crazed madwoman tearing round the house, examining every room like something possessed.

'Will you just chill,' Maisy says to me. 'The house is spotless, well, except for my room,' she mumbles.

'I know, I know,' I reply. 'It's just that, well, you know ... the house was a mess that day ... and ...'

I pause as the words clog in my throat. I try not to blink, looking away from Maisy's gaze.

'You idiot,' Maisy says, punching my arm.

'Ouccchhhh,' I reply, turning to look at her. 'Wad ya do that for?'

'To give you something real to cry about,' she states, chewing the gum that never seems to leave her mouth. 'Mum will be fine. No scrap that – Mum IS fine,' she continues.

I stare at Maisy (she actually looks well sick with blonde

hair). I'm not sure if I want to punch her in the face or burst into tears.

She rolls her eyes and sighs heavily. 'Oh c'mon then. I'll bloody help too if it means you'll stop running around like some crazy, psycho bitch.'

I smile at her. Her words are endearing. It's kind of like her derogatory remarks signify we're getting back to normal, or at least as normal as we were before Mum was attacked. When Mum was in a coma, it was like everyone was walking on cornflakes, or eggshells or whatever the bloody saying is. Maisy and I had always been offensive to each other but it was always (most of the time) done in a sisterly way. Somehow calling each other loser or idiot never sat right while Mum wasn't with us.

'Thanks then loser,' I laugh. 'Let's start with your room shall we?' I run up the stairs as Maisy follows behind screaming.

'Leave my fucking room alone.'

I fling the door open praying to God or any other religious thing I don't really believe in, that her room is at least *slightly* better than normal.

'Oh my god, I don't bloody believe it. It's like a bloody miracle or something. *Your* room is actually tidy.'

Maisy sniffs. 'Yeah, well, I just thought, you know ...' She shrugs her shoulders.

'Thought what?'

'How pissed off Mum was with all the mess in the house before she was ...' Maisy trails off. I look straight at her and realise my vision is now as blurred as hers is.

I quickly look away. 'Loser. I need to take a photo,' I say, pulling out my phone. 'It's ammmazzzing! I can actually see your carpet and everything.'

Maisy laughs. 'Idiot,' she says again before punching my other arm.

'Ouuuuucchhh! Bitch. Just coz you think you're some hard tattooed gangsta.'

'Ahhhhhh yes, the Cassie I know so well has returned.'

'I won't bloody miss you when you're gone.'

'The feeling's mutual babe.'

We hover for a moment, silently staring at each other before breaking into fits of laughter.

'C'mon Sis,' she says. I can hear the warmth in her voice. 'Let's check Connor's room.'

Connor's room, on the whole is pretty tidy really. It does have a sort of musty, fusty, mouldy cheese, smelly feet smell to it though. In fact, come to think of it, so does the room of every boy I know. Even Joe's room. Despite the fact he himself always smelled well delish, his room always had that same vague, whiff and pong of boy.

The main colours of Connor's room are boyishly blue. He has a smallish wardrobe, bedside cabinet (that has a photo of him and Mum on) and chest of drawers as well as a small silver desk and chair tucked away in the corner for his laptop. His silver framed bunk bed is one of those high sleeper ones. He sleeps on the top bunk and friends that sleep over take the bottom. His walls, like mine and Maisy's are covered with posters including characters from The Hobbit, Lord of the Rings, Star Wars and Doctor Who. Asking Alexander, Kurt Cobain and The 1975 also share the wall space as does Katy Perry and Melissa Auf der Maur.

'It looks pretty tidy in here,' Maisy says. 'You finish checking up here and I'll make a final check downstairs.'

'Okay,' I say, wandering over to Connor's desk, picking up the plastic bottle of gunk he made with Grandad. The same one he carried with him on every single hospital visit to see Mum. I hold the bottle up towards the light, squinting to see if there's anything left in it. It's hard to tell. I shake it hard before unscrewing the lid attempting to look inside. I think it's virtually all gone. I take a sniff. It smells like the moisturiser Nan uses. I put the lid back on and spot Connor's bin on the other side of the room. I throw the bottle towards it. To my surprise, with a thud, it goes in.

'Noooooooooooo!!' Connor shouts behind me. 'Don't you dare throw that away,' he says, bending down to fish the bottle out.

'Why? It's empty. Besides, Mum's okay now.'

'Yeah, well, it's special,' he says, folding a protective hand around it. 'Me and Grandad made it. And it's important stuff – it helped Mum get better.'

I look at Connor. 'I'm not sure it did you know?'

'It did,' he shouts back at me. 'I know you think all the stuff Grandad does isn't true, but it is. You don't know anything!'

I can't help laughing. 'Okay Connor, whatevs'

He doesn't reply but just looks at me for a minute. He sighs, heavily.

'If I tell you something,' he eventually says. 'You can't say anything – to anyone – ever. Okay?'

I roll my eyes. 'Okay Connor.'

'No, I mean it Cassie. You can't, not ever, ever, ever, ever, ever, EVER. Okay? Coz of Mum. It could change everything. You can't. EVER'

I can hear the front door opening downstairs. 'You really can't Cassie.'

'We're here, we're home,' Simon shouts. I look towards Connor's bedroom door then back at him.

'OKAY, I get it. I won't say anything *ever!* Now, what the hell is it?'

'It's Grandad.'

'What about him?'

Connor sighs again 'It's, well ... you really can't say anything Cassie.'

'C'mon you lot,' Simon shouts.

'Just look at Grandad's name okay? And don't say anything when you've worked it out. Not to Mum, definitely not to Grandad and not even to me. Okay? Coming Mum,' Connor shouts, barging past me and heading for the stairs.

'What? What the bloody hell's that supposed to mean?' I call out, but it's too late, Connor is already half way down the stairs.

## CHAPTER 45

### BACK TO NORMAL ... ALMOST

**LIZZIE**

Everyone has gone off to work, or school or college and the house is eerily quiet. You'd think I'd have had enough of quiet but as it descends upon me I'm more grateful for it than I realised. The last few days have been a whirlwind of visitors and phone calls wishing me well or a speedy recovery but frankly I feel worn out. I stare at the plaque on the wall, erected, as a homecoming gift, in my honour. I digest the words, chosen apparently, especially for me:

**A Mother
Is She Who Can Take the Place Of All Others But Whose Place No One Else Can Take.**

I sniff inwards. I love the sentiment but ...
'Not true though is it?' I say to no one. Although due to the

infancy of my slow repairing brain, the words that actually leave my mouth are something like, 'Not the fucking toilet.'

It's painfully obvious my wonderful family have all coped far too well without my nagging presence. I should be proud, happy and safe in the knowledge they can, would be able to go on – should the need arise again – without me. It was, after all, all I'd wanted eight months ago.

I laugh to myself. I can hear Dad's voice and one of his favourite phrases running through my thoughts,

'Careful what you wish for Lizzie, it may just come true.' And it did. All I'd wanted was a little help around the house, for the kids to show a little initiative and ease the burden of the day-to-day crap, to do a few more chores, to notice when things needed doing. The truth is they took me for granted but when the shit well and truly hit the fan the incapable proved beyond all reasonable doubt that they were in fact, very capable.

'We've got it all sorted Mum,' Cassie had said reassuringly. 'Things will never go back to how they were and there's nothing for you to do except concentrate on getting better.' It was great to see her so self-assured, so confident. But the truth is, I'd taken them for granted too.

I sit here now, staring into space. I want things back to where they were. I was, I am Mum, I am the one who nurtures. And this has fuck all to do with women's lib. I'll fight against women's oppression and stereotyping until I take my last breath (which hopefully won't prove to be too soon) but this is about me – Lizzie Lemalf – Partner, Mother, Stepmother and proud of it. I want to be the shoulder they cry on, their fortress and Zion, their helper and teacher, the gospel and preacher, the meal maker, deal breaker and if needed ball breaker, their mover and bed maker, their words of wisdom, lover to one and to the rest just Mum.

I sigh inwardly. Everyone has been so good. Simon was so nervous about leaving me on my own.

'You sure you'll be okay babe?' he'd asked. He had the look of a concerned parent leaving their child on their first day of school. It was touching but suffocating at the same time. If I'm honest I'm terrified but I don't want them to wrap me up in cotton wool, afraid to leave a mess, afraid to upset me. Yes, I'm lucky to be alive, yes it will take time, yes it's very strange when the words that leave my mouth are not the ones I have lined up in my head, but the truth is I want my life back and no-one can see that. No-one except Mum maybe.

No-one else was suspicious of my painted smile as I waved them all off, Simon and Maisy to work, Cassie to college and Connor to school, but Mum, who had dropped by with Freddy, put a familiar arm on my shoulder and said, 'Don't worry love, they'll all be taking you for granted again before you know it.'

I'm sure she's right but what an adjustment, so much has changed. I hardly recognise Maisy with her blonde hair, barely-there make-up and permanently inked arm to match her permanently inked leg. And what about Connor? So tall, his sweet little voice breaking into a man's. And of course Ruby is pregnant and Andy has gone. I can't believe it, truly can't get my head round it. I'm brutally attacked and live to tell the tale and Andy drives his car for the god knows how many millionth time in his life and is instantly killed in a road traffic accident.

I shudder, in awe of both the fragility and strength of life, never more evident than when I saw my lovely friend Ruby again. Clearly she was grieving for the love of her life, and yet juxtapose to her grief was the obvious thrill and excitement of the new one growing in the huge bump she coveted with such pride.

The minute I laid my eyes on Ruby forgiveness came so easily, even before Cassie intervened and made me listen – in full – to Ruby's version of events. Why had I been so unforgiving? Even Cassie had had the good sense to see it was just one stupid mistake. Ruby is so much more to me than that one bad faux pas. We must always try to retain the capacity to forgive, because people are not split into good or bad. We are human, and that means there is some good in the more immoral and corrupt among us and definitely some bad in the best of us.

My thoughts turn to poor Andy, again. I must go and visit him and say goodbye. Even if it does come out as garbled gibberish, Andy will be listening, he'll understand me – I know he will.

I think of my own lovely man, Simon. Such a sight for sore eyes when mine – fleetingly at first – flickered open. He didn't see me but I saw him, reading, holding and stroking my hand. Although it would be hours before I opened my eyes again, something told me that from that moment on I was going to be okay. And Mum and Dad, my wonderful parents, steadfast and strong looked so weary – who needs this kind of shit at their time of life? Jodi looked weary too, although that may have had more to do with the twins than me. And it was good to see Raj. He finally found the courage to tell his parents he was gay and they all took it surprisingly well, his Dad was actually more supportive than his Mum and his sister is chuffed to have a gay shopping companion.

And finally Cassie, my lovely woman-child has blossomed into something beautiful. Self-possessed, confident, strong and yet kind, it's almost impossible to see the old Cassie, although she does make a rather loud, guest appearance from time to time. Look out though world, I've a feeling we ain't seen nothing yet. So engrossed have I become in my self-induced inertia, I don't realise until I look down at my phone that an hour has passed. My un-drunk coffee has gone cold and I haven't moved from the kitchen table.

I hear a familiar sound and look up to see Romeow casually saunter in from whatever secret sleeping place has kept him occupied. He stops in front of me, looking up, staring intently. He then lowers his back, as if ready for starters orders and using his front paws springs upwards, landing gracefully on the kitchen table. His walk towards me is relaxed but full of swagger. He sits directly opposite me and gazes at me through yellow eyes. Cat's eyes are supposed to be the windows to the soul aren't they? Does he also see the same fragility in me everyone seems to?

'Hey Romeow,' I say. 'How are you?' Although not necessarily the exact words to leave my mouth, I think Romeow gets my gist. His response, quite out of character, is an affectionate one, nudging his nose against my cheek and purring loudly before tentatively stepping from the table onto my lap. His paws dance up and down in quick succession, ballerina pas de bourree style, before he finally curls himself into a purring ball of fuzz on my knee. For god bloody sake, even the cat is at it.

'When did you become so social? You can treat me with the same disdain you always have you know? I won't break.' Romeow purrs loudly in response. He isn't going anywhere. I'm flattered but I can't sit around *all* day.

*Why not?*

Should I stay or should I go? I stay a while longer, stroking the soft ball of fluff and enjoying this rare moment of affection. Footsteps on the drive break the silence and my stomach lurches forward. I'm relieved to hear the post-box rattle. I decide to make my move. I lift the sack of ginger fluffy skin from my knee and gently place him on the chair next to me. Romeow's eyes open temporarily and he flicks the end of his tail in obvious disapproval before quickly settling again. 'Sorry Romeow,' I say. He ignores me. I smile. Perhaps things are getting back to normal.

I sort through the pile of letters that have arrived and quickly discard the flyers and ignore those not addressed to me. My eye however is drawn to a couple addressed to Cassie from UCAS. I wonder? Hopefully the news is good?

The only letter marked for my attention is a small white envelope in bad handwriting from a PO box.

I'm pretty sure I know who it's from. I've been expecting something. Thank god Amber did go to the Police but I'm glad she spoke to Simon first. He helped her, along with the women from the refuge, to find a solicitor, and they did a deal to make sure she wasn't charged under the law of joint enterprise – Guilty by Association as it were. Simon knew I would have wanted him to help Amber.

My mind wanders back to that day and my stomach performs a tiny somersault, the events of eight months ago suddenly resurrected before my eyes with blinding accuracy. A faint whiff of body odour dances around my nostrils as does the smell of alcohol. My tongue sticks to the roof of my barren mouth and the palms of my hands sweat profusely. I count to ten very slowly as the fear I can't ignore rushes through me. Fear is okay, it'll subside – panic however is not acceptable. To my great surprise I burst into tears, great big, sobbing, salty tears. I use the back of my hands to wipe my tears away, my fear and anxiety suddenly replaced by anger and confusion. I thought I was stronger than this?

'Aaaaaaaaaarrrrrrrrrgggggggghhhhhhh! I will not let this define me you baaarrstaarrd!' I scream. Romeow jumps, his look now one of utter contempt. If he could speak I'm sure he would be telling me "to get a grip".

*And he's right of course.*

I flick the switch on the kettle. Strong, hot coffee is what's needed.

Coffee made, I grab the envelope and once again take my

rightful place next to Romeow. No longer hesitant, I rip the envelope open and take out a folded piece of typed A4 paper. I take a deep breath and begin to read:

*Dear Lizzie*

*I don't think I've ever written a letter in my entire life but if I had, this would be like the hardest one I have ever written. I can never explain to you how sorry I am, and how I wish, for your sake, you had never met me. This terrible thing would never have happened to you if you hadn't known me. You could have died.*

*I came to visit you at the hospital (it was me that called the ambulance). I sneaked in. No-one saw me; no-one knew I was there. I didn't recognise you, couldn't believe what a mess Travis had made of you. He'd been following you for some time but I had no idea he was going to hurt you. Something happened to me then, when I saw you lying in that hospital bed. I knew I had to make a change. I went to the Women's Refuge you told me about and they, and your Simon, persuaded me to talk to the Police. Then they sent me to another Refuge away from everyone and everything I knew. Which was a good thing because it meant I could start over again.*

*The refuge has helped me find a place to live. It's small but it's mine and I'm careful who I choose as friends. I'm also working a few hours a week in a shop and I'm doing a computer course (which is why this letter is so good because I have a tutor and spellchecker to help me!). My tutor is nice. She reminds me of you, kind, but strong.*

*You'd have to be strong to put up with my shit eh?*

*I've had my baby, a little girl. I've called her Elizabeth after you; although I call her Beth for short coz there'll only ever be one Lizzie. I hope you don't mind?*

*It's hard sometimes and Beth doesn't sleep well. I get sad and frightened, mostly frightened that I'll be a bad Mum.*

*That's when I think about giving Beth up for adoption or something. But, then I think of you and how you never gave up on me and I remember how sad you said you was when you got divorced and how it was just a grieving process and how it gets better in time. When I thought about it I realised that's what I'm sort of going through, a divorce, from everything and everyone I know. So I know it'll just take time eh?*

*So I pull myself together and my goal is to do well for myself then come back and see you, with Beth, and make you proud of me.*

*I'm so sorry Lizzie, really. Thank you for always believing in me though.*

*Lots of Love, Amber xxx*

I put the letter down, stunned. Dad often says good things come out of bad – look at Scott for god sake. Tears run freely down my face. I am filled with a myriad of emotions but the overwhelming one that competes for my attention is pride. I'm filled with a heart-warming sense of pride. Realistically I know it won't be easy for Amber but I love her and will always be thinking of her. I wish her all the happiness she deserves and I will always carry hope for her here in my heart.

'Good luck Amber,' I say out loud. At least, they're the words in my head but not necessarily the one's that come out of my mouth.

## CHAPTER 46

THE SEARCH FOR INDEPENDENCE

**CASSIE**

It's April 17, 2015 and Nan's second official year free of cancer – Yay! And OMG. Oh my actual bloody god. Mum is like such a moaning cow, which is like amazing coz it means things are getting back to normal. I'll never moan about her moaning again – not much anyway.

Coming home to fresh cooked spag bol and Mum dancing, as badly as ever, around the kitchen to Bob Dylan blaring out of the CD player, is what it's all about for me. The only difference now is I join in too. Home feels like home again.

Mum's more or less completely recovered now, even her brain. Mum says any damage caused to that was done a long time ago by us kids. Ha ha. So funny. Not! She does still say the odd thing from time to time though, which can be a bit embarrassing, especially if we're out in public and she drops a swear word. I just tell people she's got problems – namely Tourette's caused by two teenage, pain in the arse, daughters.

'Oh my god, is this it?' I shriek. 'It's like well aaammmaaazing. Huge. Sick. Errrrrrr, actually, no, forget I said that. It reminds me of school. I hated school. Actually it looks like well scary. Oh my god it looks like a prison. I can't go to this university, it looks like a prison.'

Simon sighs. 'Cassie!' he says. 'You've managed to turn a potential university from amazing to a prison in the space of three seconds.'

'I know but ... but ...'

'But give it a chance Cassie for god sake,' Mum says.

'Hmmmmm, okay,' I reply.

The truth is I keep finding fault with all of the universities we've looked at coz I'm actually a bit scared. Not that I'll ever admit that to Mum and Simon. I am excited too though. The Incandescent Adolescents are disbanding at the end of the summer whilst we all go off to study at different places. I'm not studying music to be famous or any of that shit. I don't want to be a star or anything (I already am in the eyes of the people important to me) but I do want to reach for them. I'm not sure what the future holds, but who is? What I do know is, I want to do something with music. Anyway, like Grandad always says, 'It's not a life. It's an adventure!!!!'

Life will definitely be a lot different for Mum, a lot quieter without me. And Maisy, of course, has already left and lives in Oz now with Crazee. We Skype and FaceTime with her quite a bit. I think Mum really misses her. She cried for about two days when she left. Maisy will never admit it but I think she misses Mum well loads too – and me (of course) and Simon and Connor.

My lovely friend Luke, after our wonderful night together, is back in the friend zone. Thankfully he's grown up enough to understand. It didn't feel slaggy or wrong to sleep with him. It was beautiful but I just needed a friend that night.

I've started to realise boys are just as complicated as girls. Not long after Mum's attack I started to realise that Joe doesn't really care for me. No, actually that's not true, he does care for me, but he also cares too much about what his friends think. Anyway since I rejected him he wants me more than ever now. What is it with people always wanting what they can't have?

Joe bombards me with texts on a daily basis and has even written me a letter and sent me flowers – like a proper bouquet, not a bunch grabbed from the corner shop. I still like him, but so much has happened and somewhere along the way I've changed. I'm not closing the door to a possibility of us, but right now I need some time to find out who Cassie is.

Dad said he'll come and visit me at Uni. Frankly I'll believe it when I see it, but who knows? I hope he does. He doesn't know about Lilly. And unless anyone else tells him he never will coz I'm not going to tell him. And of course, when I get back for the Christmas holidays I'm going to be Godmother to little Nancy. God knows why Pheebs chose me. I wasn't sure about the name Nancy – it seemed a bit old fashioned. But I changed my mind when Pheebs explained that she took the name from Charles Dickens's *Oliver*. I asked her if she meant the movie? Pheebs said no, from the book. Turns out Pheebs is an avid reader, a real bookworm. I've known her for years and I never even knew. Sometimes we're so sure we know people – and we don't, not really. I'm like, so honoured that she's asked me to be Godmother and everything but I don't know a bloody thing about babies. I keep having this reoccurring nightmare that I'll drop poor little Nancy in the font thing on the day.

I'm still in awe of Pheebs, being a parent and everything. I don't envy her one bit though; I know now how hard it's been for Mum. And I so can't believe how much poo actually comes out of such a little thing too. And it stinks like, well bad. I'm not ready to be a parent, not yet anyway. But Pheebs seems happy so I'm pleased for her.

Me, Mum and Simon take a tour of the huge Uni campus that looks like a prison. Everyone seems nice but I think I've made up my mind, this one's not for me, which is a shame coz I got talking to some really fit boys who are coming here. Oh well, I've taken their names and promised to contact them on Twitter and Facebook. As is usual with most things I think I'm going to choose the first Uni we looked at in Guildford.

We all pile back in the car. Mum and Simon turn on Radio Two and I put my earphones in. I feel, what's the word, content? Yeah, content is a good word and a good feeling.

I'm so pleased Nan is now in her second year free of cancer – three more to go and we're home and dry. Oh my god, Grandad! I've just remembered that weird conversation I had with Connor in his bedroom all those months ago, when Mum came home from hospital.

I take a note pad and pen out of my bag. Now, what was it he said? Something about Grandad's name, I think? I take the lid off my pen and start writing.

S A L O C I N L E M A L F

I stare at the name for several minutes, wondering if it's an acronym or anagram. I start to move all the letters around. I feel like I'm on an episode of Countdown. I'm rubbish at that and just as rubbish at this, until I turn the note pad around and then I see it. Oh my actual bloody god!

N I C O L A S F L A M E L

What? OMG!! Wasn't he some sort of wizard bloke or whatever? I lift my phone from my bag and swipe the screen. I jab the internet icon and type in the name *Nicolas Flamel*. I select the first website that comes up and read:

> *Nicolas Flamel, born around 1327, was a well-known alchemist and only known maker of the Philosophers Stone. The Philosophers Stone (Latin: lapis philosophorum) is a legendary alchemical substance said to be capable of turning base metals into gold and also believed to be an elixir of life (sometimes in the form of a magical or medicinal potion), useful for rejuvenation and achieving immortality.*

Immortality? But, no one is immortal, except vampires and time-lords. And what the hell does rejuvenation mean? I stab the internet icon on my phone again and search for its definition. I read:

> *Rejuvenation: The phenomenon of vitality and freshness – restoring something or someone to a satisfactory state.*

But ... this is ridiculous? I re-read the last words, "restoring something or *someone* to a satisfactory state". Was that *someone* Mum? I re-open the Flamel tab and read some more:

> *Flamel lived in Paris, France during the fourteenth century where he met and married his wife Perenelle in 1368.*
> 
> *Legend says the couple achieved immortality through the Elixir of Life – the Philosophers Stone.*

'What? What?' I shout.

'Did you say something, Cas?' Simon shouts from the front of the car.

'What?' I say again.

'For god's sake Cassie what on earth is the matter?' Mum asks.

'I errrrr ... ummmm.' I can hear Connor's voice in my head

telling me to check Grandad's name but also reminding me of my promise not to say anything once I've worked it out.

'Where was Grandad born?'

'London,' Mum replies. 'But you know that Cassie. Why do you ask?'

'Did ever live in France?'

'No, not that I'm aware of. Why?'

I look at my phone again and re-read the page. Nicolas Flamel wife's name was Perenelle. I write it down.

PERENELLE

PEREN-ELLE

'What's Nan's name?'

'What an absurd question,' Mum replies. 'You know what Nan's name is. It's Elle. But everyone just calls her Ellie. You know that though.'

'Is her name short for something else?'

'No. At least, I don't think so. Why all the questions?'

'No reason,' I reply.

'Are you sure she hasn't had a bang to the head?' Simon asks Mum. They both laugh.

'I'm not so bloody sure sometimes,' Mum replies.

I put my earphones back in and close my eyes. I've got this all wrong, surely I have? This is real life and things like this don't happen in real life. It doesn't matter anyhow coz Mum's fine and according to Connor if I want to keep it like that I can't talk about it anyway. I try to doze off but my thoughts are troubled.

## CHAPTER 47

WHO WANTS TO LIVE FOREVER ...?

**CASSIE**

We stop off at Nan and Grandad's house to collect Connor and stay for a quick cuppa and a chat. Freddy barks and wags his tail excitedly. He's like well pleased to see us. Anyone would think it's been years not hours since he last laid eyes on us. He brings his new toy over to me and drops it at my feet for me to throw. I pick it up and quickly hurl it in the air coz it's like well rank, covered in dog spit and stuff.

Grandad brings in a tray full of steaming hot mugs of tea and Nan has baked a bread pudding. Sorted. They ask me what I thought of the Uni. I tell them it looked like a prison but some of the boys were well fit. I keep looking at them all – Nan and Grandad and even Connor to see if I can see something I didn't before, if they act strange or weird. They don't though. Nothing is out of place. Nothing is different. Besides, I couldn't say anything if it was. I suddenly have an idea though.

'Just nipping to the loo,' I say.

Instead of going to the bathroom I go into the kitchen and open the small draw below the glass display cabinet and start rummaging through it. I know Nan keeps hers and Grandad's passports in here and I just want to check something. Yesss! I find their passports. I flick them open, quickly discarding Grandad's. Then I look at Nan's. According to this she was born in 1950, surname is Lemalf and forename is ... P E R E N E L L E. Oh my fucking god.

'Booooo,' Grandad shouts behind me.

'Arrrrgggghhh!' I scream, dropping Nan's passport on the floor.

'Wha chooo bleedin app to?' Grandad says.

'No one, I mean Tuesday, I mean nothing,' I reply.

Grandad looks straight into my eyes and smiles at me, a lovely, big, familiar, saggy, craggy smile. His face looks old but his eyes are young and full of mischief.

'Grandad?'

'Yes Cassie.'

'If you made a promise to someone but then broke it coz you needed to ask someone something, would it be wrong?'

'I think you're old enough to answer that question yourself Cassie.'

I sigh heavily. That wasn't the answer I was looking for. 'But, if you can accept karma ...' Grandad continues.

'What do you mean karma?'

'That every cause has an effect.' I must look as confused as I feel coz now Grandad sighs heavily.

'If you can accept the consequences of your actions then do what you must Cassie.'

'Huuummmpphh. Okay. Can I ask another question?'

'Ask away.'

'If you were rich ...'

'I am rich.' Grandad interrupts.

'Really?'

'Course I bleedin am.'

'What, like loads of money rich?'

'Money? Who mentioned money? I'm talking about family and love. Richest man in the world in that department, and that's all that really counts at the end of the day. Turn the radio up Cassie,' Grandad says, bending down to pick up Nan's passport from the floor, 'I love this song.'

'Oh, okay,' I reply swinging round in confusion. I didn't know the radio was on? 'What song is it?' I ask, reaching to turn the radio up only to find it isn't on after all. I press the power button anyway.

Grandad winks at me as the powerful vocals of Freddie Mercury sing across the kitchen.

'*Who Wants To Live Forever* – by Queen,' Grandad replies.

## CHAPTER 48

### LETTING GO

'Why are you crying?' I ask her.

'Just because,' she replies moodily.

'Come on now, stop that,' I continue, a little irritated by her childishness. 'That's a silly answer and you know it is.'

'But it's so far away,' she continues, lip trembling. 'You'll forget all about me. I won't be important anymore.'

I laugh at her. 'How can I ever forget you and why for that matter would I want to?' The tears roll freely down her face. They are tears without pride or prejudice, her vulnerability cold and bear before me.

'Because I'm a pain in the arse,' she whimpers.

She suddenly seems, tiny, fragile. My throat tightens as I attempt a useless fight against my own tears. I carefully wrap my arms around her and hold her close.

'I thought you wanted this?' I whisper in her ear. 'It's always been my dream, but I thought it was yours too?'

'It is,' she replies sobbing. 'It's just hit me though, how scary it is. All those miles away from home, not knowing anyone. Please stay in touch,' she pleads. 'Promise you won't forget about me?'

I am totally taken aback by her directness; her raw and exposed openness frightens me a little.

'Yes but think of all those new people to meet, all those wonderful experiences and opportunities just there for the taking,' I continue, in my best reassuring voice. 'And you have your mobile phone so we can text and FaceTime and email. We can talk everyday if you want?'

'I will,' she continues sobbing. 'Every day, at least twice a day,' she adds.

I laugh again and draw her to me. I gently pull the tear soaked hair away from her face and rock her gently. 'I'm so proud of you.' Evidently these are five words too many and only serve to open the floodgates of her tears even wider.

'And ... I'mmm ... so ... pr – oud ... of ... you ... too,' she replies.

I continue rocking her and stroking the side of her face.

Simon walks in and looks at us.

'She at it again?' he asks, shaking his head and rolling his eyes. 'She was the same last night you know? And she reckons you two aren't alike! It's only university, not another bloody planet; it's not even another country for that matter.' Simon's sounds exasperated but amused at the same time.

'It might just as well be,' she mumbles, her head buried in my chest.

Simon mouths to me that he'll leave us to it and departs as quickly as he arrived.

We sit, quietly, enjoying the intimacy of the moment. The smell of her freshly washed hair and her favourite perfume, slightly jaded by the passing of the hours, fills my nostrils. I slowly pull her away from me, grabbing her tear stained cheeks imploring her, without words, to look at me.

'You did it Mum,' I tell her. 'Despite all the hardship, the struggles, emotional as well as financial, you did the best possible job of raising the life you brought into this world and surpassed your ability with more love than anyone could ever dare to hope for. And this is where it was all leading to Mum, this moment. This moment when I spread my wings and – thanks to you – fly. I'm about to fly Mum and it's all because of you.'

Mum looks at me, pressing both her lips together with the vague hope, I think, of suppressing the continual flow of tears from her eyes – which of course it doesn't. She nods her head up and down in agreement.

'I love you Cassie,' she finally manages to whisper. 'I love you so much.'

'I know you do Mum,' I reply. 'I love you too.'

## CHAPTER 49

## A PERFECT LIFE

**LIZZIE**

'Okay Mum,' Maisy says. 'We really have to go now but give our love to everyone and I'll call you again in a few days.'

'Yeah, bye Liz,' Crazee speaks over Maisy's shoulder. 'Tell Simon to ged his arse in gear and sord samthin out for you two to come visit.'

Crazee's Australian accent is noticeably strong compared to Maisy's, although I have noticed a bit of a twang in her vernacular of late.

I laugh. 'Okay, I will.'

'Byyyyeeee,' they both say in unison then the screen goes blank.

That was nice. Australia suits Maisy and so, it would appear, does Crazee. I suppose that's the good thing about technology – although she's thousands of miles away she still feels close.

Oh well, it hasn't been a bad day and with today's

contribution I've already written ten thousand words for my book. I took Nigel's advice, sat down one morning and just started to write. I'm not sure the world's ready for what I have to say, but we'll see. If nothing else, I'm finding it extremely cathartic.

Now, time to pack my laptop away and get ready to feed the five thousand.

Cassie's coming home for the weekend.

I throw a couple of pizzas in the oven and switch on the CD player. Think I'll listen to *Moby* today. As I start to prepare the salad the first song begins to play. I smile. It's one of my favourite's – *Perfect Life.*

*What is the perfect life?*

Sometimes, I think we're all so busy striving for the perfect life we fail to see what we've actually got. I look up as the door crashes open, interrupting my thoughts.

'Look who's here,' Simon says, standing behind a slightly bedraggled but smiling Cassie.

'Hey Mum,' she says dragging in a bag that looks big enough and heavy enough to contain a dead body. 'Washing?' she says wincing. 'Do you mind?'

I laugh. 'Give us a hug.' Cassie strides towards me and drapes herself across my shoulders.

'Hey Cas,' a deep voice speaks behind us.

'Bloody hell Connor, your voice has like, well dropped.' He coughs. 'Ahem. Yeah, well ... how's Uni?'

'Manic, crazy but yeah, good I think.'

'Sick,' Connor replies, his face reddening a little. 'Well, err, this is, ummm, Samara – my, ummm, girlfriend,' he says, stepping aside as a slightly embarrassed blonde girl wearing black skinnies and a black *Iron Maiden* tee shirt emerges from behind him.

'Hi,' she says, lifting her hand in a half-hearted wave.

'Well is it now! Hello Samara, I'm Connor's big sister. Welcome to the bloody madhouse. Anything you wanna know about him,' Cassie nods at Connor, 'let me know and I'll happily dish the dirt.'

The front door opens again and Freddy drags Dad through it followed by Mum, Sean, Natasha and Summer. Freddy spots Romeow sprawled across his usual step on the stairs and begins barking incessantly. Romeow's look is one of utter contempt. He watches Freddy for a moment, mildly amused, mildly intrigued, before closing his eyes again.

'Stupid bleedin' dog,' Dad shouts.

'Salocin,' Mum responds.

'Sorry.'

My phone pings. It's a text from Ruby.

'Simon, Ruby's here, on the drive. She needs some help?'

'On my way,' Simon replies.

Ruby walks in with a sleeping baby Andrew in his car seat. I wipe my hands on a tea towel and take the seat from her.

'Oh my god, Ruby, he's grown so much already. And he looks soooo like Andy.'

'Doesn't he?' Ruby frowns. 'Poor little sod.'

'Wait till he's running around like this one,' someone calls behind us.

'Pheebs!!' Cassie screams as a shy little Nancy toddles in, clinging to the side of Phoebe's leg.

'Room for a few more?' Jodi shouts above the noisy and overcrowded kitchen that, moments ago, was completely quiet. Two reluctant teenagers, two enthusiastic toddlers and a rather tired looking Rob follow her.

I step back for a moment and observe the commotion unfolding before me. A wonderful, noisy hullabaloo as Moby continues to sing out his *Perfect Life*.

It's not a perfect life. If it were Andy would still be with us.

The truth is life can often be about suffering and pain. As we go about our daily struggles of job losses, pay cuts, divorce, inflation, the loss of a loved one, life seems to be about fear, frustration, disappointment, embarrassment and anger. The trick is to live each day at a time, to capture those moments that truly are important, the little things as well as the big. And don't just see them. Feel them. Experience them. Live them.

True wisdom comes from compassion, for yourself and others. If you spend your life craving the seemingly perfect life of others, wanting what others have, you are in serious danger of missing what you actually have. Wanting deprives us of contentment and happiness. Dad always says that out of bad things comes good.

Love and be willing to be loved right back. And remember ...

IT'S NOT A LIFE, IT'S AN ADVENTURE!!!!!

THE END

ACKNOWLEDGEMENTS

Firstly, I would like to thank Betsy Reavley and the rest of the Bloodhound Books team for offering to give my books a new home. Sadly, my first publisher, Urbane Publications, had to close in April this year, mainly because, like many small businesses, recent events during the past year have made it impossible for them to remain open. I will be forever grateful to Matthew Smith and Urbane Books for taking a chance on Lizzie Lemalf and her madcap family, and I wish everyone from Urbane all the very best for the future. However, I am equally grateful that Bloodhound Books have taken my stories, given them new book covers, and a new platform to, hopefully, reach new readers.

I would also like to thank the many readers that have read this, and my other books and enjoyed them. Without readers, there would be no storytellers. In fact, I am extremely grateful to *all* the bookish community, including the many writers I've met, and the many book bloggers and book reviewers. I am in awe of your support and enthusiasm, which never fails to amaze me.

I would also like to thank friends and family, whom this book is dedicated to, particularly the women in my life, including my mother, daughters, and good friends, who helped inspire this, my debut novel, a modern-day exploration of domestic love, hate, strength and friendship set amongst the thorny realities of today's divided and extended families.

Thanks also to Dave Jordan, and David James Smith, for giving me permission to use their wonderful song 'Funky Purple Haze' performed back in the day with their band Hoo Knows.

Dave Jordan: http://notownwithoutmotown.com/
https://www.facebook.com/NotownVocalGroup/timeline

David James Smith:
http://www.austingold.co.uk/
https://www.facebook.com/davefallenbreaks77

Big thanks also to Betsy for her patience, Tara and Maria for their guidance and support, and all the other Bloodhound authors for their very warm welcome.

Finally, I would like to thank you, the person reading this. I am truly grateful that you have taken the time to read my debut novel, and I really hope you enjoyed it. If you did, please consider reading my other books, and leaving a review on Amazon to help others find it too. Otherwise, please feel free to contact me. I love to hear from readers, and you can reach me via my website or my social media accounts.

Website: EvaJordanWriter.com
　　Twitter: @evajordanwriter
　　Facebook: https://www.facebook.com/EvaJordanWriter/
　　Instagram: @evajordanwriter

## ABOUT THE AUTHOR

Eva Jordan was born in Kent but has lived most of her life in a small Cambridgeshire town. She has a degree in English and History and describes herself as a lover of words, books, travel and chocolate––and the odd glass or two of wine. Her career has been varied and has included working for the library service, and in a women's refuge.

She is both a mum and step mum to four adult children, and Nanna to two beautiful grandchildren. Navigating blended family life has, for the most part, proved to be a wonderful, rewarding experience. Nonetheless, there were times when she found it extremely challenging––especially when her children were all teenagers! However, it was those very experiences that provided Eva with the inspiration for her three novels, *183 Times A Year*, *All The Colours In Between*, and *Time Will Tell*; family based dramas that take a delightfully funny but at times, tragic and poignant look at contemporary family life.

As well as writing novels, Eva also writes short stories and is a columnist and book reviewer for her local lifestyle magazine, *The Fens*.

A NOTE FROM THE PUBLISHER

**Thank you for reading this book.** If you enjoyed it please do consider leaving a review on Amazon to help others find it too.

**We hate typos.** All of our books have been rigorously edited and proofread, but sometimes mistakes do slip through. If you have spotted a typo, please do let us know and we can get it amended within hours.

info@bloodhoundbooks.com

www.ingramcontent.com/pod-product-compliance
Lightning Source LLC
LaVergne TN
LVHW040037080526
838202LV00045B/3368

*9781913942823*